The Titus Chronicles
Berserker Returns

by
R.W. Peake

Also by R.W Peake

Marching With Caesar® – Birth of the 10ᵗʰ
Marching With Caesar – Conquest of Gaul
Marching With Caesar – Civil War
Marching With Caesar – Antony and Cleopatra, Parts I & II
Marching With Caesar – Rise of Augustus
Marching With Caesar – Last Campaign
Marching With Caesar – Rebellion
Marching With Caesar – A New Era
Marching With Caesar – Pax Romana
Marching With Caesar – Fraternitas
Marching With Caesar – Vengeance
Marching With Caesar – Rise of Germanicus
Marching With Caesar – Revolt of the Legions
Marching With Caesar – Avenging Varus, Part I
Marching With Caesar – Avenging Varus Part II
Marching With Caesar – Hostage to Fortuna
Marching With Caesar – Praetorian
Marching With Caesar – Usurper

Caesar Triumphant Parts One and Two
Caesar Ascending – Invasion of Parthia
Caesar Ascending – Conquest of Parthia
Caesar Ascending – Pandya
Caesar Ascending – The Ganges
Caesar Ascending – The Han

The Titus Chronicles
Eagle and Wyvern
Viking
Berserker Returns

With L.R. Kelly
The Tenth

Foreword

When I began thinking of the Foreword for this book, I was going to be writing about the challenges of writing it while dealing with the terminal illness and decline of my 11 year-old Yellow Lab Sadie, known to the members of Legion Peake as Optio Sadie, who had been diagnosed with lymphoma late last year. At the time, we were told that it was unlikely she would live until Thanksgiving, and there was no way she would last until Christmas; she died on July 13, 2022, in her Centurion's arms as she deserved. Despite this not being unexpected, it was still hard, especially for my mother, whose dog Sadie had become with the arrival of Titus, who, as much as I love him, is a bit...much. Consequently, I took some time off from this book to grieve her loss, and to help my mother cope as well, but I had already begun "writing" what I wanted to say about Sadie in the same way I write these books, in my head first, and I had planned on doing something I have never done before, include a full-color picture of my Optio on the dedication page.

That all changed at 0643 on September 20, when I got a call from my only child, who told me that her husband of 16 years, Doug, had gone to take a nap and never woke up, at the age of 48. By 1930, I was on a plane from Seattle to London, where they live, to help my daughter, my lodestone, to begin picking up the pieces of a shattered life. This is where I'm writing this now, in their flat in London's Marylebone, and thirteen days after his death, I don't know that I understand things any better than I did as I sat on the edge of my bed that morning, trying to wrap my head around it. As I told my daughter, when I die, there will be a *long* line of people who will be only too happy to let her know, "Hey, I'm sorry for your loss and all, but your dad was an *asshole*." And that's okay; I've chosen to live my life a certain way, and that way is a practical guarantee that I have ruffled some feathers along the way.

But the same can't be said for Douglas Mark Mills. Despite being extremely successful in his chosen profession of finance, being named the Chief Accounting Officer of a Fortune 500 oil services company in his early forties, Doug was one of the most approachable, likable people I have ever known. He had a true curiosity and interest in people, and my most vivid memories of him when we were together was how he was able to strike up a conversation with absolutely anyone and everyone. Best of all, he was absolutely crazy about my daughter, but very early on in their relationship, I saw that this feeling, as intense as it was, was reciprocated by her towards him. They complemented each other perfectly, and their shared passion for travel (sometimes to places that Dad wasn't terribly happy about) made for a life filled with adventure and new experiences. When I walked into their "regular" pub that is a staple of British life and culture, seeing grown men crying unashamedly as they tried to absorb his loss just 24 hours after it happened is a memory that I will take with me to wherever I'm going...and I hope that I meet him again, because I didn't thank him enough for the life and happiness he provided my daughter for sixteen years. When people would ask me about my son-in-law, I always had the same answer:

"I won the Powerball in the Son-In-Law Sweepstakes with Doug."

He was, and I suspect will always remain one of the best men I have ever known.

Semper Fidelis
R.W. Peake
October 3, 2022

Historical Notes

As I've mentioned before, sometimes a story takes me places I didn't expect, and that is the case with *Berserker Returns*, with Titus' time in Frankia, and the region of modern-day Flanders in particular. To my dismay, I learned that as little as has survived about Anglo-Saxon England in the time of Alfred, there is even less about Frankia available. When I say this, let me be specific; I'm referring to the kind of information that anyone trying to tell a story of everyday life would find useful. However, there was material that I found extremely valuable, particularly *Vikings, War and the Fall of the Carolingians: A Critical English Translation of the Annals of Saint Vaast*, by Steve Bivans, which included several valuable appendices. I also relied on the *Chronicles of Saint-Bertin*, translated by Janet L. Nelson, along with *Carolingian Chronicles: Royal Frankish Annals and Nithard's Histories*, by Bernhard Walter Scholz, and translated by Barbara Rogers-Gardner.

As I've done with all of my works, there is a mixture of historical and fictional characters on the Frankish side of what was called The Narrow Sea. Count Baldwin II is a historical figure whose mother, Judith, was the daughter of Charles the Bald, married to two Kings of Wessex, beginning with Æthelwulf, the marriage only lasting two years before his death, whereupon she married his son, Æthelbald. This marriage was no more successful than the first one, also lasting approximately two years before Æthelbald died as well. In accordance with the times, she was sent to a convent at Senlis, twice widowed, powerless...and all of about seventeen or eighteen years old. Depending on which version one chooses to believe, Judith was either kidnapped by Baldwin I, or she eloped with him, but either way, her father was enraged, leading to a period where Baldwin was excommunicated, and the couple actually sought refuge with a Northman, Rorik, who was the King of Friesland. Eventually the matter was resolved, and whether Charles fully accepted Baldwin as his son-in-law, or was resigned to the marriage we don't know.

What we do know is that the union was fruitful, producing several children, including Baldwin, the second of his name, who was the Margrave of Flandre (Flanders), who plays a pivotal role in this story. His fortification of Saint-Omer, Kortrijk, and Ghent added to the work done by his father, who had invested Bruges and made it his seat of power, but while I was unable to find out why, it appears that when he became Margrave, he relocated to Saint-Omer, making it his base of operations. Perhaps it was because of its closer location to the coast, or to Paris, but whatever the reason, this is where I have located the young Count in the year 885.

Another aspect of this story that's historically accurate is the Count's marriage to Ælfthryth, Alfred's fourth child and third daughter of those who survived, which, in my opinion, destroys the version that Judith was kidnapped by Baldwin, because I find it highly unlikely that the pious and correct Alfred would willingly give his daughter to the son of a kidnapper. What's also accurate is the description of the territories that Alfred is offering as a dowry, this coming from Alfred's own will.

The assault on Boulogne, currently known as Boulogne-Sur-Mer, and formerly known as Gesoriacum, and perhaps, Portus Itius, is fictional, as is my supposition that it was in the possession of the Northmen during this period of time, but as much as I tried, I couldn't find any indication of who possessed it during this period. And, given its location on the Strait of Dover, the shortest distance between the mainland and England, it makes sense that this would be a hotly contested location. The fact that Boulogne was also Gesoriacum, and is a candidate for being considered the site of the jumping-off point for Caesar's invasions of Britannia, should make it obvious to readers of *Marching With Caesar* why I found it an attractive site. The Roman lighthouse that I mention is real; known alternately as the Tour D'Ordre or as The Old Man of Boulogne, it was believed to be constructed by the order of Caligula, during his aborted invasion of Britannia. The shape of the tower is as I describe it, and was actually standing for more than 1,600 years, until an earthquake destroyed all but the foundation in 1644.

While it may seem as if I made it up, the mention of King Alfred consulting Caesar's Commentaries is not as farfetched as it may seem. One of the earliest copies of the Commentaries is known as the MS Amsterdam 73 manuscript, written at Fleury Abbey in ~875, which would be the kind of priceless artifact that makes an appropriate gift for a King, particularly one like Alfred.

Finally, my mention of the remains of a Roman marching camp near modern Ramsgate is based on recent archaeological finds, which have been identified as the site of one of Caesar's encampments. Also, there are actually two River Stours; this one, and the one that will be the focal point of a battle in Volume IV of *The Titus Chronicles*.

Flanders is a famous region with a long history, but when I was looking for examples of the earliest depictions of the famed Lion of Flanders, the earliest example I could find was from the 12th Century CE, and my first reaction was, "That looks more like a dragon than a lion." Consequently, I decided to use that motif, while moving the use of it up a bit earlier. Hopefully, my readers will overlook this transgression.

I also make mention of the Burghal Hidage, although neither Titus nor any of his contemporaries knew that this was what it would be called, but the truth was that it had already begun by 885, according to the *Penguin History of the Anglo-Saxons*, pp. 152.

The oaths of fealty that Titus and Eadward exchange are accurate; there is an archived copy at Fordham University, which is what I used verbatim, save of course for the names and locations.

To Douglas Mark Mills
August 7, 1974-September 20, 2022

Table of Contents

Chapter One

It was the Year of our Lord 885, and the uneasy peace between the Danish King Guthrum, for that was how even the Saxons other than King Alfred thought of him and not by his adopted name of Æthelstan, and the Saxons had held, for the most part. There were regular small-scaled raids into Saxon lands from the Danelaw, resulting in retaliatory incursions by the Saxons, but by and large, the peace first negotiated after Ethantun still prevailed. The same could not be said when it came to the Northmen, who had managed to seize a toehold in Frankia and used it as a base of operations to sail the relatively short distance between Saxon Britain and the mainland to raid and pillage. It had been a source of contention and debate between the handful of Frankians who visited Saxon shores and the Saxons about who between the two invaders from the freezing north were the most savage, the Frankians claiming that the warriors from Norway, called Northmen, were even more barbaric than the ferocious Danes, while the Saxons scoffed at the idea that there could be any warriors fiercer than the Danes.

For men like Ealdorman Eadwig, his Thegns Otha and Ceadda, and Eadwig's son and heir Eadward, now nineteen, it was nothing more than a topic of idle interest since none of these pagan raiders had ever made it so far inland, the kind of thing the warriors liked to argue about when they were drinking ale in The Boar's Head, still their favored spot even now that Wiltun had three other alehouses, The Bounding Stag, Offa's and the least reputable of the four, The Merry Widow, although it was neither run by a widow, nor could its owner, Wigstan, be considered merry by any definition. It was also favored by the handful of men in the area who seemed to have money but were vague about how they earned it, and the rumor was that

Wigstan's real business was to serve as a facilitator for various parties who preferred to keep their source of income private. The Merry Widow had been put off limits to all warriors sworn to Lord Eadwig's Thegns, and Eadwig had actually put Eadward onto the task of finding out if there was a fire to all the smoke about Wigstan and his dealings, but the younger man had been thwarted in his task.

Now, a bit less than four years after its opening, Lord Eadwig's men largely ignored the place, while Wigstan was wise enough not to engage in anything that might revive Eadwig's interest in him and his business. Similarly to after the Battle of Ethantun, things had settled into a peaceful routine, and by this point, two years later, the subject of Titus, the tragic death of Isolde, and the subsequent killing of her husband Hereweald by Titus when the young smith confronted him, was no longer a topic of daily conversation as it had been for at least six months. Life, as Titus had known it would, went on without him, and while Eadwig had ordered a search for the vanished warrior, it could only charitably be called such; that Eadwig was relieved by the young warrior's disappearance was something he tried to keep secret, but he would not have been surprised to learn that he had not fooled anyone, particularly his son.

What neither Eadward, nor his mother the Lady Leofe, knew was that his father's relief was not because it lifted the burden of having to punish Titus, even after his heroics that Eadward and all those men present on *Sea Viper* swore saved every one of them, but because, in his own rough way, Eadwig held a strong sense of affection for this son of a one-hide *ceorl* from Cissanbyrig. Yes, the young Titus had saved his son and heir four years earlier, when he had been an anonymous, if outsized, stableboy, then had gone on to distinguish himself at the Battle of Ethantun, earning himself a spot as one of Eadwig's warriors in Otha's service, Eadwig's senior and most trusted Thegn. Additionally, while Eadwig never spoke of it, he held out a secret hope that, one day, when the time was right, Titus would reappear. The problem was, Eadwig would remind himself whenever his mind would lead him to thoughts of that episode, his initial reaction, one prompted by what he still thought was justifiable anger at Titus, was to publicly and quite loudly declare that Titus would never be forgiven by Eadwig, and if he did return to Wiltun, he would have to face justice. Those words, which he wished he had never uttered, had been spoken within a matter of heartbeats of learning that the body of Hereweald, his eyes gouged out and with a fatal sword thrust, had been found outside the home of Uhtric and Leofflaed, where Titus lived with his sister and brother-in-law.

Without waiting for more information, in the moment, all Eadwig remembered was that this was not the first time the huge warrior had been responsible for the death of one of Eadwig's subjects. The previous incident had been when Hrodulf, a dimwitted *ceorl's* son, had been manipulated into confronting Titus by the missing but not lamented daughter of one of Wiltun's bakers, Aslaug her name, who claimed that Titus had raped her, when in fact she had taken advantage of Titus' inebriation after he had a quarrel with Isolde, setting off a chain of events that culminated with Isolde's death during childbirth, which in turn had prompted Hereweald to confront Titus. In simple terms, Eadwig had lost his temper, only later learning that he had incorrectly assigned the blame to Titus; once the evidence was presented to him, Eadwig understood the essence of what had taken place, although he also intuited that he would never learn the full truth unless and until he spoke with the missing warrior. Which, he also knew, would never happen because, despite knowing he had been hasty in his judgement, the Ealdorman in all but name was a proud man, and was not going to reverse himself, but he did feel confident that he now knew enough. Hereweald, in an understandable fit of rage, had not confronted Titus— he had ambushed him—and he had done so because he blamed Titus for Isolde's death, which on its face seemed nonsensical, until Eadwig's wife, after talking to Leofflaed, learned that the reason Isolde had died was because the babe she was trying to bring into the world was too large for her frame, mother and son both dying in the process. It was a sadly common event in their world, at least the woman dying in childbirth part of it, but it was Leofflaed who supplied what Eadwig was certain was the missing piece of the puzzle.

"Isolde died in the exact same manner as Leofflaed's mother when she was having Titus," Leofe had informed her husband, though she said nothing more, having promised Leofflaed that, while she would not lie to her husband, she would not divulge the other piece of information Leofflaed had given her, about Titus and Isolde's night together before Titus and the other warriors of Wiltun had departed to serve their King on *Sea Viper*.

It took a moment, not because Eadwig was thick, but men just did not think the same way as a woman, because Leofe had already guessed the cause of Isolde's death before Leofflaed confirmed it, but she also knew better than to say anything, waiting silently for the dawning look of understanding to cross her husband's features.

"By the Rood," he groaned, sitting back in his chair. "Titus was the father, and Hereweald found out about it."

"Or," Leofe offered, "he worked it out for himself. After all," she pointed out, "Hereweald had a muscular build, certainly, but that was because of his trade. He wasn't naturally big like Titus. So..."

"So," Eadwig finished for her, nodding thoughtfully, "Hereweald is told why Isolde dies, then goes to The Boar's Head to confront Titus, with a *seaxe*, but Titus just stood there and told Hereweald to strike him down, and Hereweald lost his nerve. Then, he goes to Uhtric's holding and ambushes Titus." Shaking his head, he murmured almost to himself, "Then why didn't he stay and explain?"

Leofe knew her husband well, understanding that, while he appreciated honesty from those around him, there were limits, yet she was still sufficiently angered by Eadwig's preemptive declaration about Titus to ask pointedly, "Would you have been in the mood to listen to him? Especially since your first reaction was to declare that he was banished from Wiltun?"

For a moment, she thought she had erred grievously, as Eadwig's head shot up and he regarded his wife with narrowed eyes, although it was the set of his clean-shaven chin that was the most potent warning that his temper was in danger of being roused. Leofe had never seen Titus in the state that her son would not even speak about, but Eadwig's was formidable in itself. However, he suddenly exhaled sharply, which in turn made Leofe aware that she had been holding hers.

"No," Eadwig admitted grudgingly, "probably not."

It was as much of an admission of error her husband would ever make, she knew, so she did not pursue the matter. And, although it took several months, gradually, Titus was no longer a regular topic of conversation, nor, as far as she knew, did anyone know where he was. Leofe was a shrewd woman in her own right, so she was not particularly surprised to learn that his whereabouts were not as much of a mystery as was commonly believed. Still, life had gone on, and if it was without Titus the Berserker, perhaps that was for the best, she had come to believe. Then, the messenger from their King had changed everything.

"A large force of Northmen have sailed up the Medway and are besieging Hrofescester (Rochester)," Eadwig announced to Eadward, Otha, and Ceadda, the trio standing in front of the large chair that the acting Ealdorman used when a summons was official. "The King has called on Wiltun to answer his call for warriors."

"Is he calling the *fyrd*?" Ceadda asked before Eadwig could say anything else, and Eadward winced, shooting the Thegn a sympathetic look, knowing how much his father hated being interrupted.

Consequently, he was surprised when, rather than snapping at Ceadda, his father just shook his head and, without any rancor, replied, "There's not enough time. It will be like what you did when you took to sea on *Sea Viper*." Before Eadward could begin to think about the larger ramifications of what this meant, his father added firmly, "Except that this time, I'll be there. The King has specifically ordered that all of his Ealdormen who supply men attend to him."

"When do we leave, Lord?"

Eadward was surprised when, instead of answering himself, Eadwig turned to his son.

"What say you, Eadward? How many days do you think it will take to be ready?"

Although there had not been another opportunity to test his mettle on his own as he had when he commanded the Wiltun men serving Alfred on the sea, just the passing of time had helped Eadward mature, and he had been sporting the long mustache favored by Saxon men long enough that he no longer felt as if he was trying to affect looking older. In short, he had grown into his role as not just Eadwig's heir, but as his second in command, which was why he only thought for a heartbeat before replying.

"Three days, Father. Unless," he allowed, "the King is going to stand for our supplies so that we only need enough to get to..." realizing he did not know, he asked, "...where are we meeting him? Wintanceaster? It's on the way to Hrofescester."

"No." Eadwig shook his head. Pointing to the scroll that his steward Beorma had read to him, he explained, "According to this, Alfred said that he's leaving tomorrow at dawn, because he's going to meet with Ealdorman Sigeræd on the way."

The mention of the Centish nobleman elicited a reaction that, while muted, was impossible to misinterpret, in the form of a curled lip by Otha, a snort by Ceadda, and while Eadward was more circumspect, the father knew his son well enough to recognize the look of contempt. Not, Eadwig knew, that it was meant specifically for Sigeræd, but he had heard all about the actions of his Thegn, Beorhtweald, whose cowardice had almost cost Eadwig the life of not only his son, but the entirety of the crew of *Sea Viper*. And, he reminded himself, it had been Titus that every man, save one, credited with saving their lives.

"That means that we'll need at least another two days' worth of supplies," Eadward mused aloud. "Which means that we'll need to use the wagon instead of the cart since we're already bringing tools."

This startled Eadwig, and he saw that Otha and Ceadda were similarly caught by surprise.

"Just for extra food?" he asked, and was shaking his head in dismissal, but Eadward explained patiently, "No, not just for food, Father. Remember, we're going to Hrofescester to relieve the people there who are under siege. If I was in command, I'd essentially besiege the besiegers by hemming the Northmen in, and cut them off from supply themselves. Which," he shrugged, "requires tools to dig the trenches and build the guard towers and such."

"Alfred will supply those," Eadwig said dismissively.

"I'm sure he will," Eadward agreed, which was not what Eadwig was expecting. "But how many other Ealdormen would think to do that? And, the more tools for the men doing the work, the faster the work will go. We," he finished by holding both hands out, palms up, "will show Alfred that his acting Ealdorman of Wiltun is thinking of the larger situation, and is prepared for any eventuality."

Eadwig sat back; he had not been expecting this. Eadward's proposal was based as much in politics as it was in strategy, and as the son knew it would, it resonated with his father. Eadwig *was* an Ealdorman for all intents and purposes, yet while Alfred had fully invested him with the entire shire of Wiltscir in terms of all rents and duties, neither had the King presented Eadward with the royal charter naming him as the permanent replacement for the disgraced and vanished Wulfhere, who had chosen to throw in his lot with Guthrum at Cippanham, when the Dane had violated the Yule truce and driven Alfred and his small band of supporters into the swamps of Athelney. It was a sore point for Eadwig, and Eadward's suggestion would show Alfred yet again who the King could count on.

Nevertheless, he did not want to appear too eager, so he reminded his son with feigned skepticism, "Having the wagon means we'll be traveling slower."

"It will," Eadward agreed. "But if we bring spare oxen, we can push them harder, so that at most it will be a half-day. Besides," he pointed out, "it's likely that Alfred is going to pause somewhere between Wintanceaster and Hrofescester, both to meet with Sigeræd and to come up with a more detailed plan of attack."

This, Eadwig acknowledged to himself, was true, and he stood as he said, "Very well. We leave at dawn, three days from now. Go make the necessary preparations."

Otha and Ceadda bowed, both men knowing exactly what needed to be done, but Eadwig caught the glance his senior Thegn gave his son, and correctly interpreted it. Therefore, he was prepared when Eadward lingered, nor was he surprised to see his son shifting from foot to foot, a habit that he had been unable to break himself of from his childhood, and the sign that

Eadwig was unlikely to care for what was coming.

"Father," Eadward began, "there's something I wanted to..."

"No," Eadwig cut him off, not unkindly, but also unwilling to indulge his son when there was no chance of him changing his mind.

"No what?" Eadward asked, a bit sharply. "I haven't even said anything yet!"

"That's true. But," Eadwig held up his hand, "just in the event that you were about to ask me to send a message to someone who I effectively banished, to let him know that he's forgiven and ask him to join us at Hrofescester, then the answer is no. And," his voice hardened, "I would be *most* displeased if you continued to pursue the issue."

In another sign of his maturity, Eadward recognized the sign that this was a subject his father was not going to budge on, which he signaled with a slight bow of his head, while in a tiny show of defiance, he turned and left the hall without being given leave. Eadwig considered making an issue of it, but quickly dismissed it; the fact that Eadward had recognized the futility of pursuing the matter was enough of a victory.

Otha had been lingering outside the hall, but out of the line of sight of the open doorway, and when Eadward emerged, he fell into step with the younger man, asking only, "Well?"

"It's as you said," Eadward sighed. "Titus won't be forgiven, so there's no chance of him meeting us."

While it was true that Otha had correctly predicted his lord's reaction, he was surprised that he experienced a pang of disappointment, realizing then that Eadward was not the only one who felt better with Titus at their side when there was the prospect of battle. On Eadward's part, it was not until he thought about the moment later that day when he realized something; his father had made what was essentially a correct assumption, that Eadward knew Titus' whereabouts, which he did, though not because his friend had sent word, but the son of an Ealdorman, acting or not, had resources of his own, and while it had not come cheaply, Eadward did know where Titus was, even if it was not anywhere on this island.

Titus, who still thought of himself as Titus of Cissanbyrig and not the name by which he was gaining a wider reputation here in Frankia, as the Berserker, was bored. That he was in this state surprised him; after all, he had everything he could have wanted. He now possessed a mail shirt made by Frankish armorers, who were the undisputed masters of the art, not purchased secondhand but made especially for him, meaning that it was larger in the chest, allowing him more freedom of movement, and hung down to just above his knees, which meant that it would be mid-calf on a man of average size. There was another difference, at least when compared to his Frankish comrades, because he had insisted that it be a Saxon-style shirt, made of ringed mail and not the scale armor that was the most common on this side of the Narrow Sea. Along with the mail shirt was a new helmet that actually fit his head more comfortably, with a hinged nosepiece and mail fringe to protect his neck, which again was made in the Saxon style, without the large ridge riveted in place from front to back and a flange to protect the neck that was part of the helmet. However, his true pride and joy was the sword, also Frankian, and similar to the Danish sword that he had taken as spoils in the aftermath of Ethantun in that it was double-edged before tapering into a needle point, but it was about six inches longer and an inch wider, while the blood groove down the center of the blade ran from the hilt to about four inches from the point. The added length and width added to its heft, which meant that when it was wielded by a warrior with the strength of the Berserker, it was a potent instrument of death, and thanks to the almost constant raids by the Northmen, Titus the Berserker had had ample opportunities to use the blade, that he had named it Wyvern's Fang as a reminder, to himself as much as to others that he was still a Saxon of Wessex, bringing death to the invaders, while his reputation grew to the point that he had come to the attention of Lord Baudelius, the commander of the household warriors sworn to Count Baldwin, the Margrave of Flandre.

Flandre was well north of where Titus had first landed in Brittany, and even now, almost two years later, he did not like thinking of the days and weeks immediately after his slaying of Hereweald, although much of it was a blur. When he left Uhtric and Leofflaed's, his only thought was to get as far away from the source of what was an unbearable pain as he could, but it was without making a conscious decision that he began heading east. It was only when, several days later, he found himself looking at the same inn in Lambehitha where he had sat with Einarr and Dagfinn a few months earlier, waiting for Lord Eadward to arrive with the ransom for him that Titus realized that he had been heading for Lunden, both because of its location and status as the largest port in Saxon lands, and because there were two men there who had once been enemies but were now friends. When he thought about it later, he understood that the plan was somewhere in the back of his mind, still largely unformed, the idea of sailing across the Narrow Sea to Frankia. The first challenge had been how to get a message to Einarr, and Titus did not even know if the Dane was still in Lunden...

"Berserker!"

Jerked out of his reverie, Titus returned to reality, which was standing on a rampart, doing his turn at guard duty, something that Lord Baudelius required of all of his warriors, no matter their status or renown. It was something that Lord Otha would have required, if he was the lord of a walled manor here in Saint-Omer, which to Titus' eyes was more fortress than the home of Count Baldwin, although as Titus had learned very quickly, these kinds of fortified positions were a necessity here in Frankia because of the Northmen.

Turning in the direction of the voice, Titus saw the broad grin on the face of his friend Ranulf, who was walking down the parapet in his direction as he called out, "What are you doing tonight when you are off guard duty? Or," the grin turned into a leer, "do I need to ask?"

"Why?" Titus demanded, but he was smiling as well. "What stupid idea for fun have you come up with this time?"

Ranulf affected a hurt look, protesting, "I do not know what you are talking about!"

"That night at Melisandre's?" Titus countered, raising an eyebrow for emphasis.

"That only happened one time!"

"And once was enough." Titus shook his head. "We had to

run for our lives, all because you thought it would be funny to challenge that big Frisian on my behalf to wrestle."

"How did I know he had so many friends?" Ranulf protested, widening his eyes in an attempt to look innocent.

Titus was not fooled, and he gave Ranulf a shove.

"Because they were sitting all around him, you oaf."

"Do not blame me because they were such poor losers."

Despite the subject, both men were grinning; enough time had elapsed for Titus to see the humor in the pair of them fleeing through the darkness, after Titus had hurled his opponent bodily by lifting the man over his head and flinging him into the Frisian's companions; not, Ranulf liked to remind him, before they had snatched their winnings off of the table. Anyone who bothered to listen to their exchange would have been hard pressed to follow, because while Titus had become conversant in Frankish, there were still phrases and words that he was forced to lapse into Saxon for, while Ranulf did the same, just in the opposite direction. The result was a mishmash of language that only they understood with any fluency.

Giving Ranulf another friendly shove, Titus, as his closest companion here had predicted, confirmed, "I'm going to spend the evening with Yanna. She," he gave his friend an even broader grin, "is roasting a goose tonight!"

"By the cross," Ranulf groaned. "Why did you tell me that? Yanna's roast goose is the best I've ever tasted! And," he grumbled, "I know better than to ask if I could join you."

"If she was roasting two, I would," Titus replied, feigning regret. "But you know that one is barely enough just for me."

"That woman is a saint," Ranulf said fervently, and that Titus did not argue.

He, more than anyone, knew just how blessed he had been that Yanna and he had found each other, although he felt certain that not even Yanna knew the real reason why, and while Titus of Cissanbyrig did not normally engage in excessive introspection or ask himself how much of the events of his life had been steered by the Almighty, he could not help thinking that the hand of God had guided him to find a woman that, despite only being a couple years older than Titus, and in otherwise good, even robust health, Yanna was barren...and that was something that Titus *did* offer a prayer of thanks to God for, relieving him of one of his greatest fears.

Just as Eadward had promised, the Wiltun men were ready and departed at dawn, and as had become something of a custom, there was a small crowd gathered in Wiltun, through which Lord Eadwig led his men. For married men like Uhtric, he had said his goodbyes to Leofflaed, Wiglaf, and the newest addition to his family, their newborn daughter Deorwynn at his holding, as Otha had done with Wulfgifu, who to their surprise was pregnant, and Wistan, now fourteen and who had *almost* convinced Otha to bring with him to Hrofescester, but the Thegn had, wisely in his opinion, deferred to Wulfgifu's strong objection. Their daughter, Sunngifu, had married just a few months earlier, to the son of Thegn Bede of Hampscir, which Eadward knew had caused some hard feelings between Otha and Ceadda, who had been under the impression that, since he was widowed, that he would be a suitable husband for Otha's daughter. It did not help matters that this was still relatively fresh; the wedding had been just three months earlier, but Eadward felt certain enough that the two Thegns would not let their personal issues interfere with their duties that he had assured his father that Eadwig had no cause for worry.

Riding beside his father now as they passed through Wiltun, he gave his sire a sidelong glance, knowing that Eadwig's erect posture in the saddle was due as much to the pain from the piles that afflicted him as it was this was expected of the Ealdorman riding off to war on behalf of their King. To his relief, Eadward determined that only someone who knew Eadwig well, like himself or Otha, who was riding on the opposite side, would see the tightness around the mouth and the squint that was a bit more pronounced than the sunlight called for. It had surprised and disturbed Eadward seeing how his father had aged so rapidly in just the past year, if only because he had reached a decision, one that he was certain would shock his father. While it had been true that, once he had experienced leading the men of Wiltun in battle, during their time as Alfred's *de facto* navy three years earlier, he had begun chafing to be given more responsibility, seeing his father's rapid decline had shaken him. Whereas before, the idea of taking his father's place held enormous appeal, Eadward now recognized that the appeal came at least in part from the prospect that he was still several years away, but that belief had been shaken by his father's decline. It would only be later that he would think about this moment in Wiltun and wonder if he had somehow stumbled onto a hint about what his future would hold, only to not recognize it until it was too late?

Departing Wiltun to the calls and cheers of the small crowd seeing them off, the party soon lapsed into what was a familiar routine, although it had been some time since the Wiltun men had marched to war. Every warrior that was part of this foray, numbering thirty-four, with a half-dozen men left behind, was mounted and with their packhorse, either their own or provided by Lord Eadwig, albeit through Otha, who was the Ealdorman's horse breeder. The wagon, pulled by a pair of oxen, with another pair attached to the rear, was driven by Beohrtic, and assisted by Hakon, the Danish slave who, at long last, Eadward no longer viewed with distrust, and for which, despite his absence, Titus was owed the credit. Unlike Eadward, Titus, perhaps because of his own precarious status as the son of a disgraced, traitorous one-hide *ceorl*, had never viewed Hakon with the same level of disdain that many, or most if the truth were known, of his fellow Saxons did. In Eadward's case, he was also the son of an Ealdorman, but to his credit, the young nobleman had been brought around to a more equitable view of not just Hakon, but slaves in general. While no orders were given to that effect, the men tended to ride three or even four abreast, and always with their closest friends among their fellow warriors. Eadwig and Eadward began the journey side by side, but soon enough they were joined by Otha, while Eadward drifted back down the column, checking on the others and spending a moment chatting with them. For the most part, he listened to the tales being swapped that were the most common way to pass the time when the pace was at a moderate walk, and these were usually tales that had been told and heard before, although they differed slightly depending on who was telling it. There was one subject that, on this day, was not discussed, and Eadward was relieved that his quiet word to the

Thegns had been heeded, because even now, more than two years later, Titus, his exploits on the battlefield and off, and more commonly, his current whereabouts were still a topic of conversation at The Boar's Head among the warriors of Wiltun. While it was true that his Lord father had not specifically enjoined discussion or mention of Titus, given everything that had transpired on the subject, Eadward was doing everything he could to avoid upsetting his sire. Fortunately, the prospect of what lay ahead was what most of the talk was about. Traveling east from Wiltun, they passed the barrow of Old Sarum just to the north of the track, reaching Wintanceaster shortly before dark, and while Eadward was not surprised that Alfred had already departed, it was still a disappointment. Awaiting them was Lord Eardwulf, and while he was too old and infirm now to accompany Alfred on campaign, Eardwulf was at least able to provide information.

"The Lord King is meeting Ealdorman Sigeræd and the Centish forces at Aylesford, and he instructed me to direct your force to meet him there, Lord Eadwig," Eardwulf informed them, making a point to meet the Wiltun men outside the palace walls, and Eadward guessed the number of heartbeats it would take for his father to grouse about this once they were in private.

"When did the King leave?" Eadwig asked, which was a reasonable question; the tone, on the other hand, was borderline disrespectful, and Eadward saw that Eardwulf did not miss this, his face darkening.

However, Eardwulf was a courtier as much as he was a councilor to Alfred, and he replied blandly, "He left two days ago, and barring any unforeseen obstacles, should reach Aylesford day after tomorrow." The old nobleman paused, his rheumy eyes on Eadwig, but Eadward understood that Eardwulf was addressing him as he resumed, "It would be most...beneficial if you could make the journey from here more quickly than our Lord King will, considering that his force is larger. He has ten wagons, for example." He leaned over slightly to indicate the Wiltun force's lone wagon, nodding in approval as he added, "And I see that you thought to bring spare oxen."

Eadward said nothing, waiting for his father to speak for

them, but when nothing was forthcoming, he glanced over at his father and saw that he seemed to not be paying attention at all, and in something close to panic, Eadward said hastily, "We will push hard, Lord Eardwulf, I...we swear that we will move as quickly as possible."

This seemed to startle Eadwig, who looked embarrassed as he cleared his throat and agreed, "Er, yes, as my son says. We'll push as hard as we need to, for the King. Now," Eadwig's eyes narrowed slightly, "have you made arrangements for our accommodations? I assume we'll be staying at our usual, the Hart and Hound?"

Eardwulf shifted on his feet, looking uncomfortable, though he answered readily enough, "Yes, about that, Lord. I'm afraid that in all the...excitement of getting the King and his force ready, no arrangements were made."

For a moment, Eadward was afraid that his father's temper, which, while not as fearsome as the Berserker's, was still formidable, would erupt, the older man's face turning the kind of shade that presaged an explosion, but instead, he gave Eardwulf a curt nod, then without another word, spun about on his heels and stalked away, leaving Eadward to mumble an apology before hurrying to catch up.

When Eadward rejoined his father, he caught the end of his muttering, "...just like Alfred! He wants us at his beck and call, but expects us to spend *our* silver for the privilege! A *pox* on him!"

While Eadwig did not say this overly loudly, Eadward still glanced about in concern, but their men were gathered in a knot, chatting quietly and watching them approach, none of them looking as if they had heard, and Eadward thought ruefully, *I was a few heartbeats off.*

Just as they reached them, Eadwig murmured, "You tell them. I'm afraid that if I do, I'll say something stupid that will reach Alfred's ears."

This actually relieved Eadward, who did as his father ordered, telling the others, "We're going to be staying at Hart and Hound as we usually do. But," his tone hardened, "you're restricted to one pot of ale, and no whoring! We have to get an early start in the morning, and the King has ordered that we march hard enough that we catch him before he and his force reach Aylesford tomorrow, where he'll be meeting with Ealdorman Sigeræd."

Now, this was not exactly what Eardwulf had said, but Eadward had ambitions of his own, although this was also a test to see how closely his father had been paying attention, but it took only a quick, sidelong glance at Eadwig, who was staring moodily off into the distance and did not react at all to his son's orders to tell him that he was not. The Wiltun men did not bother getting back into the saddle; it was only a short walk to the inn, and it was just getting dark by the time the livestock was cared for and the men were settled in. They grumbled about it, but they obeyed Eadward's command, only downing a single pot of ale with their meal before retiring, crammed into every room on the entire upper floor, and four men were still forced to share the stable with Hakon and Beohrtic.

As much as they had complained the night before, by midday the next day, most of the warriors were saluting, silently, Eadward's admonition. The pace set by the young Lord was significantly faster than the day before, and the midday break was correspondingly shorter, just long enough for the oxen to be switched out, the men to refill their flasks from the stream (Ashford Stream), and water their mounts. They stopped only one other time, switching out the oxen again, then resumed at the same pace, which was a fast walk on level ground, and almost a trot on downhill stretches, following the track that, if they stayed on it, would take them to Lunden. Reaching a track that angled slightly southward in mid-afternoon, most of the talking had ceased, but Eadward was most concerned about his father, who his son saw was holding on to the front of his saddle with his free hand with a white-knuckled grip, while only responding to his son's queries with a grunt, nod, or shake of the head. For Eadward's part, he could not imagine the amount of pain his father must have been in, because he had never seen Eadwig like this before, even when he returned home bearing wounds from battle. Despite his obvious pain, Eadwig remained in the saddle, snarling at Eadward when he suggested that his father would be more comfortable in the wagon, although it was already packed almost to overflowing. Finally, just as the sun was setting, they spotted the glint of light on water in the form of the River Medway, the sign that they were now in Cent. More importantly, they would follow the river north from this point, and they made what could only be charitably called a camp, with the men once again caring for their mounts and pack animals, then themselves before wrapping themselves in their cloaks, falling into an exhausted slumber. Not, Eadward made sure, without a sentry, but he volunteered for the middle watch, universally loathed as the worst one, despite his own exhaustion. It was something that he knew his father approved of, even if he had never seen Eadwig do it himself, but his father barely seemed to notice, actually nodding off twice while in the middle of consuming his meal, cooked by Beohrtic.

Hakon took the first watch, Eadward the middle, and Beohrtic was roused for the final watch before dawn, who in turn woke Eadward first, just before dawn. The son took care not to awaken his father, including issuing harsh, whispered admonishments to the others to keep their voices down. Only when it was time to break their fast did Eadward awaken Eadwig, forcing himself to ignore how frail and old his father looked as he lay there, head on his saddle and covered by his cloak, mouth open as he snored, helping Eadwig sit up before handing him a hunk of bread, a slice of mutton, and a cup of ale. Thankfully, none of the men were in a boisterous mood, and within an hour of awakening, they were swinging themselves into their saddles, then moving out and quickly resuming their pace of the day before. It was after midday when Otha, riding alongside Eadwig, suddenly stiffened in his saddle, then stood in the stirrups as he strained his eyes, looking ahead of them.

Finally, he muttered, "My eyes are too old." Turning, he shouted, "Lord Eadward! I need you up here!"

Eadward had been riding with Uhtric, conducting a whispered conversation about the forbidden topic, and he kicked his horse, which had replaced Thunor—which meant speedy of foot—into a canter, drawing up alongside the Thegn, who pointed.

"Is that what I think it is? A dust cloud?"

It took Eadward less than a heartbeat to see that, in fact, it was, and he said excitedly, "That has to be the King! We're not far behind them now!"

Despite their fatigue, the news that they were about to catch their King, especially with him having a substantial head start, infused the Wiltun men with a surge of energy; even Eadwig offered his son a pained smile. Now that they were in the heart of Cent, the ground was flat, and it was when they emerged from a forest, with the sun still a half-hand's width above the horizon, that they spotted the handful of riders serving as the rearguard behind the last of the ten wagons. They were spotted by the rearguard not long afterward, and they turned and came in their direction at the canter, but while their hands were on their hilts, Eadward could see that this was more out of habit than alarm.

Once they were within about fifty paces, Otha and Eadward exclaimed at the same time, "That's Aedelwine!" Holding his hand up, it was Eadward who managed to call out first, "*Eho,* Aedelwine!"

The identified man, who had been part of the crew of the *Sea Viper*, smiled, calling back, "Lord Eadward! It's been awhile!"

"It has," Eadward agreed, and now Aedelwine was about ten paces away, and he turned to greet Otha before addressing Eadwig, "Lord Eadwig, I know the King will be pleased, not only to see the Wiltun men, but because you arrived so quickly." Beckoning to the trio, he began turning his horse. "I'll take you to him."

Eadward made no move to follow, deferring to his father, but Eadwig said firmly, "You're coming with me." Turning, he told Otha, "It's up to you, Otha."

"That's all right, Lord," Otha grinned. "I've met the King often enough."

He was rewarded by the snort he knew was Eadwig's laugh, and he watched as the pair hurried to catch Aedelwine. If the Ealdorman had turned to look over his shoulder, he would not have cared for the expression on Otha's face, which was very similar to the one Eadwig's son had been giving him. There was...*something* wrong with Lord Eadwig, and if it was for slightly different reasons, Otha was as worried as the son about his Lord.

Alfred, by the Grace of God, King of the Saxons, was tired, though not as fatigued as Lord Eadwig, but whereas his problems were not a result of age, and piles, he did have a griping of the bowels that future generations would speculate about, and right now, he was beset by cramping of the kind that warned him he might have to dismount and find a bush in the very near future. He actually welcomed the distraction of the clattering of hooves behind him, although as always Cyneweard, the commander of his bodyguard, automatically interposed himself between his King as what Alfred saw were three horsemen coming their way at the canter. A couple of heartbeats later, he recognized the Lord of Wiltun, and as he always did, Alfred felt the tug of regret that he had not rewarded Eadwig as he deserved. Unfortunately for Eadwig, his value as a vassal and loyal nobleman was dwarfed by the strategic importance of Wiltscir, and he had been able to dangle the shire as bait ever since the disgraced Wulfhere chose the wrong side, though not just to Eadwig. And, while Alfred would only say it to his confessor, Father Æthelred, the normally cerebral King felt an admittedly irrational stab of anger at the entire shire, and by extension, everyone in it. After all, *someone* had known of Wulfhere's intended betrayal in joining Guthrum, and it made sense that the Lord of Wiltun was one of those, and yet the first that Alfred had learned of Wulfhere's disloyalty was when he had not appeared at his grandfather's gravesite after Alfred summoned the Saxon *fyrd* and Wulfhere was not there. Yet even so, Alfred knew that it was grossly unfair to Eadwig, but in this, Alfred of Wessex was not immune to petty grudges. None of this mattered in the moment, he told himself, and he offered a genuine smile at the pair of Wiltun men, acknowledging their bowed heads with a wave.

"Lord King," Eadwig spoke loudly, so that he could be heard by more than just Alfred, "the men of Wiltun have marched hard, and we are tired...but we are here, and we are ready to serve our King!"

As he hoped, Eadwig's pronouncement earned cheers from

the warriors of Alfred's force, which consisted of his royal guard and the warriors in the service of the Hampscir, or as they were more commonly called, the royal Thegns, along with the assorted slaves and servants, and Alfred inclined his head in a regal thanks.

"As always, Lord Eadwig, you have proven your fidelity, and your dependability in a way that leaves no doubt." Turning, he addressed Eadward, "Young Lord Eadward, I have heard good things about you. Now," he said, with only partial mock severity, "why haven't you married yet?"

Despite expecting this, since the King had broached the subject at Yule, Eadward still felt his face coloring, and he stammered, "I...I just haven't found the right woman yet, Lord King."

Alfred did not address Eadward, looking to Eadwig with a raised eyebrow, and Eadward's father said bluntly, "He's too picky, Lord King. I've been telling him that for years."

"Well, perhaps there will be a maiden in Hrofescester that catches your eye." Alfred hesitated, then opened his mouth as if to say something else, but what came out of his mouth was a slightly fumbling, "Yes...well...Now that we're all together, let's hurry to Aylesford." He offered a grim smile. "I know that none of us want to hear Ealdorman Sigeræd complaining about waiting for us."

He turned his horse, and progress quickly resumed, but while Eadward was not about to mention it to his father, he had noticed the hesitation in the King's words, and while he had no real reason for it, he felt certain that Alfred had been about to mention, or ask about the whereabouts of one of the Wiltun warriors. And, while he would never know, Eadward was right, because Alfred had indeed been thinking about the large warrior whose whereabouts Eadward would have been shocked to learn Alfred knew, and quite precisely at that. Even more astounding, Alfred had seriously considered sending someone he trusted across the water to Count Baldwin, carrying a purse of gold to essentially purchase the young Saxon's services, since, after all, it had been at his suggestion that the Count take the warrior from Cissanbyrig into his service, although it had been done indirectly. What had stayed his hand was the knowledge that

Eadwig would, correctly, consider this meddling in an affair where the Ealdorman had already ruled, and there was enough tension in their relationship as it was. Besides, he had reasoned, he was not overly concerned that breaking the siege would be that difficult.

The goose was just as perfectly prepared and cooked as Titus had hoped, and he gave a slight groan of pleasure as he loosened his belt, while Yanna flushed, knowing this was a supreme compliment. Giving a glance at the remnants of the goose carcass, she thought ruefully, And now I'm going to have to find something for him to break his fast in the morning, though she did not mind. After the death of her husband, who like Titus had been a warrior serving the Count, she had been certain that she would never find anything approaching the love she and Maló had experienced. And yet, she thought as she sat across the table from Titus, she had been wrong, yet as happy a consideration as this was, she also knew that her feelings were not shared, not fully anyway, by the man across from her. Oh, she knew he cared about her, and more than he probably wanted to, because he had never made any attempt to convince her that his feelings for her more than they were, yet he seemed content to spend most of his free time with her and not with Ranulf and the other warriors. While they had never discussed it, it was mainly through Ranulf that Yanna had gleaned that the one thing about her that would normally repel a serious suitor was the one thing that had appealed to Titus. In a place like Saint-Omer, nothing was secret, so the fact that, after Yanna almost lost her life trying to bear what would be her first and only child, who was stillborn, the midwives declared the damage she suffered so massive that she would never have children was well known. That this had not dissuaded Titus was such a surprise that she did not stop to think about the possible reason why until it was too late, and she was already hopelessly in love with this Saxon warrior whose reputation had followed him across The Narrow Sea. She had gone to Ranulf several months after Titus had taken her as his woman, ignoring the whispers and the looks from the town priest, a vile little man who had tried to force himself on Yanna on two separate occasions, during the period she was still grieving her husband. Titus' arrival had put a stop to Father Hervé's attempts to bed her, which she was certain was another factor in the priest's vicious whispering campaign against her. By this time, Ranulf and Titus had become friends, close enough that the Frankish warrior knew a bit about his Saxon friend's past, although it was not much.

"I know that he had to leave Wessex after he killed a man who tried to kill him," he had told Yanna, somewhat reluctantly. He hesitated a moment before adding, with a sigh, "And I know that it had to do with a woman he knew who died in childbirth, but," he finished firmly, "that's all I know, Yanna."

Thankfully, Yanna received and understood the message, that even if Titus had confided in Ranulf further, Ranulf would not tell her. However, he did not need to; a combination of logic and feminine intuition told Yanna what she felt fairly certain was the rest of the story, that the woman in question had died bearing Titus' child, which, as anyone with eyes could see, meant that the child was probably very large and was the likely cause of the woman's demise. Consequently, it made sense why Titus would be reluctant to become entangled with a woman who could suffer the same fate, and Yanna's status as a barren woman would make her an ideal companion. For a time, she told herself that this was enough knowledge for her; to her dismay, she discovered that being *fairly* certain was not the same as knowing without a doubt, and she could not count the times she caught herself just before she asked the questions that she instinctively knew Titus did not want to answer. After all, she reasoned, once she had told him the bare bones of her past, that she had been married, and for their times, happily so, he had not seemed interested in delving more deeply into her past. Maybe, she would think, that's the difference between a man and a woman; men seemed content enough to remain in a relative state of ignorance, while women...didn't.

Now, sitting across the table, with the glow from the fireplace in the small but snug and tidy cottage located just off the northern road and within sight of the walls of Saint-Omer, Yanna felt the words forming, so quickly that, before she could stop herself, she blurted out, "Tell me about the woman you loved in Wessex, Titus."

The change in her lover was sudden, obvious...and frightening. She had heard the stories, including the one about how he ended up in the service of Lord Baudelais, after a tavern brawl when one of Baudelais' men, Bent, had instigated a fight with the huge bearded stranger who wore his hair long and in a braid. Despite being outnumbered six to one, which included Ranulf, Titus had thrashed all of them so soundly, and with such ease that, rather than have him thrown in chains, as Bent, who had borne the worst of the punishment, insisted, when Lord Baudelais had taken him in front of Count Baldwin for judgement, the Count had offered Titus a spot in his household guard. Ranulf, who had been there, insisted to this day, almost two years later, that Count Baldwin had not only not seemed surprised, he behaved as if he had expected the appearance of this Saxon warrior. In the intervening time, while there had been no major battles between the Frankish forces of Baldwin and the Northmen, there had been skirmishes beyond counting, so that by now, it was accepted as a simple fact that this stranger was the most formidable, and dangerous warrior in the Count's service. Aside from his size and obvious strength, it had always puzzled Yanna, because Titus was invariably gentle, and kind, with her, but right now, that man was nowhere to be seen; the figure sitting across the table from her was radiating a rage that, while he was not overtly snarling or cursing her, made her quake with fear. How can someone just look at you and make you so afraid? she wondered. Then, so quickly that she began to think she might have imagined it, the expression of rage evaporated, replaced by a widening of his eyes and a look of vulnerability that she would remember for the rest of her days.

"Her name," his voice had gone so hoarse it was almost unrecognizable, "was Isolde."

Only later would she realize that Titus spoke for hours, telling her everything; how, as a fourteen year-old youth who could pass for much older, at least at a distance, he had left his village of Cissanbyrig, escaping a father she at least knew he despised, and who had chosen to follow the disgraced noblemen the Saxons called an Ealdorman, Wulfhere, who in turn had decided that aligning with the Danish King Guthrum was the wise choice. While he had spoken of the Battle of Ethantun before, this time was different, because he talked about how he felt, about the rage at seeing Leofric as he fled with the Danes and how much he wanted to kill his father, but when the moment came, he was unable to do so. He spoke of the feast after Ethantun, and the awarding of arm rings, of which he now had six, including one of gold that was the most finely worked piece of craftsmanship Yanna had ever seen, that had been given to him by a Dane named Einarr. Titus had mentioned him before, but never to the level of detail as he did this night, and it was the first, and only, time he smiled while he talked. At one point, she had the urge to gently nudge him back to Isolde, but she managed to quash it, knowing that it was more likely to result in him shutting down...or worse. She was rewarded a short time later, when he returned to his happier days, before he and his friends and comrades became seaborne warriors aboard the *Sea Viper*, and about how his future seemed so bright, not only as a warrior, but with a life with Isolde in the offing.

"We had an argument," he explained, albeit after taking a long swallow of wine, which was the drink favored by the Franks, to lubricate his throat. Although he did not say her name, Yanna knew he meant Isolde, saying nothing as he continued, "about..." he shook his head, "I don't even remember, really. But I *do* remember that I was acting like a fool. Anyway," he sighed, "she walked off, and that's when a girl named Aslaug suddenly appeared. I didn't know it until later, but she had chosen me as a target for her schemes, and she had overheard my fight with Isolde." Titus paused to take another gulp of wine, and whereas before he had not avoided Yanna's gaze, this time, he refused to meet her eyes, and she understood why as he continued, "I...I lay with Aslaug because I was angry with Isolde. No," he shook his head emphatically, "I wasn't angry. I was hurt. My pride was hurt because Isolde had said some things about me that I didn't want to hear." As much as she wanted to ask what those things were, Yanna wisely held her tongue. "Aslaug was...experienced, not just about...that, but in how to flatter and beguile a man." Titus chuckled, but it was laced with bitterness. "As I found out, I wasn't quite as special as she said I was. And," he shrugged, "it was just my bad fortune that the next morning, when I was leaving Aslaug, I ran into Isolde, who was on her way back to her father Cenric's home where she cared for her two younger brothers." Seeing Yanna's look of confusion, he explained, "She had spent the night with her best friend, Cyneburga, and just happened to be walking past when I stepped out of the stable."

"Stable?" Yanna echoed, confused, and even in the dimmer light of the fire, she saw Titus flush.

"Yes, that's where Aslaug and I...were together. And," his mouth twisted into a scornful smile, "of course Aslaug heard us talking outside, and she made sure to come out so that Isolde could see her."

As much as she knew she loved Titus, Yanna still felt a somewhat conflicting series of emotions; a surge of sympathy for this Isolde at what had to be a humiliating moment seeing the man she loved with another woman, a stab of anger at Titus for his arrogance and, in her view, acting like most men, but more than anything, a sense of scorn and contempt for Aslaug. Over the course of her twenty-five years, she had known a handful of women like Aslaug; she even had an Aslaug of her own, Maela, who had tried to steal her husband the first year of their marriage. Like this Saxon whore Aslaug, Maela was only interested in men who already had a woman, and she had set her eyes on Maló, but Maela learned her error, Yanna thought with a savage satisfaction that was almost as potent now these years later sitting here with Titus, as it had been when she returned to this very cottage, bleeding and with her shift torn, but triumphant after thrashing Maela in the town square, in front of an audience of delighted townspeople. Thanks to a combination of factors—mainly being married to one of the Count's men, along with Maela's reputation—Yanna had escaped punishment for breaking the Count's peace, but best of all, she was considered a minor hero by the other wives of Saint-Omer. The difference between her situation and Titus' was that her husband had not succumbed to Maela's blandishments; at least, he had sworn he had not, and despite her suspicions, Yanna had chosen to believe him. Titus, on the other hand, had not had that luxury, since he had been caught in an incriminating manner.

"She never forgave me," Titus had continued, jerking Yanna back to the present. "And not long after that, a smith's son in Wiltun began courting her."

"What happened to the other woman? Aslaug you said?" she asked, though she remembered the name quite well.

"She thought that because we had been together that meant that I was hers," Titus replied. "But she was wrong, and I told her as much."

"How did she take it?"

Titus laughed again, except there was a scornful note that she understood when he answered, "Not well. In fact, she told another man, a *ceorl* named Hrodulf who she was stringing along, that I had raped her."

"*What*?" Yanna gasped.

As different as the Saxons and Franks were in some ways, there were more commonalities between them, and accusing a man of rape, at least outside of war, was one of the most serious that a man could face.

"That was my reaction," Titus said lightly. "But Hrodulf wasn't very clever, and he believed her."

He stopped then to take another sip, but Yanna was a good listener, and she did not miss the use of the past tense.

"You said he *was* not clever," she pointed out. "Does that mean...?"

"It means that I killed him," Titus replied flatly. "He came into The Boar's Head; that's the alehouse I told you about," she nodded, "and he accused me of raping Aslaug, in front of witnesses."

That these witnesses were some of Titus' closest friends was something he did not mention, not that he needed to; Yanna was struggling with her desire to learn the details, though she could not have explained why it mattered.

"Did you...stab him?" she asked, thinking this was the most likely explanation, yet at the same time, and for reasons she could not have articulated, she was certain that this was not the cause of this Saxon farmer's demise.

"No." Titus shook his head. "I...beat him to death."

Which was the bare bones of it; that the commonly held

belief that Titus essentially killed Hrodulf with one, or at most, two punches, which he knew was true, was something he did not think she needed to know.

"Were you punished?"

"No." Titus shook his head, deciding that an incomplete truth was sufficient. "There were two dozen witnesses who saw it happen and that I tried to avoid trouble with him. Besides," he shrugged, and gave the real reason he was not brought before The Hundred Court, "that's when King Alfred called on Lord Eadwig and the Wiltun men to go to sea to fight the raiders who sailed from here."

"Then you came back to Wiltun," Yanna prompted, understanding that Titus would have been content to leave it at that, but she had not heard the rest of the story, and it was the rest of the story she wanted to hear the most.

At first, he only nodded, then they sat in silence for some time, with Titus moodily sipping from his cup, but he understood that this was the night. He owed it to Yanna, after all; she made him happy, and this had been between them since they had become involved, like that rock just under a murky surface, indistinct but looming and ready to rip the bottom out of your ship, so he set his cup down.

"You know that I was being held hostage in Lunden, so I didn't return to Wiltun until three months after the others did, and by the time I was back, Isolde and Hereweald had already married...and she was with child. Fortunately, Uhtric had warned me on the way back from Lunden, so when I saw her in Wiltun, I was prepared, or I thought I was." He looked away from Yanna, turning his head to stare into the fire as he continued, "I was home a couple months, and it was on Yule's Eve. I had promised Leofflaed that I would go with them to Lord Eadwig's for the feast, but after Mass, we went to The Boar's Head. It was while we were there when Hereweald came in and told me that..." he closed his eyes, "...that Isolde had died in childbirth." He still was looking at the firepit, so she could see the gleam of the tears on his cheek trickling down into his beard, another difference from both Saxons and Franks, who favored mustaches of varying lengths. "And, he told me that the reason she died was because the child was too large for her."

Yanna understood then, that while she was certain that Titus had told her the truth, he had not yet been completely forthcoming.

"Was this Hereweald a...large man?" she asked gently. He shook his head, and she swallowed the surge of anger and jealousy. Doing her best to still sound gentle, she said as a statement, "So you lay with Isolde after she married Hereweald."

She was surprised when he shook his head, saying without hesitation, "No! She wasn't married to Hereweald when we were together." Understanding this would not be enough, he explained, "The night before we left to join Alfred, she came to Uhtric and Leofflaed's home, where I lived. She told me then that she would be marrying Hereweald the week after we left. And," he said with a shrug, "I believed her."

They sat in silence then. Finally, Yanna stood up, walked around the small table and held out her hand, which Titus took. Without a word spoken, he took her hand, allowing her to lead him to the bed they shared in the corner of the room.

Ealdorman Sigeræd actually made Alfred and his army wait in Aylesford for a full day and a half, infuriating not just Alfred, but his warriors, who were enraged on their King's behalf. For the Wiltun men in particular, there was no question in their minds that this was a deliberate insult; never far from their minds was what they unanimously considered the act of cowardice and betrayal by Sigeræd's most trusted Thegn, Beorhtweald, and the Centish crew of the *Dragon's Fang*, when they had set the trap for the marauding raiders from Frankia, with *Sea Viper* and *Dragon's Fang* being used by Alfred as bait. While it had ultimately been a success, it was not due to the courage of the Centishmen; even Beorhtweald had been forced to admit to Alfred that they had withdrawn from the fight before it started, claiming that the presence of more Northmen ships than expected rendered the situation untenable, prompting their withdrawal without putting up a fight. As far as the men of *Sea Viper* were concerned, the Centishmen abandoned them, and the consensus, one that had not only not changed but in fact had hardened into a fundamental truth for each of them, was that the reason for their surviving long enough for Alfred, aboard *The Redeemer*, and the rest of the Saxon fleet to arrive in time was due to the actions of one man, and one man only. The fact that Titus was not with them now actually exacerbated the hostility they felt towards the Centishmen, and this insult by Sigeræd was just another example of Centish arrogance, and their lack of trustworthiness as far as the Wiltun men were concerned. For Alfred, while he shared their indignation, he also knew that he had not been and was currently in no position to exact some sort of punishment on the Centish Ealdorman. In simple terms, even now, seven years after his victory at Ethantun and almost three years after the Saxon victory over the seaborne raiders from Frankia, his power was not yet solidified, at least not enough that he could afford to risk a rift with Cent. While this was another thing the King would never mention aloud, even to his confessor, his hesitation was due in part to what had occurred with Ealdorman Wulfhere's betrayal, and because of Cent's strategic location, with its miles of coastline and multiple anchorages, when coupled with his distrust of Sigeræd, who he believed harbored ambitions that included his crown, Alfred had decided that he must swallow his anger. Therefore, when the Centish nobleman finally arrived at the head of his own forces, he could not fault the reception from his King, and in a sign that Sigeræd recognized that he was pushing the boundaries of acceptable behavior, informed Alfred that, should the King desire it, his men would continue their march towards Hrofescester after a brief rest.

"If it is your wish, Lord King, I can send some of my men ahead under the command of Lord Beorhtweald in order to put pressure on the Northmen surrounding Hrofescester after they have recovered from the march here," he said, immediately after the courtesies were observed.

They were in Alfred's tent, the same tent he had at Hamtun, which served as a reminder to the King that there could be another reason that Sigeræd might want to send Beorhtweald ahead, and, he thought with some grim humor, he was wise to do so. He had been surprised when the Wiltun men had obeyed his orders to avoid the Centishmen in Romney on the fleet's return from their defeat of the *viking* that had originally been led by Sigurd Gunnarson, although he was happy that they did. Since then, there had been no opportunity for the Wiltun and Centish warriors to be in the same proximity, making this the first opportunity for Eadwig's men to exact vengeance on Beorhtweald. No, he thought, even as he nodded politely at what Sigeræd was saying, *I can't fault the Centish Ealdorman for making this offer*, but his mind was already thinking ahead, seeing an opportunity.

"As far as your first suggestion, Lord Sigeræd," Alfred spoke once Sigeræd was done, "I appreciate your eagerness to close with the Northmen, and I agree that having your men set out after a brief rest is a good idea." He paused before continuing, "But it won't just be your men who go, Lord. The entire army will be moving, and we will be moving immediately."

This pronouncement elicited gasps of surprise, not just from Sigeræd, but from Cyneweard, who was standing a short distance away in his customary spot. However, while Alfred had not discussed it with the commander of his bodyguard, or with Ealdorman Oswald of Sussex, who had brought sixty-six warriors, Ealdorman Cuthred of Hampscir, who was supplying thirty-nine men, or Lord Eadwig and his Wiltun men, this was not as spontaneous a decision on the part of the King as it appeared. Starting with the first bitter lesson at Cippanhamm, Alfred had determined that one of the most important strategic tools possessed by the invaders from the North was in their speed of movement, whether it be by ship or on foot. Forced to flee and spend a bitterly cold winter in the swamps of Athelney had given Alfred much food, and time, for thought, and it was from Athelney that three central ideas had developed. The first was in the recognition that this island, that he was one of the only, if not *the* only one at this point in time to think of as one kingdom he called Angle Land, had enjoyed a level of security brought about by the fact that it was an island, and before the arrival of the Northmen, had been safe from foreign marauders.

The fact that he was descended from earlier marauders known as Saxons, who, like the Northmen, had sailed across The Narrow Sea, never really factored into his thinking, although he was aware of the history. From the perspective of

Alfred, ordained by God to be King of the Saxons of Wessex, none of that mattered; what did was that his kingdom had enjoyed a level of security that allowed the land and the people in it to prosper, at least in a relative sense for the times in which they lived. Yes, the *ceorls* had to worry about raids from fellow Saxons, especially those who had the misfortune to be born near a border between shires, as feuds between Ealdormen were commonplace; in fact, in one sense the arrival of the Northmen had been a blessing because it had reduced these raids now that the Ealdormen had a larger threat with which to contend. Nevertheless, the consequence of this relative peace and stability was that the villages and towns of his kingdom, with only a handful of exceptions like Wintanceaster or important port towns, were unfortified and essentially defenseless.

Just the year before, he had taken the first steps in correcting what he saw as one of the most crucial strategic deficiencies in his campaign to repel the Northmen, which was a survey of every town, village, and settlement larger than a family farm or estate. In later years, this survey would have a name, the Burghal Hidage, and it was a sign of Alfred's ordered mind that, before the first spade of dirt was turned, the first column sunk, an exacting inventory of what needed to be defended and how it was to be defended was done. Although it was not complete, circumstances were such that the construction of the first *burh*s had already begun. This was the most ambitious part of Alfred's plan, and it would be the part that took the longest to complete; the second he had actually begun to address first, though he was far from satisfied, and that was in creating a navy that could compete with the Northern longships. The captured Danish ship that had been called *Sea Viper*, but in accordance with Alfred's wishes now had a name more appealing to his Christian sensibilities, *Ærendgaest* (Archangel), was now a part of a fleet that numbered twenty-two ships. While this was certainly an improvement, all but six of the ships, of which *Ærendgaest* was one of the six, were the Saxon design, meaning that they were hopelessly slower than the sleek dragon ships, and he had commissioned a small, select group of Saxons with nautical experience to begin designing a new kind of vessel, one that combined the sturdiness and ability to carry larger loads like the Saxon ships, but faster than the current design, knowing that they would never be as fast as a purely Danish vessel, but were not as lumbering as the current Saxon design while carrying more warriors.

The third strategic advantage of the Northmen was a byproduct of their faster ships, which they extended to dry land, and it was this that Alfred intended to copy now. Whereas in the past, a Northman commanding an army like the one outside the walls of Hrofescester could count on an almost leisurely advance by a relieving Saxon army, and Alfred was under no illusions that whoever it was, this commander already knew of Sigeræd's arrival. In fact, given that Aylesford was only six miles from Hrofescester, Alfred was about as certain as he could be that this was the case, but he was almost as sure that, if they moved quickly, they could arrive at Hrofescester more rapidly than the enemy anticipated. The Northman in command of the besieging force was in all likelihood not expecting Alfred and his army until late the next day at the earliest; if he could cut that by a full day, there was the possibility that they could catch the besieging army by surprise and unprepared.

As many advantages as the northern invaders possessed, some of which had been either negated or at least countered to an acceptable degree in the last ninety years since their first appearance on these shores, the Saxons had some advantages of their own, and one of them was in siegecraft, both in the offense and the defense, while the Northmen had scant interest in it, although just as the Saxons had adapted to the Northmen's tactics, they had begun paying more attention to the art. In fact, the latest information from Wiglaf, his chief scout, was that the Northmen had begun constructing those kind of fortifications surrounding the town, which was protected by a wooden wall. Consequently, an unexpected early arrival by the Saxon army might catch the Northmen in a position whereby the Saxons could at least inflict casualties; that, at least, was Alfred's hope.

Turning to Cyneweard, he ordered, "Go inform the Lords, Cyneweard, that we are departing in one hour."

Cyneweard, thinking that he had not heard correctly, gasped, "One hour, Lord King? That's not enough time to break camp!"

Understanding that he had been too vague, Alfred replied, "You're correct, of course, and I should have been clearer. The men of the army will be marching along with Ealdorman Sigeræd's men in one hour. The servants and slaves will remain behind to break down the camp and pack the wagons." He stood, beckoning to his body servant as he continued, "I intend to surprise whoever it is commanding these pagans outside Hrofescester by arriving sooner than he expects."

The smile he offered the Centish Ealdorman was one that Sigeræd would have cause to remember, not quite wolfish in nature, but close to it. Within a span of perhaps fifteen heartbeats, they could hear the first shouts as the Ealdormen bellowed for their Thegns, and the Thegns began shouting at their warriors as the camp erupted into a hive of activity; Alfred and his army would be confronting the Northmen before the sun set.

One day, almost two years before Titus finally told Yanna about Isolde, he had been in the courtyard of the manor, doing what he usually did when he did not have other duties, working on one of the stakes, stripped to the waist as he thrust and slashed, over and over. He would have preferred facing a live opponent, but the only man who was still willing to face him in sparring on his own was Ranulf, and he had guard duty. Similarly to when he had been in the service of Lord Otha, he had a small audience, usually a few of the members of the little army of staff that were needed to keep the Count's manor running. That was how it was referred to, at least, as a manor, although the Franks called it a *château*, but to Titus, it was what it looked like, a fortress, built for defense against the threat posed by marauding Northmen. In fact, this fortress was only about three years old; not long before Titus entered into his service, the Count had been forced to relocate further inland from the coast because of the constant depredations of the Northmen. And, in a sign of the importance of the Margrave of Flandre, what was protected by the walls of Saint-Omer was in reality a town the size of Wiltun, although every inhabitant served the Count in some fashion.

None of which was in his mind on this afternoon; all that

mattered in the moment was how his forearm stayed perfectly parallel with the ground on his thrusts, his ears listening for the sharp cracking sound that was in its own way the most potent sign that it was the Berserker working the stakes. And, as he had learned when he was in Wiltun, it was the sound created by the massive, explosive power that Titus of Cissanbyrig was able to generate that sent its own message about the identity of the warrior working the stakes that in turn brought the audience. Naturally, he was aware of the eyes on him, but he had long before learned how to ignore them, focusing on the scarred wooden stake by telling himself that this was all real; that the hunk of wood was actually a flesh and blood enemy, and the people watching him was a ploy designed to distract him by this enemy. It was also easier said than done, because it also depended on who was in that audience. When it was the farrier, or one of the cooks, or even one of the other men of the household guard, it was easy to do; when it was Yanna or Lord Baudelius, it was more difficult, but when it was Count Baldwin, as it had been on a handful of occasions, it had required his complete attention. Thankfully, the Count was not around much, most of his time occupied with whatever it was that Frankish Counts did, which seemed to be closeted away in the main building that served as both his home and the headquarters for the administration of the lands surrounding Saint-Omer, which Titus knew was called a *pagus*, and was similar to the Saxon shire, except that the Kingdom of Frankia was huge, so that the *pagus* of Flandre was almost the same size as all of Wessex. It was, Titus thought idly as he paused to catch his breath, a lot of responsibility for someone so young; Baldwin, second of his name, was barely twenty years old, but he had been the Count since he was just fourteen, although Ranulf, who had been in service to the Count for five years, had told Titus that Baldwin's father, also named Baldwin, had appointed a council, which the Franks called a *consilium*, led by a companion of the dead Count, a man named Gozbert. According to Ranulf, which was confirmed by other men of the guard, this Gozbert had had designs of his own that depended on the young Count trusting Gozbert implicitly, which had been the case...at first.

"It was a year after I joined," Ranulf had informed Titus one night, before Titus began spending most of his time with Yanna. "The Count was turning sixteen, and Lord Gozbert had arranged a feast for his name day. Now," Ranulf had lowered his voice, leaning forward as he took a glance around Melisandre's, "nobody knows with any certainty, but the rumor was that Lord Gozbert had planned on murdering the Count and seizing power."

He paused then to take a swallow of wine, but Titus saw the gleam in his friend's eye, which told him this was deliberate, so he decided to have his own fun by saying, "Clearly, it didn't work since he's still the Count. So," Titus shrugged, "what did he do? Put this Lord Gozbert in irons?"

As he had hoped, Ranulf did not appreciate Titus' ruining his story, but he took a measure of revenge by shaking his head, while the grin he gave Titus contained a hint of the kind of satisfaction when one's social betters suffered.

"Not exactly. No, he beheaded him. Along with three other men of the *consilium* who were involved."

Titus gave a low whistle, but he clarified, "You said that the Count had these men beheaded?"

"No." Ranulf shook his head. Tapping the table to emphasize the point, he said, "*He* beheaded them, with his own hand. Now mind you," he laughed, "he made a right bad job of it. It took him three strokes to get Gozbert's head off. The other three were pissing themselves, but he got better as he went along. Although," he allowed, "there are some who think that he knew exactly what he was doing in taking so long to take care of Gozbert."

Titus never asked what Ranulf's purpose was in telling him about this, but if it was to get Titus to view the young Count in a different light, it worked. His own relationship, if it could be called that, with Count Baldwin was both flattering and confusing to Titus; from his arrival and introduction by Lord Baudelais, Baldwin expressed an interest in the Saxon warrior over and above what he displayed towards the other two hundred-odd men of his household guard, something that clearly irritated Lord Baudelius, who reminded Titus of Lord Otha in some ways, aside from the fact that the Frankish nobleman was missing most of his right ear. Titus' assumption was that it was because he and the Count were close to the same age, making both of them a rarity, since only the most experienced warriors were considered for the Count's personal force; he would not learn for some time that the connection ran much more deeply, and much higher than this superficial similarity. For the first few months after his arrival, Titus was subjected to the young Count's scrutiny whenever he was training in the courtyard, albeit from the balcony of the Count's residence, Baldwin watching with an expression that gave nothing away. That, however, was back when men were still willing to spar with the Saxon warrior, but after one particularly brutal bout with Bent, where Titus put the Frankish warrior who, before Titus' arrival had been considered the most formidable warrior in the Count's service, out of commission for more than a month, Lord Baudelius had forbidden any warrior from facing the Saxon one on one.

It was on this day almost two years before his conversation with Yanna that Titus saw his first real action as part of the Count's household guard, after a villager from Watten, which was located downriver on the Aa, arrived in Saint-Omer in a state of panic, culminating in the young Count leading a force composed of half of his household guard, which included Titus.

Because Titus still knew very little of the Frankish tongue, it was left to Ranulf to inform him what the villager was shouting in the courtyard. "This man has a farm north of Watten. He said there is a dozen *Nordmanni* longboats heading upriver!"

Titus was about to ask how far Watten was from Saint-Omer, but remembered that it was about six miles, not that it mattered. The courtyard quickly filled with the others, the noise as they talked to each other excitedly making it almost impossible for Titus to pick anything out. His inability to converse with the others had been just one of the many challenges facing him when he arrived in what he only learned later was the *pagus* called Flandre, so he relied on Ranulf quite heavily in those days, who had picked up a smattering of the Saxon tongue before they met. Fortunately, they did not have to wait long before both Count Baldwin and Lord Baudelius appeared on the balcony, which Titus had already deduced was there for more than decoration but mainly for purposes such as this.

Since the Count was speaking to fellow Franks, it was left to Ranulf to whisper to Titus, "The Count says that the men who are *Eques* need to saddle their mounts to leave as quickly as possible. The *Pedes* will follow, but knowing Lord Baudelius, he is not likely to stop and wait for them."

Because this was the first time Titus had ever faced action as part of this force, despite having Thunor with him, he did not know whether he was included, and Ranulf ran to ask the two noblemen. As he watched, Titus saw Baudelius shake his head, but when Ranulf turned away, Baldwin spoke, his tone sharp, and Ranulf bowed once the young nobleman was done, then trotted over to the Saxon.

"Lord Baudelius said that since you have not undergone the trials he requires of all of us *Eques*, he wanted you to march with the *Pedes*. But," he jerked his head back in their direction, yet when Titus glanced up, they had both disappeared back inside, "the Count said that you will ride as an *Eques*."

Ranulf was already moving towards the stables as he finished, forcing Titus to scramble to catch up, but he ignored the Frank's grin that told him this had been intentional to ask, "We'll be fighting from horseback?"

"We might," Ranulf answered, though his attention was already elsewhere, grabbing the saddle for his own horse, a grey stallion named Grisel, "but it depends on those *Nordmanni* bastards."

Titus did not ask any more questions, hurrying over to Thunor with his own saddle, and while his hands moved with the practiced certainty that came from repetition, Titus' mind was working furiously, trying to recall the last time he had fought from horseback. Not, he told himself, that there's much chance that these Northmen would be bringing their own ponies on a raid; unless, of course, he realized, they plan on roaming the countryside, which was a possibility if the villager had been telling the truth about there being a dozen ships. To his relief, he was not the last one out of the large stable, joining the fifty men of what the Franks called *Eques*, completely unaware of his own connection to the people who had created this term, and in fact, many of the terms used by the Franks. Their language was closer to Latin than his own Saxon tongue, which had posed a problem for him from the beginning, finding the Danish tongue somewhat easier to understand than the Frankish, though this was all the time he gave to such thoughts, running to the large building that served as the barracks for his part of the household guard, joining the others in putting on their armor and gathering their weapons. Since this was still early in his service to the Count, he was still wearing the mail shirt he had taken from the Dane he slew at Ethantun, while the helmet was one he had traded for, having lost the one it replaced at sea when he had been knocked overboard during the *Sea Viper* fight. He was already wearing his sword, also from the Dane, checking to make sure the sword slid easily from the scabbard, but he had since added a Danish ax, which he thrust under his belt. The men around him were doing much the same thing, although they were also talking excitedly to each other, in their tongue of course, and Titus heard himself being mentioned, although not by his name but as "Saxon"; he had not done anything to warrant being called "Berserker" to this point, although this was about to change, something that neither he nor anyone else knew.

He was not surprised when, after he picked up his shield and began heading for the door, his path was blocked by the Frankish warrior Bent, a name that Titus thought was especially appropriate now, given how his nose now took a decided turn about midway down, thanks to him. The reason he was not surprised was due to the fact that there had been bad blood between the two, literally from the moment they met, when Titus had sought refuge from a downpour at what he would later learn was Melisandre's as he drifted north from Brittany, not really knowing where he was heading. It had been Bent, along with his close companion Sigismund and a couple of other warriors, who had initiated the trouble that ended up with Bent's nose matching his name, while Sigismund was unable to eat solid foods for a week, and Melisandre's was in a shambles. Since that moment, Bent had taken every opportunity to try and belittle the Saxon, yet despite not facing the Northmen in battle to that point, the Frankish warrior had seen support for his campaign against the Saxon melt away, just by Titus' sheer competence in the training yard.

Even another sound beating had not dissuaded Bent, this one with a wooden sword, which was why he stood there now, a sneer twisting his thick lips as he said, "I will be watching you...*Saxon*. You may have fooled the others, but you have not fooled me!"

"That is good." Titus nodded in seeming agreement, and as he intended, he saw the look of surprise and confusion flash across the Frankish warrior's features.

"Why do you think this is good?" Bent scowled suspiciously, reminding Titus that while Bent was not particularly intelligent, he was just clever enough to recognize that this was not the response he expected, and rightly suspected that he was being mocked in some way.

"Because," Titus answered evenly, fighting the smile that tried to creep into the open, "you might learn something, Bent. Remember how easily I've beaten you when we spar?" He shook his head, and in mock sadness, said, "I am surprised that you have survived this long, but maybe it is because these *Nordmanni* are not as fierce as the *Dani*."

This, as Titus knew it would, enraged the Frank, just as it would have angered even men like Ranulf, who Titus was beginning to consider a friend by this point, since the question of who was fiercer, the Danes or Northmen, was as much a point of contention here in Frankia as it was in Saxon lands. Among Bent's other shortcomings, he was not a particularly quick thinker, and this was exacerbated when he was angry, so he was left standing there, spluttering impotently as he tried to think of something clever to say, while Titus gently but firmly pushed him aside. The problem, Titus thought as he strode over to Thunor, was that he knew that Bent was not alone in his suspicion of him, and he was honest enough with himself to know that he did not help his own cause. His stubborn refusal to cut his braid or shave his beard; even his insistence on carrying an ax, which was uncommon among Wessex Saxons, and practically unheard of with the Franks, when added to the normal suspicion of outsiders that, frankly, was shared by his own people on the other side of The Narrow Sea, all added up to a healthy distrust of the Saxon by a fair number of his comrades. And yet, despite knowing that he could make his life easier, that streak of mulishness that his sisters, Uhtric, and Isolde when she had been alive, had teased him about unmercifully, showed itself now. None of this was in his mind as he leapt aboard Thunor, in armor and with his shield in one hand, without touching anything with his free hand, giving Ranulf a grin as he landed in the saddle, thinking about how often he had practiced that back in Wiltun, something he had no intention of ever telling the Frank.

"You like to show off," Ranulf grumbled, "but let us see how you fight from horseback."

It was, Titus knew, a fair point, so he did not say anything; besides, he had barely gotten settled into the saddle when Lord Baudelius shouted something that became clear when the men immediately arranged themselves into a mounted column of twos, with Ranulf nudging Titus into the spot next to him just as the gates swung open, and with the Count and Lord Baudelius leading the way, the force of *Eques* left Saint-Omer, heading for Watten. They had gone barely two miles on the hardpacked dirt road that paralleled the Aa when there was a shout from one of the pair of scouts that the Count had sent ahead as they came galloping back towards the column. Because of their position, near the tail end, it was almost impossible to see anything at the front, but as Titus strained his eyes to look beyond the small cloud of dust raised by the pair of scouts, he gradually recognized that what he was looking at was not just dust, but smoke.

Reaching out, he grabbed Ranulf's arm and with his free hand pointed slightly above the heads of the riders in front of them, exclaiming, "Look! That is smoke, not dust!"

At first, Ranulf did not react, and in fact was about to disagree, but the Saxon's pronouncement was validated by the shout by Lord Baudelius again, and once more, Titus did not comprehend the meaning of the words; the fact that the column went from the brisk trot it had been maintaining to a hard canter that was just short of a gallop confirmed to him that the Northmen had stopped at Watten and were putting it to the torch. Titus' immediate thought was that this sight of destruction of the village would spur the Count to do something rash; thankfully, even if he had had the urge to charge headlong towards Watten, Lord Baudelius stopped him. There was a brief conference at the head of the column, then four *Eques* detached themselves and headed for the trees. The pause was welcomed by most of the men; Titus was an exception, feeling the rush of...something that he only realized now that he had been missing in this period of relative period of peace. Sparring was better than nothing, but it did not fulfill what he was only now recognizing in its absence was a deep need that, when he thought about it, he likened to those men who craved ale or some other intoxicating beverage above and beyond what was considered normal.

"The Count sent those men ahead to scout," Ranulf commented, but Titus only responded with a nod, watching the trees intently for any sign that the scouts had run into trouble.

They returned seemingly unharmed, though at the gallop, drawing up in a spray of dirt, pointing back at Watten as they informed the two noblemen of what they had seen. Given their location in the column, it would have been impossible for Titus to hear, even if he could have understood the words, so he resigned himself to wait to find out. Whatever the news was, it engendered another discussion between Baudelius and Baldwin, and it was during this when the rearguard shouted something. The entire column twisted in the saddle, and more than one hand dropped to sword hilts at the dust cloud that was approaching from the south and Saint-Omer, but as Titus guessed, it was the remainder of the Count's force, the *Pedes*, numbering more than a hundred fifty men, if the Count had not ordered more than a dozen men to stay behind. There was a further delay as they waited for the infantrymen to arrive, led on horseback by Lord Arnoulf, who Titus had been informed was essentially the third in command, followed by another conference, while the smoke above Watten thickened and drifted higher into the sky. Finally, Lord Arnoulf went galloping back to his command, then they moved at a trot past the horsemen, their faces dripping with sweat from the exertion of hurrying from Saint-Omer.

"They already look exhausted," Titus murmured, half-hoping to hear Ranulf disagree, but the Frank nodded soberly.

"They do," he agreed. "But," he shrugged, "they will do what they need to do."

"Which is?" Titus asked, realizing that they had never discussed tactics to this level of detail.

"They will tie up the *Nordmanni*," Ranulf explained. "Then, once they are engaged, Lord Baudelius will take us around so that we can hit them from the rear. At least," he shrugged again, "that is what we normally do."

Titus' first thought was that they would be better served to already be moving, but even as the thought entered his mind, the *Pedes,* after aligning themselves in the Frankish version of a shield wall, began marching into the trees, whereupon both Baudelius and Baldwin thrust their swords into the air, then pointed to their left, moving in that direction as they did. Still in their column, the *Eques* followed, moving west away from the river, and Titus wondered how far they were going to travel before turning back north towards the coast. Reaching the western edge of the forest in about a mile, Titus looked to his right, and while they were too far away to make out much, he guessed that perhaps half of the buildings of Watten were aflame now. Whether it was due to the incompetence of whoever was commanding these Northmen, or as he deduced from what his Frankish comrades were saying, God performed some minor miracle that temporarily blinded the Northmen to the sight of a force of cavalry circling around the village would never be known. He supposed it was possible that it was the case of divine intervention, but he believed it more likely that it was a combination of the smoke and the confusion inherent in the sacking of a village. Ultimately, it did not matter why, what did was that they swung around so that the village was to their south, where they encountered a few dozen panicked villagers who had managed to escape.

What Titus noticed, and a glance over at Ranulf told him that his companion had as well, was that the vast majority of these escapees were men who had chosen to flee rather than stand and fight for their wives and families. It was, he was forced to admit, understandable, but to a warrior like Titus, that did not make it any less inexcusable, and he took a grim sort of satisfaction when Count Baldwin swung his sword at a particularly insistent *servus* who was grabbing the Count's leg with one hand while pointing towards the village, his tone sounding more akin to what the Count would use when giving orders. At the last instant, Titus saw the young nobleman twist his wrist so that he struck the man on the side of the head with the flat of his sword, but the *servus* still dropped to the ground like a sack of grain. While Titus made sure to guide Thunor around the prone villager, the men ahead of him were not quite as careful, so that by the time he reached the man, his features were obscured by blood, and he was clearly dead. The other men who had fled had gathered together in a huddled mass, staring at their saviors with a hostility that was made even more virulent because of their impotence, none of them being armed with even a spear. This was all the attention Titus gave them, as now he heard Lord Baudelius shouting orders, but as he usually did, he looked to Ranulf for clarification, especially because, of the few Frankish words he knew at this point in time, he had never heard the commands used for the *Eques*.

Ranulf understood, so once Baudelius was finished, he said, "The Lord has commanded that we form in the Boar's Head." Immediately realizing this would have no meaning to the Saxon, Ranulf struggled for a moment before, inspired, he put his hands together, but with just his fingertips touching while his palms were a few inches apart.

"A wedge," Titus understood immediately, thinking that this would be what he would have ordered, though his pleasure was short-lived because, as they maneuvered their horses into position, Titus found himself squarely in the middle, with Ranulf and Sigismund to his left, and Sigismund on the outside, while Bent and Gerulf were to his right. Making it worse, Bent was immediately next to him, with Gerulf on the outside.

Somehow, Titus was certain that this was no accident, which seemed to be confirmed when Bent muttered, "I am watching you, Saxon, in case you try some sort of trick to help these *Nordmanni* dogs!"

If that was all Bent would do, this was not a problem for Titus, yet he suspected that the Frank had something planned;

if he had managed to get Sigismund where Ranulf was, he would have been certain of it. There was no more time to think about it, as Baldwin thrust his sword into the air, bellowing something that Titus learned was the order to begin at the trot. Since this was his first time doing anything like this, Titus relied on Ranulf, and he saw that his friend had put his spear into the scabbard behind his right leg.

Seeing Titus looking in his direction, Ranulf had to shout to be heard. "Your spear will be useless where we are. Use your sword, and be ready because those bastards will do everything they can to break us apart!"

This was the moment they went to the canter, the noise increasing, but for Titus, the most distracting part was how, being as tightly packed as they were, he could not see anything beyond the riders immediately ahead of him, so how would he know when they came into contact with the Northmen? This thought had just flashed across his mind when the *Eques* went to the gallop, which was the signal for all of the men around him to begin bellowing at the top of their lungs. Like a huge, many-legged beast, the Franks went plunging into what Titus could at least see was now a maelstrom of smoky chaos, thick enough to make his eyes sting, and the volume not only increased, there were added elements, in the form of the shrieking of the women and children who had been abandoned by their husbands and fathers, and men bellowing in what Titus could tell was the tongue the Northmen shared with the Danes.

Despite now being three rows back, and even with the other noise, Titus heard the meaty, deep sound as both Baldwin and Baudelius' mounts smashed into what would turn out to be a hastily created line of men as the fight for Watten began in earnest. And, at first, all went according to plan, as the power created by the momentum of the mass of horseflesh sent the Northmen reeling backwards, and while he was not doing so, Titus would not have been gotten beyond the count of ten before he found himself unexpectedly confronted by the appearance of a snarling face, lips peeled back to reveal teeth that had been filed to look like fangs, although it was the wolfskin headdress, complete with a wolf's skull attached to the helmet that informed Titus that his foe, who in that instant was swinging his ax, was an Úlfhédnar, a Wolf Warrior. This realization did not stop Titus from reacting immediately, understanding that the Northman was aiming for Titus' right thigh, his Danish sword moving even before he had a conscious thought in an upward sweep that struck the stout ash handle of the bearded ax just below the head. The shock that ran up his arm turned it numb, and it was only by virtue of his own prodigious strength that he was able to deflect the downward motion of the ax with just the strength of his arm, despite his foe putting all of his body into the blow. It was not all good news for the Saxon, however; while the blade did not cut into his leg, the head of the ax caromed sideways and in the process, the spike that topped the ax grazed Thunor's head just behind the ear. More startled than from any pain; afterward, Titus found only a tiny scratch that had drawn a small amount of blood, the stallion suddenly reared, bellowing his own cry of frightened anger, but it forced Titus to drop the reins to grab the saddle in order to avoid being thrown.

His foe, moving with a speed that seemed inhuman and, as Titus would learn later, was aided by a concoction that Úlfhédnar drank before going into battle, dashed under Thunor, intending to gut the horse, when Ranulf, seeing that Titus was in no position to stop him, leaned over and launched a thrust of his own at the Northman. It was not a killing blow, being at the end of Ranulf's reach, but the tip of his blade bit into the warrior's bicep in the eyeblink before he swung the ax up in an underhand blow aimed at Thunor's belly. Now it was the Northman's turn to bellow in pain, but more importantly, he was forced to scramble out of the way as Thunor's front hooves came crashing back down to the ground. The horse, aware of the threat to his most vulnerable spot, performed a movement that Titus had never seen Thunor do before, and the only way he stayed in the saddle was because he was still holding on to the saddle as his horse used his powerful hindquarters to make a slight hop while twisting his body to his left at the same time so that when all four hooves were back on the ground, the Úlfhédnar was now essentially back in the same position where he began, except this time, Titus was ready, his sword already swinging downward in a similar motion that the Northman had attempted when trying to cut his leg off.

Whether he was weakened or distracted by his foiled attempt to kill Thunor, Titus neither knew nor cared, because what mattered was that he was slow in bringing his shield up over his head, too slow, and in less than an eyeblink, his head went tumbling up into the air, the spurting blood from the stump of his neck seemingly standing out even more to Titus' because of the grayish-brown dusty air. When he kicked Thunor, his horse did not hesitate, slamming into the headless corpse just as it was collapsing to the ground, though Titus barely noticed, seeing only that the gap between himself and the second rank had grown and knowing that other Northmen would see the same thing and rush in to exploit it. This kind of fighting was unlike anything Titus had experienced; the only time he had fought on horseback it had been to cut down fleeing Danes after Ethantun, but these Northmen were not running, they were standing and fighting, darting in and out, trying to get under the Frankish horses, or separate and isolate a single horseman. Just then he saw Bent, his blade already bloodied to the hilt, suddenly veer away from his right side, turning so that his horse was perpendicular to Titus and Thunor, while on his left, Ranulf was still oriented in the same direction as he was, but half of a horse's length ahead of him. Bent was flailing with his sword in a frenzy of motion, alternating his strokes between his right side, where he sent a Northman leaping backward to avoid the slashing blade, then twisting his upper body to do the same to an enemy warrior wielding a spear. To Titus, it appeared that Bent was in danger, yet despite his feelings for the Frank, he kicked Thunor, intending to run down the spear-wielder, deeming this Northman to be the bigger threat because of the reach of his weapon, but just as he did, a shout, a scream really, came above the already deafening sounds of the fight. Naturally, it was in Frankish, but Titus understood every word.

"The Count is down!"

Normally, Titus loathed men who yanked their horse's reins, knowing how tender their mouths were, but this was what he did then, and whether it was painful or not, to his eternal credit Thunor reacted instantly, spinning about to plunge into what had become a tumult of confusion where dust mingled with smoke from the burning village around them, and disembodied voices were shouting in two different tongues while barely discernible figures were milling about, the metal of helmets, armor, and weapons catching a stray ray of sunlight that penetrated the choking cloud for the briefest fraction of an eyeblink. Moving more by sense than sight in the direction it seemed the repeated cries about the Count were coming from, Titus used his sword judiciously, not wanting to become engaged, thrusting it at any Northman who got near enough they might be a threat to his attempt to reach the Count, while trying to identify those men he could see were mounted.

However, while he thought he recognized Baudelius, he could not be sure, although he knew that it was the bodyguard commander's voice that was shouting, "Save Count Baldwin!" over and over.

It would help if I knew where he was, Titus thought sourly, although he recognized the possibility that because of the lack of visibility, Baudelius did not really know either. Then, as if by some unseen force, or perhaps a random breeze that just happened to blow strongly enough and in the right direction, for the briefest moment, Titus could see more than a couple feet beyond Thunor's nose. What he saw initially froze his blood, and he actually stopped Thunor's movement; indeed, if a Northman had been paying attention to the large Saxon, they probably could have ended him because he was staring so intently at the sight about a dozen paces away and directly in front of him. The shouts had been accurate; the Count had been unhorsed, and in fact, he was standing hard up against the body of his horse, using the corpse as a protection from an attack to his rear and holding a spear and shield as he crouched in a ready position, while what Titus identified as two men of the *Pedes* had reached him and were standing on either side. What initially puzzled Titus was how the rest of the *Eques* did not seem aware of the precise location of their threatened Count; it would not be until later, from Ranulf, that he learned that the bulk of them had been following the sound of Baudelius' voice, who was in fact leading them away from the Count, which he would later attribute to the appalling visibility, which was accepted by most, if not all of the men who had been present. Why Lord

Baudelius was heading in the wrong direction, and bellowing for the rest of the *Eques* to follow him was of no consequence to Titus; all that mattered in that instant was what Titus saw, a pair of Northmen rushing at the Count, one from his weak side and one from his strong side, while another half-dozen launched short throwing spears at the *Pedes*, and most importantly, what the sight of his embattled Count unleashed in him. This would be the day where Count Baldwin, second of his name, and the men of his bodyguard would learn that the rumors they had heard about this Saxon were true, that he *was* the Berserker, and as the Berserker, he was an unstoppable force on the battlefield. It would be a day where, once again, everything changed for Titus as it pertained to his relationship with the most powerful man in his life, and once again...he would have no memory of it.

Chapter Two

Just as Alfred had intended, the arrival of him and his army caught the Northmen outside Hrofescester unprepared, but much to the surprise of Eadward, the Saxon king did not seem all that interested in taking advantage of this by going into battle immediately. While it was true that the men were tired, Eadward felt certain that they would summon the energy to throw themselves at the Northmen, but Alfred did not give the order, although he did array his men in a line across the neck of land formed by a loop of the River Medway where Hrofescester was located, a few hundred paces south of the similar line of Northmen who were outside the walls of the town but were now facing the newly arrived Saxons. However, it was Eadwig who not only understood their King's strategy but agreed with it, which he explained to his son as they walked to where the King was standing, waiting for his tent to be erected.

"The King isn't going to waste men, not when we can achieve the same ends another way," Eadwig said.

"And what way is that?" Eadward asked, unconvinced.

"If you'd be patient, we'll find out soon enough," his father snapped, but then relenting slightly, he added, "But if I had to guess? I think he's going to besiege the besiegers."

Which, as Eadward learned moments later, was exactly what Alfred intended.

"We are going weaken the Northmen before we attack," he announced. "And to do that, we must cut them off from supply, which is why Lord Æthelweard should be sailing with *The Redeemer* and four other of our ships, and they will be joined at the mouth of the Medway by one of Ealdorman Sigeræd's Thegns, Lord Cœnred, who will be sailing aboard *Dragon's Fang* and who will be bringing another four ships of their own. This should be a sufficient force to bottle up the Northmen's own fleet, which numbers fourteen ships." Eadward was close enough to his King to see the flicker of irritation when he mentioned the Centish ship and about which Eadward had seriously conflicting feelings himself, recalling how Alfred had been enraged by the Centish Ealdorman's refusal to surrender the ship, which like *Sea Viper* had been captured from the Danes. This was just another example of Centish perfidy as far as Eadward was concerned, and he was not alone in this judgement. Not that his opinion mattered, he knew, and he silently listened as Alfred continued, pointing to where the men of his force were arrayed, ready and waiting for an attempt by the Northmen to engage with the newly arrived force. "We are going to build our own fortifications."

Eadward was not surprised that there was a stirring as some of the Thegns, who were part of this small but select group, murmured with what the young lord was certain was concern at the idea. Alfred, clearly seeing this, offered them a slight smile as he explained, "I can see that some of you think this is foolhardy, but let me put your minds at ease." Indicating the Centish Ealdorman, Alfred said, "Lord Sigeræd has assured me that his Thegn who's commanding the garrison inside Hrofescester, Lord Rægenhere, is not only an experienced man, he's quite bold. Whoever it is commanding those Northmen will be forced to divide his forces if he wants to stop or at least disrupt our work in hemming them in, and if he does that, Lord Rægenhere will not hesitate in taking advantage." Shaking his head in a slightly exaggerated manner, he assured the men, "No, they will try to convince us that they are going to attack us, but they will not. Now," he turned back to the south, pointing to the dust cloud made by the approaching baggage train, "our implements will be here soon, and we will do as much work as we can before dark."

Since he did not ask anyone other than Otha and Ceadda, Eadward could only assume the other Thegns, all of them more experienced than he was, agreed with his own.

"The King is right; they're only going to try and convince us that they're attacking us, but they don't have the numbers to take us and to fend off an attack by that Rægenhere from inside the town at the same time. They'd be slaughtered."

"Do you know him?" Eadward asked Otha, who had offered his opinion.

"I know him by sight, but not to speak to," the Thegn replied. Then, he added grudgingly, "He has a good reputation as a warrior..." Eadward was certain he knew what was coming, and he was not disappointed when Otha finished, "...for a fucking Centishman."

Alfred was proven correct, in all instances. The commander of the Northmen, who they would learn a few days later was named Hallsteinn Olafson, and had sailed across The Narrow Sea from a place called Boulogne, which Eadward knew had been taken by the Northmen early in their raiding and served as one of the largest and busiest of the ports from which the pagans launched their forays against his island, had made a big show of lining his men up, where they stood, slapping their shields with their swords, axes, and spears, bellowing their challenges and promises to wade in the guts of the Saxons. By this point in time, Eadward was experienced enough to have learned a smattering of words in the Northmen's tongue, though he understood the Danish version more easily, but with them bellowing all at once, he could not pick out much of what was being said...not that there was any need. It did serve to delay the Saxons from beginning their own work, but Eadward had learned why Alfred had insisted that the forces he summoned bring more slaves and servants than would be considered necessary, so that Hakon and Beohrtic were among those with spades who began digging into the earth and piling up the spoil on the southern side, which would form the basis of the wall.

By the time the Northmen gave up the pretense that they had any intention of trying to stop the Saxons, there was only enough daylight left to finish what was the most important part, the ditch and wall, which extended almost a half-mile across the neck of land. The Wiltun men were dirty, exhausted, and angry because the servants and slaves had been hard at work as well, which in turn forced them to prepare their own meal, and that was before they were informed by Eadward that they would be standing guard on the dirt wall for the first watch; that he had volunteered them was something he did not feel it necessary to share, nor that it had been at his father's direction.

"If my old bones are right, we're going to be here a long time," his father had told him in their tent which they shared. "I'd rather have them tired now rather than later, after we've been on half-rations."

It would turn out to be a wise decision, one that Eadward would remember. Their guard shift that first night passed slowly, if uneventfully, aside from the catcalls and jeers from the Northmen who would come rushing towards the ditch, trying to elicit a reaction, but while the Wiltun warriors were too experienced, some of the warriors of Thegn Beorhtweald's Centishmen hurled their short throwing spears out into the darkness, the only damage inflicted being their pride when they were rewarded by mocking laughter from the Northmen. Otherwise, the sun rose as it always did, and now that the Northmen had seen what Alfred intended, they abandoned any pretense that they intended on attacking and began work on creating another set of fortifications similar to what they had used to hem in the defenders of Hrofescester, except these were oriented in the opposite direction. None of the men present, save one, was aware that what was taking place was remarkably similar to an event that had occurred more than nine hundred years earlier, across The Narrow Sea in Frankia, nor that what was being done by the Northmen was called a contravallation. The exception was Alfred, who had been given a precious copy of the great Caesar's work, *De Bello Gallico,* just a matter of a year earlier, as a gift from the Margrave of Flandre, Baldwin, second of his name, although this was not on his mind as he watched both his army and the enemy as they worked to improve their respective positions.

The two ditches were separated by a distance of about two hundred paces, placing both sides out of enemy archer range, although neither Saxons nor Northmen relied on the bow much for war. What pained Alfred and was the cause of him staring morosely at the Northmen busily at work was what was required to relieve the people of Hrofescester; this area outside the walls had been fields that had just recently been planted, but the ground now was despoiled, the tender shoots of budding plants trampled into the ground. It would be, he thought grimly as he stood on the freshly packed earthen rampart watching his men drive sharpened stakes into the base of the dirt wall at the edge of the ditch, a hard winter for these people, and that was after enduring the hardship of being besieged. Like Eadwig, Alfred had experienced siege warfare before, although this was his first such operation as King, and he knew that it was a tedious, grim, and dirty business, a race against time as supplies dwindled, followed almost inevitably by the onset of sickness from the poor sanitation conditions endemic in the camps of both besieged and besieger.

The people inside the walls at least had the river to transport their waste out to sea, along with a series of wells inside the walls that drew on the groundwater, plentiful enough next to a river, although as Wiglaf had reported, the Northmen had dug their latrine pits next to the riverbank, along with channels that transported their waste downriver past the town walls, so the smell would be atrocious. And, he understood, it was inevitable that some people within the town would fall ill, even with the wells, although it vexed Alfred greatly that he did not understand why. It was at this moment, which made sense given his train of thought, that he began thinking about reading the Roman general's account of the conquest of Frankia, although it was called Gaul then. Specifically, he tried to remember reading anything about Caesar's Roman soldiers being afflicted during their sieges of Alesia, Gergovia, and a number of other locations, but as far as he could recall, Caesar spoke of hunger and exhaustion, but never of a bloody flux of the type that Alfred knew he and his men would be facing, with the risk growing every day of the siege. In fact, the Saxon King was acutely aware of the risk he was taking by not engaging the Northmen immediately, and he knew how, if given the choice, most of his warriors, baseborn and noble, would prefer a sword through the guts and dying in that manner rather than spewing noxious shit as a man's own body seemed to eat itself as they lay on a cot shivering and crying for God to end their suffering that could last for weeks. It was a risk, he well knew, but while Alfred was personally brave, and recognized that men followed him at least in part because he had proven his courage in battle, he was not normally an eager warrior, especially when it came to sacrificing the men who followed him. If he could achieve defeating these invading savages without spilling a drop of blood, he would be more satisfied with that victory than if he and his warriors slaughtered every Northman; what mattered more than anything was that he *was* victorious.

One frustration he was grappling with was the fact that these were not Danes, they were Northmen, and at this moment, he was ignorant of the identity of the leader of this force, although even after he learned the man's identity it was not particularly helpful knowledge. No, if they had been Danes, then he could have sent an emissary to Æthelstan in Lunden, and there was a possibility that the Dane who called himself King of East Anglia might have personally intervened, even if these Danes had come from Frankia. Northmen, however, were different, and his attempts to glean information about them had met with mixed success, and while he did not care to think about it overmuch, he did offer prayers for the men he had sent across the water to Frankia to gather information who did not return. If Alfred of Wessex possessed one weakness that, if an enemy found it, could be exploited by them, it that was that, when Alfred did not know something he considered important for him to know, it could drive him to distraction as he focused almost exclusively on what he did *not* know as opposed to what he did. So far, this had only resulted in what bolder men like Ealdorman Eadwig would call a hesitance on his part, or in this case, an abundance of caution in choosing to wear his enemy down over time. Whether this was going to work was something he would not know for weeks, and it was this uncertainty that caused the sudden flare of pain in his gut, Alfred was sure of that. Unfortunately, he had long experience in such things, and in fact had been expecting something like this as soon as his mind went in the direction it had gone. Turning away from the Northmen, Alfred walked across the earthen rampart, down the dirt ramp and headed for his tent. To the men around him, all of whom stopped what they were doing as they bowed their heads, a habit that Alfred hated since it took them away from their work, the King presented his normal demeanor; only men like Eadwig would have noticed how one hand that seemed to be tucked into his belt in a casual manner was actually pressing against his stomach, and would have recognized it as the most potent sign that it was because he was in pain. Fortunately, none of those who would have seen and understood this were anywhere about, and Alfred was able to enter his tent, allowing his servant to drop the flap, despite it making the tent stuffy, before he collapsed onto his cot, his face shining with sweat.

"Tell Father Æthelred I need him to attend to me," he managed through lips pressed tightly together.

The servant, knowing the signs, rushed out of the tent.

Across The Narrow Sea, Titus, now riding immediately behind Count Baldwin in an unmistakable mark of favor and one that not even Bent was foolish enough to challenge after Watten, was scanning the land to their right side as they rode at a steady walk, heading almost due west from Saint-Omer. They were heading for Boulogne, and this time, it was not like their haphazard dash to Watten almost two years earlier, because this time, they were embarking on a campaign. Accompanying the Count's personal bodyguard were the men of the *lantweri*, the Frankish version of the *fyrd*, numbering more than nine hundred men, so when combined with the Count's bodyguard, a force of more than a thousand were on the march. It had been weeks in the making; while Titus had learned by this point that the young Count was receptive to the Saxon's counsel when it came to personal combat, and was interested in hearing how Saxons waged war, he was not at all eager to hear about it when, in Titus' opinion, the Saxons did something better, and when it came to summoning the *servii* from the *pagus* of Flandre, to Titus, the Franks seemed almost leisurely in their actions. Not, Titus admitted to Yanna, that he had all that much experience; the only *fyrd* that he had been a part of was the one seven years earlier, when Alfred had summoned it after Cippanham. Still, it was something, and from the young Saxon's perspective, what took the Franks more than six weeks to do, when looking at the number of men answering the call, King Alfred had done in half the time. Not that it matters now, he thought as he scanned a small forest off to their right looking for movement, not now that they were finally on the march.

With the composition of the force being what it was,

composed almost entirely of infantry, with the entire complement of Baldwin's *Eques* of fifty horsemen joined by the *Eques* of the half-dozen lesser nobility that the Franks called *domini* of the *pagus* of Flandre, there were more than eighty warriors who, if required, could fight from horseback, although as Titus had learned, the Franks were like the Saxons in preferring to do their fighting with both feet on the ground, the fight at Watten being unusual in that regard. The rest, marching in a ragged column five abreast, were led by the hundred fifty *Pedes* of Baldwin followed by those belonging to the other lords, altogether numbering almost another four hundred, with the six hundred men who, aside from slightly different dress, could have been *ceorls* like Isolde's father Cenric and his friend Heard, sturdy farmers who, in their own way, were every bit as tough as the men riding with Titus. The purpose of this *lantweri* was straightforward, and had been building for some time, until the Frankish King Charles, called Charles the Fat, which Count Baldwin had gleefully confirmed was an accurate nickname, sent an official courier the Franks called a *Legatus*, ordering that the Count take whatever steps necessary to drive the Northmen from Boulogne. The order had come in late February, unleashing the activity that now ended with this, the first day of what would be a three-day march from Saint-Omer.

Suddenly, Titus' eyes caught something, although he could not have articulated what it was, not at first, but then it happened again, and while he did not shout, he spoke loudly enough for the Count, Lord Baudelius, and the five men around him to hear, "Lord, I see some movement in the woods to our right front!"

Both noblemen stopped their conversation, their heads moving in unison, which in turn triggered a reaction from whoever it was just inside the trees, as the shrubbery and low hanging branches suddenly moved in a violent manner that was not due to the light breeze, while Titus was certain that he saw the hindquarters of a horse as its rider wheeled it about.

"Berserker! Take your *Exploratores* and go after him!" Baldwin shouted, speaking rapidly, but even though Titus' fluency had markedly improved, he already knew what the order was, so he was already kicking Thunor, with Ranulf next to him, going to the gallop as they went streaking towards the trees.

He knew from observation what the role of the *Exploratores* was, again completely unaware of his connection to the originators of the term, and that it was essentially identical to the role Wiglaf and his men played for King Alfred, but this was his first time as such. Indeed, he had only been told by Count Baldwin as they were actually heading out of the gates of Saint-Omer, who also ordered him to pick five other men. Naturally, Ranulf was his first choice, now firmly established as Titus' closest friend; the other four, however, had taken some thought, with Titus selecting Hekfrid, a narrow-faced, sallow warrior who was one of the best horsemen of the group, along with Hekfrid's companion Lambertus, a quick-witted, cheerful man about four years older than Titus who reminded him of Dagfinn. The final pair were Theutbald, the oldest of the group and almost the polar opposite of Lambertus, rarely smiling but agreeable enough, and Wala, Theutbald's younger brother who, if anything, was more taciturn than Theutbald. None of which mattered; Titus had seen them in action, and on horseback, which was why he barely slowed down when he reached the edge of the forest, aware that it was possible that the stranger he had sighted had company, but not only did he not think it likely, he had confidence in his companions. And, even if there were more horsemen he had not seen, hitting them at close to full speed would negate a possible advantage in numbers. It was not necessary, thanks to Thunor, who, without any guidance from Titus, suddenly veered slightly to the left, and when he looked in front of his horse, he saw a flash of blue, which he recognized as the trailing edge of a cloak, streaming behind the fleeing rider.

"This way!" He did think to shout in the event that the others were farther behind him, but when he risked a quick glance over his shoulder, he saw Ranulf there, bent low over Grisel's neck and grinning at him, which Titus returned.

The undergrowth was denser now that they were in the woods, and Titus understood that he was likely at a disadvantage, not knowing if there was clear ground up ahead, so that when Thunor slowed slightly as he began to pick his way more carefully around the trees while avoiding obstacles underfoot, Titus did not force him back to his original pace. Besides, he could see they were gaining on their quarry, and Titus took the opportunity to check to see that Hekfrid and the other four *Exploratores* were close by, with Hekfrid on his right side and Lambertus on the opposite side. Returning his attention to their prey, he caught a flash of silver-gray when the rider turned his head to look over his shoulder, giving Titus a bare glimpse of a bearded face, although it was the unexpected smile that he would remember given what was about to happen. He saw the Northman's hand raise then come down hard on his mount's rump, the horse responding by increasing its speed.

"*Berserker!*"

What happened over the next few heartbeats occurred so quickly, and was so unexpected that it was all jumbled in Titus' memory, but the bare bones of it was that, from their right quarter, bursting out from what had seemed to be an impenetrable wall of low shrubs and small trees, at least a dozen mounted men materialized no more than fifty paces away.

"*Ambush!*"

Acting completely on instinct, somehow Titus understood that he would not have time to draw his sword, and although his shield was strapped to his forearm, it was on the side opposite from this sudden attack. Later, he could not recall if he had forcefully pressed his knee into Thunor's left side in a command they had practiced more times than he could count that told his horse to turn sharply to the right, or Thunor had acted on instincts of his own, but whatever the case, it put Titus in between a pair of Northmen going in the opposite direction. In the span of the less than a full heartbeat he had, Titus thrust his right hand out perpendicular to his torso in a hard shoving motion, and somehow struck the Northman on his shoulder just as he intended. It was a glancing blow, and if it had been delivered by anyone else, it might have rocked the Northman in the saddle, but this was from the Berserker, and it struck the rider with enough force that he reeled to his left, grabbing wildly for the front of his saddle with his free hand to retain his seat.

Titus was already past, so he did not see that the Northman missed and toppled from his saddle, though he heard the shrill screams, first from the Northman as he fell under the hooves of the horse next to him, followed immediately by the horse, who stumbled over the body. By the time Titus managed to slow Thunor enough so that he could turn around, he only saw the aftermath; two men and one horse on the ground, the animal writhing in agony with its right front leg dangling at a grotesque angle, while the man Titus assumed was the one he had struck was lying facedown, his body spasming in a manner that the Saxon had seen before that told him he was out of the fight permanently. The second Northman, who Titus assumed was the rider of the horse with the broken leg, was on his hands and knees, his helmet a couple paces away, shaking his head trying to clear it. Hesitating only long enough to draw Wyvern's Fang, which he had been carrying for more than a year now, Titus kicked Thunor and, as he passed by the Northman, leaned over and executed a hard, downward thrust, the point punching into the base of the man's neck, whereupon the man collapsed facedown, not even quivering. Then, returning his attention to the larger situation, he saw that his fellow *Exploratores* had managed to coalesce, forming a makeshift protective circle, which was surrounded by the still numerically superior force of enemy horsemen.

Theutbald was furiously engaged with a Northman who was armed with a spear, which he was thrusting repeatedly at the Frank, altering his aim as rapidly as he could, but to this moment, Theutbald was able to block the attacks. Theutbald was also slightly more separated from the others, and even in this brief heartbeat of time, Titus saw another enemy horseman, obviously seeing this gap as well, kick his mount and head for it, which would thereby place him on Theutbald's weak side and slightly behind him. Fortunately for Theutbald, Titus was moving as well, and while there was not enough distance for Thunor to reach full speed, he still covered the space so quickly that the second Northman did not have the time to twist in the saddle to present his shield, and just that quickly, Titus made his third kill as the point sliced through the mail vest just below and a bit behind the Northman's armpit. His foe would have shrieked in agony, but Titus' blade punctured a lung, so what came out was a breathy moan, but then Thunor was past them and his rider was already looking for another target. It was during this brief moment that Theutbald, taking advantage of the distraction on the part of the spear-wielding Northman, who obviously had been counting on his comrade to dispatch the Frank, managed to get inside his opponent's spear to drive his into the man's chest, sending him tumbling backwards off his horse. Now that Theutbald was free, he waded into the clash between Wala, Hekfrid, and three Northmen, still using his own spear and the advantage in reach it gave him to good effect, jabbing it at one of the Northmen, and while it was at the outer range of his reach, Theutbald did manage to distract his foe just enough that it gave Hekfrid the opening he needed to drive his sword under the small round shield of the Northman, who recoiled backward, dropping his own weapon to clutch his stomach, his hand instantly turning red from the blood pouring from the gaping wound. Titus saw none of this because, for the first time, he noticed something; the warrior in the blue cloak they had been pursuing was not part of this group of Northmen.

In a flash of realization, Titus, certain that these men were buying the escape of their comrade with their lives, shouted, "Ranulf! With me! We need to catch that *bâstart*!"

Ranulf did not hesitate, and while he did not like doing so, Titus forced Thunor to move more quickly than the horse wanted, although it was Titus who paid for it when they shot past a small tree and one of the thin branches slashed across Titus' face, which he could tell by the feel had drawn blood.

"You did that on purpose," he muttered to Thunor, but he also made sure to lean forward and place his head closer to his horse to avoid being struck again.

The pain was enough to fill his eyes with tears, and he tried to blink them rapidly to clear them, but it was Ranulf who spotted the fleeing Northman first.

"There he is! He's turning west!"

Titus was aware they had been generally heading north, so he looked to his left, yet it still took a heartbeat for him to spy their quarry, while Ranulf had already made a shallow turn, so that by the time Titus changed direction, he was a few lengths behind his friend, and perhaps three hundred paces away from the Northman. Because they were still in the confines of the forest, it meant that the fleeing rider would suddenly disappear from view, either behind a wall of brush and trees, or because there was a dip in the undulating ground. At times like this, it was impossible to judge exactly how long they had been in pursuit, but Titus guessed they were perhaps a mile and a half north of the column, and now that he had turned to head west, at least a half-mile ahead of Count Baldwin and the army. Thunor's normally dull golden coat was now a darker, almost bronze color, and his head was beginning to bob slightly, the first signs of fatigue, and Ranulf's Grisel was in a similar condition. However, what Titus had no way of knowing was when they would reach open country, or if in fact they would before they closed with their quarry. And, he could plainly see, they *were* closing, because as he had perceived from his first glimpse, these Northmen were riding their own native mounts, which were little more than ponies, something had puzzled Titus, though he was far from alone. They had been here in Frankia for decades, as they had been on his island home, yet they had never seemed interested in the advantages of the larger, sturdier, and ultimately superior horses like Thunor, not that he was complaining. The pursuers reached a dip in the ground, with Ranulf about two lengths ahead of Titus, and on the upward slope Titus pulled even, just in time to see that their foe was now less than a hundred paces away. Most importantly, just ahead of the Northman they could see the bright sunlight of open ground. While he did not like to do it, Titus used the flat of Wyvern's Fang, which he was still holding, to smack Thunor's powerful hindquarter, wincing at the half-shriek, half-bellow of surprise, pain, and more than a little anger, but it served its purpose as Thunor opened his stride.

"We cannot let him get too far out into the open!" he shouted, but while Ranulf said nothing, he gave a grim nod.

When they burst out into what appeared to be an open, fallow field that, if it had been cultivated at one point it had not been in many years, yet another reminder of the impact the marauding Northmen had had on this formerly peaceful land, they were within fifty paces and the Northman's pony was clearly foundering.

Ranulf carried a few short throwing spears in a quiver

attached to the edge of his saddle, and he reached for one now, but Titus, thinking he knew what his friend intended, shouted, "No, Ranulf! Let's take him alive! He can tell us what's ahead of us!"

Again, Ranulf made no verbal reply, nor did he even acknowledge the Saxon, instead using the shaft of his throwing spear in the same manner as Titus had used Wyvern's Fang on Thunor, creating a burst of speed from his mount that closed the gap to perhaps twenty meters, whereupon in one, fluid motion, Ranulf stood up straight in his stirrups, still holding the reins with his left hand, then hurled the missile with all of his might, the momentum causing him to bend at the waist so that, for a heartbeat, it appeared as if he would pitch over his horse's head, though he did not. From Titus' perspective, he was certain that Ranulf had misjudged, it looking as if he had thrown well ahead of the Northman, who just happened to glance back, and now they were close enough for Titus to see the fear in his eyes and how, despite the beard, he was barely older than the Saxon. It turned out that Ranulf had not misjudged, at all; again, from where Titus was on Thunor, it looked as if the pony ran directly into the path of the spear as it dropped out of the sky, and he also learned that Ranulf had heard him because, instead of striking the rider, the point of the spear buried itself just in front of the point of the animal's left shoulder. Somehow, Titus had no idea how, the smaller horse did not collapse immediately, managing to keep moving at least two more lengths before, finally, its left front leg gave way, the stricken beast letting out a scream of pain that was almost human as it went crashing into the ground, even as its rider went sailing through the air to collide, with a sickening force, onto the uneven earth, though he did manage to tuck his head and hit the ground on his shoulder then tumbled over and over, limbs akimbo, before coming to a stop, face up. The impact with the ground drove the point of Ranulf's spear deep into the animal's body, and as Titus slid to a stop next to it, prepared to put it out of its misery, it exhaled its last breath in a gout of blood and froth, its hooves giving one last quiver as if it was still trying to escape its fate. Without being aware of doing it, Titus had dismounted then found himself standing over the Northman, who was conscious, but judging by the manner in which he kept rapidly blinking, Titus' first thought was that his wits had been scrambled. It was with some chagrin that when Ranulf, swinging out of his own saddle, came and stood next to Titus and blocked the sunlight, stopping the Northman's blinking that he realized that he had just had the sun in his eyes, while the look he was giving the two warriors now told Titus that his senses were with him.

The point of Titus' blade was already at the man's throat, and he asked, in Frankish, "Do you speak the Frankish tongue?"

It was an old but effective trick, something that he had actually been taught not by Otha, or by any of his Frankish companions, but Einarr the Dane, back when he had been his "guest" in Lunden.

"If a bastard shakes his head, or says no when you ask him if they speak your tongue, then he's probably lying, at least a little," Einarr had told him. When Titus had asked how one would use that, he had shrugged and said, "We usually start by peeling off some skin. That is how we learn if they are truly lying."

It was something that Titus would do, though not as his first resort, but the Northman made no response at all, not even a shake of the head, looking up dumbly at the pair.

"What about the Saxon tongue?" Titus asked, though he was not surprised that this earned him no reaction.

"I say we cut his balls off, and *then* we ask him questions," Ranulf suggested, staring down at the Northman balefully. "I wager that he will learn our tongue as if by magic!"

However, they had been friends long enough that Titus knew Ranulf was not serious, and that he was using another tactic to achieve the same result, trying to determine whether this Northman truly had no idea what they were saying, or he just had his wits about him and was disciplined enough not to react.

The Northman swallowed, which Titus could feel through his sword, but he said nothing, nor did he make any movement of his head, choosing to continue to stare up at them, only his eyes moving, back and forth from Titus to Ranulf.

On an impulse, Titus asked in Danish, "Do you understand the Danish tongue?"

He got his answer in the manner in which the man's eyes widened slightly, but Titus also noticed he maintained enough self-possession not to nod his head, since even that could draw blood.

"Yes."

And, while Titus was somewhat relieved, his Danish was rudimentary, nor had he had an opportunity to use it, and while it was very similar to the language spoken by the Northmen, he had been informed by Dagfinn, who had been his primary teacher in the Danish version, that those differences, while small, could be important.

"I think," Dagfinn had told him one night when they were both uproariously drunk, "that more Danes and Northmen have been killed by each other because a word has a different meaning than those you Saxons have killed put together!"

It was, he felt somewhat certain, an exaggeration, yet at the same time, Titus felt the responsibility of being the commander of the *Exploratores*, and as Count Baldwin had said just that morning, which seemed like days before, that Titus' ability to communicate with these savages was a factor in his decision.

Now, looking down at the Northman, Titus began by asking bluntly, and in Danish, "Who are you, and what were you doing spying on us?"

By the time Titus was done, he was certain of two things; killing this Northman, whose name was Halfdan, was the only way to shut him up. The other was that, if Halfdan was telling the truth, Count Baldwin and his Franks had been presented with an enormous opportunity.

The first week after Alfred and his army's arrival at Hrofescester would prove to be the most eventful, as the commander of the Northman belatedly seemed to recognize his predicament, which most of the Saxons, including Eadward, put down to the arrival of *The Redeemer* and the other ships that effectively cut off Northmen supply up the Medway. Two days after the arrival of the fleet, the Northmen had attempted to break the blockade, though not with the intention of evacuating, but to enable one of their ships to slip past the Saxon blockade, and while none of the crew on that ship was captured alive to be questioned, the assumption was that the leader of this force was sending for reinforcements. They *had* learned by this time that the man's name was Hallsteinn Olafson, though in itself this did not mean anything; that he had sailed from Boulogne was significant only in the sense that Alfred knew that this was one of the largest among what he thought of as the nests of vipers dotting the coast from which the pagans launched their *vikings* against his kingdom. Stopping their ship, in fact damaging it so badly that it sank in the middle of the river, was certainly a positive thing, and it helped boost morale any time the Saxons managed to thwart these savages. The next night, another attempt was made, not to try and escape by ship, but by a half-dozen Northmen who, under the cover of darkness, swam across the Medway. That they were caught coming out of the river was a credit to Ealdorman Sigeræd, who had urged Alfred to place a series of outposts along the opposite riverbank, each of them with four warriors, and it was the men from two outposts who converged on the Northmen, slaying four of them outright, while the fifth was wounded and died soon thereafter. It was from the sixth man they learned more, and while the information was valuable, it was also of a nature that Alfred summoned his senior noblemen to his tent.

"As you know, the leader of this attempt to take Hrofescester is named Hallsteinn Olafson, and that he and his army sailed from Boulogne, which as we all know, is the closest port to us of any size." He took a breath before continuing, though he made sure to maintain the same composed demeanor and matter-of-fact tone, "This Hallsteinn is a sword Dane, sworn to Sigfred the Úlfhédnar." He stopped then, knowing that there would be a reaction, and he was not surprised when he saw that it was young Lord Eadward and his Thegn Otha who had the strongest response, although there were a ripple of murmurs among the others as well. The name of Sigfred the Úlfhédnar was known among the Saxons, although to this point, most of his depredations had been either in Frankia, or farther north, especially in Northumbria. For the Wiltun men, and to a lesser extent for Alfred himself, there was more to this revelation than just his formidable reputation. During the intervening time after Titus had returned from Lunden, followed by his flight after beating Hereweald to death, thanks to the unofficially sanctioned but nonetheless vital commerce between the Danelaw and Saxon lands, they had heard bits and pieces about Titus' time as a hostage in Lunden. Specifically, they had heard about his combat with Leif Longhair, who had been a close friend of Sigurd Gunnarson, who was more widely known as Sigurd the Bold. Sigurd had been the leader of the *viking* that had sent the Wiltun men to sea, also learning later that, like Hallsteinn, he had been a sworn man of Sigfred. Beyond that, and just a few months earlier, they had learned from a merchant that men in Sigfred's service had come to Lunden to speak with King Æthelstan.

This merchant, the same man who Einarr Thorsten had used to begin the negotiations that resulted in Titus' release, brought another message from the Dane, where he informed Lord Eadwig that, despite it being two years earlier, Sigfred had finally decided that he needed to exact vengeance on the Saxon who called himself the Berserker for killing his son...Leif Longhair? Wasn't that his name? Alfred thought. Since Titus was long gone, he could not inform him that, according to Einarr's message, it was more likely that Sigfred was angrier about Titus slaying Sigurd at the monastery at Stanmer, because the warlord had more regard for Sigurd than he had for his youngest son. Which, as anyone who had met both Sigurd and Leif Longhair knew, was completely understandable. Nevertheless, whatever the reason, this Sigfred was offering a substantial reward for the capture of the Saxon named Titus, who called himself the Berserker. Just as those who knew the two Northmen could attest which of them was the more valuable man, those who knew Titus would tell anyone who cared to listen that the appellation of Berserker was one that he did not care for, nor had he given it to himself. In his note, albeit dictated to a Saxon in Lunden who knew his letters, Einarr had actually mentioned that, like Sigfred the Úlfhédnar, Einarr himself had been offended that a *Saxon* was calling himself a Berserker; until, that is, he had been aboard *Sea Viper* and, like Eadward, Otha, and the other Wiltun men, had witnessed for himself that Titus was worthy of that title. None of which, Alfred reminded himself, mattered at this moment; it was enough that he saw the mention of Sigfred was not lost on Eadwig, Eadward, or the two Wiltun Thegns seated with them.

Continuing, he said, "The men last night were sent by Hallsteinn to try and reach Lunden. And," he took a breath, bracing himself for what he was certain was coming, "they were to ask King Æthelstan for aid in breaking our siege of their encampment."

The reaction was immediate, and was exactly what Alfred had expected, although none of the noblemen jumped to their feet, which was something of a relief. Their words, however, were another matter.

"Lord King!" Ealdorman Cuthred, who had arrived with his men just a day earlier, was a man that Alfred knew could be counted on for holding the most virulent and unfavorable views of the former Guthrum. "This must not go unanswered! We must let Guthrum know the penalties for aiding *any* savages who sail from Frankia, no matter who they might be sworn to!"

Alfred stifled a sigh, then explained patiently, "Lord Cuthred, just because this Hallsteinn sent men to *King Æthelstan*," he emphasized the title and name as a reminder to his lords that he required them to refer to the Danish king in the acceptable manner, "to ask for help, there is no indication that there was any chance of King Æthelstan agreeing!"

If this had any impact on Cuthred, it did not show, the Ealdorman snorting, "He clearly believed that Gut...Æthelstan would at least consider his plea, Lord King! Surely you see that!"

In fact, Alfred did not, and despite it being clear that Cuthred had a fair amount of support in his distrust of Æthelstan, he made this clear.

"I am not going to risk provoking King Æthelstan based on the fact that this Northman sought aid from him. Nothing I have seen or heard indicates that Æthelstan is any happier about these incursions from across The Narrow Sea than we are. Indeed," he pointed out, "the fact that we are having this discussion at all is why I'm not inclined to believe he had anything to do with this. And that," his voice hardened in a sign that this was their King speaking, and that his word was final, "is all I intend to speak on this subject." He paused to scan the faces, and satisfied with what he saw, he continued, "Now, we need to send out foraging parties for our own needs..."

For the next several moments, the King and his commanders concerned themselves with the myriad details that a siege entailed. Once they were dismissed, Alfred beckoned to Lord Eadwig and his son, indicating that they stay behind. Naturally, this engendered murmurs and glances, particularly among Cuthred and Sigeræd, who Alfred considered the two Ealdormen who bore the closest watching, and his spies had in fact been assiduous in gathering bits of information that convinced him that his vigilance was at least justified. Cuthred's ambitions had less to do with Alfred's throne than his coveting Wiltscir, so it made sense that the glare he gave Lord Eadwig, albeit at his back as the Ealdorman left the tent, was baleful in nature. Alfred did take note of something else; young Eadward pausing to turn and look directly at Cuthred, and while the young nobleman was turned away from him, Alfred saw the Ealdorman's face coloring, and he fumbled with the flap of the tent before thrusting it aside and exiting. Alfred had had somewhat limited contact with Eadward; as King, he was acutely conscious to always address himself towards the current Lord of Wiltun, making a show of paying attention to Eadwig more than his son, feeling that it was not only politic but that it was the least he owed the older nobleman, the only real concession he made in recognition that he was treating this man, who had shown nothing but loyalty, so poorly. Alfred had also noticed the almost alarming decline in Lord Eadwig just in the interval between Yule and now, though he still made sure to address him as soon as they were standing before him.

"There is something else we learned from Hallsteinn's man before he...succumbed," was how Alfred put it, ignoring the flicker of amusement from Eadwig, knowing that there were men who thought him squeamish. "It concerns Sigfred...and your man."

Even Kings, Alfred thought with wry amusement, had to learn when to be mindful of their subjects' feelings, which was why he did not mention the name of that man, though he saw there was no need, given how Eadwig stiffened, but it was the expression on the son's face that offered the most powerful testimony that sire and offspring were at odds on the subject of Titus of Cissanbyrig.

"Oh?" Eadwig replied stiffly, his tone flat and neutral. "What now?"

"Just that Sigfred the Úlfhédnar hasn't paid anyone the bounty he promised," Alfred explained. Despite himself, he glanced over at Eadward as he added, "And he's now increased the bounty...to one hundred pounds of silver."

For Eadwig's part, the moment he understood that the subject would be Titus, he was determined not to betray any interest or concern, but he could not stop the gasp from escaping his lips at what was a staggering sum.

"By the Rood!" he exclaimed, yet for one of the only times in his association with the pious King, Alfred did not admonish him, and in fact made what was a very rare jest.

"Yes," he said dryly, "by the Rood indeed, Lord Eadwig. One might say that is a...kingly sum."

Both father and son laughed, not just out of politeness but from real appreciation at Alfred's wit, then without thinking, Eadwig said ruefully, "It's probably a good thing I banished him, because that would be a tempting offer." He clearly understood the import of his words, his face coloring, and he glanced over at his son who looked to Alfred as if he had been slapped. "I apologize, my son," he muttered. "Those were poorly chosen words."

"Yes," Eadward replied tonelessly, but Alfred could see he was shaking slightly, and Alfred felt certain that the young lord was struggling to contain his rage. "They were, but no apology is necessary, Lord. You've made your feelings abundantly clear on the subject."

Alfred felt the embarrassment of the person who has inadvertently created an awkward situation, and it was because of this that, for a brief moment he considered divulging to the pair that he actually knew Titus' location, at least in a general sense. It did not last long, however, mainly because it would not help matters at all.

"Yes, well," he cleared his throat. "The good news is that Sigfred has been thwarted in his designs to this point." Deciding on the fly that sharing this piece of information could not hurt, he said, "And I don't think that Hallsteinn can count on Sigfred sending reinforcements any time soon. According to the prisoner, Sigfred didn't sanction this *viking* because he's in Frisia, gathering men and ships for something that this man didn't know about."

"So he says," Eadwig snorted.

"Considering that he died, and in a most...painful manner," Alfred countered quietly, "without divulging anything other than Sigfred left Boulogne for Frisia, I tend to believe that he did not know."

He stood then, in a sign that the conversation, and the audience was over, and the pair, interpreting this correctly, bowed and left the tent, leaving Alfred to gaze at their retreating backs, a frown on his face. Perhaps, he thought, it's time to have a private conversation with young Eadward.

"I'm sorry, Eadward," Eadwig said awkwardly, and it took an effort on Eadward's part not to come to a dead stop, but the expression on his face elicited a rare chuckle from his father, who joked, "Surely it's not *that* rare that I apologize is it?" Then, before his son could respond, Eadwig added ruefully, "Actually, now that I think about it, I suppose it is."

Now, Eadward laughed, a hearty one that was not forced and which caused his father to join him, offering nearby onlookers a rare sight, of the dour Ealdorman in a mirthful mood.

Once they subsided, Eadward decided to take a risk by asking, "What is it that makes you so harsh when it comes to Titus, Father? Why can't you forgive him?"

This startled his father, and for the first time he glanced over at Eadward, remembering their many conversations, and immediately understanding why his son would see it that way, which he acknowledged.

"I can understand why you would have that impression, my son," he replied soberly. "But while I confess that I was angry at the lad, and," he admitted, "for longer than I should have been, that hasn't been the case for some time." He paused then, and by doing so, gave Eadward the impression that his father was waiting for him to work it out for himself. Eadward tried, the pair walking a few paces in silence, but finally he shook his head in frustration, though he said nothing. "If I made it known that I forgave Titus, and rescinded his banishment, what do you suppose he would do?"

Eadward thought for a moment, and now a glimmer of an idea came to him as he replied slowly, "He might come back to Wiltun."

"He might," Eadwig agreed. "And if he did, how long do you think it would be before that heathen bastard Sigfred would hear of it?"

Understanding then, Eadward sighed, "Not long. And then," he nodded grimly, "Titus would be in even greater danger since his whereabouts would be known to Sigfred."

"Yes," Eadwig seemingly agreed, but added forcefully, "but that's not my primary concern. You know better than anyone that Titus can take care of himself, and this Sigfred would have to send more than just two or three men. No," he shook his head, "my concern is for my people who would be hurt in the event that happens. And Eadward," his tone became almost gentle, "I don't think that you can argue that Titus is almost as dangerous to his friends as he is to his foes."

Eadward's first impulse was to argue, but even as he opened his mouth to do so, he realized that it was, frankly, inarguable.

Instead, he asked, "So you have just been saying that it's about not being seen as weak and vacillating?"

Now it was Eadwig's turn to hesitate, but like his son, he decided that honesty was the best option, and he admitted, "No, I won't deny that that's part of it. Especially now as I've gotten older, and my time on this side of the dirt is coming to an end. No," he held up a hand to stop Eadward, who had in fact opened his mouth to protest, "don't argue. We both know it's true. I'm...failing, Eadward. I don't expect to see another Yule feast. And," he put a hand on his son's shoulder, squeezing it hard as he assured Eadward, "that's God's will, my son. I have no complaints, and I thank Him that I've been able to see you become the man that I hoped you'd be."

It took a supreme will of effort on Eadward's part to maintain his composure; that he was conscious that there were eyes on the pair, which was always the case when their men were anywhere nearby, was the only reason he was able to do so.

Finally, he managed to say, "I had a good teacher, Father."

"Oh, I agree," Eadwig replied, smiling. "Otha *did* do a good job," earning the father another laugh from his son.

They had reached their tent by this point, and while Eadwig went inside, Eadward informed his father that he needed to check on the men, who at that moment were responsible for reinforcing a section of the dirt wall by creating a latticework made of strips of wood at a spot where the wall kept collapsing down into the ditch. His father was not fooled; he had seen how shaken his son was, but he went along with the fiction, needing his own time alone, and he gave a nod before disappearing inside the tent. Eadward did head towards their men, but he took far longer than necessary to cover the distance, his mind absorbed with so many thoughts, some of them conflicting, and he would look back at this conversation for the rest of his days and wonder if he had missed something.

The opportunity afforded Count Baldwin and his army was created by the absence of Sigfred the Úlfhédnar, and most importantly, the bulk of his forces, from Boulogne.

"The prisoner told us that there should have been a garrison of more than a thousand men left behind," Titus had explained to the Count and Lord Baudelius during the impromptu conference conducted on horseback, although about fifty paces away from the column to avoid prying ears. "But then one of the noblemen left behind decided to go on a *viking* and took almost half the remaining garrison with him."

"To where?" Baldwin asked, but Titus could only shake his head.

"Halfdan...that was the prisoner's name," Titus explained when he saw the looks of confusion on the faces of the two noblemen, "did not know other than it was nowhere in Frankia. They were heading across The Narrow Sea, but he swore he did not know where. If he did," he added grimly, "it was a secret he felt worth dying for."

It was Baudelius who asked, "Do you know the identity of

this Northman who would disobey Sigfred?"

Actually, Titus did, nodding as he supplied, "Hallsteinn Olafson."

The name had meant nothing to Titus, or Ranulf for that matter, but it clearly did to both noblemen, eliciting a grunt from Baudelius, who said, "That makes sense."

Baudelius was not inclined to explain to the Saxon; he was by nature more suspicious, and he had never warmed to Titus as the young Count had, so it was Baldwin who explained, "Hallsteinn has the ambition of Lucifer, Berserker. Our spies have informed us that he has clashed with Sigfred on multiple occasions because he believes that he has earned more glory for Sigfred than for himself, yet the Úlfhédnar refuses to give him the rewards he feels he deserves."

While Titus had never heard of Hallsteinn, he was well aware of Sigfred, though not simply because he was one of the most powerful warlords among the Northmen, which he was, but because of his title by which he was known. It had been Dagfinn who explained that the Úlfhédnar would be considered by Saxons, and Franks, to be of the cult by which Titus himself was becoming known.

"But they are very different," Dagfinn had warned Titus in Lunden. "The spirit animal of the Berserker is the bear. And," he allowed, "most men who claim the bear as their spirit animal are like you." He indicated Titus' muscular frame, then held up a hand to simulate height. "The Úlfhédnar worship the wolf, and the men who claim the wolf as their spirit animal are leaner, and not as tall, but that is not what makes them more dangerous than the men who worship the bear."

Despite how often he told others, and himself, that he had nothing to do with his nickname, and how he did not care for it, Titus still found himself bristling at what he took as a sign of disrespect, this dismissal of the Berserker as being the more dangerous of the two.

"What makes you say that?" he challenged Dagfinn. "A bear could tear a wolf apart with out any effort!"

"That is true," Dagfinn agreed, or at least seemed to, but then he added, "a bear can defeat *a* wolf." He paused for perhaps the span of a full heartbeat before going on, "But how often have you seen a bear fight one wolf?" The Dane was rewarded by the sudden change in Titus' expression, telling him that he had scored, so he continued, "What makes the Úlfhédnar so dangerous is that they're as cunning as wolves, and they *never* fight alone, not unless they are forced to. Do *not*," he had shaken his head to emphasize his point, "take them lightly, Titus."

It was this conversation that was on Titus' mind when he said, "That sounds like a dangerous thing to do for this Hallsteinn, defying Sigfred like that."

There was agreement at this, but it was Baudelius who thought about it, then said slowly, "That is true. Which means that Hallsteinn must have plans to either defy Sigfred and is challenging his leadership...or," he glanced at Baldwin, "what we have heard is correct, that Sigfred is far from here."

"Frisia," Baldwin breathed the word. "Sigfred is in Frisia. This Hallsteinn has taken half of the garrison across The Narrow Sea, and," his voice was rising in pitch, a sign of his growing excitement, "there are only about five hundred *Nordmanni* defending Boulogne." Addressing Titus, the Count said quickly, "I am afraid that you and your *Exploratores* will not have time to rest, Berserker. We must know if this is true, or is some sort of ruse."

Titus knew better than to let his dismay show, although he did ask, "May we have time to water the horses and give them a few moments to rest? And," he thought to add, "Hekfrid was wounded in the fight with the *Nordmanni* who ambushed us. It's not serious," he assured the Count, "but he did lose a fair amount of blood."

"Lord Count," Baudelius interjected, not doing much to hide his impatience, "every moment counts. They will have to ride through the night to reach Boulogne as it is, then depending on how long it takes to perform a thorough scout, they might not return to us for another half-day after that."

Baudelius said no more than that, but Titus had the distinct impression that there was an unspoken message to the Count, and judging from Baldwin's slight nod of the head, he had received and understood it. This, in turn, got Titus thinking, and it did not take him long to at least believe he understood

Baudelius' concern, which in turn caused him to grab at his saddle as unobtrusively as he could as his head felt like it was suddenly spinning.

They're concerned that Sigfred might be about to attack Saint-Omer!

On the heels of this thought was the image of Yanna as he had left her in her cottage, her eyes shining with unshed tears as she jokingly admonished him that he did not need to try and add to his reputation as the Berserker. Ranulf had taken a woman, and they had had a child; they were at Saint-Omer as well, as had dozens of the men of Count Baldwin's personal bodyguard. Suddenly, Titus had a glimpse into the challenges, and the crushing responsibility that came with all of the luxuries and privileges accorded a Count, or a Saxon Ealdorman for that matter. What was, after all, the right answer? Had this all been an elaborate trick, starting with the spy who had informed Baldwin that Sigfred the Úlfhédnar had taken a sizable portion of his fleet and his men, sailing north along the coast, leaving behind Boulogne and a garrison of a thousand? And now, according to Halfdan, that had been cut in half because of Hallsteinn, but was that really the truth? Of this second part, Titus was as certain as he could be, though he also recognized that it almost did not matter if the first was not. Realizing that, as much as he wanted to give Thunor and the other *Exploratores*' mounts a rest, there was simply too much at stake.

"We will leave immediately, Lord Count," Titus announced, while at the same time deciding that he would make do with four men and leave Hekfrid behind to bind his wound from a spear thrust to his leg that, thankfully, did not sever the large vessel but still had bled copiously. "But with your permission, I would like to leave Hekfrid behind with the rest of the army, and we will take the Northmen's ponies that we gathered up as spares so that we can make good time."

Since he had addressed the Count, when Baldwin inclined his head, he replied with a nod of his own then turned Thunor away to head to where the men of his small force were waiting when Baudelius spoke up.

"Berserker, you are one man short now."

Unsure why the lord, who was more highly ranked than a Saxon Thegn, but not of the same status as a Count, was pointing out the obvious, Titus decided to take the safest course, saying only, "Yes, Lord, we are."

Later, Titus would wonder if this had irritated Baudelius to the point he made this move; somehow, he suspected, this was not the case.

"I know that," Baudelius snapped. "Which is why, if Hekfrid will not be with you, you need another man so that you are an even number and can work in pairs." His face gave nothing away, yet Titus was certain he heard a note of satisfaction in the lord's tone, as Baudelius continued, "That is why Bent will join you."

It was only through a supreme effort that Titus did not groan aloud, but he did not bother looking to Baldwin for help, for a number of reasons, although the main one was that Titus had learned that Baldwin rarely, if ever, overruled Baudelius on such matters. From Titus' perspective, Baldwin, who Titus had to continually remind himself was actually a year younger than he was, twenty to his twenty-one, was still unsure of himself in many ways, and in fact was intimidated by Baudelius, who had served his father in the same role for years before the first Baldwin had died, back when the current Count was just fourteen. His judgement seemed confirmed when Baldwin looked pointedly away, which also meant he missed the cruel smile Baudelius gave Titus.

In a measure of small revenge, Titus replied tonelessly, "Yes, Lord," then turned Thunor's head away without being dismissed, which meant that when Baudelius offered an oath at the Saxon's impertinence, he could not see Titus' broad grin, knowing this would rub the stiff-necked Frank the wrong way even further. He did not look forward to trotting down the column to where Bent was sitting, Sigismund next to him, nor what he had to tell his rival.

"Hekfrid was wounded," he said peremptorily, then felt a stab of chagrin at the look of alarm, not just on Sigismund's face, but on Bent's, another reminder to Titus that the Frank's enmity extended only to him, and for the most part, Bent liked the other warriors of the Count's bodyguard well enough, and also for the most part, it was reciprocated. This was why he added hastily, "It's not serious, but we have a hard ride ahead of us, and Lord Baudelius said that you should replace him."

He did not wait for an answer, telling himself he needed to inform the other *Exploratores* what was taking place, which was true, and it included informing Hekfrid that he should seek aid from one of the slaves in the baggage train who served as orderlies. Not surprisingly, the others were not happy when Titus informed them that the period of time they had been standing there, dismounted and talking amongst themselves, was all the rest they would be getting. Before a count to one thousand, the *Exploratores* had remounted, with each man holding the reins of one of the slain Northmen's ponies as a spare, the column had resumed the march, and his comrades were regaling Bent with tales of the attempted ambush by the Northmen.

Ranulf, riding alongside Titus, waited for perhaps a half-mile before he finally demanded, "Well? Whose idea was this for us to keep going?"

Just by his friend's tone, Titus knew Ranulf was certain that he knew, but Titus shook his head and said flatly, "It was not Baudelius. At least," he amended slightly, "not in front of me. Maybe they had talked about it while we were gone, but it was the Count who told me. And," he hesitated, not certain that it was wise to share this with his friend; then, he decided he needed to confide in someone, "he's right in sending us on to Boulogne, because there is a possibility that Sigfred leaving for Frisia is a ploy."

He stopped then, offering a silent prayer that Ranulf would immediately understand the implications, even as he knew it was unlikely; his friend would never be considered a swift thinker, though to his credit, he never pretended to be, always happily and quickly deferring to others when a problem or situation of moderate complexity presented itself.

And, as he feared, Ranulf's mind did not go where Titus' had, offering a shrug and saying, "So he is probably going to your lands instead of Frisia. Which," he laughed, "makes more sense anyway. There is nothing in Frisia but stinking mud and outlaws that smell even worse."

"That's not what the Count and Lord Baudelius are worried about," Titus replied quietly, only then becoming aware that the chatter of the other *Exploratores* had died down, and a glance over his shoulder confirmed his fears, that they were now paying attention.

"Then where else could that *bâstart* go?" Ranulf wondered, truly perplexed now, and for a moment, Titus was certain that he would have to spell it out.

As it turned out, it was Theutbald who uttered a half-gasped oath, then asked, "Do they really believe that that demon is heading to Saint-Omer?"

"No," Titus said sharply, more than he intended, and he explained, "I mean, it was only mentioned as a possibility, that is all."

"Well," Wala spoke up, "did they send any of us back to Saint-Omer to warn the garrison we left behind?"

Titus was torn, mainly because he thought that the fifty *Pedes* and five of the more experienced warriors who served in the *Eques* and had been left behind would be unable to do anything other than slow Sigfred down perhaps a half-day at most, but he decided a lie was in order, though he said vaguely, "I heard them talking about it when I rode away. But," he admonished, "they did not seem to think it was a likely possibility, and I agree with them."

"Then why are we going on ahead?" Wala demanded.

It was, Titus thought, a good question, and he was forced to think of an answer that made sense.

Finally, he answered, "Because the story that *Nordmanni* told me about one of their noblemen taking half the garrison to go *viking* across The Narrow Sea sounds too good to be true to both the Count and Lord Baudelius. They just want to be prepared, that is all."

"Maybe," Ranulf ventured, wearing the kind of frown that Titus learned meant that he actually had something that was usually worth hearing because he had thought it through, "they're sending us ahead to save time, so that if it *is* true that there's only five hundred of those turds left behind, we won't need all of us to take the town, and they can send the bulk back to Saint-Omer."

This made sense to Titus; most importantly, it appeased the others, and they soon lapsed back to whatever they had been speaking about, which in this case was bickering about who did what when striking down the *Nordmanni* ambushers. Titus was not pleased to learn that, despite their best efforts, there were two Northmen of the ambush party unaccounted for, with the rest being slain, or wounded so badly that they were unable to stay on their horse, and without exception, these men were put to the sword. From what he could gather, the reason the two Northmen escaped was concern over Hekfrid, who had suffered his wound against one of them, but Theutbald swore that while one of the escaping Northmen may have gotten away from the fight, he was bleeding too heavily to stay in the saddle for more than a mile, if that much. Theutbald was wrong; they spotted a lone horse, just off the track with its head down, grazing, and without Titus giving the command, the *Exploratores* spread out into a line, approaching with weapons drawn, but it was Lambertus who spotted the body lying in tall weeds no more than a pace off the beaten track they were using.

"That's the turd," Ranulf announced. "The one Theutbald was talking about." He laughed, reaching out to shove the taciturn Frank sitting on his horse next to him. "You said he wouldn't last a mile, but we're at least four miles away!"

"Lick my ass," Theutbald grumbled. "He's dead, isn't he?"

Because it had been Lambertus who spotted him, he was the man who claimed the spoils, dismounting to search the body, Titus noticing that the man had not even started stiffening yet, indicating that he had not succumbed long before, which in turn reminded him of the other Northman.

It was with this in mind that he said, "Bent, I want you and Wala to go," he pointed up the track in the general direction of Boulogne, "a couple hundred paces that way and keep watch while we wait on Lambertus."

Wala automatically kicked his horse, but Bent did not move, snarling, "I do not take orders from you, Saxon!"

Before Titus could respond, Ranulf moved his horse, positioning it in between Bent and Titus, and while he did not draw it, his hand was on his sword, and, Titus noticed, he had placed himself so that he was facing the opposite direction, but on Bent's right side.

"Count Baldwin put Titus in command of us as *Exploratores*, Bent," Ranulf said calmly. "And I know that you heard him say that because you were next to me this morning when he did."

"I was not listening," Bent replied carelessly, then offered Ranulf a smirk, though his eyes were on Titus. "I do not hang on every word that boy says like some of you. I," he jerked a thumb at his chest, "am Lord Baudelius' man, just as I was when that boy's father was the Count!"

Before Ranulf could say anything, Titus spoke up, "So, you are saying that you are not loyal to Count Baldwin, Bent?" Making a show of looking at the others in turn, he asked, "Is that what you lads heard as well? That Bent here does not take orders from the Count but from Lord Baudelius?"

"That's not what I said!" Bent protested, then realizing that was essentially exactly what he had said, he amended, "At least, that's not what I meant!" He betrayed himself then, licking his lips nervously as he looked around at his comrades. "You men know me!" Suddenly, he thrust a finger at Theutbald, "And I know *you* agree with me, Theutbald! Do not deny it! The Count is too young to be making decisions! I've heard you say as much!"

Just as Titus was certain Bent intended, the attention of the others, including Lambertus, who had paused in his stripping the Northman's corpse and was standing there, looking up at Theutbald, who had turned a deep shade of red.

"I...I do not know what you're talking about," he stammered. "I have never been anything but loyal to the Count! It's *you*," Theutbald pointed an accusing finger back at Bent, "who licks Lord Baudelius' ass, and loves to stir up trouble just because that's what he tells you to do."

"You *lie*!" Bent snarled, and for a moment, he seemed as if he was intending to draw his sword, but Ranulf stopped him by simply drawing his own blade partially out of his scabbard.

Bent was many things; initially, Titus had thought he was a coward, but he had seen differently at Watten, and he was certainly a blusterer and a bully. However, he was no fool, which was why he made an exaggerated point of raising his hand away from the area of his waist, though he glared at Ranulf. Titus nudged Thunor, walking slowly over so that his horse was nose to nose with Bent's, and he relished how Bent suddenly did not look as confident, or as defiant.

"Go with Wala," he said coldly, lifting his right arm to point west, "up the track. Now."

Please refuse, Titus silently prayed. Please give me an excuse to humiliate you again, because you clearly have forgotten yourself. The silence dragged out for several heartbeats, with nobody moving or seeming to breathe, no man present wanting to be the one responsible for causing the bad blood that had been between these two men since the Saxon's first appearance in Melisandre's to erupt into what would likely be open bloodshed. Not, at least, right now. Many of the other men in Baldwin's bodyguard would have been surprised to know that Titus was acutely aware that Bent had supporters among them, men who shared their distrust and their dislike of the Saxon warrior who had achieved a place of eminence among them, and that many of these men would love to see Titus fall at Bent's feet. What none of them, even Ranulf, knew was that Titus of Cissanbyrig had been the object of jealousy and hatred from his earliest days, starting with his father Leofric, and he had been forced to learn how to use that hatred from others, turning it to his own advantage. It was, Titus and only a very select few knew, from where the power of Titus the Berserker came, and now, staring calmly at Bent, he could feel the first tickling sensation as whatever it was inside him that made him the Berserker began to stir. Whether Bent himself sensed this or saw something in Titus' expression, Titus would never know, but what mattered was how, without saying a word, Bent pulled his reins so that his horse's head turned away just as he gave the animal a kick in the ribs, moving away at a walk. Wala fell in beside him, the pair heading up the track, and Titus could hear the exhalation of the others, while he was forced to hide his own emotions, a mixture of disappointment and relief in equal measure. Lambertus resumed his search, giving a shout of delight when he pulled off the boots from the corpse, though it was not the boots or their quality, but what tumbled out onto the ground with a tinkling sound they all knew came from coins, and Titus could see that at least one of them was gold. Scooping them up off the ground, Lambertus gave them a brief examination, then glanced up at Titus, beckoning to him. Walking Thunor over to the Frank, who was the same age as Titus, Lambertus held out his palm, upon which lay a coin.

"I don't recognize this one, Berserker. Do you?"

Leaning over slightly, it only took a heartbeat for Titus to identify it, immediately beset with a queer sensation that he could not have identified, but he was happy how calm he sounded as he explained, "That is a Saxon shilling, Lambertus. And that," he pointed to the profile, "is King Alfred of Wessex."

Chapter Three

Outside Hrofescester, the days turned to weeks as the combatants on both sides settled into what was a grim business for besieger and besieged alike, and where the outcome hinged on a simple but brutal fact; which side could endure the most suffering? By the end of the second week, the Saxon position that hemmed in the Northmen besieging Hrofescester had been improved to a point that any other work was more for the purpose of keeping men busy than actually making the position more defensible, or to make repairs because of a series of heavy rains. Downriver, the Saxon ships had been secured in a line, their bows pointing upriver and with lengths of cable looped around the prows of each ship that attached one to another, and with planks that enabled men to move from one ship to the next as rapidly as possible. The ships were guarded day and night, with the men essentially living onboard, but aside from the attempt to break the blockade during the first week, Hallsteinn had only made one other try, sending fire rafts drifting downstream. These did cause a fair amount of excitement, but because of the orientation of Hrofescester in the middle of a loop of the Medway, the Saxons in Alfred's army were in a perfect position to come to the aid of the crews, and the fires were quickly extinguished. Otherwise, it was a case of both sides carefully watching their foe, looking for an opportunity to inflict damage, usually with a missile by the handful of warriors who happened to be skilled with a bow. It was during the third week that Lord Eadwig developed a cough, the only consolation being that he was far from alone; the first cases of the bloody flux came a few days later, beginning with two of Alfred's personal bodyguards and a Centishman. Otherwise, the most virulent enemy facing Eadward and the other Wiltun men was boredom, and it was a sign of that boredom that men began volunteering for duties that, under normal circumstances, no Saxon warrior would deign to perform. That was why, one day after a night of heavy rain, Uhtric, Hrothgar and Ealdwolf were down in the ditch, out of sight of the Northmen, resetting the sharpened stakes placed in the wall on the Saxon side that had become loose the night before. Consequently, they were knee deep in foul-smelling water, and it was impossible to do the work without getting coated in mud, but trying to break up the monotony was not the only reason they were down in the ditch; it also gave them privacy to discuss something that none of them wanted overheard.

As usual, it was left to Uhtric to finally break the silence, saying in exasperation, "Well, Hrothgar? You're the one who suggested this as a way to talk...so talk."

Titus' brother-in-law was not surprised when Hrothgar blinked in surprise as if he had forgotten this, but he finally said tentatively, "Lord Eadwig doesn't look well."

"Oh, really?" Ealdwolf snorted, making a show of flinging a spade full of dripping mud at the warrior who, prior to Titus' arrival, had been considered the strongest man in Lord Eadwig's service. "What gave you that idea? That he's always coughing and looks as pale as death?"

"Yes." Hrothgar nodded, reminding his companions that, for all of his qualities, the large Saxon was incapable of determining when he was being mocked, taking what the others knew were jests such as this as being serious queries. "That's what I'm talking about." Despite their spot, Hrothgar glanced over his shoulder and up at the lip of the ditch, and then lowered his voice. "I don't think he's going to survive this siege if it goes on another month."

This, Uhtric knew, and a glance at Ealdwolf told him that the other warrior was of the same mind, was likely true. In fact, Lord Otha had confided in Uhtric, telling him that Eadward and his father had had a blazing row about whether or not Eadwig should return to Wiltun, which the Ealdorman had flatly refused to do.

A moment's silence ensued, then Uhtric said quietly, "I don't think Lord Eadwig plans on surviving this siege, Hrothgar."

"*Cum lā!*" Hrothgar exclaimed, using the Saxon euphemism for disbelief. "How can you say that?" His expression suddenly changed, remembering how he had seen Uhtric, who he and most of the other Wiltun men considered the most likely to be made a Thegn himself, talking in hushed tones with Lord Otha. This caused him to ask cautiously, "Is that what Lord Otha says?"

"Not in so many words," Uhtric admitted. "But he definitely believes that Lord Eadwig is certain that his end is near, and," he shrugged, "if it is, he'd rather die with a sword in his hand."

This, they all agreed, was understandable, and it prompted Hrothgar to ask Uhtric, "How would you want to die, Uhtric? I," he declared emphatically, "would rather go out fighting, with a pile of these Northmen bastards at my feet than getting old and becoming feeble like my father."

"I'd like to die fucking my wife," Uhtric answered without hesitation. His companions both roared with laughter as Uhtric tried to stifle a grin as he insisted, "I mean it! If I could pick the way I die, I can't think of a better way. Can either of you?"

When put that way, neither Ealdwolf or Hrothgar could argue the point, but Hrothgar was nothing if not stubborn when he was trying to make a point, and he pressed Uhtric, "Besides that way, wouldn't you rather die in battle than because of the bloody flux?"

Sensing that this was at least part of the reason that Hrothgar had broached the subject, Uhtric replied, "Yes, Hrothgar, if those are the two choices, I'd rather die in battle than shitting my guts out bit by bit." He hesitated before asking, almost gently, "Is that what you're concerned with? That you might be stricken?"

It was a sign of his distress that Hrothgar did not try and bluster or deny this, instead giving his friend a sober nod.

"So do I," Ealdwolf spoke up, understanding the same thing Uhtric had, admitting, "I think about it a lot, actually." Turning to Uhtric, he asked, "What about you, Uhtric?"

"Of course I do," Uhtric replied. "And," he emphasized by pointing up out of the ditch towards their camp, "anyone over there who says they're not worried about it is either a fool or a liar."

"That Centishman, Wigmund? The one missing half his nose? He says that he's safe from it because he carries a flask filled with a potion that a witch prepared for him," Hrothgar said, reminding Uhtric that, among his other quirks, the large Saxon was a gullible sort who believed in all manner of folk cures and superstitions, not that this was uncommon.

"And you believe a Centishman?" Ealdwolf scoffed. "Did you forget what they did to us?"

"No!" Hrothgar protested indignantly. "I haven't forgotten anything! I just thought it was...interesting."

"Hrothgar, if God wills you, or me, or Ealdwolf...or Lord Eadwig should die that way, we will. I," Uhtric shrugged, "prefer not to dwell on something that I can't control. Now," he said pointedly, "we need to finish this up so we can get out of this ditch. I think," he made a show of sniffing, "those bastards over there have been flinging their turds over into our ditch."

"Bah," Ealdwolf snorted. "It's not them, it's those fucking Centishmen. They're filthy animals themselves and not much better than any Dane."

They returned to work, but while Hrothgar had not said as much, Uhtric was certain that he knew why the large Saxon had thought Uhtric would know something the others did not, and it was because he was considered a likely candidate for elevation. Which, Uhtric could have told them, was true, because Otha had mentioned it. Replacing the slain Aelfnod who, depending on who was speaking of it, had been overcome with grief at the slaughter of his monk brother at Stanmer and allowed himself to be cut down, was long overdue, and it was no secret that both Otha and Ceadda had been regularly pressing the matter, yet once again, it was Lord Eadwig who had refused to name a replacement for Aelfnod. Why he was refusing to do so was anyone's guess, and Otha had his own theories, but so did Uhtric, one that he had not even shared with Leofflaed. In his heart, Uhtric was almost certain that Lord Eadwig wanted to die without naming one of his warriors as Thegn, thereby giving his son Eadward the opportunity to do what he could not, for a variety of reasons. And, Uhtric also knew that if his suspicions were correct, the man who Eadward would elevate the moment he had the opportunity was not at this siege, nor even on this island at the moment.

They were all weaving in the saddle by the time the *Exploratores* stopped just before dawn, none of them exactly certain where they were in relation to Boulogne, having switched out mounts twice with the spare Northmen ponies. The track they had followed had taken them through a thick forest that extended for miles, which actually made them more secure, since the chances of any *servus*, even if they lived in the area, venturing out into these woods in the dark of night was next to nothing. Nor, they knew, would Northmen, both for the same reason as the Frankish *servii*, but also because of their lack of familiarity with the area. It was difficult for each of them to keep their mounts under control as they rode through the thick forest, with wolves seemingly all around them, howling to each other and communicating that intruders were passing through their domain.

They also heard the heavier grunting of a bear, which prompted Ranulf to joke, "One of your relations, Berserker?"

This had momentarily relieved the tension and the fatigue they were feeling, but the most potent sign of how exhausted they were came when Titus called a halt, and Bent did not offer an argument, or even a cutting remark. They found a dip in the ground in the early morning light that was deep enough that the horses were hidden from view from the track, with a stream nearby, and once again, there was no resistance when Titus announced that they would rest there for the first part of the day, even taking the first watch, although he also made the watch periods shorter. For another time, Titus felt the weight that comes from command; the truth was that he was sure that he was at least as fatigued as his comrades, and probably more so, given his actions with the pursuit, capture, and questioning of Halfdan, yet he sensed that taking the last watch, which would allow him to immediately go to sleep, would cause friction. He was not above a bit of petty revenge, however; he gave Ranulf the last watch, and gave Bent one of the shifts in the middle that would require him to rouse himself after a short period of rest. To his dismay, he did not immediately fall asleep, his mind racing with all the things that could go wrong once they began their scouting of the town, but mainly because he had been toying with an idea. Finally, however, he drifted off, awakened by a kick to his foot by Lambertus, his preferred method of being roused and one that his comrades, Saxon and Frank, had learned was the safest way of waking him. He was embarrassed to see that the others were already up, all of them occupied with gnawing on a hunk of bread or meat as they whispered among themselves. Ranulf was standing at the edge of the depression, facing in the direction of Boulogne, but his posture was relaxed, telling Titus that he did not see anything potentially dangerous. Titus reached into his saddlebags, withdrew the loaf of bread that Yanna had baked, tearing it in half, devouring it in a few bites, and washing it down from his flask, which was filled with water. Swallowing the last morsel, he stood and called to Ranulf, motioning him to come to where they were gathered in the middle of the depression.

"I have an idea of the quickest way for us to find out whether this Hallsteinn is really gone, or if this is part of some ruse on Sigfred's part," he began.

Naturally, the others were attentive, though he noted Bent's expression of surly suspicion; by the time he was through, Bent actually looked happier than he had in some time. Ranulf, however, had a completely different reaction.

"You have lost your wits," he said flatly, and Lambertus and Wala nodded their agreement, while Theutbald looked thoughtful.

Knowing that his friend's concern was genuine, Titus did not take it amiss, and he understood that losing his temper or attempting to impose his authority over his tiny command would be counterproductive.

"I know it might seem that way," he replied blandly, inwardly smiling at the look of shock on Ranulf's face at his words, "but how many times have you told me that I look more like a Northman than a Frank, or a Saxon for that matter?"

He could tell by Ranulf's expression that he had scored, but his friend was not ready to concede the point, not yet.

"Even if you manage to get inside the walls, you said yourself that your Danish is not that good, and they," Ranulf pointed in the direction of the town, "are Northmen, not Danes."

This, Titus knew, was true, but like Ranulf, he was not willing to concede the point; besides, he had the advantage of thinking about this at length, though he was only now aware that he had been doing so, somewhere in the recesses of his mind.

"The Danes and Northmen mix together all the time," Titus countered. "In any given ship's crew, there will be Northmen on Danish ships, and Danes on Northmen ships, so that's not unusual. Besides," he indicated himself, "along with my hair and beard, there are many Danes my size." This was not exactly true, but it was a matter of degree, and he could see Ranulf beginning to waver, while the others seemed content to let him lead this discussion, except for Bent, who Titus was certain wholeheartedly supported the idea since he believed it would get his hated rival killed.

"How do you plan to get into the town?" Ranulf asked, and while Titus was not religious in any real sense of the word, he did offer up a prayer of thanks, because he bent down and, from one of his saddle bags, extracted a cloak...a blue cloak that had been worn by a Northman named Halfdan.

"I'm going to wear this, and my helmet is almost identical to what Halfdan was wearing," he explained. "He's not as tall as I am, but I'll be bent low over the horse, and he was stocky in build. And I'm going to be riding his horse and coming at the gallop," he paused, "while the rest of you chase me."

This was the moment when the others decided to weigh in, and for a moment, Titus thought that their arguing would be loud enough to be heard in the town, almost a mile away.

Titus finally settled the question when, more out of exasperation than any real belief it would end the debate, he cried out, "Someone give me a better idea, then!"

They were making their preparations not long after that. Just before they mounted, Ranulf came to him and only half-jokingly said, "If you get killed, I am going to tell Yanna it was your fault and we all tried to talk you out of it, but you said you would kill us."

As Ranulf hoped, this made his friend laugh, and Titus clapped him on the shoulder, saying lightly, "You worry too much. It will work. Just," he lowered his voice, "keep an eye on Bent. I don't know how he could, but if he sees a way to betray me without being obvious about it, I know he will."

"I will," Ranulf assured him, then they clasped hands, and Titus swung onto Halfdan's pony, who was at least rested, though he heard the soft grunt the animal made at this sudden extra weight.

They did not hurry; they were still screened by the thick forest for another quarter of a mile, then they stopped.

"Give me fifty paces head start," Titus said, but Ranulf rubbed his chin, and said doubtfully, "That's not very much."

This was the moment when Titus realized that he had been thinking about Thunor, and not the horse he was actually going to be astride, and he amended, "Make it a hundred."

He also reminded himself that he was not riding his normal horse, and the short spell he had ridden Halfdan's mount to give his own horse a chance to rest, they had not been going at the gallop. With a curt nod, he kicked the Northman's pony, heading along the hardpacked road for the eastern gate. Knowing they were too far away, Titus did not make a show of glancing over his shoulder, although he did check, and he also realized that they would have been better served if galloping their horses for a bit first, if only for appearances' sake when they got closer. There was a handful of people already out on the road, and he barely noticed the smattering of huts distributed on either side, though they were all set a good distance off, and he had a fleeting thought, wondering why these Frankish *servii* were still here and had not fled to a part of Flandre not under Northmen control, but put it quickly out of his mind, reminding himself that the same question could be asked about the Saxons living in the Danelaw. There was a gentle rise that obscured all but the very top of the eastern wall, and he felt his horse begin to labor before they reached the top of the rise, the wall now just a half-mile away. Now he could see the heads of the Northmen who were manning the wall just above the gate, and this was when he began making a show of looking over his shoulder. When he did, his heart sank; to his eyes, it was clear that Ranulf and the others were curbing their mounts, and he realized with a sudden twisting in his gut that he had not thought things through.

The *Eques* of Count Baldwin were mounted on the best quality mounts that could be found in Flandre, and while they did not rely on cavalry that much, another similarity with Titus' Saxons, compared to the Danes and Northmen, who only viewed their mounts as a means of transportation, even now, the difference in quality was obvious. The muzzle of Titus' mount, almost identical to Thunor in coloring though much smaller, was already rimed with white foam, its mouth open, but he could feel it stumble slightly, despite the ground being level and the roadway relatively smooth. Looking under his arm, he saw Ranulf making a show of whipping Grisel, but to Titus, it was so overdone, he felt certain that the Northmen watching on the wall would recognize it as a ruse. Titus did not like striking animals, even this one that he had no attachment to, but he gritted his teeth, and with a considerable amount of force, smacked the pony on the rump. The horse screamed in shock and pain...but it somehow managed to increase its speed, and now came the next moment of truth, the gates looming larger with every stride.

"Open the gates!" Titus bellowed in Danish, even as he tried but failed to recall if there was a significant difference between the Northman version of this command. "Open them! Open them, you *oskilgetinn*!" Was that the right word for bastard? he thought.

Whether it was or not, he saw one of the men on the rampart turn about to look down and make a gesture. The wind was shrieking in his ears, of course, so he did not hear the short throwing spear that went streaking past him about a half-arm's length away, gasping in shock at the surprise. Despite the speed at which he was closing with the gate, he gaped back over his shoulder, immediately understanding when he saw Bent, an evil smile on his face even as his arm pulled back to hurl another missile. Instinctively, Titus pressed his knee against Halfdan's pony's ribs, and while it was not by much more, this second missile missed by a wider margin, but Titus was rewarded when three Northmen on the rampart suddenly lifted their left arms while drawing their hands back in a gesture that needed no explanation.

"Bows! The bastards have bows!"

Titus recognized Bent's voice, and the near panic in it, but he forced himself to keep his attention ahead of him, thinking that it might rouse suspicion if he seemed concerned about the fate of his pursuers, and he was rewarded by the sight of the gates cracking open.

"That's right! Run, you cowardly dog! Run! I'll kill you yet, I swear it on the Cross!"

It was, Titus thought with a touch of bitter amusement, Bent at his most cunning, since he recognized the Frank's voice. When Ranulf would undoubtedly challenge him about threatening to kill his friend, Titus was certain that Bent would solemnly declare that he was just doing his part in aiding the ruse, just as he had been in throwing those two spears at Titus, and from Bent's perspective, the beauty of it was that this made sense, at least superficially. The question that lingered in Titus' mind was whether Bent had purposely missed him, or if he was trying to hit him, then later declare that it was an accident, which was also plausible, given they were at the gallop. He tucked this away because there were more immediate concerns, namely that the gates had opened until there was a gap wide enough for a lone man to exit, but not enough for a man on horseback to pass through them. Titus was now about fifty paces away, and while he had taken care to keep his head down close to his horse's neck, not lifting it to look up at the rampart, he knew he was getting close enough that this Northman standing in the gateway would recognize him at any instant. This was when Titus made a show of actually leaning forward even more then looking under his armpit, as if he was checking to make sure his pursuers had given up, and he was relieved to see that they had already turned about and were moving at a trot back away from the town.

This, he knew, would be the moment that a man who was truly fleeing pursuers would ease his mount up and slow down, although what Halfdan's mount was doing right now could only be charitably called a gallop, and Titus did feel a stab of remorse at what he was about to do. He *did* slow the horse, but while he sat up straight, he immediately turned his head to continue looking over his shoulder, as if he was not convinced that these

Frankish warriors had given up the pursuit, yet what he was really doing was straining his ears, listening for a sign.

He heard it, or at least partially, when the man at the gate from the sound of it shouted something, but most importantly, he added, "Halfdan?"

Titus, still not turning, nodded, but he did point and say in Danish, "I do not trust these Franks! I think they are going to trick us!"

He was rewarded by a screeching noise that he had heard before, the sound of hinges holding up a heavy wooden gate protesting as the gate was swung open even wider, presumably to allow the man the Northman at the gate now thought was Halfdan to enter. Even as Titus turned his head back towards the gate, his right hand was swinging down, once again but with even more power striking the exhausted horse's rear, and once again, it screamed in pain and surprise. He was back at full speed within a heartbeat, now barely twenty paces away from the gateway, but he still saw the Northman standing there, his hair and beard a flaming red and wearing a leather vest with iron rings sewn to it, noticing how his eyes widened in surprise; whether it was in his recognition that he was not looking up at Halfdan but a stranger, or that the horse, small as it was, was now hurtling at him at full speed and he understood that he would be unable to leap out of the way, Titus would never know. From his perspective, one instant the Northman was standing there, mouth open, then he felt the shuddering impact as Halfdan's pony slammed into the man, causing the animal to stumble slightly, then Titus could feel it recover its footing; besides, he was already looking past what had been the first obstacle. To his relief, he saw only two other Northman standing in the middle of the street, although one of them was just bringing his spear up, but by this time, Titus already had Wyvern's Fang in his right hand, and he leaned over slightly as he brought the blade down in a chopping blow that struck the Northman at the junction of the warrior's neck and shoulder. His horse's momentum helped Titus wrench the blade free, but he made no attempt to engage the other Northman, seeing that he was fumbling to withdraw his ax from his belt, and he was to Titus' left while Titus was already yanking the horse's head to the right. He had never been to Boulogne, but from the beginning of his plan, he had gambled that it would be like every other walled town he had ever been in, which meant there would be a street running the length of each wall, forming a ring road that, like the wall, encircled the town. In the two heartbeats of time he had once he rode through the gateway, he had seen that the street to his right was almost completely clear of traffic, and what little there was seemed composed completely of townspeople, all of them on foot.

He had no intention of fighting his way in; as confident as he was in his abilities, he was no fool, so he kicked the horse savagely in the ribs and for a brief instant, he thought the animal would collapse, feeling it shudder and pitch forward, sending him lurching forward as well. He braced himself, yet somehow the horse regained its footing and resumed moving, not at a gallop but still quickly enough that one of the townspeople did not heed his shouted warning quickly enough, caroming into the outer wall after being struck by his mount's shoulder. The corner, he thought, he had to make it to the corner, and he heard shouting, both in Frankish on the part of the frightened people on the street, and the roaring curses of the Northmen he had left behind. Then, when he was within a half-dozen paces of the corner where the eastern wall connected with the northern, he sensed something slashing past him while at the same time he felt a puff of air, seeing an arrow from one of the three archers strike the wooden wall of the building at the corner, noticing the shaft still quivering slightly as he rushed past. He did not see the second arrow, which was on target but a bit too high and struck the northern wall a couple feet from the junction with the eastern wall, Titus being too busy guiding the horse around the corner, his eyes already looking ahead and relieved to see that, while there were people on the street here as well, there were no Northmen warriors.

They almost made it all the way around the corner to safety from the archers, but while the first two arrows missed, the third one struck the left hindquarter of the horse, burying half its length in the flesh of the animal, and this time when it shrieked in pain, Titus heard the different tone that told him the horse had suffered serious injury. When it inevitably stumbled, however, on this occasion, it was unable to maintain its footing, the left rear leg collapsing under it, yet somehow, Titus managed to kick his feet free of the stirrups and throw himself clear as the horse collapsed onto the hardpacked dirt of the street, the impact driving the arrow even deeper into the lower belly of the doomed animal. Although he managed to get free of the horse, it did not mean that Titus escaped cleanly, falling in the street on his left side with enough force that it knocked the wind out of him, while his helmet struck a glancing blow against the side of the same corner building, but on its northern side. Stars of a thousand colors burst in his vision, exacerbated by the fact that he couldn't get his breath on his first, or second try, yet somehow he still scrambled to his feet. Grabbing on to the side of the building to stabilize himself, he finally drew a breath, which helped his vision clear, but then he heard shouting, and while it was muffled by the presence of the building in between him and his pursuers, he could tell that the Northmen up on the rampart were now racing down it towards the corner. This got him moving and heading for the opening between this building and the next, which was his target for the next part of his plan to escape. Staggering a bit, he still managed to get there, though it was more of an alley than a street, but it would serve his purpose of getting out of sight.

A pair of townspeople, a man and woman and Frankish by their dress, were standing there, seemingly frozen in place with almost identical expressions of shock on their faces, mouths hanging open, and Titus, taking a risk, called to them in their tongue, "I have been sent by Count Baldwin! I am here on a scouting mission! Tell those Northmen dogs that I kept going towards the docks!"

Then, he was dashing down the alley, dodging and hurdling the piles of refuse and mounds of turds that were dumped from the nightsoil buckets of the people who lived along this alley, seeing another intersection where another street or alley dead ended into this one. Although he could have continued in his current direction, essentially heading back towards the eastern gate but with a solid line of buildings blocking the view of any Northman, even those on the rampart, provided he hugged the side of the buildings nearest to it, he instead ducked down this intersecting alley to the right, wanting to put at least another corner between himself and any pursuers, who he could hear bellowing something at the townspeople, undoubtedly demanding to know where he had gone. If they had their wits about them, he thought, maybe they'll tell them what I told them to, that I went farther west in the direction of the docks, but he also acknowledged that neither of them looked as if they were swift thinkers even under the best of circumstances. What he had assumed was another alley was actually more of a street, one that went for several blocks, paralleling the northern wall but a couple of blocks south of it, yet once again, he did not travel very far, choosing instead to turn down another narrow alley that took him farther south into the town, hurrying about half its length towards where he could see another intersection before he finally stopped. He chose this spot because there was another pile of trash, composed of broken pottery, old clothing and assorted other detritus, and he quickly unfastened the blue cloak, then with some reluctance, took off the helmet as well. While his armor was Frankish made, it was not the scale armor they favored but mail, and cut in a style that would not look out of place among Northmen, while his sword was of a type carried by many warriors of their day, but it was what he did next that he hoped would complete his disguise.

Swinging the leather bag he carried over one shoulder around to the front, he dug into it and pulled out his arm rings, all of which he put on, save one, the golden one Einarr had given to him. For what seemed much longer than was wise but was probably only a couple of heartbeats, he stared down at it, assailed by memories that were of absolutely no use at this moment, yet he could not seem to move, despite hearing the shouting not only getting nearer, but there were now new, additional voices, coming from an entirely different direction. He would never know what caused him to do it, but instead of putting it back in the bag, he attached it to his bicep, the gold glittering in the sunlight, the entwined wires looking like a thick golden rope about as big around as his little finger, with the two bulbous ends looking a bit like acorns. Fortunately, his reverie was broken when another shout sounded, except this one was just around the corner from where he had come, and Titus broke into a sprint; reaching the next corner, he turned it...and collided with another man who had just happened to be walking past this spot. The impact sent both of them reeling, and although Titus managed to stay on his feet, he staggered sideways and slammed into the wall of what turned out to be a wineshop, while the man he collided with was knocked on his back. It was the third man that Titus had not noticed at first who posed the most immediate threat, drawing his sword as he stepped over and straddled his prone companion.

Time seemed to stand still then, as, instead of drawing his own weapon, Titus stared in disbelief, saved only by the fact that his prospective foe was doing the same, but it was Titus who managed to find his voice first, gasping, *"Dagfinn? What are you doing here?"*

The Dane, helmsman of *Sea Viper* and one of Titus' closest friends among his ostensible captors during his time in Lunden, as was his habit, recovered quickly, saying dryly, "I could ask you the same thing, Titus."

Only then did Titus turn his attention to the man he had collided with, and seeing his face, he did not know whether to laugh or cry, as this one, also a Dane and older than the other two, was glaring up at him as he propped himself up on his elbows.

"Einarr?"

"Who else do you think it would be, you shit for brains Saxon? You," the Dane growled, "are still a *burlofotr*...and you're on dry land!" Thrusting an arm out, he commanded, "Now, help me up, boy."

Titus did as he was told, and Einarr had just come to his feet when, from immediately around the corner where Titus had come, they heard pounding footsteps, and Titus spoke urgently, "I need your help."

He was unable to explain why, because just then, a half-dozen puffing warriors, all of them armed with shields and spears, rounded into view.

"You there!" Their leader, who Titus offered a quick prayer of thanks that he did not recognize as the man he ran down at the gate, pointed with his spear. "I know you two! You are from Lunden and serve King Guthrum, yes? You," he indicated Einarr, clearly trying to think, "are Lord Einarr Thorsten; that is your name?"

"It is good to see that you are not completely witless," Einarr replied coldly. "Seeing that you are the one who met us at the docks four days ago, I can see why you might be confused, it being so long ago."

The man flushed, but he did not offer a retort, turning instead to Dagfinn, saying, "And you are Dagfinn Grimmarson. I remember you now." Then, he looked at Titus coldly, "But I do not recognize you. And," he turned and gave Einarr a cold stare, "as you said, I was at the dock to greet your ship. I am certain I did not see this man with you." Returning his attention to Titus and, seeing his youth, he demanded, "What is your name, boy?"

"His name," Einarr said coldly, "is none of your business." He took a step towards the Northman. "But, despite this fact, I will tell you. His name is...Svein. Svein Thorsten." Titus saw the man's eyes go wide, while Einarr confirmed, "Yes, Svein is my son. My oldest son, and I am telling you that he was with us when we arrived." Suddenly, Einarr pointed to the golden arm ring. "If you want more proof, ask any man in my crew. That arm ring is worn by the heir to the Thorsten name. Now," he asked in a reasonable tone that was easy to tell did not fool anyone, "you are not calling me a liar, are you?"

For the briefest moment, Titus thought that the Northman might challenge Einarr, but it did not last long, and he muttered, "No, I am not, Lord Einarr. But we are searching for a man who likely murdered one of our scouts and is now loose in the town."

"We will keep our eyes open," Dagfinn promised, then asked with a sincerity that only those who knew him well would know was feigned. "Can you give us an idea what this man looks like? So that I can alert our men?"

The leader looked embarrassed, admitting, "I...I did not get a very good look at him, I'm afraid. And the man who did," he shrugged, "he's not likely to wake up anytime soon...if at all."

With a curt bow of the head, the Northman led his charges back in the direction from which they came, and once they turned the corner, Titus murmured, "I think we need to leave the area. I stashed the scout's cloak and helmet nearby, and if they start looking, it won't take them long to find it."

The pair of Danes exchanged a glance, but Dagfinn gave a slight shrug, and Einarr turned and said, "Follow me." They had not gone more than a couple paces when Einarr said, almost gently, "Titus, while it is good to see you, I think you have some explaining to do."

"I know," Titus answered quietly. "And I'll tell you everything."

Despite Titus' protests at what he thought of as the foolhardiness of doing so, Einarr and Dagfinn took him to the house where they were staying, just across the street from the docks that lined the river called the Liane, where their ship was moored. Titus could tell that it had been an inn, which included a kitchen area, but it was now treated with the same indifference and lack of concern about keeping it up that was a hallmark of the Northern invaders. However, what his eyes were drawn to more than that was the sight of the high stone tower that he had been told about by Ranulf but had never seen, realizing now that Ranulf's description had been far from thorough. It was, Titus thought, even as Dagfinn was talking to him, the strangest thing he had ever seen, looking like a series of octagonal but slightly smaller blocks of stone stacked atop each other that towered above the town wall. The fact that it was constructed in stone told him that it had to be the work of the Romans, if only because there was something about the style of what he knew was a lighthouse that reminded him of the things he had seen first in Bathenceaster, then Lunden.

"Sigfred keeps this place for honored guests," Dagfinn had explained, completely oblivious to where Titus' eyes had been drawn, then grinned. "And we do not have to lift a finger. These Franks make better slaves than you Saxons!"

Knowing what Dagfinn was trying to do, both taunt Titus but also to assure him that he was not in danger of discovery by the Northern occupiers, the Saxon did not rise to the bait, although it did take his attention away from the lighthouse, which he also noticed did not have a flame burning. Besides, he was more concerned with Einarr, who had refused to say a word to him as they made their way away from the hubbub of the search for Titus, nor had he given him so much as a glance.

"Why are you two here?" he asked Dagfinn, not missing that the Dane's first reaction was to glance over at Einarr.

"It is...complicated," Dagfinn finally answered. "And," he actually sounded apologetic, "it is Lord Einarr's decision whether or not he tells you anything."

Titus' own look over to Einarr, who stood just a couple inches shorter than Titus, told him that, at least for the moment, nothing would be forthcoming. It took all of Titus' willpower not to behave in a manner that would draw suspicion when they walked past a Northman, or a group of them heading in the opposite direction, but none of them gave the three more than a passing glance, informing him that his attempt to blend in was working. He also kept a silent count of the numbers of Northmen they encountered, although he did not peer in both directions whenever they encountered an intersection. Naturally, he would have to perform a more thorough inspection, but nothing he saw indicated that there was anything, like a ruse where men were hiding away, in the works, and when they reached the docks, which served as the port because the river emptied out into The Narrow Sea less than a mile away, Titus saw that there were only a half-dozen warships, and about twice as many merchant vessels. Well, he thought to himself, at least we know that Sigfred really isn't here, though he was one of those who never believed that was a possibility. Without saying anything, Einarr entered through the open door of the inn, Titus noticing the remnant of a sign hanging askew above the doorway, and seeing that a picture of a fish had been part of it, which made sense for a seaport town. He was unsure of what to expect, but the reception he received was nothing he imagined, beginning when Sigmund Grimmarson, Dagfinn's brother, looked up blearily from the game of *Talkfast* he was playing with two other men, the Danish version of the dice game that, had he known it, was very similar to the game Titus' ancestor played on occasion.

He was obviously inebriated, making his reaction comically slow, blinking several times before a broad grin of recognition split his weathered features, and he bellowed, "Frigg's cunt! Look who it is! The *Burlofotr* himself!"

Despite the circumstances and his nervousness, Titus' own face split into a smile as he strode across the room, moving in between the tables that were largely empty, but he was unprepared to be swept into an embrace by Dagfinn's normally reserved brother, though he did not mind, squeezing Sigmund hard enough back to make him gasp for breath before he released the Dane and examined him more closely.

"You're missing a tooth," Titus observed, and Sigmund, still grinning, retorted, "That may be, but I took more than a tooth from that *oskilgetinn* who knocked it out! I took his life!"

Without thinking how Sigmund might take it, Titus glanced at Dagfinn, who confirmed, "It was in Lunden. There was a feast, and there was a girl..." Dagfinn shrugged, and while he was smiling, Titus sensed there was something more there. "The other man drew a knife after my brother knocked him down."

"And I beat him to death!" Sigmund declared, holding up both of his hands. "With just these!" He turned his head and spat on the floor. "I did not need anything more to take his life!"

Unsure what to say, Titus said simply, "It's good to see you, Sigmund."

"And you, Bers..." Sigmund stopped himself, glancing over at Einarr, but the Dane did not seem to hear, having dropped onto a chair and poured himself a cup of what Titus' nose told him was ale.

Before Titus could comment, another figure entered from a doorway in the rear of the front room, the manner in which he was adjusting his trousers telling Titus he had gone for a piss, and like Sigmund, it took him a moment for his eyes to take in the figure standing next to Sigmund.

"*Heill ok sæll,* Oddbjorn," Titus said, using the more formal greeting, not because he did not care for the Dane known as Oddbjorn the Bald, which was understandable because his head was as smooth as an egg, and not because he had shaved it, but they were not as close as Titus was to Dagfinn and Einarr.

"Berserker!" Oddbjorn exclaimed in surprise, but again Einarr made no reaction, and while he did not hesitate to come to Titus, he instead thrust out a hand, which Titus accepted, not pulling the Saxon into an embrace. "I never thought I would see you again, but if I did, especially not here!"

"That makes two of us," Titus answered honestly, though he smiled as he did so.

"Ragnar is around somewhere," Dagfinn told Titus, referring to Ragnar Oleson, the Dane who had served as the steersman on King Alfred's ship that the King had named *The Redeemer*, and Titus did not miss how his friend had taken him by the arm to gently steer him to where Einarr was sitting.

There were other Danes that Titus recognized, although some of them he only knew by sight, but he noticed that while, for the most part, they seemed pleased to see him, returning his nod of greeting with one of their own and a friendly grin, it was not unanimous. There was one Dane in particular, who Titus noticed was sitting by himself at a table tucked into the corner farthest from the entrance but nearest to the doorway from which Oddbjorn had come, and he was certain he had never seen the man before, but the Dane, a thin-faced man about ten years older than Titus with a long, livid scar down the right side of his face, gave him a stare of such malevolence that it stirred that thing in Titus. That man, he thought, hates me for some reason, but then he had no more time to worry about it, taking the seat that Dagfinn had pointed to, while he dropped down into the one opposite Einarr. All worries about the lone Dane evaporated when Titus' nose previously alerting him to the presence of ale was confirmed after Dagfinn poured a cup, then shoved it in front of him.

"By the Rood, I've missed ale," Titus murmured, only after taking a long, deep draught of the sour, potent brew then slamming the empty cup onto the table.

"You can have as much as you like," Dagfinn muttered. "When Sigfred left, he took everything worth drinking, and this cow piss is all that's left."

He did not know with any certainty, but Titus suspected that Dagfinn was helping Titus by introducing Sigfred, but before he could broach the subject, Einarr asked abruptly, "I can guess, but why don't you tell me why you are here, Titus? And," he added before Titus could answer, "where have you been for the last two years since you left Wiltun?"

Only later did Titus realize that he should not have been

surprised that Einarr was aware of Titus' movement, at least that he had left Wiltun. Even by the time he had vanished, Titus had learned just how much interaction there was between the two implacable foes of Saxons and Danes, his education about this fact of life having been begun by Hakon.

Sitting at the table, Titus did not reply immediately, thinking carefully about how he would respond, ignoring Einarr's clear impatience before, deciding there would not be much harm, he replied, "I am now in the service of Count Baldwin, Margrave of Flandre and one of the Frankish King Charles' sworn men," deciding not to add the sobriquet by which Charles was better known. He saw the look Einarr exchanged with Dagfinn, and understood that it was meaningful, though not how, but he nonetheless continued, "The Count's spies informed him about Sigfred taking most of his men and ships, supposedly for Frisia." He paused, gauging their reaction, which he was disappointed to see was essentially nonexistent, forcing him to go on. "The Count decided that this presented an opportunity, so he has gathered an army, and is marching here. Yesterday, we managed to capture a scout, and from him, we learned that one of the men Sigfred left behind took a substantial force with him to go *viking* somewhere."

This did elicit a reaction, in the form of another exchange of glances, except this time, Einarr gave an almost imperceptible nod, so it was Dagfinn who asked, "This man you mentioned, who left here to go *viking*. Did you learn his name?" Titus nodded, and was about to supply it himself, but Dagfinn beat him. "Was it Hallsteinn Olafson by any chance?"

"How did you know?" Titus gasped. Then, more importantly, "And why are you here?"

"That is...complicated," Einarr began, but now Titus' patience, never his strong point, was near exhaustion, and he snapped, "Yes, you said that already. But that does not answer the question, Lord." He congratulated himself for remembering that Einarr was a nobleman, elevated to the status of *Jarl* by Guthrum for his service with Alfred, and it also served as a reminder to himself that Einarr was an important man in his own right and worthy of respect for that alone. "Why," he repeated, "are you here?"

"My King has...concerns," Einarr answered reluctantly. "And he sent me to determine if what he has heard is in fact something that he should worry about."

"He sent us because of Hallsteinn," Dagfinn put in, except that rather than illuminate the matter, Titus was even more confused, but Dagfinn stopped then, giving Einarr an inquiring look.

"Go ahead," Einarr sighed. "You may as well tell him."

"Hallsteinn and about five hundred of *Jarl* Sigfred's men are besieging Hrofescester," Dagfinn explained. "And King Alfred arrived with an army of his own, and they have now surrounded Hallsteinn's army outside the town."

Titus knew of Hrofescester of course, but it was in Cent, and the deepest into Cent he had ever been was at the monastery at Stanmer, so his knowledge of the town was limited to knowing its name, and that it was on a river, or so he believed anyway.

"It is on the Medway, is it not?" he asked, and Dagfinn nodded. Understanding there was more to the question, Dagfinn dipped his finger into his ale, and used it to trace what looked to Titus like a horseshoe as he explained, "This is the Medway where Hrofescester is," he indicated the dry space in between the loop, "situated in the loop of this river. So," he dipped his finger again and drew a straight line across the open end of the horseshoe, "Hallsteinn hemmed them in on land, while his ships cut the Saxons off on the river. But then," he did not dip his finger again, just using it to indicate another straight line, just below the first one, "Alfred showed up, and his army did the same thing to Hallsteinn what Hallsteinn did to Hrofescester. And," he added, "he brought enough ships to create their own blockade of Hallsteinn's ships."

Dagfinn paused to take a drink, and Titus mused, "So, Alfred is besieging the besiegers."

"Exactly." Dagfinn nodded. He hesitated, but again Einarr nodded, which Titus missed. "Hallsteinn sent a man to Lunden, asking for our help to break the siege."

It was Titus' misfortune that he was taking a swallow of ale of his own, and he went into a coughing, choking fit as part of the liquid went down his windpipe.

"He did *what*?" Instantly realizing the more important question, he asked, "And what did King Guthrum say?"

"He did not say anything," Einarr spoke now, his voice cold. "Our King has a treaty in place with your King..."

"I don't know that he *is* my King," Titus interjected, then added more quietly, "at least not anymore."

Einarr's expression softened, and he lifted a hand and gave Titus' arm an awkward pat.

"Yes, well, as I said, we have a treaty with Alfred...But," he sounded cautious, "Guthrum sent us here to find out whether this *viking* on Hallsteinn's part was done by Sigfred's order, or if he was acting alone."

This, Titus knew, would be a matter of interest to Count Baldwin as well, and he asked, "And?"

"And, according to Bjorn Sigurdson, who was left behind by Sigfred as second in command, Hallsteinn disobeyed Sigfred. Although," Einarr acknowledged, "Hallsteinn had warned Sigfred that if he left him behind, he would do that very thing."

"So," Titus breathed, "it is true. There are only a few hundred men to defend the town." It was difficult, but he forced his mind to return to the two Danes. "So why are you still here? If you determined that Hallsteinn is acting without Sigfred's blessing, is that not what King Guthrum wanted to know?"

"Yes," Einarr replied, then after a pause, added, "and other things." Titus was about to press, then in a flash of insight, understood this was the time to do the opposite, so he sat there, regarding the Dane silently, saying nothing. Finally, Einarr grumbled, "Fine. If you insist on pressing me, I will tell you." He paused to take a sip from his cup, then continued, "Just like your Count, King Guthrum has his own spies, and there has been talk of something...big happening, not just with Sigfred. Have you ever heard the name Rollo?"

Now, Titus *had* heard that name before, but it was a common name among the people of the North, and he was certain he understood that Einarr meant someone specifically, so he shook his head.

"He is Norse, like Sigfred. And," Einarr added ominously, "he is Úlfhédnar as well, like Sigfred. He was also seen in

Frisia, and our King's spies tell him that the two are joining forces for something. If that is true," Einarr sighed, "that is something we need to know."

Suddenly, Titus was certain of something else, that Einarr was not being completely forthcoming with him; at the same time, he understood that what Sigfred was up to was far more complicated and far-reaching than just an attack on Saint-Omer. After all, he had enough men with him now to attack Saint-Omer without help from this Rollo, nor had there been any real need to go to Frisia and, he also realized, that given Guthrum's interest, the Danish King of East Anglia had to at least suspect that the Northmen were looking at Wessex, Mercia, Northumbria...or East Anglia as a target.

In a signal that he had said all he intended about the subject, Einarr said, "Now, tell us how you ended up here in Frankia, serving some pig turd Frank."

Titus hesitated, though not for long, deciding that there was nothing harmful in his tale, and he spoke for several moments, pausing only long enough to drain or refill his cup, the two Danes exchanging a rueful glance at this reminder of just how much intoxicating beverage that Titus could consume, no matter what it was, without it affecting him like most men. He spoke of how he seriously considered coming to Lunden and seeking them out, then decided against it, choosing instead to take a merchant ship from Hamtun that was sailing for Brittany, the first vessel that was sailing across The Narrow Sea that was large enough and had room for Thunor and his packhorse. Landing in Brittany, he found himself almost immediately at odds with the most powerful lord in this strange place whose tongue was unique to its people, and who fiercely resisted every attempt by the Frankish Kings to subsume them into the West Frankish Kingdom. His name was Judicael, and when, through intermediaries of course, he approached Titus with an offer of service in his household guard, Titus declined, whereupon he was almost immediately attacked by a trio of armed men who had been lying in wait outside his inn in Brest. He had killed one of his attackers, wounding a second, while the third fled; Titus paused only long enough to grab his belongings, then fled Brest on Thunor and with his packhorse, not stopping until he had made at least twenty miles, making a cold camp where he spent a sleepless night, listening for sounds of pursuit. The next two weeks were spent in a game of cat-and-mouse, as the lesser lords in Judicael's service through whose lands Titus was passing hunted for the interloper who had had the temerity, and bad judgement, of spurning their lord. Somehow, even Titus could not really say how he managed it, he evaded his pursuers, reaching the eastern border between Brittany and Western Frankia about two weeks later and without any more bloodshed. From there, he drifted north, without any kind of real plan, and he could not tell his Danish friends exactly why he decided to stop at the tavern called Melisandre's in the walled town of Saint-Omer. Once again, the stranger was viewed with suspicion and hostility, except this time, Titus did not run; he chose to stand and fight.

"And," he finished with a shrug and unusual understatement, "that is how I ended up in Count Baldwin's service."

They sat in companionable silence for a moment, then Dagfinn cleared his throat before he said awkwardly, "We heard about what happened with Isolde, Titus. And," he glanced over at Einarr, "we made offerings in her name to our gods."

Partially because it was unexpected, this moved Titus, and he felt his throat tighten up, but he managed to thank them. Taking another swallow, he was about to talk more when, for a reason he could not have articulated, he looked over at the table in the corner from where the unknown man had been glaring at him sullenly almost since their arrival.

More out of idle curiosity, Titus pointed at the table, and said, "That man who was sitting there is gone now. Who is he? I don't remember seeing him before."

This was met with a snort by Dagfinn, who replied disgustedly, "His name is Floki, but it should be Turd Breath, at least that is what we call him. He is Bjorn's man and has been our shadow." Suddenly, Dagfinn frowned. "But he rarely leaves that spot, at least as long as Lord Einarr is here..."

Suddenly, from outside came the sound of pounding footsteps, moving at a run and with a level of noise that could only come from several men, causing every head inside to turn towards the door.

"Where did you say he was?" Titus heard the voice, recognizing it as the man Einarr had forced to back down; only then did Titus automatically turn his head to look back at the corner, his heart sinking when he realized the meaning of the empty table.

"He's in the inn!" While Titus did not recognize the second man's voice, panting as it was, clearly both of his companions did, as they simultaneously leapt to their feet.

"That is Turd Breath's voice!" Dagfinn gasped. "That *oskilgetinn* betrayed us!"

Einarr did not hesitate, snapping, "Follow me, both of you!" To Sigmund, Oddbjorn and the others who Titus had recognized, all of whom had come to their feet, although Sigmund was weaving like a man on a heaving deck in a storm, Einarr ordered, "Delay these turd lickers!"

Without waiting for any acknowledgement, Einarr led Titus and Dagfinn towards the door at the rear.

"Do not worry, Berserker," Oddbjorn promised as he passed the bald Dane, "we will do what is necessary."

As grateful as he was for this, Titus also did not want his Danish friends to put themselves in a situation that would put them in danger with their Northmen hosts, but he followed Einarr nonetheless. Just as Dagfinn slammed the inner door, they heard shouting as Bjorn Sigurdson and his men entered through the entrance, but once the door was shut, his eyes took a heartbeat to adjust to the gloom, just making out Einarr's figure as he navigated down a narrow aisle between a series of shelves and a stack of crates. Bending down, Einarr grunted as he shoved a crate aside, revealing a trap door, which he lifted.

"Follow me," he said before sitting down and dropping his legs into what, to Titus' eyes, appeared to be nothing but a gaping hole. Seeing Titus hesitate, he explained, "There is no ladder, but it is not a far drop, and we will have to crawl on all fours. Now, hurry!"

With that, he was gone, but even as Titus moved to follow, he gave Dagfinn a quizzical glance that, despite the darkness, the Dane interpreted correctly.

"My brother was poking around the day after we got here,

and he stumbled into that crate and moved it a bit, and when he looked down, he saw the edge of the trapdoor," he explained.

The last part was muffled because Titus had dropped down into what he felt more than saw was a square hole barely large enough for two men, although he heard a scuffling sound as Einarr had already begun crawling. Einarr's bulk blocked out most of the light, but Titus caught a glimpse of a dim source of illumination up ahead of the Dane, and he followed obediently. From behind and above them, they could hear the crashing sound of footsteps on the wooden floor, along with more shouting, though it was too muffled to be distinct. Titus understood why the light was so dim when Einarr suddenly vanished in front of him, taking a right turn, and once he got there and navigated the turn, he could see, about fifty paces ahead, an opening, though Einarr's bulk still blocked a clear view, while what light there was had a greenish tinge to it that he would understand shortly. He caught up to Einarr when the Dane stopped suddenly, just a pace from the exit, and Titus pressed a cheek up against the dirt wall to peer around the other man, and while it was not much, he saw enough to understand that the entrance was screened by a stand of small trees and shrubbery that was hard up against the mouth of the tunnel, yet if he looked carefully and peered through the leaves that they were now at the docks, which he could see were about fifty paces away from the entrance.

"Wait here," Einarr ordered, then crawled out into the open, squeezing himself in between the trunks of two trees before standing, the upper half of his body disappearing from sight.

Titus watched Einarr turn around to look back in the direction from where they had come, and as he did so, Dagfinn, who had caught up, whispered, "When Sigmund found this, we made sure to move *Fenrir* over to the berth right across from it. In case," he heard by Dagfinn's voice his friend was grinning, "we had to do what we are doing now."

"But what about the others?" Titus asked, but before Dagfinn could respond, Einarr's face appeared in the opening.

"It is safe," he announced, then added, "for now."

Crawling out, Titus stood, blinking against the sun as he

got his bearings. Since he had never been down to the river here, he saw for the first time that the town was built on a low bluff, no more than thirty feet above the riverbank, while there was a section where the dropoff was almost vertical, and it was into this stretch the tunnel had been dug.

"Go with Dagfinn," Einarr ordered, pointing to the low, sleek ship at the last berth nearest to the tunnel. "He will hide you while I go get the men. We," he said grimly, "are leaving this place now."

Before Titus could respond, he was trotting away, though not for the tunnel. Instead, he ran upriver to where Titus saw what was essentially a narrow dirt street that wound up the bluff to the town, then Titus was following Dagfinn. Reaching the ship, Titus dropped down into it, remembering as he did how long it had been since he had been on the water, reminded of the difference between dry land and shipboard when he staggered slightly from the motion, which Dagfinn saw.

"Still the *burlofotr,* I see." He shook his head with mock sadness. "I had hoped that you would not forget everything you learned with us."

In answer, Titus grabbed his crotch, watching as Dagfinn went to the center of the ship to the hole where the mast, which was stepped, was placed. Directly in front of it were barrels and crates securely lashed down, which Titus knew would be empty, with the barrels filled just before departure, while the crates, also empty, would be packed with provisions. Using his dagger, Dagfinn pried the lid off of one of the crates, and when he did, Titus saw that what had appeared to be two crates, with two separate lids, was in fact one large one...large in a relative sense.

"Get in," Dagfinn ordered, but this time, Titus did not move, looking at his friend in undisguised horror.

"Are you *mad*?" he gasped. "I'll never fit in that!"

"It will be cramped," Dagfinn agreed equably enough, then assured Titus, "but you will fit."

"How do you know?"

"Because," Dagfinn showed a touch of impatience, "you do not have any other choice. Not," he added, "if you want to get out of here in one piece."

Just then, the shouting that had been in temporary abeyance resumed again, and even from a distance, Titus recognized Einarr's bellow.

"I'll have to unstrap my sword," Titus said dubiously, but he was doing so as he said it.

And, Dagfinn was proven correct; while it was extremely cramped, he did fit, if he lay on his side, although the ridge where the two crates were joined but made to look as if there were two dug into his back.

"There's a hole right on the mast side, do you see it?" Dagfinn asked. "You will get air through there."

It took him a couple heartbeats, but while he saw it, to his dismay, it looked impossibly small, and he asked doubtfully, "Are you sure?"

"Yes," Dagfinn snapped. "Now I'm putting the top on. From now on, you cannot move, and you know that you cannot make a sound. Einarr will do what he can to delay them, and to keep them from doing much poking around here on *Fenrir*, but do *not* give them any reason to tell us to open this up!"

"I...understand," Titus replied, taking solace in wrapping his hand around the hilt of Wyvern's Fang, but that comfort was not destined to last long.

Even as Dagfinn finished hammering the lid down, then grabbed a couple coils of rope and dropped them on top, Titus was covered in sweat that was not due to the temperature or the stuffiness in the crate. For the first time in his life, Titus of Cissanbyrig learned something, that he was terrified of enclosed spaces.

Back in the depression outside Boulogne, Ranulf occupied himself brushing Thunor; after, of course, attending to his own Grisel, while the others alternated standing watch or lying on their cloak. His eyes kept going to where the sun was sinking lower and lower in the sky, knowing that time was running out, and not for the first time, he cursed himself for not being able to come up with another, better plan than the one that Titus had concocted. The only man who seemed pleased was, not surprisingly, Bent. He's smiled more in the last hours than he has in his entire life, Ranulf thought sourly, certain that he knew why; he was convinced that Titus had been caught and was dead...if God had blessed him. Titus had been clear in his instructions, however, which was why his friend kept watching the horizon, while at the same time pausing from the slow, careful brushing to cock his head and listen for something, anything that would indicate someone was approaching. An hour before sundown, Titus had warned, was the last moment they should wait for him; after that, they needed to make their way back to Count Baldwin and the army and report.

"Report what?" Ranulf had demanded.

"That I failed," Titus answered calmly. "Tell him that it was all my idea, and tell him that it did not go as planned."

When Titus had said that, Ranulf did not really believe that it would happen; even more than the other men in Count Baldwin's service, Ranulf had utmost faith in his large friend's abilities, yet now here he was, faced with the prospect of returning to the army to inform Count Baldwin of that very thing. Hard on the heels of that thought came another that, in many ways, was even worse; whenever what they would do at Boulogne was finished, they would be returning to Saint-Omer, and Ranulf would have to tell Yanna that Titus was dead. It was as this thought was going through his head that he happened to glance over at Bent, who happened to choose this moment to chuckle at some private joke. Before he had any conscious thought to do so, Ranulf dropped the brush, strode over to the reclining warrior and stood over him, fists clenched.

"Get up," he snarled. "Get on your feet, you whorespawn, you *bâstart!*"

More shocked than angry, Bent climbed to his feet, but he had barely come erect when Ranulf's fist shot out, catching Bent on the point of the chin, whereupon he dropped right back to the ground, stunned.

"Ranulf! What are you doing?" Theutbald, who was closest to the pair, gasped, retaining his wits and keeping his voice down. "Have you lost your mind?"

He was moving, arriving to interpose himself just in time as Bent, shaking his head to clear it, had started to climb to his feet, his face darkening as his anger began replacing the shock, but when he lunged, Theutbald was ready, grabbing one of

Bent's arms that was outstretched and reaching for Ranulf's throat and, with a savage twist at the waist, used the warrior's own momentum to send him stumbling past the pair. Wala was the next quickest to react, grabbing Ranulf around the waist when Titus' friend thought to take advantage of Bent being off-balance once again, leaving Ranulf to flail wildly at Bent, who was just a matter of inches out of reach.

"Don't think you fooled anyone, you piece of shit!" Ranulf raged, and since he was restrained by Wala, he had to satisfy himself with pointing a shaking finger at Bent's face. "I saw you when you threw those spears at Berserker! You were trying to hit him!"

"If I was trying to hit your *paederastus,* I would have," Bent snarled, which elicited a chorus of gasps from the three onlookers at one of the worst slurs one man could utter to another in their world.

Ranulf's reaction was to twist so violently that he almost wrenched himself free from Wala's grasp, and Theutbald, realizing that they were dangerously close to blood being shed, actually drew his own sword. While it was not done with this intention, the rasping sound of the blade leaving the scabbard arrested the attention of everyone, most importantly the pair of men who, in that moment, had only one thought: to kill their opponent.

"The two of you need to think very carefully what you plan to do next," he said with a calmness that he did not feel, "because I will cut down the winner if you two try to kill each other."

Working in Theutbald's advantage was that neither Ranulf nor Bent held a shred of doubt that he would do that very thing, yet at the same time, Bent's pride was smarting, while Ranulf's desire to kill this man, who he viewed as a malcontent and troublemaker, had not abated. However, just as Titus was aware that Bent had allies among the Count's bodyguard, Bent knew that Ranulf's view, which he had never bothered to hide, was equally shared, and most importantly in this moment, at least two of those men were currently present.

"He struck me without any provocation!" he declared, then spat a gobbet of blood onto the ground. "I hadn't said a word about anything, and he just walked up to me and struck me!" He glared around at the others. "Do any of you dare deny that?"

"No," Lambertus admitted, but it was Wala who said, "I saw what you did as well, Bent."

"I was doing the Berserker a favor!" Bent protested. "I made it look as if we were really trying to stop him from getting to the town!"

"You can understand why Ranulf would be suspicious," Lambertus was the man who could be counted on to try and smooth matters over between comrades who disagreed, "can't you, Bent?"

All Bent had to do in that moment was to simply agree that, yes, given their history, he could see why that Saxon bastard's minions would harbor those thoughts, if not in those words...but he could not do it. It just was not in Bent's nature to not only admit fault, but to even see it in himself. If he had one talent, it was an ability to convince himself that he was always the aggrieved party whose motives were always pure, even if *sometimes* they might be hard to explain, and in Bent's mind, it was simple, and straightforward. That Saxon had supplanted him, *him*, as the most feared warrior serving that pup Count Baldwin, and for that, Bent not only would not, he *could* not forgive Titus the Berserker, even as a part of him acknowledged that it was not really the Berserker's fault, other than the fact that he had shown up. No, the Berserker, Ranulf, and every man of the bodyguard would have been shocked to know that Bent secretly blamed none other than Count Baldwin, and to only a slightly lesser extent, Lord Baudelius, for his predicament. At this moment, however, he knew that the man he had to convince was the one holding his sword, point down but clearly ready, and he addressed Theutbald now.

"I'm not going to try anything. But," he turned and indicated Ranulf with his head, "what about him?"

Theutbald looked over to Ranulf, who unlike Bent, did not say anything, just gave a slight shake of his head, and there was no mistaking how everyone relaxed.

"Ranulf," Theutbald said, almost gently, "it's time for us to get back to the army. We can't wait any longer if we don't want to be crashing around in the dark trying to find them."

"I know," Ranulf sighed, then without another word, and in a signal that sent its own message, he turned his back, walked back to where Thunor and Grisel were hobbled, and picked up the brush, which he stuffed into his saddlebag.

Within fifty heartbeats, they were all mounted and, after a quick glance around, rode away from the depression, heading east for the army.

Titus would never admit it to anyone, but when they finally opened the crate where he had spent the previous several hours and thought that he was asleep, which would add to his legend, albeit in a minor way, he had been passed out, not slumbering. It was only through the intervention of God Himself that the sound created by the lid being pried off had roused him back to consciousness, so that when he looked up, blinking blearily, Dagfinn had burst out laughing.

"He is sound asleep!" he called out, and Titus heard the roars of laughter from what he foggily understood had to be a full crew, which in turn alerted him to the manner in which the ship was rolling.

We're out to sea, he thought with numb surprise, taking Dagfinn's offered hand to help him out of the crate, and he could not stop the groan from escaping his lips as muscles that had been frozen in one position were suddenly stretched. This was bad enough, but it was when he gathered his wits enough to take in more than his immediate surroundings that he gasped again, though not from pain this time. Only half of the sun was visible, the waves tinged with gold from the rays of the setting sun, and after a moment's thought, he remembered that it had still been early afternoon when Dagfinn had stuffed him into the crate.

"Where are we?" he asked Dagfinn.

"We are about three miles north of the town."

"How long have we been at sea?"

"Not long," Dagfinn replied, then grinned. "It took us a while to find the rest of the crew so we could leave."

"They didn't try to stop you?"

"Oh," Dagfinn said with a casualness that did not fool Titus, "Bjorn Sigurdson made noises about trying to stop us, but

Lord Einarr convinced him it would be a bad idea to anger King Guthrum." With his head, Dagfinn indicated the stern. "Lord Einarr wishes to speak with you."

Titus followed the Dane to the rear, exchanging greetings in the form of good-natured insults and taunts with the men at the oars who had not been at the inn, some of whom jokingly blamed him for disrupting the fucking they had been doing. Einarr was talking with Sigmund, who held the steering oar, and Titus took the time to scan the coastline, which was perhaps a half-mile off the right side, but he did not see anything he recognized, or had heard mention of, though this did not surprise him. The Franks were, if anything, worse seamen than the Saxons, although at least in their case they had the excuse that they had never been to sea, unlike the Saxons, who had sailed across The Narrow Sea to carve out a home.

Einarr turned to address Titus, but before he could speak, Titus said earnestly, "Lord, I want to thank you for saving my skin back there." He gave an involuntary shudder. "I don't even like thinking what they might have done to me."

"Well," Einarr joked, rare enough in itself to be notable, "I could hardly let them harm my son...eh, Svein?" Titus laughed, more because of Einarr even attempting such levity, but Einarr's own smile vanished as he asked, "Now what, Titus?"

He was prepared with his answer. "If you can put me off anywhere here where it's safe, I need to go find Count Baldwin and the army."

"We can do that," Einarr answered readily enough, but there was a hesitation there, unusual in itself with the Dane, that alerted Titus. "But I have a...proposition for you."

"A proposition?" Titus repeated warily; a glance at Dagfinn did not offer any hints.

"Yes, a proposition," Einarr snapped with some asperity. He took a breath, turning to look at the coastline as he did so. "Do not rejoin your Frankish Count. Stay with us...where you really belong."

In that moment, Titus realized that he was half-expecting something like this, yet even so, it staggered him, almost literally.

"That...that is a great honor, Lord Einarr," Titus began.

"And," he admitted, "it is tempting. But," he shook his head, "I am afraid that I cannot accept. Count Baldwin has treated me well, and," he shrugged, but he made sure to look Einarr in the eye, "I am not ready to return to Wessex, not yet. Maybe someday, but not now."

Einarr looked disappointed but not surprised, just offering the Saxon a curt nod.

"Very well. We will lower the boat and Dagfinn will row you ashore."

"What will you do now, Lord?"

Einarr gave Titus a grimace that might have been his version of a smile, though Titus did not think this was the case, and the Dane countered with a question of his own.

"What are you going to tell your Frankish count?"

"That there is no ruse on Sigfred's part, and that Hallsteinn did leave with about half of the garrison," Titus answered immediately. "And this is a perfect time to attack."

"Which means," Einarr pointed out, "that we have no more business in Boulogne. So," he pointed west, "we will return to Lunden to tell King Guthrum that we do not know exactly what Sigfred the Úlfhédnar is doing in Frisia, but that he *is* there, and not anywhere else...yet."

Sigfred's whereabouts was certainly something of concern, to both the Danes in East Anglia and, more crucially from Titus' perspective, to his Count, but he felt confident that the Northman was sufficiently far enough away that the Franks could deal with what had become an increasingly sharp thorn in their collective sides in the form of Boulogne. What he did not share even with Yanna was that, for Titus, originally of Cissanbyrig, taking Boulogne from the Northmen would remove an important base for the *viking* that was still plaguing his home island. Now that he was aware that the Danes in East Anglia were at least as concerned about the possibility that Sigfred may land in force somewhere along their coast, it made Count Baldwin's plan even easier to defend.

Sigmund intruded into his thoughts when, from his spot at the steering oar, he said casually, "I made sure to move that crate back over the trapdoor before those *oskilgetinn* showed up."

"You mean they didn't know about it already?" Titus asked in surprise.

"No," Sigmund replied, but Titus was not convinced.

"How do you know?" He pressed Dagfinn's brother.

"Because if they had known about it, Berserker, they would have moved the crate and gone after you," Sigmund said impatiently. "It is the shortest way to get to the docks, and if they had known about it, they are not likely to go back outside and take the long way, are they?"

This was true, and Titus felt his heart quicken, and he turned to address Einarr, his mind moving almost as quickly as his pulse.

"Lord," he pointed to the small skiff that was lashed against the side of the larger ship, "I would like to buy your skiff so that I can row it ashore myself."

This clearly caught Einarr by surprise, his mouth dropping open, though he shut it quickly, his brow furrowing as he demanded, "Why? What could you possibly need..." He stopped abruptly, his face clearing as he understood. "Ah," he said softly, "I see." A new expression came over his features now, one that Titus recognized from his time in Lunden, that of Einarr the bargainer, confirmed when the Dane asked coolly, "And what are you offering?"

Without hesitation, Titus took off one of his arm rings, albeit a silver one and not one of the two golden rings; besides, he would have never offered the ring that Einarr had given him, not only because it was worth many times more than a small boat; indeed, it would have provided the bulk of the purchase price of this ship, but because Einarr would rightly take that as not just an insult, but a repudiation of what his gift of that ring meant. He held the ring out to Einarr, but the Dane made no move to accept the offering, looking down at it in Titus' palm before raising his head to look up at Titus with a raised eyebrow.

Pretending to fume, Titus grumbled, "Fine."

He took off another silver ring and held both out, and these Einarr accepted, but then to Titus' surprise, he withdrew his ax from his belt, and kneeling down, put one of the rings on the deck, and with an ease that spoke of long practice, brought the ax down perfectly in the middle of the ring.

Standing back up, he handed Titus half the ring, and said simply, "It is yours."

It was almost completely dark when, only after exchanging heartfelt farewells disguised by barbed jesting and crude insults, Titus rowed a short distance up a muddy stream (Wimereux), until he saw the large darker shape against the night sky that he knew were treetops. Dragging the boat up onto the muddy bank, even with his prodigious strength, it was a struggle for him to move the craft far enough away from the bank and take advantage of the cover provided by a stand of what he found out the hard way was some sort of thorny bush. Stifling the curse from the scratches, he paused to catch his breath and to think about how to proceed. If God favored him, he reasoned, this stream ran due east, which meant he could follow it, and depending on how long its course ran, it might put him very close to Count Baldwin's army. Understanding there was only one way to find out, he began walking, scanning the surrounding countryside for any sign of life, human or otherwise, and it was not long before he heard the first howls of a wolf pack, somewhere to the south of him. This, in turn, reminded him that if this stream did run perfectly east and did not angle south at all, he would have to cross the stream to turn in that direction at some point since the stream was north of Boulogne, and the route the Count was taking was essentially a straight line between Boulogne and Saint-Omer, which was almost perfectly east of the town. He was aided by the light of a rising three-quarter moon with few clouds, and with the gentle breeze that cooled the night air, it helped keep him from overheating in his armor, which he realized he had been wearing for the better part of two days, although he was fortunate in that regard, not even really noticing its weight, and the lack of flexibility was just part of the price for protection.

By his estimate, he had gone about two miles from the boat when, once again, there was a single howl...much, much closer than the previous one, and Titus felt the hair on the nape of his neck stand up straight. Despite knowing that he would not see anything, he looked across the stream, which at this point was barely ten paces across, although it was still a welcome barrier, but as he expected, he saw nothing, not even movement of any of the underbrush lining the opposite bank. Before he had gone another hundred paces, there was another howl, but any thought that this might be the same wolf was dispelled when, again immediately across from him, there was an answering call. This was the moment he drew Wyvern's Fang, the feel of it in his hand giving him a surge of comfort, but it took an effort on his part not to speed up, having heard somewhere that this was what wolf packs wanted, for their prey to panic and bolt. By the time he had gone another mile, Titus was certain of a couple of things; the stream was not angling south enough, if at all, which meant he would have to wade across...and there was a pack of wolves on the other side of the stream, stalking him and waiting for their moment.

The ride back to the army by the *Exploratores* was a silent one, with an air of tension so thick that Ranulf thought it could be cut with a knife; although, he thought with sour amusement, if anyone drew even an eating knife, there would be bloodshed. Yes, he had heeded Theutbald's warning, both the explicit and implicit, and he was keeping a tight rein on his emotions, yet every time he glanced over at Bent's shadow in the darkness, he felt an itching in his sword hand. He also knew that it was irrational to blame Bent for Titus' likely demise, yet he could not seem to help himself, and judging from the constant scrutiny he felt from Theutbald, Wala, and Lambertus, they were as concerned about him doing something stupid as he was. Only Bent seemed oblivious, but Ranulf was certain this was a pretense, if only because of the manner in which his head kept turning in Ranulf's direction.

"We must be getting close," Lambertus whispered, then asked hesitantly. "Shouldn't we?"

"We should," Theutbald confirmed, but if he was going to say anything else, off to their left and to the north, they heard a lone howl.

It had been relatively quiet for the last couple of hours, and this resumption, even if it was a single wolf, elicited a low chorus of groans and curses.

"I thought those beasts had finally found something to eat,"

Wala grumbled. "And as long as it's not me, that's all I care about!" Suddenly realizing how that sounded, he added, "I mean, as long as it's not one of *us*. That's what I meant."

"Yes," Lambertus countered dryly. "We know what you meant."

Before Wala could protest, there was another howl, again from a single wolf, but it was instantly answered, and to Ranulf's ear, this reply seemed to come from the same spot where the first howl had come from, while the other one came from a short distance away from the original wolf, perhaps closer to them. Even as this thought crossed his mind and what it might mean, the night air was shattered by howls too numerous to easily count, and impossible to separate and identify.

"They must have found something," Theutbald commented. "And now they're calling their friends for the hunt."

"Better whatever beast that is than me," Wala murmured, reminding Ranulf that being devoured by wolves was the other Frankish warrior's particular fear, one that he talked about quite a bit, and always in gory, lurid detail.

It was, Ranulf thought uneasily, one thing when they were sitting in Melisandre's, snug and safe inside and surrounded by stone walls, and they heard the occasional howl, but now, despite being heavily armed and armored, and numbering five men, it was another matter entirely, and Ranulf did not need to verbalize this to know his companions were every bit as nervous. What happened next occurred so quickly that Ranulf would never be able to untangle the sequence of events, but it began when, without any warning whatsoever, Thunor, who had been obediently following Ranulf on a lead rope, came to an abrupt stop, his head lifting with ears pricked forward, looking off to their left, which jerked the rope out of Ranulf's hand since Grisel kept going. At what Ranulf was certain was the exact same time, amid the chorus of howls, there came a bellow from another animal, one that was most decidedly not a wolf, a bellow of rage and defiance that Ranulf thought might have been a bear...and Thunor instantly broke into a gallop, lead rope trailing behind him after jerking it out of Ranulf's gloved hand. All that was in Ranulf's mind was, I can't lose his horse too!, so before any of the other *Exploratores* could react, let alone respond with anything other than inarticulate shouts of surprise and fear, Titus' friend was in hot pursuit.

Anyone who knew Titus the Berserker and were informed of the events of that night might have had a variety of reactions, but none of them would have been surprised to learn that his solution to the problem of being alone and surrounded by a pack of wolves who, for whatever reason, had decided that this lone human on foot was suitable prey, was to attack the entire pack. And, once Titus had time to think about it, he was able to provide his reasoning to those interested in learning what he could have possibly been thinking in a manner that, even if the listeners did not completely agree with him, would acknowledge that it was not quite as reckless, foolhardy, and mad as it sounded...not quite. In the moment, what actually happened was that Titus first lost his patience after spending what seemed to him to be a couple of thousand heartbeats on the opposite side of the stream, shouting, waving his sword, and otherwise doing whatever he could think of to dissuade what he counted was a pack of at least fifteen wolves from the idea that he would make an easy kill, although he was also certain there were more, less bold members of the pack lurking out of sight. Once he determined that they were unwilling to try and swim the stream to force the issue, he used it to his advantage, taking the time to pick up rocks and fling them at the dark shapes, rewarded twice by sharp yelps of pain before, unsurprisingly, they retreated out of his range. Using his leather bag, he stuffed it with rocks, which also meant he had to sheathe his sword, but instead drew the ax from his belt, which he had learned to use with his left hand with ample dexterity...or so he hoped. Then, after taking a deep breath and, unusually, offering a prayer to God that he not end up in the bellies of a pack of wolves, he began wading across, hurling rocks when a couple pack members became impatient, creeping forward once he was midstream, with the water just above his knees.

Just before he reached the opposite bank, one of the beasts came charging in his direction, its eyes seeming to catch the glow from the silver moon, and Titus, fighting the urge to immediately hurl one of his rapidly dwindling supply of stones, waited until the wolf was barely ten paces away and about to leap when, putting his body and strength of his arm into it, he flung the rock. The force created by the opposing momentums of wolf and stone, along with the power that Titus could generate, meant that the rock, which hit the animal unerringly between the eyes, crushed its skull, the rock burying itself in the brain of the animal, which hit the ground, dead, tumbling with limbs askew before skidding to a stop a pace from Titus' dripping feet just as he stepped out of the water. This unleashed another torrent of howling, yet even in this moment, Titus' ears informed him this was different; this was the pack sounding its grief at losing a member, coupled with a rage that meant that, when another animal began moving, head low with teeth bared, then breaking into a sprint at Titus, the Saxon was ready. He did not draw Wyvern's Fang; not only was there no time, there was no need, because this animal was coming from his left. If it had been daylight, Titus' timing would have been perfect, with the bearded ax blade slicing through the beast's neck just behind the ears, but because of the darkness, it was slightly off so that it did not decapitate the animal cleanly. The body's angle of momentum was altered enough by the force of the ax blow that the corpse shot across Titus' front less than a full hand's width away, and he felt the hot blood splash on his face and chest, yet it did not repulse him, not anymore, because in that same instant, the Berserker had been unleashed. He was aware that he was bellowing something; more accurately, he was inarticulately snarling, matching the ferocity of his enemies, and the body of the second wolf was still rolling in the dirt when Titus drew Wyvern's Fang and went charging at the nearest wolf, with one and only one thought...to kill. His target hesitated, unable to decide whether to flee or to fight this two-legged creature that was behaving in a way so far outside this animal's experience that his hesitation sealed his fate as Wyvern's Fang stabbed down into its body, severing the wolf's spinal cord less than an eyeblink before the point pierced its heart with unerring accuracy, so sudden was the death that the wolf did nothing more than let out a low whimper as it died. It was at this moment when, from behind the remaining wolves, who were already moving to fully encircle him now that Titus was no longer with his back against the stream, that they became aware of another sound, along with a sensation coming up through the pads of their paws, a vibration that signaled a new kind of danger.

Even before Thunor, with Ranulf just behind him, came thundering out of the gloom, most of the surviving wolves melted into the darkness, sprinting away in both directions along the stream, though not before one more wolf, which Titus would never know was the mate of the bitch that he had just slain, leapt at the man, teeth bared and snarling its defiance as it died, skewering itself on Wyvern's Fang, which Titus had just withdrawn from its mate and brought up into position to face this new attack, then using the massive strength of just his right arm, held the animal up so their faces were inches from each other, each creature staring into their enemy's eyes, both pairs blazing with hatred and battle fury. This was how Ranulf found his friend, the sight so disturbing that he yanked his horse's reins, while even Thunor, who could usually be counted on coming to his master at almost a gallop to thrust his nose into Titus' chest, drew up short, although Ranulf was certain that, like all horses, the stallion was thrown off by the combined smell of wolf, blood, and death. For a time that seemed to stretch forever, Ranulf sat there, hearing but barely registering the drumming hoofbeats of the other *Exploratores*, yet Titus did not seem to notice anything at all, so intent was he on his slain foe as he stared at the animal, whose head was still erect, jaws snapping weakly, telling the Frank that it was still alive. He heard Titus, but was not close enough to hear what he was whispering, then at last, with a breathy groan, the wolf's head dropped; only then did Titus, his arm trembling violently from the effort of holding this animal feet off the ground, lower the wolf with a gentleness that Ranulf would always remember but never understand. Titus withdrew his blade from the wolf's body, and only then did Thunor move, taking a tentative step towards Titus, nickering softly in a manner that Ranulf thought was a question, struck by the thought, Thunor is asking Titus if he is all right.

"*Wes hal*, my champion," Titus said, and despite himself, Ranulf slumped in the saddle, relieved at this sign that his friend had returned from wherever he had been.

"Christ's blood! What happened here?"

So engrossed in the scene before him, Ranulf had completely forgotten the presence of the other *Exploratores,* while Titus had been in his...place...where he was Berserker and nothing else.

Ranulf, seeing that his friend was in the kind of state he had been immediately after Watten, answered Bent for him. "Those wolves we were hearing were attacking Berserker here. They," he added pointedly, "made the same mistake I've seen some men make."

"You killed these beasts?" Bent asked, swinging down, counting and, before he could think better of it, gave a low whistle. "You killed four wolves?"

"Without a spear or bow." Ranulf nodded.

The rest of the men had dismounted as well, dividing their time between examining the dead animals and, more surreptitiously, examining Titus, who was now absorbed in talking to Thunor, apologizing to his horse for not having anything to give him. It was when Bent dropped into a crouch next to the corpse of the wolf that had been the last Titus had killed that the atmosphere immediately changed. Ranulf, who had also dismounted by this time, was trying to decide the best way to remind everyone that, as arresting as this scene might have been, they had yet to reunite with the army, and he saw the glint of moonlight on metal in Bent's hand, realizing what the warrior intended on doing. It was very common for men to adorn themselves with wolf tails, and to use their pelts to trim the collars of cloaks, and their teeth as necklaces, yet he somehow knew that these wolves were different, at least as far as Titus was concerned.

Bent reached out with his free hand to grab the tail, preparing to saw it off at the base, which caught Titus' attention, and the Saxon said flatly, "Do not."

"Do not what?" Bent asked, affecting an air of innocence that fooled nobody.

"Get your hands off that animal," Titus replied, sounding

more tired than angry.

As much as Ranulf despised Bent, it was because of his concern for his friend that he wanted to shout, "Do you not have eyes, you fool? Do you not see what this man did to a *pack of wolves, by himself?*"

Ranulf would have been shocked to learn that, inside Bent, there was a voice essentially screaming the same thing, yet he could not seem to heed it.

"Why should I?" Bent asked, then feigned a laugh that was obviously counterfeit. "It is dead, you fool. It does not need a tail!"

Titus did not reply, instead staring down at his foe, and finally, Ranulf broke it by reminding them, "We still haven't found the army yet. We need to get back to the Count." Somewhat ashamedly, Ranulf thought to ask, "Did you find anything out, Titus?"

"Yes." Titus nodded, but his eyes never left Bent. "There are only about five hundred Northmen in the town. Hallsteinn is in Cent, besieging the town of Hrofescester, Sigfred really is in Frisia...and I know how to take the town."

"Then we need to stop wasting time," Theutbald said, and the others joined in a chorus of agreement that, thankfully, Bent correctly interpreted.

Standing erect, Bent offered an elaborate shrug, and said, "Very well. I can always come back..."

"If I see you wearing anything that I even *think* comes from these animals," Titus did not raise his voice, but there was no need to in order for the others to hear him, "I'll kill you, Bent. Do you understand me?"

"I know you might *try*," Bent sneered, but there was a false bravado behind his words...and he was moving to his horse as he said them.

The others remounted, and while Ranulf, Lambertus, and Wala all noticed, none of them commented when Titus knelt, placed a hand on the last wolf he had slain, and with head bowed, whispered something. Then, he stood and strode to Thunor, leaping into the saddle in what was a calculated display on his part, happy that he managed to do so without touching the stirrups with his feet, or his saddle with his hands, which he would not have wagered on himself to do. Riding in a southeasterly direction, they began searching for the army.

An hour later, it was Wala, riding a short distance ahead, who called out, "I see a glow!"

This was what they had been looking for, the glow on the horizon created by the fires of a large body of men, and they broke into a trot, slowing only when they reached another strip of heavily forested land, with the camp on the other side. Titus was near the end of his tether, unable to remember the last time he had been this exhausted, but he still had much to do before the prospect of any rest. Ranulf was next to him, and he knew this was no accident, that his friend had an idea of how fatigued Titus was, and was ready to offer assistance any way that he could.

"Did you get any sleep at all?" he finally asked Titus.

"Some," Titus lied. "When I was being smuggled out of Boulogne on..." Suddenly, he realized that he had not talked about running into Einarr, literally, and even with his fatigue, he grinned in the darkness. Rather than finish, he went on hurriedly, "I need to tell you the other part first."

He went on to describe everything that had taken place on his disappearance into the town, and how he had literally collided with Einarr.

"Wait," Ranulf interrupted. "Einarr. I know you've mentioned that name before, but I don't remember where." With some chagrin, Titus reminded Ranulf of Einarr's identity, and the role he played not just in Titus' past, but in the larger sense; later, he blamed his fatigue for not setting the stage properly, as Ranulf instantly grew suspicious. "What is that Danish *bâstart* king's man doing over here? Are they some sort of secret allies with Sigfred?"

"No!" Titus shook his head. "No, they are not!" In a slightly more moderate tone, he realized that he needed to make an effort to concentrate. "In fact, they are as suspicious of what Sigfred is up to as the Count is, but the other reason they came here was because of Hallsteinn's besieging of Hrofescester. Ranulf," he assured his friend, "they're not going to betray us."

Ranulf was not convinced, but he also understood that this,

in fact, was above his station and was a matter for Lord Baudelius, or Count Baldwin, so he nodded, which was enough for Titus, who went on to finish the story, stopping with the encounter with the wolves. Which, not surprisingly, Ranulf was still intensely curious about, which was what led him to blurt out, "What were you doing with that last wolf you killed, Titus?"

Titus did not seem surprised by the question because he was not; he had been expecting it for some time.

"I was asking the Norse gods to transfer the spirit of that wolf to me," he replied, as if this was the most natural thing in the world.

"*What*?" Ranulf gasped, then took a quick glance around, only then noticing that, since he was matching Titus' pace, he had not noticed that his friend had slowed Thunor so they were slightly separated from the others. "Titus," he said nervously, "that is blasphemy! God will surely punish you for that!"

Titus gave a bitter laugh at this.

"You mean, more than He already has?" he asked mockingly. "I killed my mother. I killed the woman I loved. This bastard Sigfred the Úlfhédnar has raised the bounty on my head, even though he hated his son Leif. I just thought," he finished with a shrug, "that if I am ever going to face a wolf, I could use some of a wolf's strength."

When put that way, Ranulf thought, it was hard to argue, but he still warned, "Just do not tell anyone else about that, Titus. All right?"

"I will not," his friend replied.

They lapsed into silence, and a short time later, after negotiating their way through the forest on the western side of a large clearing, they entered it to see, spread before them, the camp of Count Baldwin and his army. Now, Titus thought grimly, comes the hard part.

Normally, Baldwin, second of his name and Margrave of Flandre, despised being roused from his slumber; this was an exception. The news his body servant brought him that the *Exploratores* had returned was more important than such trivialities as losing sleep, although he did change from his sleeping robes into his tunic and trousers. When Baudelius arrived outside his tent, a sumptuous affair that even Alfred, King of Wessex might have envied, Baldwin had arranged for pitchers of water and wine, cups, and an amount of food, knowing that, had he been in their place, he would have appreciated the gesture. It was the kind of thing Baldwin did that marked him as different than other men of his rank; part of it was his youth and the insecurity that came with it, but it was more than that. His first shock came when the *Exploratores* entered, immediately bowing their heads, and he saw that the Berserker looked as if he had been dipped in blood.

"By the Cross, Berserker!" he exclaimed, earning a frown from his personal chaplain, Father Rudolf, which he pointedly ignored. "Are you wounded? Do you need my healer?"

"No, Lord Count," Titus replied automatically. "It is not my blood."

Baldwin stared at the Saxon for a moment, not sure if he believed him, but then moved on, asking crisply, "Well? What did you learn?"

That every man, save two, all looked at the Berserker was something that Baldwin did not miss, though he made no comment about it. One of them was Bent, who looked deliberately at the dirt floor of the tent, while the other was Baudelius, who was glaring at Bent as if he had done something to draw Baudelius' displeasure. For his part, Titus would have been shocked to learn that, not only did Count Baldwin know quite a bit about Bent, but despite their different stations, Saxon warrior and Frankish nobleman shared very similar feelings about him.

That, however, did not matter now, and Baldwin said, "Clearly, Berserker, you are the one the rest are looking at, so what is it?"

Titus talked for the next few moments, regretting that he had not availed himself of the refreshment, if only to wet his throat, and Baldwin had given the others leave to guzzle as much as they wanted while Titus spoke. By the time he was finished, or almost finished, it was next to impossible for the Count to hide his excitement, while even the dour Baudelius had the grimace that was his version of a smile on his face.

"So," Baldwin summarized, "my spies have told the truth! This is not a ploy on the part of Sigfred! He is really gone, and Hallsteinn really did take half of the *custodes* with him," using the Frankish term for the garrison. Standing up, he began to pace, hands behind his back, as he continued, "We will reach Boulogne just before nightfall tomorrow, and there will be no time for them to summon help. Our ladders will go against their wall at dawn, day after tomorrow."

"How did the Berserker here escape from the town? I would like to know."

Baldwin spun about to glare at Baudelius, who had asked the question, but despite his irritation, he acknowledged that it was a valid question, and he looked at Titus.

"Well, Berserker? How did you get away?"

There was, Titus realized, nothing for it, though he was not all that surprised. It had been a bit silly to expect that he could have avoided bringing Einarr and his other Danish friends into it.

"Lord Count, I am happy to tell you, but I have a request," Titus said, without any conscious thought to do so, and even he wondered where the idea had come from.

"Oh? What is that?" Baldwin asked, eyebrow raised.

"I wish to speak to you about it privately. Just," he turned and looked directly at Baudelius first, then Bent, "the two of us."

Chapter Four

Across The Narrow Sea, the event that every man, be they Saxon or Northmen, experienced in such matters had been dreading, when the bloody flux that had struck down the men of Alfred's bodyguard and the Centishman began to spread like wildfire through both camps outside Hrofescester. It was this event that forced Hallsteinn's hand when, two months after beginning the siege, Eadward and his father were awakened by an uproar outside their tent.

The son leapt to his feet and rushed to the flap, while Eadwig stirred, asking groggily, "Wha...what is it, boy?"

Rather than answer immediately, Eadward stepped out into the early morning light into a scene of activity as men seemed to be doing what he was, trying to determine what the excitement was about.

Otha and Ceadda came trotting up, but when he asked them if they knew anything, Otha chuckled. "We were hoping that you would know, Lord."

They learned from one of Alfred's men, Cynebald, who had served with them on *Sea Viper* and who happened to be trotting up at that moment, bringing orders from Alfred.

"The Northman Hallsteinn has begun the attack on the town! King Alfred orders that you arm your men. Lord Eadward," he did offer a perfunctory bow, "the King summons you and your father to his tent as soon as you are able."

"Tell the King we will be there momentarily," Eadward promised, but Cynebald was already moving in the opposite direction from the King's tent, heading for the men from Hampscir and Ealdorman Cuthred, who were on the other side of the Wiltun men.

"You know what to do." Eadward was turning back to the tent as he said this, while his two Thegns were in motion as well.

Entering the tent, he was dismayed to see that his father, while sitting up, had not even swung his legs out of his cot, and he glared at Beohrtic, who had been pressed into service as Eadwig's body servant. The servant gave Eadward an apologetic glance as he hurried to the cot, but when he extended a hand to Eadwig, the elder man slapped it away.

"I don't need help getting out of bed, oaf," Eadwig growled, but Eadward heard the slight groan as his father swung his legs off of the cot. Turning to Eadward, he demanded irritably, "So? What's all the excitement about? Why is everyone shouting out there?"

"The Northmen are attacking Hrofescester, Father," Eadward replied. "The King requires our presence immediately."

"Immediately?" Eadwig echoed, then shook his head. "I haven't broken my fast yet! I'm not going to go into battle on an empty stomach! You..." He snapped his fingers at Beohrtic, and it was clear to Eadward that his father was struggling to remember Beohrtic's name, an increasingly common event, borne out when Beohrtic supplied his name without any hesitation or surprise. This prompted Eadwig to snap, "I know who you are, oaf! You didn't need to remind me, I would have come up with it! Now, go fix some oat cakes, and," he paused to think, as Eadward watched in growing dismay, "I think a nice side of bacon as well." Somewhat embarrassed, he turned to his son. "What about you, boy? Does that sound good?"

"Father, we don't have time for..."

"Nonsense!" Eadwig snapped. He pointed a finger in the direction of the King's tent, and Eadward noticed the slight tremor. "Do you know how much time I've spent waiting on our King, boy? Do you? Well," he huffed, "he can afford to wait for a man who's going to be doing the fighting for him to fill his belly on what might be his last day!"

Such was Eadward's consternation that he did not place any significance on this last statement by his father, although in his defense, the Lord of Wiltun had made such bombastic declarations in his son's presence more times than he could count.

Understanding the futility, Eadward glanced at Beohrtic, who gave a silent nod of his own comprehension, while aloud, Eadward said, "Yes, well, please hurry, Father. I'm going to go attend to the King on our behalf." He gave his father a smile that he hoped did not appear as false as it felt. "Someone needs to remind him that we Wiltun men can be counted on, eh?"

"You do that," Eadwig agreed absently, his mind already going somewhere else.

Eadward donned his mail, then snatched up his helmet and sword belt, hurrying out of the tent, running into Otha, who, unlike Eadward, was fully attired, save for his spear and shield, which would be the last things he would take up once they learned what they would be doing.

"Where's Lord Eadwig?" Otha asked, a perfectly reasonable question, but Eadward snapped, "It's not your place to worry about my father, Otha! He'll be along immediately, that's all you need to know!"

Otha was more shocked than angry or offended, and the pair walked in silence for a few paces, slowing when Ceadda called to them, coming at a quick trot.

"I'm sorry, Otha," Eadward said quietly before Ceadda joined them. "My father is just not...himself right now, but that's neither your fault nor your problem."

"No apology necessary, Lord," Otha assured him quietly. "I've seen it as well."

Eadward desperately wanted to ask Otha for advice, but Ceadda had arrived by then, and before he could comment, Eadward said, "My father will be along shortly, Ceadda. He was...indisposed when the summons came."

He saw Ceadda's head turn sharply, feeling the Thegn's eyes on him, but thankfully, this was all Ceadda did; besides, they were at the tent, which was rapidly filling up. Alfred, standing in the middle of the tent, had Cyneweard next to him, along with a filthy, muddy man that Eadward did not recognize. Because of the distance between the Saxon camp and the walls of Hröfescester, the noise of fighting was only faintly audible over the hubbub of voices as the assembly talked among themselves, but it became more audible when Alfred raised a hand for silence, which was granted immediately. With his father's voice in his head, Eadward had pushed himself forward to stand in the front row facing Alfred, ending up next to Ealdorman Sigeræd to his right, who barely deigned to acknowledge him, while Cuthred, huffing and puffing, arrived a moment later, ending up on Eadward's left.

"Where's your father?" the Ealdorman demanded, loudly enough for Alfred, who had been listening to the muddy man whispering in his ear to hear as well, and Eadward saw the pale blue eyes of the King on him.

Pointedly ignoring Cuthred, who Eadward knew coveted being given Wiltscir by the King, Eadward said, "Lord King, my father is..."

"Here, Lord King!"

It took an effort for Eadward not to sag in relief, and he heard the buzzing noise of the lesser noblemen arrayed behind them moving out of the way for Eadwig, who firmly moved Cuthred aside so that he could stand next to his son. Eadward heard Cuthred hiss in rage, but Eadward was watching their King, and he saw what he was certain was a slight smile on Alfred's face at this clear assertion by Eadward's father.

"My lords," Alfred began by indicating the muddy man, "this man is in my employ. He is a Dane," there was a ripple of murmurs at this, which Alfred ignored, "who has performed services for me in the past. Until this morning, he was part of Hallsteinn's band of pagans, escaping only after fulfilling the task I had given him, at great risk to himself."

He nodded to the Dane, who Eadward thought he recognized now that Alfred had identified his role, and he had long heard rumors that Alfred had many such men in his purse.

"Hallsteinn is attacking Hrofescester," the Dane began, in heavily accented but understandable Saxon. "He was forced into it by his men, because the bloody flux has weakened them. I," he drew himself up, "warned Lord Rægenhere last night..."

"How?" Ealdorman Sigeræd demanded, not hiding his skepticism. "How did you manage to warn my man without being caught?"

"Because," the Dane answered simply, "I am good at what I do."

"You mean that you are good at sneaking into places you

aren't supposed to be!" Sigeræd snapped. "You mean that you're a thief!"

Rather than be offended, the Dane actually laughed, and Eadward saw that most of his bottom teeth were missing.

"I am," he admitted cheerfully, "and a very good one."

"Lord King, I do not trust this man," Sigeræd insisted, which Eadward found curious.

Why, he wondered, is Sigeræd fighting about this? We can all hear what's happening.

This seemed to be Alfred's thought, because once again, he lifted his hand in a signal for silence, then after a moment, he chided the Centishman, "Lord Sigeræd, I believe just by listening you can hear what's taking place." He paused long enough for Sigeræd to offer a perfunctory bob of his head that Alfred accepted as his yielding the point then continued, "We will array for battle immediately, with my bodyguard in the center, Lord Sigeræd's men on the left wing, and Lord Cuthred and Lord Eadwig's men on the right wing."

Eadward mentally counted the time before Lord Sigeræd objected; he got to two before the Centishman protested, "Lord King, Hrofescester is a Centish city! It should be Centishmen who bear the brunt of the fighting, not..." He stopped himself in time from committing a mortal error by saying "outsiders," or worse, choosing, "...men who aren't from Cent! Men who are not related by blood to the women and children who are right now cowering inside those walls!"

Alfred listened impassively, but he was unmoved.

"While I understand your passion, Lord, my decision stands. Now," he raised his voice, "men of Wessex. Our Centish countrymen need our help! What say you to their plea?"

He was drowned out immediately, and while his expression did not change, Eadward was in a unique position, standing as he was next to the Centish Ealdorman while facing his King to see the glint of sardonic amusement in Alfred's eye as he looked Sigeræd directly in the eye in an unmistakable message. You may be Ealdorman of Cent...but I am King. The assembly broke up, with the attendees heading rapidly towards their men, Sigeræd practically stomping up the muddy path, clearly fuming with rage.

"That is a sight that does these old eyes good." Eadwig laughed at the nobleman's retreating back.

Before they had gone a dozen paces, they heard someone call Lord Eadward's name, and they both turned to see that it was Cyneweard, the commander of the bodyguard beckoning to him. Eadwig, assuming that he meant both of them, an assumption that Eadward shared, began walking back to Cyneweard, who suddenly looked embarrassed.

"Er, Lord, the King asked specifically for Lord Eadward...alone."

"Ah," Eadwig fumbled. "I...see." Eadward would always remember the smile his father gave him, as he attempted to joke, "The King has figured out who the real mind is among us Wiltun men, eh?"

"I'm sure that it's nothing important, Father," Eadward said, truly believing it.

"We'll be ready by the time you come back," Eadwig assured him.

Hurrying back to the tent, Eadward found Alfred in the last stages of donning his armor, although he did not do it himself, not really, standing with arms outstretched as one of his attendants made a last adjustment to the mail coat, of Frankish construction but which hung down to his knees even after it was bunched above his sword belt.

"Lord Eadward," Alfred spoke formally, "the reason I called you back was to inform you that you are in command of the Wiltun men." He paused, and closed his eyes for a heartbeat before adding, "Not your father." Now, he looked directly at Eadward, asking pointedly, "Do you understand, Lord?"

"Yes, Lord King." Eadward bowed, from the waist instead of just his head, wanting to assure his King that he understood not only the order, but why the King gave it.

"Also," Alfred said as the attendant strapped his sword to his waist, giving it a tug, "Lord Cuthred is in overall command of the right wing. However," he dismissed the attendant with a shooing motion so that he could walk over to Eadward, and his voice lowered to just above a whisper, "I also have...concerns about Lord Cuthred, specifically as it concerns one order in particular that I gave him."

"Which is, Lord King?" Eadward asked, completely mystified.

"Because you're on the right wing, you're near the river, and nearest to the Northmen's ships. I gave Lord Cuthred orders that I do *not* want him to attempt to fire those ships."

Confusion was added to mystification; what the King was saying ran counter to common and accepted practice among Saxons. Whenever presented with the opportunity, one always made sure to destroy the number one weapon that the dreaded raiders from the North had at their disposal, their ships that gave them the mobility that was unparalleled in their world.

Consequently, even as he knew what his answer should have been, Eadward heard himself ask in bafflement, "But why, Lord King? Why wouldn't we want to destroy their ships?"

Under other circumstances, Alfred would not have taken the time to explain; after all, he could tell just by the noise that his men were almost completely assembled and ready to cross the ditch using the three large wooden ramps that had been constructed for the purpose. However, while Alfred had no way of knowing what lay in this young nobleman's immediate future, he was aware in a general sense that this battle, however it turned out, would be Lord Eadwig's last, and that if God willed it, Alfred would have to rely on this youngster and the warriors under his command in the future, and even in that moment, in the back of his mind, there was one warrior in particular whose service Alfred foresaw needing, even if he was not present for this moment.

Still, he could not completely curb the impatience he felt as he explained, "If we destroy their ships, we give the Northmen no choice but to fight to the death, which will cost us more lives than it already has. By sparing the ships, we give Hallsteinn and his men the chance to escape. And," he held both hands out, "ultimately what we want is to relieve the suffering of those poor souls in Hrofescester, do we not?"

When explained this way, Eadward saw the logic, but he was also aware that time was not on his side, yet he still felt he had to ask, "And you worry about Lord Cuthred not following your orders?"

Alfred hesitated, then said carefully, "Lord Cuthred is a

great warrior, and when the moment comes, I am...concerned that he might temporarily forget my orders. But," he reached out and placed a hand on Eadward's mailed shoulder, "if you and your men reach those ships first, then he will not be led into temptation."

The King smiled at his own small jest, using the words from the *Pater Noster*, which Eadward returned.

"You can count on us, Lord King," Eadward assured him.

With that, he was dismissed; it was not until he was almost back to where the Wiltun men had already assembled before he realized that he had no idea how he would do any of it.

As such things went, the Battle of Hrofescester was not the kind of affair that the bards would compose songs about. In fact, it would become a point of contention, as it alternately became an article of faith on the part of Centishmen inside Hrofescester that they had not really needed the help of the King of Wessex, which would become just another bone in the collective throats of those who were present who fought for King Alfred who insisted that they were crucial to success. The casualties were light, for the most part, but the only source of agreement on the part of both factions on the same side was that what fighting there was saw the fiercest combat on the riverbank on the eastern side, where about one hundred Northmen, led by Hallsteinn, fought their way to the riverbank and the ships that had brought them from across The Narrow Sea. What Eadward learned that day was that obeying his King's orders to allow the Northmen an avenue to escape was easier said than done, and even a more experienced commander would have been hard pressed to appear to put up a fight that did not draw the suspicion and the wrath of Ealdorman Cuthred.

Eadward had given strict orders he did not want to be disturbed, and he had yet to clean himself up, but it was more important to him to offer prayers for his father, whose body *had* been cleaned and prepared before being wrapped in his shroud. Beohrtic had helped him, cleaning the grime from his father's hands while Eadward lovingly cleaned the blood from the puckered wound to his chest, the result of a sword thrust delivered by the Northman Hallsteinn himself. He took some solace in the fact that, for once in some time, his father looked at peace, his features composed, and Eadward swore he wore a slight smile on his face. It's as if, Eadward suddenly thought, he had achieved something that he had been striving for, and this thought alone threatened his composure. Now, with his father prepared for his final journey back to Wiltun, Eadward knelt next to his cot, offering up his prayers to God for the peaceful passage of his father, at least with part of his mind. There was another portion that was thinking ahead, grappling with what it meant now that he was Lord of Wiltun, more than a Thegn, yet not quite an Ealdorman. That, he thought grimly, needs to change, and if anything, his father's corpse helped his cause, because Eadward possessed the kind of resolve that is the province of the young to right what he felt with all of his being was a great wrong. He heard the flap being thrust back, despite his strict instructions to Beohrtic, who he had placed outside, that he was not to be disturbed for any reason, and he turned his head to issue a rebuke, but when he did, he immediately understood why Beohrtic had not obeyed him.

"Lord King!" he gasped, jumping to his feet. "I...I..." He could not get the words out, but what saved him was that Alfred, King of Wessex was as discomfited as the young nobleman, understanding that he was intruding on a private moment of grief.

Suddenly, on impulse, Alfred asked, "I see that I disturbed you at prayers. May I...pray with you? For the repose of your father? He was," the King said with quiet conviction, "a good man, a faithful servant of God."

He stopped then, and Eadward felt an unexpected flare of anger, which was the only way he would have said what came out of his mouth.

"And a faithful servant to his King."

Eadward instantly wished he had bitten off his tongue rather than say that, although as he knew, it was not the words themselves but the manner in which he said it, with an accusatory tone that was a reckless and, he was certain his father would say, foolish thing to do. And, for a long moment, Alfred's face transformed into a mask, his eyes turning cold and boring into Eadward's, before, with an almost imperceptible exhalation of breath, the King relaxed.

"He was," Alfred agreed softly.

Then, without another word, he walked over and dropped to his knees. For the next few moments, the King of Wessex and one of his subjects said the prayers for the repose of the dead. Once they were finished, Eadward had no idea what to do, then decided that he would do as the King did, but Alfred did not move.

Instead, he spoke quietly, though he still looked straight ahead, over the body of Eadward's father. "You are now Lord of Wiltun, Lord Eadward. That...changes matters for you."

Eadward *thought* he understood, yet despite his youth, he was wise enough to comprehend that there were things that he would be confronted with that he had not thought of; and, he realized, there was nobody better positioned to know what it was like to be saddled with responsibility at a young age that he thought would be years away than the man kneeling next to him.

"Lord King, what do you advise?"

Alfred nodded his approval; the lad began by asking the right question, although he did not answer directly.

"You will be challenged," Alfred said. "Was there anyone your father was concerned about? Among his fellow noblemen?"

The thought that this might be some sort of trap crossed Eadward's mind, but he almost immediately dismissed it; it was inconceivable to him that this pious King had some sort of ulterior motive that would be to his detriment.

Years later, he would laugh at this naiveté even if it did pay off, but in the moment, he answered honestly, "Ealdorman Cuthred. My father was certain that he was trying to...persuade you to name him Ealdorman of both Hampscir and Wiltscir."

"Your father," Alfred acknowledged tonelessly, "was right. Lord Cuthred has been petitioning me for some time." The King hesitated, then decided that brutal honesty was in order. "His petitions had become more...urgent in the last few months because of your father's failing...health."

"Well," Eadward said bitterly, "his health isn't a concern of Lord Cuthred's anymore."

"As King," Alfred said, "I must make decisions that are best for *all* of my people...even if," he added meaningfully, "my personal feeling might lead me in another direction." He turned to face Eadward, though they were still on their knees. "I believe that you have it in you to be a valuable ally to me, young Eadward. But at the same time, you *are* vulnerable right now. Your men are loyal, anyone can see that, but your father's refusal to name a replacement for Thegn Aelfnod has...troubled me. I cannot lie about that."

Suddenly, Eadward had a flash of insight, and in a leap of intuition, he offered, "I'm recalling Titus from his banishment, Lord King, if I can find him."

It would be some time before Eadward would learn that this was exactly what Alfred wanted to hear, and he offered Eadward a small smile that, despite the circumstances, he thought was appropriate.

"I believe that I can help you locating young Titus, Lord Eadward."

The King left shortly thereafter, and within a matter of heartbeats, Eadward summoned Beohrtic, who entered the tent and said, "Lord Eadward, I beg your pardon! I know you gave strict instructions..."

Even with his grief, Eadward laughed. "Beohrtic, if you had kept the King out of my tent, I would have given you ten pounds of silver just to look at your balls...then I would have had you flogged." The servant laughed, and it did Eadward good to hear that sound, but he had called him in for a reason. "I need you to find Uhtric, Beohrtic. I have a task for him."

"Oh?" Beohrtic asked in surprise, although he was moving towards the flap.

"Yes," Eadward said absently, his mind already moving to other things, "he's going to be taking a trip."

The small skiff could carry six men comfortably; it carried ten men, and while it meant that there was ample help at the pair of oars, it also required constant bailing as Titus and the handpicked men with him fought the current as they rowed south back towards Boulogne, struggling to say outside the surf line as the invisibly powerful undercurrent kept pulling the craft closer to the beach. It was the night after the *Exploratores* had reunited with the army, which was now in a camp just outside the walls of Boulogne, preparing for the assault that would take place the next day. That, at least, was what the Franks wanted the defenders to believe, and the Count was certainly prepared to send his men with ladders to scale the walls, but if they did so, it was because Titus and his small force failed in the real task, using the secret tunnel by the docks to reach the eastern gate and open it for the *Eques*. All of this was to be accomplished under cover of darkness, and signaled by one of the warriors accompanying Titus, a *Pedes* who was one of the thirty men who performed primarily as archers. This man would shoot a flaming arrow into the air, which in turn would unleash the *Eques* who would come thundering down the road, followed by the *Pedes,* all of them men of the Count's bodyguard; only then would the *servii* of the *lantweri* be called upon. What was left undecided by the time Titus and his nine men departed was whether the *lantweri* would use the ladders to scale the wall, and in the process clear the ramparts, or follow their more experienced, and better armed and armored counterparts through the gate. Of the *Exploratores*, only Ranulf and Lambertus were part of this, but the man Titus was concerned with the most, Bent, did not even try to come along, and Theutbald flatly refused, on the basis that he was a Frank not a Northman, while Wala claimed that he got frightfully seasick. Frankly, Titus did not begrudge any of them; if he had been able, he would have been left behind as well, although in his case, it was due to the fact that he was still extremely tired. He had gotten some sleep, but a combination of details that needed to be attended to, the nerves brought on by what would undoubtedly be a dangerous task, and that he and Ranulf had ridden back to where they found the wolf corpses undisturbed, which they skinned and took their pelts, meant that he got little sleep.

The moon was waxing, so it was a bit brighter than the night before, which was a mixed blessing and would force a decision about where to beach the craft, although he unerringly led them to the boat. Hampering his ability to choose a spot was the fact that Titus had been stuffed in that false crate when

Einarr's ship had departed from the dock upriver, and he had been unconscious, something he did not like thinking about, especially at this moment. He had questioned Dagfinn about how he would know when they were nearing Boulogne just before he rowed ashore, but hearing about a spot, especially when the person describing it had seen it in broad daylight, was not the same as seeing it with one's own eyes, and things looked very different in the dark. The docks lay upriver from the mouth, a distance that Dagfinn guessed was about a half-mile from the river's mouth, but that also depended on the tide. It was next to impossible to tell in the dark, yet it seemed to Titus that the tide was, if not at its peak high, was still rising, which would also influence his decision. The town, or more accurately, the low rise it was built on, became visible out of the darkness, and Titus noticed there were no lights of any kind, which was to be expected now that there was an enemy army camped outside the walls. He had not been present for it, choosing to sleep instead, but he had been informed there had been discussion by Count Baldwin, Lord Baudelius, and the handful of men like Ranulf and Theutbald about the possibility that Bjorn Sigurdson, once he saw the number of fires from the Frankish army outside their walls, would surrender. It was discussed at some length, with Baldwin in particular emphasizing that the futility would be apparent to the Northman, making a request for terms an obvious choice. On the other side was Lord Baudelius, and after listening to Ranulf explain their arguments, Titus found himself in agreement with the older nobleman, though not with much happiness about it.

"They do not have enough ships to transport everyone away, and this is the most important port in this part of Frankia for the Northmen. Those pagans have been using it for years, and losing it would be a massive blow to them. And," Ranulf had grinned, "the man who lost Boulogne for Sigfred the Úlfhédnar better hope that he falls in the fight."

This had been the argument put forth by Baudelius, and it was one Titus believed was the correct one, and now they were getting closer to learning who was right.

Realizing it was time for a decision, Titus announced, "We will enter the river, then see how far we can go upstream before we land."

Since they were now directly north of the northeastern corner of the town wall, they could finally see the lighthouse towering above the walls, despite it being at the far end of Boulogne, nearest to the river, the gray series of octagonal stones reflecting the moonlight in such a way that it seemed to glow slightly, though as Titus had hoped, there was no light blazing atop it. It also told him that they had another few moments of rowing, with a man at each oar, two men bailing as the spray kept slopping over the low sides, and everyone else, including Titus, staring intently up at the seaward wall as it slid by ever so slowly. They were much too far away to see if there were men on the wall or atop the lighthouse, but Titus doubted it, for the simple reason that Count Baldwin's army did not have any ships, so Bjorn could at least be confident that there would be no attack from this direction. Which, to a point, was true, he thought with grim amusement. He felt the sudden shudder of the boat when it encountered the outgoing current of the river, which signaled that it was time to turn into the river's mouth, and also that it was time to switch out the pair of men at the oars, who gasped their thanks. They had already almost capsized once, and Titus held his breath, but despite rocking and taking on even more water, they righted the craft and, while it was more slowly, began making headway upriver.

The effort was such, however, that Titus did not wait very long before he hissed, "We'll put in now!"

With the last of their energy, the oarsmen drove the boat up onto the sandy bank, and Ranulf leapt out first, steadying it for the others to climb out, while Titus kept staring up at the wall, now no more than two hundred paces away and about sixty feet above the spot where they were now standing. Titus led the way, with the others following in single file, and it took an effort on his part not to run, knowing that in the darkness, it was rapid movement that was most likely to draw a watchful eye. Alternating his attention between the wall and the spot near the dock where the tunnel was located, Titus noticed that the berth where Einarr's ship had been was still empty, which was a relief even if he expected as much, but there had been another longship, three berths down, and it was gone now, although it probably did not mean anything. After all, he reasoned, where would the ship go for help? Frisia was several days' sailing away, and by the time Sigfred could do anything about it, the town would have fallen, and...it was at this moment that Titus realized something; he had no idea what Count Baldwin had in mind for Boulogne. While the obvious answer would seem to be take the town and garrison it with enough men that they could defend this strategically vital port, he was also aware of how thinly stretched the Franks already were as it was just defending the handful of ports along the coast in this region that were under their control. The men of the *lantweri* were almost identical to the Saxon *ceorls* of the *fyrd*, in that they were only useful for a short duration of time, and would be extremely reluctant to be pressed into service defending a town that was not in their own area, leaving their own farms and businesses untended. Thrusting that out of his mind as irrelevant to what he had to do, he led the others to the clump of trees, then with some difficulty, squeezed himself in between the trunks of the pair of trees directly blocking the tunnel entrance. He had already warned them that they would be forced to crawl on hands and knees, but it was with some embarrassment that he also realized he had not thought matters through. When they had escaped from the inn, while Titus had been wearing his armor, he had not been carrying his shield, and it was when he dropped to his knees that he realized that it was not just a matter of shoving the shield ahead of him. It took some experimentation before he finally turned the shield at an angle, then shoved it into the tunnel, and over his shoulder, he whispered instructions on what to do; to his chagrin, he learned that it was only his shield that required this treatment since it had been made for his body size, yet despite this temporary delay, they were crawling towards the storeroom in a matter of heartbeats.

The darkness this time was total, but while they were robbed of their sight, they were not robbed of their hearing, and since Titus was leading the way, it was natural that he was the first to encounter...something ahead of him. At first, he was thankful that his shield was ahead of him, hearing a squeak of surprise and fear, but more quickly than he could react, whatever it was came scuttling back in his direction, and he felt tiny, clawed feet scrabble across his hand. It took an enormous effort for him not to cry out in his own startlement and the revulsion most men had for scurrying rodents, which he was at least sure this was, but immediately behind him, Ranulf was not as circumspect, uttering an oath that sounded much louder than it was. All down the line behind him, the others had similar reactions as the undoubtedly terrified creature sprinted down the tunnel, heading for the opening, and it almost made it. Later, it was Gerulf who admitted responsibility for the sharp squeak, accompanied by a wet, crunching sound as the warrior instinctively reacted to the tiny creature touching his hand. Aside from that one episode, the party moved as rapidly as the cramped conditions in the tunnel allowed, though it took a bit of maneuvering of Titus' shield to navigate the ninety-degree bend, but finally, he was in the larger opening, directly under the trapdoor. While the space was just large enough for two normal-sized men, it meant that it was left to Titus alone to raise the trapdoor, engendering another moment when Titus realized that he had not been paying attention when Dagfinn had shoved the crate aside. He gave a tentative shove upward against the trapdoor, first with one arm, then with two, yet it did not budge.

Mouthing a curse, he turned about and leaned forward to whisper in Ranulf's ear the problem, but assured him, "They only use this inn for guests like Lord Einarr, and they do not have enough men to put any in here anyway, not with our army outside. I am going to have to shove the crate over."

Ranulf nodded, forgetting the total darkness, but Titus' face was close enough to detect the slight disruption, then he turned back around and positioned himself under the trapdoor while coming to a crouch while placing both hands on the trapdoor. His legs were bent slightly, and he would use them to begin the lift, but the rest would be using the power of his arms, so to compensate for that, after he took a deep breath, he straightened up as violently as he could while shoving his arms straight up. The result was immediate...and noisy as the crate, as heavy as it was, went flying upward and to the side from the swinging trapdoor, which was not light in itself, where it was stopped only by crashing into the wall. Almost simultaneously, there was a sharp, shrill cry, and not by an animal, from a short distance away; to Titus' ears, it sounded as if it came from either the doorway leading into the main room, or just outside the doorway.

"*What was that?*"

Titus was already moving, leaping up to catch the edge of the opening with both hands and levering himself up out of the hole, so it did not immediately register that the words were not in Northman or Danish but Frankish, too intent was he on drawing Wyvern's Fang as part of the same motion that had launched him up out of the hole. It was still dark, but it was not the total darkness of the tunnel, and he dimly made out two figures standing, seemingly frozen, just inside the storeroom, but then one of them moved.

Only then did it occur to Titus that the person, a woman by the sound of her voice, had spoken in his adopted tongue, and also in Frankish, he called out in a low but urgent tone, "Stop! You have nothing to fear from us! We are with Count Baldwin!"

While it stopped the figure from moving, Titus clearly heard the suspicion in what turned out to be a man's voice. "Who is this Count Baldwin? And why should we care?"

By this time, Titus heard what he assumed to be Ranulf clambering out of the hole, confirmed when Ranulf said indignantly, "Count Baldwin is the Margrave of Flandre, you fool! And he's here to free you from the Northmen and that bastard Sigfred!"

"Lord Sigfred treats us well," the man argued, and as Titus' eyes adjusted to the slightly better light, he began to make out details. This man was large, not in Titus' way but in the manner of a man who has eaten well, which was not how the people of places occupied by Northmen tended to look. "We have never benefitted from Count Baldwin, the son or the father!"

"Well, you're about to now," Ranulf assured him.

Titus sensed Ranulf turn his head to whisper, "What do you want to do with them, Titus?"

Whether it was Ranulf's question or just a coincidence, they would never know, but without any warning whatsoever, the bulky man bolted deeper into the main room, clearly heading for the outer door. Titus reacted first, but the woman, who they all assumed was the man's wife, seeing this large, shadowy shape appearing to come for her, let out a blood-curdling shriek of terror and collapsed to the wooden floor, just as Titus was extending a hand to move her out of the way so he could get past her. The result was that he instead tripped over her body, a knee slamming into her head and knocking her senseless, while, without the aid of sufficient light, Titus found himself grabbing wildly for something that could arrest his fall. There was nothing there, so he collapsed on top of the woman, who would have shrieked even more loudly, thinking that this beast was about to rape her, but fortunately, she had the wind driven from her lungs by his crushing weight.

"Do not let him get away!" Titus shouted, but Ranulf was already moving, followed by the four other warriors who had emerged from the hole by this point.

Between the darkness and unfamiliarity with their surroundings, Titus could follow their progress towards the front of the inn by the crashing of chairs and tables, punctuated by the curses and shouts of pain from the pursuing warriors, but he saw Ranulf briefly outlined in the open door just before he darted outside.

"*Help! Sound the alarm! Franks are inside the walls!*"

"You're a Frank, you stupid bastard," Titus muttered in his native tongue as he began to get to his feet.

Without any warning, the woman underneath him, now understanding that this huge warrior was not trying to rape her, went on the offensive, reaching out blindly, not with the intent to inflict damage on her accidental assailant, but to stop him from joining the pursuit of what was, in fact, her husband. Unfortunately for Titus, and even more so for her, when her hand came in contact with something foreign and she grabbed it, it was the part of a man they hold the most dear, and is the most sensitive to them in every sense of the word. Bellowing with the shock and pain, Titus' reaction was completely instinctive, to stop this bitch from crushing his balls, and since Wyvern's Fang was in his hand, it was a simple matter of making a hard downward thrust, feeling the woman's death spasm vibrate up through the blade, accompanied by a gurgling, choking sound. It would not be until later that he would understand the circumstances, and that he had killed a woman, but in the moment, his overwhelming emotion was relief that she relinquished her grip on his testicles. Even so, he was unable to immediately follow his comrades, gasping the order to the remainder of the men who had just clambered out of the hole, with Gerulf last, to follow the rest of the men outside. Gerulf paused, eyeing Titus, who was bent over at the waist trying to catch his breath.

"Are you all right, Berserker?"

Not trusting himself to speak, Titus nodded, while outside, there was more shouting, but while it was impossible to make out the words, it was clear that some voices were not just outside in the street but deeper in the town. This more than anything got him moving, although he was still slightly hobbled, and Gerulf followed him out into the street. The sight that greeted him was the rest of his force standing around a prone figure that, in the moonlight, Titus recognized as the portly Frank, the pool of blood that was still growing slowly shining black in the moonlight.

"He would not be quiet," Ranulf said apologetically, but Titus waved it off, more concerned with the growing noise up the street that he had intended to use to get to the eastern gate.

Staring into the darkness, he thought he saw a glimmer of something, which quickly resolved itself into the flickering light of several torches reflecting off the sides of the buildings, followed a couple heartbeats later by a large group of armed Northmen turning the corner to block the street that Titus intended on using.

"Do we fight?" Ranulf asked quietly.

"No," Titus answered immediately, trying desperately to recall the route he had taken, partly on his own, but then with Dagfinn and Einarr that was essentially the reverse of what he would be taking now, and in full daylight. With more confidence than he actually felt, he said loudly enough for them all to hear, "I know how to get to the eastern gate another way. Follow me!"

He was moving as he said it, heading down the street and out of sight of the Northmen who had clearly been anticipating that the interlopers would try to fight their way through them, judging by the shouts of surprise, interspersed with jeers at the Frankish cowards fleeing in the night. His men hot on his heels, Titus ran down to the corner where he and his two Danish friends had emerged, and he was caught by surprise at the random thought that that event had been barely two days earlier. This much was easy to remember; it was the twists and turns down the narrow alleys and streets that did not penetrate all the way through the town that he worried about. Most worrying was the fact that, thanks to that fat Frankish traitor betraying their presence, they were still hours from the break of dawn and the beginning of the attack...and he only had ten men.

"Lord? You sent for me?"

Uhtric was standing just inside the flap, but while Eadward was still kneeling at his father's side, he had stopped praying some time before, and now he was just thinking about what he would tell his mother concerning the one thing he was certain about, that his father had deliberately stepped into the thrust of that Northman bastard Hallsteinn. However, suicide was a mortal sin, consigning his father to the fires of Hell and eternal damnation, so it would be a conviction that Eadward would carry to his own grave, never mentioning it to his mother or anyone else, not even his confessor.

Turning his head to see Uhtric standing there, awkwardly shifting from one foot to another, Eadward was struck by a memory, of how this had been a habit of his own that his father had despised, literally beating it out of his son and heir. This brought a smile to Eadward's face, as odd as it may have seemed, and he rose to his feet to greet Uhtric.

"Lord," Uhtric said awkwardly, "I just wanted to express my sorrow at...at...well," he indicated Eadwig's corpse, "for what happened to your lord father. Lord Eadwig was a good man, and he was a fair one to us."

"Thank you, Uhtric," Eadward replied, fighting the lump in his throat, even as he wondered how long it would be like this, with men behaving as Uhtric did, unsure what to say or how to behave. "He thought very highly of you, Uhtric," Eadward said, but he felt he had to be honest when he added, "but much of that was because Otha thinks so well of you, and he trusted Otha's judgement."

"T-thank you, Lord," Uhtric stammered, uncertain what he was supposed to say to that.

"Yes," Eadward cleared his throat, another habit that his father harped on, "well, the reason I called for you is that I have a...task, one where you're the only man I trust to do it."

"You want me to find Titus," Uhtric said evenly, without a hint of hesitation or doubt.

Eadward's mouth dropped, and he gasped, "How did you know that?" Suddenly, he felt a stab of anger. "Beohrtic told you!"

"No, Lord," Uhtric assured him. "He didn't say a word, I swear it on the cross." He shrugged and said, "It just makes sense. We all know that it was your father who didn't want him back here. So," he concluded, "now that you're the Lord of Wiltun, we all assumed this would be one of your first decisions."

Despite himself, Eadward felt a grin split his face as he said, "You mean you were all wagering."

Uhtric laughed, partially out of politeness but not completely.

"We wouldn't be Saxons if we didn't bet on anything and everything, Lord." They lapsed into silence, then Uhtric asked, "When do you want me to leave, Lord? As soon as we return to Wiltun?" Before Eadward could reply, he asked, "And does anyone have any idea where he is?"

Eadward hesitated, not looking forward to this part of it, but he actually answered the second question first.

"Actually, there is a bit of good news there," Eadward explained. "For some reason, King Alfred says he knows where Titus is...and that he's making a ship available to take you to him with my offer to come home." Without thinking, and momentarily forgetting how clever Uhtric was in his own right, Eadward said, "And he's not just offering any ship! You'll be on *The Redeemer*, and she'll have an escort of four ships, including *Sea Viper*."

Uhtric frowned, not saying anything for a moment, and when he did, he spoke slowly, as the thoughts in his mind fell into place.

"*The Redeemer* is here at Hrofescester already," he said, staring down at the dirt floor. Then, he looked up at Eadward. "I'm not returning to Wiltun with the rest of you, am I, Lord?"

Not seeing any point in delay, Eadward shook his head, admitting, "No, Uhtric. But," he added, "it's not just because of me. The King is the one who...suggested that you leave immediately."

"Well, that will save me from being flayed by Leofflaed at least," Uhtric replied dryly. Then, with a grin, he added, "But, Lord, I do have one request."

"What is it?" Eadward asked, thinking he had an idea.

His suspicion was confirmed when Uhtric answered, "That you be the one to tell my wife. As long as she knows it's for her brother, she won't hurt you...probably."

Eadward laughed, but there was a nervous quality to it. What neither of them knew at this moment was that, as far as their King was concerned, Uhtric's task, while important to the new Lord of Wiltun and to his King, was not the only reason Alfred was reaching across The Narrow Sea.

In what would turn out to be a blessing, Titus got lost, taking a wrong turn down an alley that he thought he had used in the opposite direction, but rather than emptying onto the street that led directly to the eastern gate, it dead-ended into the back of a building. Similarly to his entrance into the town, he could hear the uproar as more Northmen were alerted to the presence of intruders, and he sent Gerulf, along with Sigemund and Gozlin, to stand at the nearest intersection back the way they had come, looking for sign that the Northmen were closing in. The rest of the party huddled together, waiting as Titus and Ranulf talked in whispers about what to do. Titus' eyes kept going to the back of the building as they discussed matters, then he reached out with a hand and pushed against the rough-hewn plank that formed the back wall.

Making his decision, he whispered, "Pry enough of these planks off the back of this building so we can get inside. We're going to get under cover while we decide."

Four warriors had brought axes with them, and used them

to pry several of the planks out from the back until there was enough room for them, even Titus, to squeeze through, but Ranulf insisted on entering first.

"In case there's any traitorous Franks in the place," he had whispered grimly. "We can't afford to be betrayed again."

To their relief, this building turned out to be a smithy on the first floor, with the smith and his family found upstairs, cowering in their single room. The smith stoutly insisted that, unlike their betrayer, he was happy to see fellow Franks, and after a whispered discussion, with Gerulf and a couple other warriors arguing that they should at least be tied up, Titus decided to have Sigemund stand guard over them for the moment while the rest discussed the next step.

"If I remember correctly," Titus whispered, frustrated because the darkness precluded him from sketching out what he thought was the layout of the buildings between where they were and the eastern gate, "we are three blocks north and about four blocks west of the eastern gate." He glanced around, asking, "Has anyone been here?"

He was not surprised when they all murmured they had not, but it was still disappointing, then Gerulf whispered, "What about that smith? He says he is happy we are here; let him prove it!"

Titus' immediate reaction was a feeling of chagrin for not thinking of the obvious, but he did not hesitate, sending Gerulf up the stairs, the warrior returning with the smith, and no light was needed to sense the man's fear.

Understanding that this was a situation for which he was not suited, Titus whispered to Ranulf, "You talk to him. I'm no good trying to talk to someone already frightened out of their wits."

As was his habit, Ranulf made a joke. "You frighten everyone, Berserker, not just people who are already scared!" Turning to the smith, the warrior asked bluntly, "We need to get to the eastern gate the fastest way, but also the best way to avoid those pagan savages out there." He jerked a thumb in the general direction of the street.

To Titus' ears, if anything, it sounded as if even more men were now involved in the search for them, and judging from the direction of the sounds, it seemed that their enemy had essentially surrounded their location, although they sounded as if they were still several blocks away.

"If...if you want to go the fastest way," the smith stammered, "then you will be likely to run into Northmen." He went silent, thinking for a moment before he said, "But there is another way. Some of us use it from time to time when we do not want these pagans to know what we are doing." The smith hesitated, then seemed to come to a decision, asking, "You are Count Baldwin's men?"

"We are," Ranulf assured him. Indicating himself first, then Titus, he said, "We are members of the Count's household guard, serving as *Eques*."

This clearly surprised the smith, who murmured to Ranulf, "I did not know the Count had Northmen in his service."

Despite the circumstances, this created a ripple of chuckling, and while Titus was too distracted to laugh, he did smile as he reassured the smith, "I am not a Northman. I am a Saxon."

"You?" the smith gasped, eyes widening enough to be visible in the gloom. "You are the one they call Berserker?"

"Yes," Titus answered tersely, wanting to get back to the more germane topic, but the smith was not finished.

"You are the one Lord Sigfred has offered the bounty on!" the smith exclaimed. "God must be watching over you, Berserker, for Sigfred the Úlfhédnar not to be here!"

"Or he's the one whose gods are watching out for him," Titus snapped, feeling his temper rising. He took a deep breath to compose himself, then said pointedly, "You mentioned another way to get to the eastern gate that the Northmen do not know about."

"Yes," the smith nodded, then cautioned, "but it is not...pleasant. It is underground."

"Underground?" Ranulf asked, puzzled. "You mean like that tunnel by the dock that we used?"

"Ah." The smith nodded. "I was wondering how you got inside the walls. We have managed to keep that tunnel a secret as well. But no, this is from before, when the Romans lived here. That," he added hurriedly, "is what Father Altmarus says."

"Where is it?" Ranulf asked. "How do we get to it from here?"

"You have to go back..." the smith began, but stopped. After a heartbeat, he sighed and said, "It is better that I lead you. It is difficult to find even in daylight. But," he addressed Ranulf, "if I do this, do I have your word that you will tell Count Baldwin?"

It was a reasonable request, and Ranulf, after a glance at Titus, he assured the smith, "We will make sure he knows."

"Let me go tell my wife," the smith mumbled, then headed for the stairs.

While he was gone, it was Gerulf who asked, "How do we know we can trust him? What makes him different than that fat turd who betrayed us? He has been living here just like that piece of shit."

It was a fair point, but Titus did not hesitate, nor did he try to soften it, saying flatly, "We do not have a choice, Gerulf." Pointing outside to the ragged chorus of Northmen, each group calling to another, he asked, "Do you think we can get past them any other way?"

"No," Gerulf admitted.

If he was going to say something else, he had no chance because the smith returned downstairs, this time with Sigemund.

"We need to go out the way you came in," the smith said, for the first time sounding confident, and it prompted Titus to ask his name. "I am called Gilo of Boulogne."

Then, he led them out into the night, heading for the entrance into the sewer of the Roman town of Gesoriacum, yet another time where, without knowing it, Titus of Cissanbyrig was walking in the footsteps of one of his ancestors, unaware that Gesoriacum, under the name of Portus Itius, had been the spot when the first of his line had come to the place that Titus still thought of as home, led by the Roman general named Julius Caesar.

His name was Eudes; he was sixteen, and this was the first time he was old enough to be called for a *lantweri*, and he initially had been quite excited to be part of it. That had been before the harsh training, which to Eudes seemed to consist of beatings for doing something wrong, despite the fact that the warriors of Count Baldwin's bodyguard rarely gave instructions on how to perform the various movements the right way. Instead, they bashed you when you did what you *thought* you were supposed to do, while calling you an oaf and a turd and all manner of things that Eudes had never heard before in his life. They were not all like that; some of the men they called *Pedes*, who wielded spears and shields like the men of the *lantweri,* did a better job of explaining what was expected of them. For the most part, the *Eques* had had little to do with the men of the *lantweri*, with one exception, the warrior named Bent, who, it seemed, had only one hobby, tormenting the youngest members of the *lantweri*, forcing them to perform menial tasks but expecting an impossible standard, then humiliating them for their inevitable failure, and Eudes was sure that he had never hated a man in all of his sixteen years as much as he hated Bent. But, he thought miserably, God surely hated him for hating Bent; why else would he be standing not more than two paces away from the arrogant *Eques* and his friend Sigismund, who, Eudes admitted, did not seem that bad a sort?

Eudes was standing guard next to a pile of ladders that would be used for the assault, in the event that whatever it was Bent and Sigismund seemed to be waiting for did not happen. Naturally, the teenage spearman was not privy to what it was, and Bent had been careful to keep his voice to a whisper as he stared at the eastern wall of the town, now about two hours before dawn, but he had heard the *Eques* whisper a name more than once; more accurately, an appellation, and even with his voice low, Eudes heard the contempt when Bent uttered "Berserker." Ironically, Eudes' own feelings about the Saxon warrior were more complex, a mixture of fear, awe, respect...and underlying the others, a deep-seated desire to be a warrior like the Berserker, feared and respected by all, even Bent, because somehow, Eudes instinctively understood that the Frankish warrior's hatred for the Berserker was based in Bent's fear of the Saxon. Eudes, like all of his fellow *servii*, was uneducated, but as anyone who had anything to do with another youth from a farm, even if it was in Wessex, being unlettered did not always mean unintelligent, so despite not being told anything, Eudes had deduced that whatever it was that the *Eques* was waiting for in Boulogne, the Berserker had something to do with it. What, he wondered, is that weasel turd Bent waiting for? He could not deny that the idea that, if whatever it was the Berserker and whoever was with him was successful, if it meant that Eudes would not be scaling a ladder in the morning and thereby putting off his first battle, as eager as he thought he had been at the prospect, he would not complain about the delay. His ridged helmet that he thought he had become accustomed to wearing seemed to have gotten heavier just in the time he had been standing next to the ladders, while behind him, and about twenty paces away his comrades, also from the village of Renescure, were sleeping, or at least lying there pretending to sleep. In some ways, he was grateful for being given this duty, knowing that there would be no way he could get to sleep, and even under normal circumstances, he had a habit of tossing and turning that had earned him punches from his two younger brothers in the bed they shared at their parents' farm. He untied his helmet and took it off, wishing that men of the *lantweri* had the scale armor that most of the men of the Count's bodyguard had, with one notable exception, and he wondered why the Berserker chose to wear the same kind of chainmail that some Northmen wore, although he had been told by a more experienced veteran of the *lantweri* that it was also what the Saxons across The Narrow Sea wore. He was just putting the helmet back on after mopping his brow, despite the cool night, when from the direction of the town, what Eudes thought was some sort of shooting star went streaking into the sky, then quickly realizing that this one was going in the opposite direction than those he saw at night, and it was yellowish in color, whereas those he had seen before were white and always plunging to earth.

Despite his hatred and fear, he felt he was wise to ask, "What was that?"

The thing was still in the air, but it had suddenly stopped its upward arc and began descending down, so Eudes knew that the two *Eques* could see it.

Bent's response made no sense, asking with a nonchalance

that Eudes did not believe, "What was what?"

"*That*!" Eudes gasped, pointing at it just before it vanished behind a copse of trees off to their right that was in between the Frankish army camp and the town. "Surely you saw it!"

"I didn't see anything," Bent scoffed, then turned to Sigismund and asked mockingly, "What about you, Sigismund? Any idea what the boy here is talking about?"

To Eudes' shock and guarded optimism, Sigismund did not immediately play along with his friend, saying cautiously instead, "Bent, that might have been the signal Berserker was supposed to send up."

"Now?" Bent replied caustically. "This far before dawn?" He laughed, but there was a hollow quality to it. "I expect the boy here to be seeing things, but not you, Sigismund!"

What Sigismund said to his friend Eudes could not hear, but whatever it was, it did not sway Bent, who insisted stubbornly, "I didn't see anything because there was nothing to see! You two are old women! And," now he turned on Eudes, pointing at the young sentry, "if you know what's good for you, you'll keep your mouth shut, *boy*! If you rouse the army now, I'm going to be sure and tell Lord Baudelius who was responsible for disturbing his sleep, and he takes his sleep seriously, especially before battle!"

Perhaps if Eudes had not borne the brunt of the cruelty and scorn of this warrior before, he might have not done what he did, and sealed his fate in the process, though he would not know that for some time to come.

Deliberately, Eudes turned his back to Bent, filled his lungs, and shouted, "The Berserker has given the signal! The Berserker has given the signal!"

Now, he thought, at least I'll find out what that signal means.

Even given how things turned out, the men of Titus' party agreed that it had been a good plan, and that it had only been ruined by a quirk of fate because one lone Northman, part of one of the search parties, who had to take a piss. Because they were still a few hours before dawn and the appointed time they would attack the gate, they briefly discussed staying at the smithy, but this was quickly discarded when, from a street over, there was the kind of crashing noise that they knew came from a man or men kicking in a door.

"They are searching houses now," Gilo said nervously. "We need to leave."

"Is there enough room where you are taking us for us to hide?" Titus asked, and the smith nodded.

"It will not be pleasant," Gilo warned them. "And there is always water...and rats down there."

Assuring the smith they would not be put off, they left through the makeshift entrance, while it was Ranulf who thought to arrange the planks back in place. It would not stand up to close scrutiny, but between the darkness and all that was happening, they felt confident that they had at least taken appropriate precautions that would not lead enraged Northmen to the smith's family. Titus had very briefly considered leaving a man behind but decided against it, so the ten of them followed Gilo out into the night, with Titus just behind the smith. To his surprise, Gilo moved more swiftly than Titus expected, though not incautiously, stopping at the first intersection to peer in both directions, then moving at a quick walk across the open space. Thinking rapidly, Titus grabbed Ranulf, Sigemund and Gerulf to line them by his side, whispering to the others to copy him.

"If we go one at a time, it's more chance we'll be seen," he whispered, and the others, seeing the sense in this, quickly complied.

They did this three times to cross streets or alleys that intersected the path Gilo was taking them on, until he suddenly came to a stop and dropped into a crouch. Thinking the smith had seen or heard something, they followed suit, but then Gilo beckoned to Titus, who duckwalked over to the smith, whereupon Gilo pointed down at the street, even as he was using his eating knife to clear dirt away. This was the moment Titus realized that what he thought was a dirt street was not, the proof being what turned out to be a square stone cover once they uncovered it, with Titus helping Gilo by using his ax.

"We make sure to have someone pack the dirt down after one of us goes in," the smith whispered, but Titus was noticing that, around the edges of the cover, there were bricks, and he suddenly had a memory of Lunden and the sections of paved streets that, for whatever reason, were still visible and not covered in a layer of dirt and filth.

He was struck by the first of what would be several random thoughts, which was to wonder why the inhabitants of Boulogne seemed content to allow a layer of about two inches of muck to form over a paved street, although this was quickly driven from his mind by the second thing he noticed, the stench; it was not as overpowering as an open sewage ditch, but it was close.

Still, he hesitated only long enough to ask, "How far of a drop?"

Gilo shook his head, saying, "If you lower yourself down, you will only drop about," he held his hands about six inches apart, "that far. And," he warned, "you will have to bend over." Titus saw a flash of teeth in the moonlight. "We will just have to bow our heads a bit." Titus moved to drop into the hole, but the smith stopped him. "I will need to go first so that I can feel the right way."

"Feel?" Titus frowned, confused.

"We have cut grooves in the walls that tell us which way we need to turn to get to where we want to go," Gilo explained, and Titus had a flash of insight; the smith was a smuggler, along with being a smith.

Not, he understood, that it mattered, and he nodded at Gilo to continue, and the smith vanished into the sewer, Titus, hearing the splash, followed by a whispered oath and a bout of gagging that, despite the circumstances, made him grin. He followed after handing his shield down to the smith, managing to barely avoid the gagging part, and found himself in a space that was slightly larger than the one under the inn, but unlike the tunnel there, the walls, and the surface he was standing on was made of stone, and circular in nature. He could touch both walls with his arms only half-extended, while Gilo had been right; he had to drop into something that was not quite a crouch, yet even then he felt his helmet scraping the top of the circular tunnel. The darkness was near absolute, even with his eyes adjusted to the gloom, but he heard the scraping sound accompanying sparks as Gilo struck his flint, illuminating his face in an eerie fashion until, on the third try, a spark caught the oil-soaked wick of the small lamp that he had brought with him. The light it gave off was barely that of a candle, yet Titus found himself glancing up nervously, but saw only Ranulf and Gerulf peering down, waiting their turn.

"All right, I am ready," the smith announced, and in proof, he immediately took what Titus had seen was the right hand tunnel of a four way junction.

He thought he had a basic idea of where they were now in relation to the gate, but Gilo seemed to be heading in the wrong direction, since Titus would have chosen moving straight ahead in the same direction they had been traveling up on the street. Resigning himself to having to trust the smith, he reached out and grasped the man's shoulder, and he immediately regretted it, feeling the smith trembling violently. No, he told himself sternly, he's not leading us into a trap. Don't be a fool, Titus; he's just scared like any sensible man should be. Just behind him, he heard Ranulf splash down into the sewer, making a gagging noise of his own, but now Titus was too intent on watching the smith to make a comment. One by one, as the smith walked slowly down the tunnel, Titus heard his comrades arriving, and while he could not tell who it was, one of them actually retched, prompting a response of sorts from a denizen of the sewer, who sounded an indignant squeak from somewhere behind him. Rats, Titus reminded himself, even as he remembered to count the number of splashes he heard behind him as the rest joined them from the street; the smith said there would be rats, which made sense. Wherever there were humans, with all of their waste, both in the form of the turds that Titus imagined were floating around his feet, and in the scraps of food and other refuse, there were rats. Still, he thought in an attempt to look at things in a more positive light, if everyone in Boulogne was using this sewer system, they would be literally wading in shit, not to mention the presence of the open sewage canal that emptied into the river at the downstream end of the docks and despite himself, his mind, seemingly on its own, once again began exploring exactly why this was the case. After all, here was what appeared to be a perfectly operating system whereby all of the piss and shit expelled by a few thousand human beings could be transported out to sea, out of sight, and most importantly, smell of the occupants...so why weren't they using it?

Any more exploration of this topic was cut off by a series of events, beginning with a faint shout from behind, and most importantly, above Titus and his men, just as he heard the tenth and final splash as Gozlin, who he had designated as rearguard, dropped into the sewer, followed immediately by the Frank shouting, "*Northmen*! One of them spotted me just as I was coming down!"

Above, the lone shout of alarm had been quickly joined by a chorus of voices, and Titus inadvertently gave Gilo a shove, hissing, "You need to go faster! They found us!"

The smith *did* begin moving more quickly, but from behind them, the vibrating thud of pounding footsteps joined the shouting as their enemies above sounded the alarm, undoubtedly calling not only for reinforcements, but to send other Northmen into position to cut them off. Reaching another intersection, they were delayed when Gilo began running his hand along the righthand wall, searching for whatever symbols these people used. Suddenly, it became discernibly brighter in the tunnel, and Titus whirled his head around to see with horror the light from a single torch, held by one Northman, with another warrior just behind him, their shouts echoing down the tunnel, though he could not make out what was being said.

"Hurry!" he shouted now that there was no need for silence. "What is taking you so long? Do you not know which way to go?"

"The marks are hard to find," Gilo protested. "Over time, they are covered with...there! I found it!" Without saying anything more, he took a left, while the others followed, except for Titus, who stopped, pressing himself against the wall to let Ranulf and the others pass.

When he saw who he was looking for, he reached out and grabbed the man's arm.

"Josse, how many arrows did you bring?"

Josse, the only member of this party not of the *Eques* but of the *Pedes*, was ostensibly there for one purpose and one purpose only, to launch the signal that the eastern gate had been seized.

He was older, in his mid-thirties, and it was more his reputation for dependability than anything else that had led Ranulf to suggest him to Titus, and now he did not hesitate, answering, "I brought fifteen."

"Good." Titus turned him around by the shoulder and pointed down the tunnel where the Northman leading with the torch was visible less than fifty paces away. "Kill that bastard. It won't stop them, but it will slow them down."

Gozlin was just reaching them, squeezing past as he muttered an apology, leaving only Josse and Titus standing in the intersection of the two tunnels. The archer had been carrying his bow, but unstrung, which meant that it took him a crucial few heartbeats to do so, although this actually aided his cause by shortening the range as the Northmen approached at something slightly faster than a cautious walk. Titus watched the circle of light thrown by the single torch advancing closer, and he had to fight the urge to snap at Josse to hurry, but once the bow was strung, Josse moved with a fluid, smooth motion that minimized the amount of time it took him to draw an arrow from his quiver with his right hand then bring it in front of him to nock it. It was as he was bringing the bow vertical that he realized that the tunnel was not high enough, but without any hesitation that Titus could see, he dropped into the kind of crouch that Titus was using, and even as his fingers nocked the missile on the string, he thrust his left arm out while drawing the string back to his cheek. Even if he had thought to do so, Titus doubted he would have made it to a count of two from the time Josse began his motion to the instant he released the string. In the close confines of the tunnel, even with the noise made by the advancing Northmen as they sloshed through water that was mid-calf, the sound made by the string snapping forward as it hurled the arrow faster than the eye could track under the best of conditions at this range was significantly louder. What transpired next happened within an eyeblink; a sharp, gurgling cry, followed by a plunging into almost total darkness as the stricken Northman dropped the torch into the foul water, the flame hissing as it was extinguished, but it was the roar of collective rage and anguish at the death of a comrade that echoed off of the stone walls of the sewer that made Titus' ears ring slightly.

Grabbing Josse by the arm, Titus had to almost shout to be heard. "Perfect, Josse! We need to hurry to join the others now!"

It was too dark to see Josse grin, but he allowed himself to be tugged around the corner and follow the large Saxon to where, barely visible because of the bodies in between them and Gilo, they saw the dim light of his lamp, which seemed a bit ridiculous now to Titus after the lurid light of that torch. The party had reached another intersection, where Gilo was once more struggling to interpret the notches.

"The symbol for the tunnel that goes to the eastern gate is the same one for His name," he muttered when Titus reached his side. "Father Altmarus showed it to me and told me what it means." He was wiping away the slime coating the tunnel walls, while Titus tried to hide his impatience and refused to think exactly what that slime was.

Behind them, they could hear what now sounded like an argument, but more importantly, there was a new light source that was growing in intensity, and he called, "Josse! Be ready! If one of those *bâstarts* poke their heads around the corner, you know what to do! But," he thought to warn, "only if you have a clear shot. You do not have that many arrows we can waste one."

Josse nodded his understanding, and he moved next to Gozlin, waiting for what came next.

"I found it!" Gilo exclaimed, pointing down to the barely legible marks that, to Titus, looked like nothing more than three vertical lines, where the middle vertical line was longer, and a single horizontal line that connected the vertical lines about midway.

"That is supposed to be the name of Jesus?" Titus asked doubtfully.

"That is what Father Altmarus told me," Gilo replied, though he was taking the right tunnel as he explained. "He said it is in Greek...whatever that is."

Josse gave a shout then, and Titus turned just in time to see the archer bring up his bow, draw his right arm back and loose the nocked arrow in one motion, but this time, they all heard the sharp cracking sound of the iron head striking the stone of the tunnel wall accompanied by a small shower of sparks, the Northman who had poked his head around the corner jerking it back just in time. While it did not draw blood, it did slow the Northmen again, enabling Gilo to guide the party down the stretch of straight tunnel that was perhaps fifty paces in length before, for what Titus had counted would be the fifth time, they reached another intersection.

This time, however, Gilo called over his shoulder, "The gate is to the left, at the end of the tunnel that is just about twenty paces away. There is a cover like the one we lifted to come down, and then the gate is..." he pointed directly up just as they reached this last intersection, "...just above us."

The original plan had been for Gilo to stay down in the sewer, make his way back to his home, and in exchange for his help, Titus and Ranulf both swearing that they would personally ensure that the smith and his family were protected once the town was taken.

This seemed to be out of the question now, but when Titus suggested that he should emerge with them, Gilo shook his head. "No, I know how I can avoid these savages down here...but I need to go now."

There was no need for argument; Titus owed the smith a debt, but he also had more pressing matters on his mind, so he nodded, then thrust out his hand.

"Go with God, Gilo of Boulogne," he said with feeling, "and I hope to see you again soon."

"As do I...Berserker," Gilo replied with a smile, handing him the lamp as he did.

"My name is Titus," the Saxon said quietly, then with a shove that was almost friendly, said, "Now go."

The smith did, and this time, he did run as he crossed the intersecting tunnel, which was a good thing because a spear hurtled out of the darkness, but like Josse's arrow, struck nothing but wall.

"All right, we have to hurry!" Titus was already moving, and just as Gilo said, at the end of the tunnel, there was the cover, but while he could reach it, it was just a bit too high even for him to shove out of the way. Snatching Gerulf's spear, he used the butt end to thrust upward and send the stone cover flying up and away from the opening into the darkness, where they heard it land on the dirt of the street, showering Titus with filth in the process.

"We have to move fast now," he said almost to himself even as he was coiling his legs to leap up as high as he could.

Josse, distracted by what the Saxon was doing, did not see the pair of Northmen who, running out of patience, stepped into the intersection, nor did he see one of them draw his arm back and take aim, but Gozlin did, shouting a warning as he used his shield to shove the archer aside, sending him hard against the curved wall of the tunnel. He had the time to do that, but not enough to bring his shield back to protect his own body, and the spear punched through the scale armor, low on his side.

He did not cry out, making more of a low, breathy moan, so it was Josse who shouted, "No! Gozlin! Gozlin has been hurt!"

Titus, however, was already leaping upward at this same instant, preparing to grab the edge of the opening when he heard the shout, meaning that it was too late to do anything about it, so he levered himself up and out onto the street, not even aware that he had drawn Wyvern's Fang.

"Ranulf! What's happening?" he shouted down, but got no immediate answer.

At this moment, while he could see the gateway and that it was exactly where Gilo had indicated, there were no men visible in the street, and Titus guessed they were either up on the rampart or standing in the recessed part of the gateway itself just out of sight, crediting the general uproar and turmoil that kept any Northman up above them from glancing down anywhere close to them, choosing instead to either look out where, presumably the Count's army was beginning to stir, or deeper into Boulogne in an attempt to try and locate Titus and his men. This, he knew, could not last, and he was torn between dropping back down into the sewer, but then Ranulf's face appeared, peering up at him with a grim expression.

"Gozlin took a spear to the side," he said curtly. "It is not good, and he says he is not strong enough to get up out of this fucking place, but that he can still fight. He is going to hold these turd lickers off as long as he can."

Titus had known they would lose men, but to lose Gozlin, and this soon even before they began the fight for the gate, was a bitter blow. Still, he understood, and he gave a nod, then reached down for his shield, which Ranulf tossed up, then pulled his friend up to join him.

"Get Josse up here next," Titus ordered. "He is the most important man right now, and we cannot afford to lose him."

Ranulf nodded, calling down to the others, and the archer was brought to the opening, where he joined them next. While Titus watched the gateway, the others helped their comrades down in the sewer to come up to the street level, but there were still three men left when, finally, the Northmen down below in the sewer belatedly made their final assault in their attempt to stop their foes from reaching the street. Titus glanced over his shoulder just in time to see what should have been the last man aside from Gozlin, who he could hear screaming curses above the clashing sound of iron on wood down in the sewer, an *Eques* named Acfrid, suddenly yank his arm from the grasp of Berwald, who was helping him up, disappearing back down in the sewer.

"I'm not leaving Gozlin!" Acfrid shouted just as he vanished from Titus' sight.

Less than a heartbeat later, he bellowed something unintelligible, and Titus immediately understood why, cursing himself for not thinking about how close the two *Eques* were, as close as Titus was with Ranulf, which in turn caused him to glance at his friend, who gave him a helpless shrug.

"I would not leave you," Ranulf said quietly.

Titus did not say anything, mainly because he knew that it was true, and that he would do the same; besides, he also understood that there was nothing that could be done now, and eight men would have to be enough. Besides, it was also at that moment that the Northmen on the rampart, who had in fact had their attention divided between watching the Frankish army outside the walls and deeper in the town, searching for them, finally took notice of a band of armed men striding towards the eastern gate.

If anyone had bothered to ask Bjorn Sigurdson, he would have happily told them that he had no desire to be in charge of the defenders of Boulogne. No, he had been perfectly content when Sigfred the Úlfhédnar had named that son-of-a-whore Hallsteinn as the commander in his absence, despite the fact that Bjorn privately believed that Sigfred was making a horrible mistake in his choice of a man who had made no secret that he believed he was the Úlfhédnar's equal in all matters. That, however, was not something that one told Sigfred, not if you did not want to see your guts falling out on the floor...and that was if you were fortunate. Consequently, no more than two weeks after Sigfred departed with the bulk of the hundred fifty longships and forty-odd captured Frankish ships that were good for hauling cargo and animals but little else, Hallsteinn took more than half of the remaining garrison in twelve longships, leaving only three behind, swearing that he would only be *viking* for a short period of time.

"There is a town in Cent called Hrofescester," he had informed Bjorn the day he had announced his intentions to the men of the garrison, many of whom, Bjorn knew, had been angry at being left behind by Sigfred. This was particularly true once the rumors began to spread of what the *Jarl*'s real plan was, and that it had nothing to do with Frisia, aside from being a place far from the prying eyes of even the Frankish king. "It is fat and soft, and just waiting to be plucked like a virgin on her wedding night," he had told Bjorn, with that infuriatingly smug smile he liked to give others.

Bjorn had heard of Hrofescester, but nothing he had heard in the description of it had indicated that it was soft.

"I heard that it has stout walls, and is in a loop on that river they call the Medway," he said cautiously. "That makes it easy to defend, no?"

"Bah!" Hallsteinn had waved a dismissive hand. "They will shit themselves when we show up! And," he added expansively, "I may just accept a payment to leave them alone if it appears to be too much trouble."

"That would be good," Bjorn agreed noncommittally.

Hallsteinn must have sensed his ambivalence, and rather

crossly, he argued, "Yes, it *would* be good! Besides, Hrofescester is Centish, and you have heard the rumors that their *Jarl* and the Saxon King Alfred do not trust each other because Alfred believes this *Jarl*..."

"Sigeræd," Bjorn supplied, earning a nod but that was all.

"Yes, that's it. Anyway," Hallsteinn "Alfred believes this Sigeræd has eyes on taking his throne, yes?" Bjorn had heard this as well, and he gave a nod. "So," Hallsteinn spread his hands out, palms upward as he asked in a manner that Bjorn correctly guessed meant he expected either agreement or no answer, "why would this Alfred lift a finger to help Sigeræd under those circumstances?"

It was, Bjorn had acknowledged to himself, a valid point, although he would not have argued it either way. Hallsteinn, he could see, had made up his mind, and he also was a cunning bastard who had correctly divined the simmering discontent on the part of a substantial portion of the garrison. Bjorn was under no illusions that, if he had tried to stop Hallsteinn from absconding, he would have gotten his throat cut and been dumped in the river, a not infrequent occurrence under the best of times. Thanks to the visit from the Danish *Jarl* Einarr, Bjorn had learned that Hallsteinn had grossly underestimated several things; first, the Centishmen of Hrofescester had not quaked in fear at the very appearance of his longships, but it was the second development that meant the most, and that was the relatively rapid response by the Saxon King Alfred, who, in fact, did not want to see Sigeræd and his people suffer, no matter how he viewed Sigeræd. Of even more interest, at least in that moment, was what Bjorn considered to be the rather elliptical message that the *Jarl* had come to deliver, one that, if he was reading what *Jarl* Einarr had not said correctly, would have widespread ramifications for both sides of The Narrow Sea. None of which, he reminded himself as he strode back towards the eastern gate, mattered at that moment; what *did* matter was where those turd-licking Franks were lurking, although he had just made a decision to stop running about the town in the dark like a beheaded chicken. After all, he reasoned, he knew where these *oskilgetinn* were most likely headed; it did not take a military genius to know that their goal would be to open one of the gates, and the eastern was the most logical of the two main entrances, since the western gate serviced the docks and the Franks had not arrived in ships. There was one small gate, more of a postern door on the northern side, but it was much too narrow to feed enough men through to take the town. No, he thought again, it will be the eastern gate, and he had sent runners from his own party of thirty men to find the others scattered throughout the town, ordering them to meet there.

After all, he glanced up at the night sky, and while his view of the eastern horizon was blocked, a lifetime spent in the elements told him that there would be a pinkening of the sky soon. And then, he knew, those Franks with their pup of a Count would be coming. Striding at the head of his own band, he reached the junction with the street that led directly to the eastern gate and turned right, just in time to see what, for the span of a crucial heartbeat he thought was one of the other search parties, led by one of his men...but who? he wondered. Only Thrymyr was that large, but he had gone with Hallsteinn, and there was no other man his size left of the current garrison. This was the moment that a series of seemingly disconnected facts, more accurately bits of talk and gossip fell into place, and in that moment, Bjorn Sigurdson suddenly knew who he was looking at. For the remainder of his life, he would never know whether it was the Norns—Urðr, Verðandi and Skuld—sitting at the foot of Yggdrasil, the tree of life, and weaving the great tapestry that used the threads of every living soul who caused the man he was certain was the Saxon known as Berserker to turn and look directly at him, or if it was just a simple accident. What mattered was how, without any hesitation, the Berserker broke into a run, heading right for him, with his sword raised and eyes seeming to catch the light from the torches held by Bjorn's men. The Berserker was coming for Bjorn Sigurdson, and for the first time in many years, Bjorn was afraid.

While Titus had recovered first, he had been just as surprised at the appearance of the party of Northmen approaching the gateway from the town, recognizing Bjorn in the torchlight, though he did not recall making a conscious decision to head immediately for him. It was an instinctive reflex; he saw an enemy, and that enemy must be killed.

Without glancing over his shoulder, Titus bellowed, "Berwald, Isnard, Méliau, guard the stairs to the rampart! Kill any of those whorespawns who try to come down! The rest of you with me!"

He had broken into a run before he was finished, his braid flying behind him, shield held out from his body so he could build his speed and drawing his sword, while Ranulf was just a half-step behind him, and with Sigemund next to Ranulf, with the latter holding his spear in such a way that he could either hurl it or thrust with it. Ranulf would have preferred to form a line across the street in between the buildings, but he had seen Titus like this before, and more out of resignation than any fervor, he was determined not to lag behind. Titus aimed for Bjorn, who was fumbling for his bearded ax that was thrust into his belt, but the big Saxon was moving too quickly, so he only had time to swing his shield up just in time, as Titus did the same, except that the Saxon pulled the shield tight against his shoulder. The Northman immediately behind Bjorn was hampered by holding a torch, just moments earlier having switched it to his right hand because his left arm had grown tired, but what doomed him was when the huge Saxon that, in this warrior's last moment, *did* remind him of Thrymr as he had Bjorn, struck Bjorn's shield with his own and sent the Northman leader reeling into the torchbearer. It was a reflexive reaction to reach for Bjorn with his free hand to steady him, but his eyes also went to the staggering man, so he did not even see Sigemund's spear thrust that skimmed over Bjorn's shoulder and into his own mouth. His body, which collapsed immediately into a heap as the torch dropped onto the muddy street, became an obstacle as Bjorn staggered several steps backward, only caught by the shield of another of his men. Titus' own Wyvern's Fang was moving as well, in a shoulder-high thrust that was angled slightly outward from the center of his body, aiming for the warrior who had been just behind Bjorn but to his left and next to the torchbearer, the point slicing into his throat, so that within the span of a heartbeat, two Northmen were dead. Bjorn's stumble backward gave him an extra instant to draw his ax, but the Saxon was on him immediately, forcing him into a wild, unaimed swing that the Berserker caught with his shield. The angle was such that the beard of the ax bit into the shield, and while his eyes did not move from Bjorn, at the lower edge of his vision Titus saw the beard protruding from the back, the angle of it informing him what to do next, and instead of keeping the shield in front of his body, he swung it out and away, seemingly exposing him to an attack from one of the other Northmen. This was the moment Ranulf drew even with Titus, stepping into the spot to the Saxon's right, his own shield protecting his friend who performed a hard lunge of his own, but coming from down low with the point angled upward, in what Titus' ancestor would have called a first position thrust.

With Bjorn's ax trapped by the friction created by Titus' move, the Northman only had his shield, but he managed to drop it low enough to block the thrust, although the power behind it, since the Saxon had added to his already massive power with a vicious twist of his hips, shoved the shield back towards his body. This was exactly what Titus had intended, because without hesitating, he stepped into this new gap, and using the hinged nose flange of his helmet to his advantage, he whipped his head forward, striking Bjorn flush in the face in an explosion of blood, mucus, and teeth, eliciting a muffled shout of agony. Once more, Bjorn felt himself staggering backward, but he was too experienced to drop his shield to clutch his face; his ax, however, was another matter because it was still trapped in Titus' shield, yet he somehow managed to retain his grip on it, and aided by his body weight falling backward, was able to yank his weapon out of the shield, tearing a chunk of limewood out with it. Titus neither noticed, nor would he have cared, angered as he was that this Northern bastard managed to keep hold of his ax, and he was determined to press his advantage; that it put him deeper into the knot of Northmen did not seem to concern him in the slightest. Ranulf, having taken note of Titus' behavior and anticipating this, had just feinted a thrust of his own that forced his own opponent, a tall, lean Northmen with a plaited beard whose weapon was a single-bladed ax, to take a step backward. This warrior's fate was sealed when, for reasons that Ranulf would never know, the Northman behind him gave the man a violent shove with his shield, bellowing something that sounded like a curse aimed at his comrade as he did so, sending the Northman directly back at Ranulf. In a reflexive reaction, Ranulf brought his sword up, the point extending beyond his shield a couple of feet, the result being that the Northman essentially ran himself onto the Frank's sword, the point plunging through the boiled leather vest with iron rings as if it was not there, and Ranulf watched his foe's eyes go wide from the shock of not just what had to be a pain Ranulf shuddered to think about, but the realization that his own thread had just been snipped short. Thankfully, Ranulf was not blasted in the face by a shriek of agony because the wind had already been forced from his lungs by the impact, but with their faces just a foot away, he did not care for what he knew was coming, though he nonetheless ripped his blade horizontally across the Northman's midriff, twisting his hips to add enough power to a maneuver that his friend could do with just the strength of his arm. Even without air in his lungs, somehow the Northman's scream was shrill enough to make Ranulf wince, ignoring the slimy, warm and wet feeling of the man's internal organs and intestines as they came rushing out through the rent in armor and stomach, and he used his shield to send the dying Northman reeling back a final time into the man who had sent him to his death.

Sensing a movement to his right, Ranulf risked a quick glance to see that it was Lambertus, whose own weak side was protected by the building on the right side of the street, while Sigemund had moved to Titus' left, and by doing so, they now had effectively blocked off the street from Bjorn's force that was reeling and disorganized from the ferocity of Titus' initial assault, with four bodies lying at their feet. This, Ranulf could see, was about to change, as the Northman that Titus had pointed out and identified as the commander of the garrison was clearly recovering his composure, even with the blood streaming down into his beard from his ruined nose and mouth, and the Franks were still significantly outnumbered. It was at this moment, out of the darkness and from behind them, there was another roar of voices, originating south of the gateway, and while it was impossible to tell what tongue the newly arrived party was speaking, Ranulf knew that there was only one possibility. Nevertheless, his attention did not waver from what was taking place in front of him; he saw and heard the Northman Bjorn raise his ax, bellowing as he did so, in what Ranulf was certain was going to be an attack on Titus, who in that instant was slashing with Wyvern's Fang at the Northman across from Sigemund, which meant that Titus had turned to his left slightly, moving his shield out of position. Because he was more concerned with protecting his friend who did not seem interested in protecting himself, Ranulf did not see the blow from Bjorn's bearded ax as it swept down, striking his helmet with a terrific force, nor did he feel the impact with the muddy street as he collapsed next to Titus. Titus, however, did see it, and Bjorn Sigurdson's fate was sealed in that instant, and if the Northman had been listening, he might have heard the snip of the Norn Urðr's shears cutting his thread as the Berserker added to his legend, and raising Sigfred's bounty in the process.

Chapter Five

"Lord Count, I must say it again! It is too soon to launch the attack! It is not even light yet!" Lord Baudelius had actually interposed his horse between the Count and the rest of the *Eques* in a last-ditch attempt to stop Baldwin. "We cannot see whether the gate is open!"

"This man," Baldwin pointed down to Eudes, who was thankful that it was still too dark for anyone to see how violently he was trembling, which had nothing to do with the impending battle, "saw the signal." The Count turned in his saddle to indicate another mounted man, "And Sigismund here confirms it as well."

"Bent does not," Baudelius replied stiffly, then it was his turn to look at the warrior sitting next to Sigismund, who was aware that he may have permanently ruptured his friendship with the other warrior. "Do you, Bent?"

"No, Lord." Bent shook his head emphatically. "I saw no such thing. And," he added pointedly, "I was paying much closer attention than Sigismund...or the boy here, for that matter."

"Lord Count," Baudelius tried to sound reasonable. "If we go galloping up to the gate, and it is closed, we will be vulnerable to those Northern savages on their ramparts. No," he shook his head as he said dramatically, "*you* will be the one most under threat. And you know that I promised your father that..."

"Lord," Baldwin cut him off, quietly but firmly, "I am a man grown now, and while I appreciate your counsel, and your desire to keep me safe, *I* am the Margrave of Flandre, ordained by God and the King of the Franks. The decision is mine, and mine alone. And," now he raised his voice, "prepare to advance!" Addressing the grizzled veteran who served as the commander of the *Pedes*, Baldwin ordered, "Liébaut, you and your men set out now. I am giving you a head start so that when we arrive at the gate, you will be close behind."

Liébaut inclined his head but did not move, asking instead, "Do you want us to carry any ladders at all, *Dux*?"

Under other circumstances, Baldwin would have appreciated this sly dig at Lord Baudelius, who consistently refused to use the honorific that denoted not only a Frankish nobleman's social status, but acknowledged his prowess as a military leader.

This, however, was not the foremost thing on his mind, and he thought for a heartbeat, then answered, "Take six of them. The *lantweri* will carry the rest." At this mention of the levy, he addressed the warrior standing next to Liébaut, who might have been Liébaut's brother but was in fact a second cousin, and who served as the overall commander of the *lantweri*, "Prothaud, you will wait until a count of one hundred after I lead the *Eques* forward, then follow us, and as we planned, you will evenly divide your ladder men on either side of the gate. The sooner you have your ladders up against the wall, the better. Is that understood?"

"Yes, *Dux*," Prothaud replied, though he did risk a nervous glance up at Baudelius, who scowled at him in a seeming response.

Baldwin turned his mount away, prompting Liébaut to go trotting over to the *Pedes*, where he delegated men to grab ladders from the pile. The infantry force was ready quickly, the men hefting their shields and wiping their palms on the hems of their tunics before gripping their spears and forming into what served as their primary formation for movement, five men across, then began marching down the road towards Boulogne. The *Eques* moved into position, waiting for a count of one hundred, but Bent made a slight detour, riding over to where Eudes was still standing in his original spot, uncertain whether he was supposed to move since the Count had not dismissed him.

Maneuvering his horse so that he could tower over the youngster, Bent leaned down closely enough so that Eudes could see the malevolence in his gaze, but the *Eques* kept his voice low so that only the youth could hear him say, "You are going to pay for calling me a liar, *boy*."

"I...I didn't call you a liar!" Eudes protested, then realized with a sinking feeling how he had, in fact, done essentially that very thing. Yet, despite his fear, he felt a flicker of anger, which was what fueled his courage enough to say defiantly, "I know what I saw! Someone in that town loosed a fire arrow into the sky!"

Bent acted as if he had not heard Eudes, saying simply, "Remember what I said, you little turd. You are going to pay."

Jerking his horse's head, Bent kicked the animal hard, so that he leaped forward, Bent guiding his mount to resume his normal spot next to Sigismund, who was regarding him with a level gaze, though he said nothing.

When Sigismund did not turn his attention away from Bent for several heartbeats, Bent, whose nerves were already frayed because of what lay in their immediate future, snapped, "What? Why are you looking at me like that?"

"If anything happens to that lad..." Sigismund began quietly.

"What?" Bent cut him off with a sneer. "What will happen, eh, Sigismund? You've never seen the day when you could handle me in any kind of fight. So," he challenged, "what are you going to do, eh?"

Rather than be angered at the slur, Sigismund seemed saddened, as if finally reaching a conclusion that he had been fighting against for some time, which was exactly what was taking place.

"I will inform Count Baldwin that I heard you threaten that boy, Bent. I will accuse and stand witness against you if that *Lantwerus* dies under suspicious circumstances...like a blade to the back. In fact, if he dies by falling off a horse, I will accuse you."

Bent could only stare at the other man in open shock for a moment, then, recovering slightly, rejoined, "And you think that Lord Baudelius would let that pup execute me? *Me?* His most valuable and greatest warrior? You know how many Northmen I've slain! How many bandits!"

"I think," Sigismund replied quietly, "you underestimate

that 'pup,' my old friend. You always have. Besides," he shrugged, though his hand had inched a bit closer to the hilt of his sword, knowing what might happen, "you might have been his greatest warrior, but since Berserker arrived?"

As he suspected it might, Bent's face contorted with what was a mortal insult to a man like him, the statement that he was no longer supreme, yet somehow Bent managed to refrain from lashing out.

Instead, he gave a mocking laugh. "That Saxon whorespawn is probably dead by now!"

"That's why you lied about seeing the signal." Sigismund nodded, taking this as confirmation. "And that's why you're not in any hurry to get to the gate." Any other conversation was cut off by the sound of Baldwin's voice giving the order to begin moving at the trot, so all Sigismund said was, "You better hope that he *is* dead, Bent."

Sigismund would never know just how fervently Bent had prayed and continued to do so for this to be the case, but there was no more time for talk, as Baldwin immediately ordered them to the canter, and they reached the *Pedes* with their head start about one hundred fifty paces away from the gate and walls, veering around them. This was when Sigismund realized that it had gotten light enough that they could see more clearly; namely, he saw a row of helmeted figures lining the rampart, most thickly above and on either sides of the gateway. More crucially, he could see that the gates were still closed, yet even as this thought came to his mind, he saw movement from the gateway as both doors began to swing open.

"At the gallop...*attack*! For God! For Frankia! For Flandre!" Baldwin bellowed as the *Eques* dug their spurs into the flanks of their mounts, the antipathy between Bent and Sigismund temporarily forgotten as the two warriors exchanged a grin, dropping their spears down to the horizontal.

Bent and Sigismund were in the third rank, so their view was partially obscured, but Sigismund saw that the man who had shoved open the righthand gate was the archer from the *Pedes* who had gone with the Berserker's party, but he could not see who was on the opposite gate; he would only learn later that it was not even a member of the Berserker's group, but a smith named Gilo who, having evaded capture down in the sewers, had ascended to the street. Just inside the gateway, Baldwin suddenly veered his mount, a fine black stallion that was in fact the brother of the mount slain at Watten, hard to the right, but the warrior immediately behind him in the second rank was forced to attempt to leap his horse over what it took Sigismund an extra heartbeat to identify, a pile of bodies that were heaped thigh-high. It was less the height than the width of the pile, the animal's front hooves plunging down to land on a prone man who, as those in the immediate vicinity learned, was still alive, letting out a shrill scream of pain, and because of the uneven surface, the horse lost its footing, its left hoof slipping out from under it and sending its rider flying. The area around the gateway was jammed with bodies, yet while many of them were lying in the street, more were still standing, swinging their axes and swords, or thrusting with their spears at the newly appeared horsemen, the noise of battle exacerbated by the sound bouncing off the wall and enclosed gateway, making it impossible for any communication. Between the normal chaos of battle, the dim lighting that was steadily growing but was still provided mainly by the torches placed in stanchions along the wall, and the Northmen trying to kill him, even as his body reacted automatically, with his shield arm moving to block a thrust aimed not at him but at the shoulder of his horse while making a spear thrust of his own into the face of a wild-eyed Northman, what Sigismund was seeing was more a series of rapid impressions, but there would be one that would last with him for the rest of his days, probably because he was not the only man to see it and talk about it later. About fifteen paces away from the gateway and directly across from it, there was a knot of Northmen who, quite oddly in Sigismund's view, did not seem concerned by the sudden appearance of Frankish horsemen who were trying to jam themselves through the narrow passage. Instead, they were facing with their backs to the gateway and the newly arrived Franks, hacking and swinging at something, or someone, but it was not until Sigismund cut down his wild-eyed foe then kicked his horse away from the gateway, placing it slightly to his left rear, that he was able to see a lone figure, and even if he had an unobscured view, he would have instantly identified that it was the Berserker. He was not wearing his helmet, and in the flickering light of a nearby torch, Sigismund saw the gleam of blood that partially obscured the Saxon's face, and had either lost or thrown his shield away, and was now holding the sword Sigismund knew he had named Wyvern's Fang in his right hand, with the ax that he favored in the other, swinging both of them with apparent abandon, yet somehow managing to inflict damage with seemingly every swing, as evidenced by a Northman who reeled backward, both hands clutching his throat and taking a couple of staggering steps before collapsing on top of at least two dead comrades.

Sigismund was forced to tear his attention away, parrying a thrust from another enemy spear, but in doing so, he extended his spear shaft away from his body. The Northman next to the spearman reacted instantly, swinging his ax down and severing the Frank's spear a foot behind the point, leaving Sigismund with nothing more than a staff. However, this was a frequent event, one for which experienced warriors like Sigismund were prepared, and he did not hesitate to drop the shaft and reach for his own sword, named Corpse Maker, drawing and swinging down with it in one smooth motion, striking the ax-wielding Northman who had not yet recovered from his own attack a powerful blow that, while it did not land cleanly on his helmet, sent him staggering away, only to be cut down by Bent, who, Sigismund had noticed had forced his horse forward, slightly ahead of and a bit to Sigismund's left. Like Sigismund, he had discarded his spear, and he was using his own sword, which was about six inches longer than Sigismund's, to lethal effect. He could have been forcing his way to get nearer to Count Baldwin, who was in a somewhat vulnerable position himself, and was obviously trying to cut his way to the Berserker; although, Sigismund thought, *the Saxon doesn't look like he needs any help.* Just behind him, he felt as much as heard the arrival of the *Pedes,* with Liébaut immediately leading men up the set of wooden stairs to the rampart, the din of fresh combat coming from a new direction. Without any warning, which was how it usually worked with Northmen, which the Berserker had assured him was the same with Danes, the warriors defending the area around the gateway suddenly broke, without any discernible signal, turning and sprinting away. Where Sigismund was now located, just a handful of paces to the right of the gateway, the Northmen that had been facing him headed down the street paralleling the base of the wall, heading north. The other *Eques* around him, bellowing in triumph, or making the kind of whooping call they used when hunting game by running them down, went pounding after them...but Sigismund did not, though he could not have said why, at least at first.

The collapse of what was essentially one wing of the Northmen's resistance meant that the defenders on the opposite side of the gate were now facing the bulk of the mounted Franks, while the *Pedes* were spreading along the rampart in both directions, where resistance was now in pockets composed of a handful of Northmen. With no immediate threat, Sigismund turned his attention to what was taking place farther down the street that led deeper into the town from the eastern gate, but his view was partially blocked by the building on the corner. He urged his mount back towards the gate, stopping once he had a clear view, although there were other horsemen, including Count Baldwin and Lord Baudelius in between him and the Berserker, but he was in time to see the Saxon snarl something over his shoulder at the Count, who was nearest to him, but while he could not hear the words over the other noise, it was clear by Baldwin's response that it was a warning of some sort. Only then did his attention shift to see that, amidst what he estimated to be at least thirty corpses, there was a man on both knees, his head hanging down. Pointing his sword at the man, Titus snarled something, his voice unrecognizable, but what he was demanding became clear when the other man looked up, the entire lower half of his face unrecognizable because of the blood that had soaked his mustache and beard. It was obviously a Northman, and from the number of arm rings he wore, Sigismund guessed this had to be one of the leaders of the men that Sigfred had left behind, and like the other Franks around this scene, he waited to see what would happen.

"*Do not interfere!*" Titus had snarled at Count Baldwin, though he did not know in that moment that was who it was.

He had sensed movement, turning his head just enough to see a horse at the edge of his vision, and knew that it was not a Northman. Every other Northman within his range of sight was down, either dead or moaning from a wound serious enough to keep them out of the fight, but his attention was on one man, and one only, who was now on his knees less than ten paces away. That the street between them was covered by bodies, at least two and in the area immediately around Titus three or more deep, was not important; all that mattered in this moment was that Bjorn Sigurdson got to his feet, because there was no satisfaction in killing a kneeling man, especially not with what Titus had planned. It was not actually accurate to say that Titus did not care about the bodies around him; he was concerned that among the dead and wounded Northmen, there were Franks as well. Lambertus, Sigemund, and, most importantly, Ranulf were lying among them, but it had been this...this turd-licking whorespawn Bjorn who had struck Ranulf down, and now that Titus had slaughtered his men, it was Bjorn's turn.

"Get up!" he shouted, remembering to say it in Danish. "Get on your feet, you *oskilgetinn*! Time for you to die!"

Truthfully, Titus' strength was almost gone, and he had begun to point Wyvern's Fang at the Northman, but he did not trust that he would be able to do so without visibly shaking, and he did not want to give Bjorn any encouragement that he might escape his fate. No, he had to move, and move quickly, and end it before that thing came that was as inevitable as the enormous strength that came from his rage, that it deserted him and left him as weak as a kitten, wanting to do nothing more than find some hole, crawl into it and sleep. Thankfully, Bjorn did so, slowly, climbing to his feet, though he did not seem to pay any attention to Titus, finally standing erect and swaying side to side, but Titus saw that he had his ax in his hand. The one, Titus reminded himself, that had struck down Ranulf in a last-moment attempt to reanimate that...*thing* that lived inside him, that was always lurking there that had first awakened when he was barely fourteen and almost beaten another boy from Cissanbyrig to death. That memory came rushing back to him, catching him by surprise as he tried to remember; what was his name? Oswiu! That was it, but what had enraged Titus so much? Had he said something about Leofflaed? Was that what it was? It did not come to him, nor did it create much of a stir in him, so he shoved the thought aside, refocusing what was left of his rapidly diminishing rage on Bjorn, who, sensing an opportunity because of his distraction, had leaned down to snatch up a shield, but he quickly discarded it with an oath, seeing in what was now brighter than torchlight but still not full daylight, the large crack that signaled it would shatter at the first blow.

"Go ahead, get another one, you *Ergi*." Titus' voice, as hoarse as it was, was still laced with contempt, and he was pleased to see Bjorn stiffen at what was one of the worst insults a Northman or Dane could hurl at another man. In fact, he had learned through Einarr that being named as either an *Ergi,* a physical coward, or, to some men even worse, an *Argr*, what Titus' ancestor would have referred to as a minion, was so insulting that it had been codified into law that gave the accused the right to trial by combat. Which, in this case, was exactly what Titus wanted, and when Bjorn did not respond verbally, he taunted him further. "Hurry up, *Sorðinn*! Pick one up! I do not want you to have any excuses."

Just as Titus had anticipated he would, Bjorn combined grabbing up a shield that was closer to the Saxon with a lunging attack, but unusually, and because he was still in something of a crouch, the Northman executed a horizontal swing of his double-bearded ax at Titus' left knee. To the watching Franks, it seemed a devastating attack, coming from an unusual angle and height as it did, especially since the Saxon did not have a shield that he could drop down to block the blow, but Titus was not surprised, having anticipated what Bjorn would do. He was further aided by another aspect of this state of being that he was in, though it was fading, how his foes seemed to be moving so much more slowly than he did, behaving in such a way that it was as if they somehow communicated their intentions before they actually began moving. He had once tried to describe it to Uhtric and Leofflaed one night, the only two people with whom he would discuss it at all.

"You know how when we're training a *ceorl* or a youngster in a new movement?" he had begun by asking. Uhtric had nodded, while Titus explained to Leofflaed, "We break down whatever it is, say, a spear thrust and recovery, into a series of smaller movements, and we have them do them very slowly, one smaller movement at a time and stopping between each part so that we can look at them and correct something if needed. Then," he had continued, "we have them start doing them faster, and we don't stop them anymore. That way, they learn how to perform a thrust properly. Well," he had finished with a shrug, "when I get...like that, it's exactly the same to me. It's like they're new men moving very slowly, like they're practicing."

This was what enabled Titus to anticipate not only what Bjorn was going to do, but in enough time that, when the ax flashed past him, his leg was not there, Titus shifting his weight to his right leg and twisting at the waist as he raised his left foot off the ground and moved it backward. The spike on the top of Bjorn's ax barely grazed Titus' right knee, but in performing this attack and putting all of his power behind it, Bjorn had twisted himself so that his back was essentially to Titus, and most importantly, the shield he had snatched up was completely useless because it was out of position on the opposite side of the Northman's body. Bjorn shouted, his frustration and despair clear in his voice, knowing that his best and only hope had failed and all the Berserker had to do was make a quick thrust with his sword down between his shoulder blades. However, Bjorn was not to be that fortunate, and the watching Franks— Count Baldwin, Lord Baudelius, Theutbald and the other *Exploratores* who were now present, Sigismund, and perhaps most importantly, Bent—would all witness the aspect of the persona of Titus of Cissanbyrig when he was the Berserker that gave the Saxon the most pause and the most sleepless nights, exhibiting a level of cruelty that, even for a world as cruel as theirs was, left those who witnessed it speechless.

It began when, instead of using Wyvern's Fang and ending Bjorn's life, Titus swung his ax, not with the blade side, but with the butt, which had a protuberance that, while not a full spike, still extended three or four inches from the shaft, and he swung it underhanded so that it came up from below and in between Bjorn's legs, striking the Northman in his testicles, instantly crushing them. Bjorn's cry of frustration instantly transformed into a scream so shrill that several of the Frankish mounts began tossing their heads or pawing nervously at the street, a couple making the kind of hops that forced their riders to curb their horses, and if that had been all Titus did before dispatching his victim, it would have been something men talked about for some time to come, but the Berserker was not through. Any idea of a fight left Bjorn's mind, as this time he did drop both shield and ax to reach for his crushed manhood, yet before he could, Titus swung his ax again, still with the butt, and shattered Bjorn's left elbow joint, causing the Northman's lower left arm to bend at the elbow but in the opposite direction it was meant to go. Bjorn had fallen back to his knees, his initial scream now a keening wail of such pain that even men who were not known as pious reached for the crosses they all wore under their tunics and armor, or making the sign of the cross.

"P...p...please, Berse..." Bjorn, remarkably, had not toppled over and was still slumped and kneeling, his good remaining hand down between his legs, cradling his ruined manhood.

"*Don't call me that!*" Titus bellowed down at Bjorn, almost a scream that contained its own anguish. "*I never wanted to be called that!*" Now, Titus pointed Wyvern's Fang, and they could all see in the growing light how it was shaking; later, Sigismund would wonder if this was what triggered what was coming. "You killed my friend! You bashed his head in with your ax!" He pointed down at the weapon, lying on top of the corpse of one of Bjorn's own comrades that was partially covered by another Northman's body. "That ax, right there!" Suddenly, Titus' tone changed, becoming less hostile as he asked, "You want to go to Valhalla, yes?"

"Y-yes," Bjorn managed, a remarkable feat in itself that he was able to retain enough of his wits to respond. Nodding weakly, he whispered, "P-please...Saxon. Send me to Valhalla, as a warrior."

"Then pick it up," Titus ordered. "Pick up your ax, and I will end your pain, *Ergi*."

This was something of a test on Titus' part, but Bjorn did not show even a flicker of anger, telling the Saxon that there was no more satisfaction to be had, nothing more to extract as payment, except for one last thing. With an effort that was impossible for the onlookers to imagine, Bjorn managed to lean over just enough, and with a sharp cry of pain, released his grasp on his testicles to reach down and grasp the handle of the ax. He looked up at Titus expectantly, but the Saxon shook his head.

"No," he said coldly. "Lift it off the ground. Prove to your gods that you're worthy of Valhalla. Lift it as a warrior should."

Somehow, and even Bjorn could not have said where the strength came from, he managed to raise his arm, his face contorted from the agony, fueled only by the thought that, in just a matter of a heartbeat or at most two, his suffering would be over, and he would be feasting in Valhalla, where his father and brother, both named Sigurd, would be waiting for him with a horn of mead and eager to hear his tale. Perhaps under other circumstances, he would have cautioned himself because of the way this Saxon *oskilgetinn* was treating him, or would have correctly interpreted the look in the Berserker's eyes, but he had already endured a level of agony very few men had experienced, and none would ever want to, no matter what reward might await in exchange.

Raising his arm, he managed to get the head of the ax an inch off the ground, and even with the agony, he bellowed, "I am Bjorn, son of..."

He got no further, because the Berserker struck, swinging his sword, but it was not to end his agony. Instead, the blade sliced down and through Bjorn's wrist, severing his hand still clutching the ax, where both fell back onto the corpse next to him. For an instant, there was no pain, at least from this new indignity, and Bjorn could only stare dumbly down at the spurting stump of his wrist. Finally, after what might have been a heartbeat, or might have been an eternity, the real meaning of the Saxon's act, and the cruelty behind it, hit Bjorn, unleashing a level of despair that made the agony he was in more of his spirit than his flesh.

Titus' face would have been a mask even without the blood that obscured any expression, unaware that he was unintentionally copying a Roman general celebrating a triumph, but there was no mistaking the satisfaction in his voice as he bent down, his face inches away from Bjorn's to snarl, "No Valhalla for you, *Sorðinn*. No, you are going to Niflheimr, with the other *Ergi*, but I am sending you with a message." Bjorn, tears now streaming from his eyes and panting from the combination of agony and despair, looked up at him uncomprehendingly, prompting Titus to lean over so that his mouth was now next to the Northman's ear. "I want you to tell Leif Longhair that Titus the Berserker sent you to give him this message. Tell him that I am going to be sending his father to join the both of you...soon."

There was a flicker of a dawning understanding in Bjorn's eyes, but it was destined to last only as long as it took for Titus to draw Wyvern's Fang across the Northman's throat, the Saxon not even bothering to try and get out of the way of the spray of blood from Bjorn's throat. The Northman's head dropped, his body slumped forward, but Titus gave him a rough shove that sent him toppling over to land on top of his severed hand and ax. It was only at that moment that Titus became aware that it was silent, at least in a relative sense immediately around him, and he straightened up and was just beginning to turn around when Bent took leave of his senses.

For the young Count, watching the Berserker essentially torture the Northman whose name the Franks learned was Bjorn, when Titus shouted his name, presented him with a dilemma. According to his cleric, Father Rudolf, who was the abbot of the abbey of Saint-Bertin, protected within the walls of Saint-Omer and under the Count's protection, a good Christian should never rejoice in the suffering of other men, even pagan savages, their punishment being up to God, yet at the same time, the Count thought of himself as a warrior, one who had seen what these animals were capable of doing, and especially in the heat of battle, he found it next to impossible to disapprove of what the Saxon was doing. Besides, while he had not spoken to the Berserker yet, nor had he even seen any of the men who had been with the Saxon on their mission infiltrating the town, although he thought he had spotted one of them—he believed it was the man Méliau who was sitting with his back to the base of the wall next to the gateway with a makeshift bandage around one leg—otherwise, the only man left of that party still standing was the Berserker. And, while he was young, Count Baldwin was an experienced warrior, and between the torchlight and the growing daylight, he could read what had taken place very easily; a glance at Baudelius, who looked as shaken as Baldwin could ever remember seeing him, told him that he was not alone in understanding that almost all of the carnage they were seeing was done before their own arrival. The fighting was still ongoing, but their charge through the gate had shattered the Northmen who had tried to stand their ground in the gateway, while the arrival of the *Pedes* and Liébaut's quick decision to lead his men up to the rampart, seeing that the *Eques* were not pressed, had ensured the collapse of the defense of Boulogne. Oh, there would be fighting for the next few hours; at least, he thought grimly, there would be if I intended to capture the town, but he had already made his decision regarding this place of such strategic importance to the Northmen.

Baldwin had slain or wounded a half-dozen men, yet even during the fighting, he had divided his attention between his own situation and that of the Berserker, and while he had not seen it all, he had seen enough to know that what he had first witnessed at Watten was not a fluke or a once in a lifetime event. No, he now knew, there was something in this Saxon warrior that made him unique, and even in the moment, there was a part of the young Count's mind that always remained apart from the rest of his consciousness, one that was planning ahead, thinking of what not just his next move but the move after that should be, and without knowing it, he was struck by a thought that a few years before, a King in Wessex had experienced; if I had more men like the Berserker, there is no limit to what I could accomplish, but having just him is still a powerful weapon. Like most of the onlookers, and proving that there were some things that went beyond class distinctions, when the Berserker swung the butt of his ax to crush the Northman's balls, Baldwin winced, while one hand unconsciously moved towards his own crotch, while he noticed a similar movement from the men around him, telling him that he was not alone in his reaction. Baudelius had muttered something, but the Northman's shrieks drowned him out, and when Baldwin glanced over, he saw that the older man had placed his left hand over the gold cross he wore under his armor, which surprised the Count since, under other circumstances, Baudelius was not very pious.

While they watched as the Berserker systematically crippled his foe by smashing his left elbow joint, Baldwin did notice out of the corner of his eye that Bent was moving his mount a bit closer, positioning himself to Baldwin's right yet still slightly behind him so that, if the Count wanted to look at the man who had been his most potent warrior before the arrival of the Saxon, he would have to twist in the saddle to do so; only later did he understand this had been no accident on Bent's part. Before he could have counted to five, Baldwin sensed more movement, but when he tore his attention away from the Berserker to glance over his shoulder, he saw that it was just Sigismund, who was on the other side from Bent and had moved a bit closer to his friend. Perhaps if there had not been something else going on, like the Berserker bellowing something in the Northman's tongue at his beaten foe, Baldwin might have noticed the peculiar expression on Bent's face, or how Sigismund was not watching the Berserker like everyone else, but his close companion. However, he was not; he was watching as the Berserker taunted the Northman to the point that, even in as much agony as he must have been in, the warrior Bjorn somehow found the strength to reach down for the ax that was lying conveniently atop a corpse of one of his own next to him. Despite himself, and despite his hostility towards these Northern invaders, Baldwin felt a surge of grudging admiration for the raw courage this Northman was displaying, although he had heard Berserker mention Valhalla, these pagans' version of Heaven, which, Baldwin would never admit to anyone, especially Father Rudolf, sounded much more entertaining than the Christian version. He also knew that the way Northmen got to Valhalla was dying with a weapon in their hand, so Baldwin was slightly puzzled that the Berserker seemed to be extending this small mercy. That thought was barely formed in his mind when he learned differently, as the Berserker swung his sword, not to sever the Northman's head from his neck, but the hand clutching his ax, eliciting a chorus of gasps and muttered exclamations from the men watching the spectacle. The Northman's reaction was much like Baldwin's, staring dumbfounded at the stump where his hand had been as the blood spurted a foot out from his arm in a rhythmic spray for perhaps two or three heartbeats before raising his face to the sky and unleashing a howl of such despair and torment that Baldwin felt the hair on his neck stand up...along with an unexpected stab of pity. He watched the Berserker take a step closer to his foe, ignoring the spray of blood that doused the front of his armor, which was already so thoroughly coated with gore that the gray of the mail was no longer visible, lean down and while he did not whisper, he did not speak loudly enough for Baldwin to hear, even if he had not been speaking in the Northman's tongue. His head was still next to Bjorn's when he brought his right hand up, his sword still in it, and drew the blade across the Northman's throat, then gave the dying man a brutal shove that sent him toppling sideways, leaving the Berserker the last man standing in what the Count had no experience to know mimicked the square created by hazel rods used by Northmen and Danes for personal combat, although the boundaries on two sides were created by the buildings lining the street that ran west into the town from the gate. Only then did the Saxon seem to realize that he had an audience present, but he gave his Count or Lord Baudelius barely a glance before he leaned down to drag a body off another one as he began to search for his best friend Ranulf who, Baldwin assumed, must be lying somewhere among the carnage.

After it was over, Sigismund could not articulate to anyone, even to himself, why he felt it necessary to change his position in response to Bent nudging his horse to get closer...but for what? Sigismund wondered. Perhaps this was what prompted him to do the same, he would think later. While he was moving, he saw the Berserker shatter the Northman's elbow, though it barely registered as his sense that Bent was planning something grew, along with his unease, even if he could not possibly imagine what it could be that Bent had in mind. For his part, Bent's attention seemed fixed on the Berserker, which was understandable, but even to Sigismund, who knew him so well, he could not interpret the expression on the other warrior's face. He was aware that the light was growing to the point that the torches were not necessary, while the noise of fighting had faded and seemed to be mainly on the opposite side of the town, down near the docks, which made sense as the defenders tried to flee now that the town was obviously lost to a numerically superior force. There had been some talk by Lord Baudelius about sending the men of the *lantweri* around the town to the river, with the intention of cutting off any escape, but Count Baldwin had demurred, deciding that allowing them to leave was adequate for his larger goal of removing Boulogne as a threat.

Among the more senior warriors like Sigismund, there was more awareness of the larger, strategic issues that faced his Count, challenges that had been daunting for his father and were even more so because of his youth, and in the case of Boulogne, there was simply not enough manpower to hold Saint-Omer, Bruciam (Bruges), Ganda (Ghent), and Cortryk (Kortrijk), all of which had garrisons of at least a hundred men, and now this town as well. It would, Sigismund felt fairly certain, be put to the torch, razed so that it could not be of any use for Sigfred, or any other Northman for that matter. Perhaps his thoughts strayed for that moment, he would think later, which was why he missed Bent leisurely lean over and grasp a spear that had been hurled down from the rampart, missed its target, and buried itself in the thick layer of dirt covering the paved street.

It was not until Bent lifted his arm, drawing it back, that Sigismund turned his attention to see what his friend, his comrade, was about to do, and without thinking, he reached out and grabbed Bent's forearm, stopping it from moving forward, hissing, "*Bent! What are you doing?*"

He was reminded of Bent's cat-quick reflexes, and the dagger he carried strapped to his saddle as, without any hesitation or a word of protest at being stopped, he drew it with his left hand and brought it down across the knuckles of Sigismund's own left hand, not hard enough to sever his fingers, but enough to cut through the leather of his gloves and cut deep gouges on all four fingers to the point that the bone was showing. Sigismund howled in pain...and released his grip of Bent's arm, grabbing his injured hand with his other as Bent once more drew his arm back, his eyes fixed on the figure of the Berserker, who, completely oblivious to the drama playing out behind him, was shifting another body in search of Ranulf.

"*Bent!*" Count Baldwin's voice was almost as shrill as the Northman's had been, and even with the pain, Sigismund heard his panic, but unlike Sigismund, the Count was separated from Bent by several feet, not close enough to reach out and stop him.

What took place over the next heartbeat or two happened so quickly, only when those present compared their stories and contributed their own accounts did they have an idea what happened. Bent's arm swept forward, releasing the spear at such a short range that it was impossible for him to miss, yet he did, but only because at that exact instant, the Berserker collapsed, facedown on top of what they discovered shortly afterward was the lower body of Ranulf, as they learned that all of the blood caking his armor, arms, legs, and face did not all belong to his foes, the spear streaking past the Berserker to bury itself in another corpse. If that was all that happened, it would have been enough, but as Sigismund stared at the man he had considered his closest friend in shock and horror, already thinking about what his punishment by the Count was likely to be, Bent's own face took on a puzzled expression as he let out a sharp gasp. It was only when he lowered his head, oh so slowly, to look down at the tip of a spearpoint that was poking through his scale armor, dripping blood, that Sigismund began to understand; naturally, his next act was to look past and slightly behind Bent to see the man standing there, still in an extended lunge position, both hands on his spear, steady and unshaking.

Naturally, his first thought was that this was a Northman who he assumed must have been lying among the corpses in the gateway and playing dead, but he realized that this was not the case, barely recognizing his own voice as he gasped what he thought was the name of the youth of the *lantweri* who had drawn Bent's ire, "Eudos?"

Then, Bent toppled from the saddle as the youth released his grip on his spear, Sigismund's friend dead before he hit the ground, his face turned in such a way that Sigismund could see one eye that seemed to stare directly, and accusingly, up at him.

For Eudes, the occasion of what would be his first and last battle in the *lantweri* was quite a letdown, at least at first. Then, however, he had gotten inside the walls of the town, not by ascending one of the ladders, but by essentially walking through the gateway with a handful of other men of the *lantweri* who slipped among the *Pedes*, taking advantage of what he had no experience to know was the normal chaos that came from a battle. In the moment, he could not have articulated why he did so, but when he thought about it later, he realized that it was because somehow, through the mass of horsemen and Northmen defenders jammed together in the gateway, he had caught a glimpse of *him*, the Berserker, ax in one hand and sword in another, his braid out behind him as he spun first in one direction, then another, swinging his ax so quickly that it was only a blur while executing a thrust with his sword that sent a Northman armed with a spear and shield staggering backward. Without having any conscious thought of doing so, Eudes stopped just inside the gateway, while the other *lantweri* he had joined scrambled up the set of wooden stairs that led up to the rampart, leaving him as one of the only ones besides the *Eques* led by the Count and Lord Baudelius down on the street. He was nothing more than a spectator as he watched the horsemen with the Count, including the hated Bent and his friend Sigismund, as they slashed and thrust down at the ragged line of Northmen who had juxtaposed themselves between the gate and where the Berserker was himself surrounded by only God knew how many Northmen. Using the bulk provided by their horses, Eudes could only watch admiringly at the skill with which these men used their mounts, maneuvering them simply by using the pressure of their knees to guide them, although the *Eques,* and their horses, were not completely unscathed. In fact, he had to throw himself out of the way of a terrified horse, blood streaming down its left shoulder as it galloped back out of the gate, while its rider was cut down by a Northman's ax after losing his seat.

The fighting around the gate was furious, but it did not last long, Eudes witnessing the moment when the feared Northmen, for whom it was a commonly held belief drank the blood of their enemies, ate the flesh of infants, and routinely had sex with animals, went from fearsome savages to men whose only concern was seeing another sunrise. Faster than he would have believed possible, the area around the gateway went from being crammed full of men and animals to a place where most of those remaining were dead, wounded too badly to move, or like Eudes, drawn to the spectacle of a single warrior slaughtering any Northman who stood against him. Two of the men remaining behind were next to the gate, where one was standing and another kneeling next to a third warrior whose back was leaned against the wall, and Eudes moved closer to get a better look and saw that the seated man had suffered a leg wound that the kneeling man, who, to the youth's surprise, was clearly not a warrior, wearing a civilian's tunic, but with a thickset frame and bulging forearms that practically screamed his identity as a smith, was using a belt that had been placed around the wounded man's thigh just below his crotch, pulling it tight as the man groaned with a pain the youth could not imagine. Even in the dim light, he could see the deathly pallor of the stricken warrior, while the standing man, who was holding a bow that identified him as a man of the *Pedes*, looked on with obvious worry.

Eudes was torn between wanting to move to a spot where he could better watch the Berserker and speaking to these men who he correctly guessed had been part of what was now clearly the plan to open the gate; the chance of watching his hero won out. It was as he was picking his way through the bodies that he saw Bent suddenly urge his horse to move to a new spot, causing Eudes to freeze, worried that the warrior would see him and demand to know why he was lingering in a spot where men like him had no business, but the warrior did not even glance in his direction. Instead, his attention was riveted on the Berserker, who Eudes saw was now down to one opponent, a man with a beard matted with blood that he could see was from a ruined nose and shattered teeth. Despite his distraction, Eudes did note that the fact that he could see the white bits of teeth sprinkled in the Northman's beard was the most potent sign that dawn had arrived, but he was far more interested in what Bent was doing. Apparently, so was his friend, as Eudes, who remained frozen in his spot, watched Sigismund essentially copy his companion, although he was on the side opposite Eudes.

Count Baldwin was sitting on his horse almost directly in between Eudes and where the Berserker and his foe were, blocking the youth's view, but that was not why he moved, although he could not have explained exactly why he felt the need to reposition himself closer to Bent, about two paces to the left and just behind the warrior who was still staring fixedly at the Berserker. Eudes' own attention on Bent was broken by the shrill scream from the Northman when his testicles were crushed, but since he did not see the actual act, he was not one of the onlookers who gasped or made some sort of exclamation, turning his attention to the Berserker and seeing only the aftermath as the Northman grabbed for his balls. However, he was just in time to see the Berserker shatter his enemy's left elbow, and he felt his stomach lurch at the sight of it bending in the opposite direction than it was intended, but he managed to swallow the bile back down without humiliating and drawing attention to himself. He had heard the Berserker shouting, but while it might have been in the Saxon tongue, he did not think so based on the manner in which the Northman reacted, though now the Berserker began speaking more calmly, if only slightly so, and he heard the word "Valhalla." Like the Count; indeed, like every Frank who had the misfortune to live in this age where these pagan marauders were a daily part of their existence, Eudes had a similarly scarce knowledge about Valhalla, but unlike the Count, he was not aware about the requirement for a Northman to hold a weapon as they died. When it became clear that the Berserker was actually inviting his foe, who was on his knees clutching his balls with his remaining good hand, to pick up the ax next to him, he could only gape in amazement as he wondered if the Berserker had taken leave of his senses. Yes, the man was obviously crippled, and he was on his knees, but everyone knew that only a fool trusted one of these Northern savages! This was how he missed Bent leaning over to pick up the spear, Eudes' attention completely on the Berserker as he saw that the Saxon warrior had not lost his wits, and had goaded the Northman into grasping and lifting the ax as he shouted what Eudes deduced was his name, which even in the moment, Eudes acknowledged was a courageous thing to do considering the agony the Northman must have been in, and the Berserker had clearly done this with the sole purpose of enabling the Saxon to swing his sword downward with so much speed that Eudes could not follow it as more than a blur, severing the Northman's hand, still clutching the ax, from his wrist.

There was an instant where, while it was not actually so as the fainter sounds of the fighting deeper in the town were clearly audible, to Eudes, it fell completely silent, almost as if they were in church during a moment of silent prayer, which was shattered by the howl of utter despair from the Northman who raised his face to the sky, sounding to the youth more like an animal than a human being. Although it seemed like much longer, it could not have been more than a couple more heartbeats as the Berserker took a step to stand over the Northman, lean down and whisper something, then slice the Northman's throat, the dead man's head falling onto his chest as the blood seemingly sprayed everywhere. When he did not fall forward, the Berserker gave him a hard shove that sent him over onto his side, but the Saxon was already moving away, leaning down to grab a corpse and toss it aside as if he was searching for something...or, Eudes realized, someone. It was the movement that turned out to be Bent's arm lifting and pulling back that caused Eudes to look away from the Berserker, though it took the youth a moment to first recognize the spear in the warrior's hand, and more importantly, who his target was, and it seemed as if he was frozen in place, his feet rooted in the dirt street, consigned to just watch as he saw Sigismund lean over slightly and grab Bent's right forearm with his left hand. As quickly as Bent actually reacted, to Eudes, it seemed that Bent moved in an almost leisurely fashion as his left hand reached down and grasped the handle of the dagger that only then did the youth notice was strapped to the warrior's saddle, right next to his left leg, draw it from its scabbard and reach across to bring it down in a slashing blow across Sigismund's fingers, causing Bent's companion to release his grip, shouting in pain as he did.

"*Bent!*"

Eudes recognized that it was the Count who shouted this, the loudest noise since the Northman had howled his last because of where it came from off to his left and not because it sounded like the Count, being almost as high-pitched and shrill as a woman or child, but he did not even glance in the Count's direction, his attention now completely on Bent. Although he did not remember doing so, he discarded his shield so that he could hold his spear in a two-hand grip, the point tilted upward as he took the two steps to get within range for the kind of thrust the men of the *lantweri* had been trained to execute against a mounted enemy. It would be, he saw, desperately close, his attempt to stop Bent, the *Eques'* arm already drawing back, and in the back of his mind, a calm voice told him that it would all depend on how long Bent took to aim the spear. The Berserker was still at the edge of his vision, but he forced himself to keep his entire attention focused on the mounted warrior, and he saw his arm begin to move forward at the precise instant that Eudes initiated his own, upward thrust, aiming for a spot midway between shoulder blade and rump where it met the saddle and just to the left of the spine. It was, he was certain, the best thrust he had ever executed in his short career as a warrior, stomping down with his left foot as he shot both arms forward and upward, his left hand guiding the point to the spot he was looking at, while his right arm provided the power, and augmented by the violent twist of his upper body.

The point struck Bent in the back a fraction of an eyeblink after the spear left Bent's hand as his arm continued downward so that it ended up as if Bent was pointing at his target. Eudes felt the resistance of iron point striking iron scale, but it only lasted a fraction of an eyeblink as his spearpoint punched through the armor, then sliced through muscle, bone, and internal organs until it struck the hard breastbone of Bent's chest, although the momentum was such that the point continued for a couple inches more to burst out of Bent's body. He felt the sudden, hard vibration through the shaft of the spear as the warrior reacted to the violent introduction of this foreign object into his body, yet his reaction was surprisingly muted; Eudes did not even hear Bent's soft gasp, only seeing how his helmeted head dropped down to look at the point protruding from his chest.

Sigismund, his mouth open in shock, looked down at him, and gasped, "Eudos"?

He doesn't even remember my name, Eudes thought numbly, still trying to grapple with what he had done, and more importantly...why? This was when it came back to him, and he turned his head away from Bent, just as the warrior toppled from the saddle and Eudes, feeling the tug on the spear, released his grip, the sound of the first man he had ever slain striking the ground not even registering because he was looking for the Berserker. It took him a long heartbeat to locate him, but then he saw him, lying prone and sprawled across another body, a fellow Frank by the look of him, who was lying face up, and Eudes did notice that this man's eyes were open, though as he had observed, this did not mean anything. A wave of such despair washed through him at the thought that he had failed, that he had killed one of his own in order to save the life of the Berserker only to fail, all the strength drained from his legs, and he dropped to his knees. I, he thought numbly, am a dead man.

When Titus opened his eyes, it took him several moments to orient himself, although his first difficulty was in just trying to open his eyes, which seemed to be gummed shut, and without thinking, he lifted his right hand to pry them open. The bolt of pain that shot through him at this simple movement accomplished it for him, as his eyes shot open, the pain such that he did not even register the stinging sensation that came from several eyelashes that had stuck together being ripped out. If he had been asked to locate the pain, his reply would have simply been that it was everywhere, but after a couple of heartbeats, it resolved to the point where he pinpointed the location of the worst pain as down low on his right side, followed a close second by a pain that seemed to run along his left ribcage, an inch or two below his left nipple and radiating towards his back. This seemed to cause him the most distress breathing, he realized, while any kind of movement caused his right side to send the signal it was unhappy.

"Ah," a male voice that he did not recognize said, "you are awake. Praise be to God!"

Again, without thinking, Titus turned his head towards the voice, and this time, there was no mistaking that the knifing agony came from the back of his skull, which caused him to gasp, which in turn made his left side erupt in enough pain that caused him to cough, which quickly turned into a groan and ignited a fiery torment centered on his right side that he became nauseous...and this was the last thing he remembered of his first period of consciousness. The second time, two things had changed; it was not as difficult to open his eyes, and it was dark wherever he was, although not completely, there being either a candle or a lamp nearby. He also remembered not to make any sudden movement, turning his head slowly, and carefully towards the source of the light, which alerted someone, because he heard the creaking sound that indicated someone was standing up from a stool or chair, then the sound of shoes on a wooden floor as they crossed the room. I must be in Boulogne, Titus thought, which meant the town had been taken, but hard on the heels of that thought was all that had occurred to ensure that this had happened.

Before he could think this through any further, a figure suddenly appeared, looming above him, and he saw that it was a man, but he recognized the voice, which repeated cheerfully, "You are awake again! Praise be to God...again!"

The voice belonged to a man, a stranger that Titus had never seen before, but he did recognize the robes the man was wearing that identified him as a monk, which was odd to Titus, knowing that considering what Northmen and Danes did to any man of God they found, the likelihood of this monk having been allowed to live here in Boulogne was so low as to not merit consideration. Not, he realized, that this mattered at the moment.

"I am Brother Albertus," the monk, who, to Titus, appeared to be in his mid-thirties—judging from his teeth, which were in contrast to an otherwise youthful countenance—beamed down at him. "I have been caring for you since you arrived. And," he lowered his voice as he glanced around, "I can tell you, Father Rudolf told me many times how unlikely you were to survive!"

"F-father Rudolf?" Titus rasped, unable to recognize his own voice, which sounded to his ears like a frog that was being strangled, also realizing how parched and dry his mouth and throat were.

"Yes, Father Rudolf," Brother Albertus replied, sounding a bit cross to Titus. Suddenly, he looked concerned, and he asked anxiously, "Do you not remember who he is, my son?"

"N-no, I remember," Titus assured him. "I just don't remember him being with us in Boulogne." Before Albertus could reply, he thought to ask, "The town fell, didn't it?" Again, before the monk could say anything, the memory of what it cost came to him in a rush, and he did not try to hide his bitterness. "Lambertus, Sigemund, and Berwald are dead; I know because I saw them fall. And," he had to swallow twice, yet as dry as he was, he still felt the sting of tears, "my best friend Ranulf is dead." He looked at Albertus, and despite knowing this warrior only by his formidable reputation, the monk heard the hopeful tone in his voice. "What about Gozlin and Acfrid?"

While he had not been told the identities of the party who had been with this wounded Saxon, who, frankly, Albertus was astounded to see still among the living, expecting him to have expired several times during the period he was under the monk's care, he had asked questions of those who had been there, and he took a guess about this pair's identity.

"Were those the two men of your party who held off the Northmen pursuing you in the sewer?" Titus barely nodded, and Albertus was sorry to inform him, "I am afraid they perished down below, my son. But," he brightened, "surely you rejoice in knowing that they are now sitting at the right hand of our Father, honored by the angels of Heaven for their heroic act, along with your other friends. And," Albertus added with a grim satisfaction, "I was told that between them, they sent more than a dozen of those heathen unbelievers into the fires of Hell." Albertus suddenly realized something, and was about to correct the warrior who he was not sure how to address, because the Saxon had been in error about the fate of one of his comrades...or had he, really? Deciding it was better to get it out of the way, he adopted a gentle tone, "You mentioned your friend...Ranulf, yes?" Titus slightly moved his head again, and Albertus assured him, "He is not dead, my son." He held up a hand, seeing Titus' eyes widen, cautioning, "But that does not mean he might not be, soon. And," he warned, "even if he survives, he might never be the man you knew."

Titus had, in fact, been lifting his head, determined to get off his cot to go find Ranulf, trying to ignore the almost blinding pain that flashed through his skull, and he fell back, staring at Albertus as he demanded, "What does that mean?"

Instead of answering directly, Albertus asked, "What do you remember of that...fight? Or battle?" He gave a self-conscious smile. "I am not a warrior, nor do I pretend to be, so forgive me if I do not know how to refer to it."

"Either one," Titus replied absently. He did not say anything for a moment, then admitted, "I do not remember much, if anything, Brother Albertus." Titus knew that he could never explain why he did not remember, but he nevertheless tried to explain, "I have these...moments, when I am in battle, Brother. And when they come along, I...I don't remember anything afterwards. At least," he amended, "not much. Only bits and pieces."

"I have heard about your...moments," Albertus said quietly, deciding to use the same term that the Saxon had. Without thinking how the large warrior might take it, he gave a quiet laugh. "In fact, that is all the men who were there in Boulogne have been talking about, even now."

Titus frowned, temporarily forgetting the topic at hand.

"What do you mean, 'even now'?" he asked challengingly, as if Albertus was hiding something from him. "And this is the second time you referred to Boulogne as if we were somewhere else, but where would we be?"

"Why," Albertus replied in surprise, "in the Cell of Saint-Bertin, of course! You are here in our hospital."

This was almost too much for Titus' mind to comprehend, but he still had enough of his wits about him to understand that more time had passed than he had thought.

"Did they transport us here during the night?" he asked, and now Albertus was the one who had cause to hesitate as he realized that the Saxon was not likely to understand the circumstances.

"When do you think it is, my son?"

"The day after the battle?" Titus ventured, but the monk

heard the question in his voice.

"No, my son," Albertus shook his head. "You have been unconscious for three full days," he said gently. "You were moved here by wagon, along with the other wounded. Although," he brightened, "there were blessedly few of them, praise be to God!" Suddenly comprehending how this could be taken, Albertus added hurriedly, "Not that the sacrifice of you and your comrades is not a tragedy, nor that it is not appreciated by the Count. In fact," he leaned closer to Titus, dropping his voice as if he was sharing a great secret, "Father Rudolf himself told me and my fellow monks that Count Baldwin plans on giving you and your friends an ample reward for your bravery!"

There was a time when this would have been music to the ears of Titus of Cissanbyrig, but that had been before, before he had lost so many friends and seen so much suffering.

He changed the subject by pointedly asking, "You said that Ranulf isn't dead, but that he's badly wounded?"

For the first time, Albertus looked uncomfortable, and he hesitated before he replied, "Perhaps it is a bit too soon to discuss such matters, my son. You are still not out of danger, and upsetting you may hurt your own..."

"Tell me," Titus cut him off, making his voice as cold as he could manage under the circumstances. "Tell me what you meant that he may never be the same."

He saw the knob on Albertus' throat bob up and down as the monk swallowed, but instead of answering directly, he asked Titus, "You said you only remember bits and pieces. Do you remember what befell your friend?"

This forced Titus to consider, and he almost immediately wished he had not, because the image of Bjorn's ax striking Ranulf's helmet came rushing back, although what followed was more the memory of the sudden unleashing of his rage, and how the scene in his mind, of Ranulf collapsing on top of Lambertus, who had fallen to a spear thrust to the body a few heartbeats earlier, seemed to evaporate in a red mist that was always the precursor to the moment that the part of him that was the Berserker took control.

"He...he was struck on his helmet by a Northman with a bearded ax," he said slowly.

"Yes, he sustained a grievous injury," Albertus nodded, his voice solemn. "But the helmet did protect him somewhat."

Despite himself, Titus felt what could almost have been a grin tug at his lips, because it had been a long-running debate between the pair, as Ranulf insisted that the Frankish helmet, with its ridge that ran from front to back that served as the method by which the two pieces of the helmet were held together with rivets, was superior to the single piece helmet that Titus wore.

"While it saved his life," Albertus continued, "it did not prevent his skull from being fractured, along with a very long cut to his scalp that had to be sewn back in place." Now, the monk thought, comes the hard part. "But while he is conscious, or appears to be, he is unable to speak, or to follow simple commands."

"What do you mean he appears to be conscious?" Titus demanded.

"I mean," Albertus answered quietly, "that while his eyes are open, and they will follow someone as they move across the room, for example, he otherwise gives no indication that he is aware of his surroundings. Our most experienced healer, Brother Membresius, has extensive experience with battle wounds, and he said he has seen this kind of thing before. And," Albertus held out both hands, palms up in a gesture that Titus understood all too well, "it is in God's hands whether or not your friend regains his wits."

"What kind of monk has experience with battle wounds?" Titus asked scornfully. "He may not know what he's talking about!"

"Brother Membresius was not always a monk, my son," Albertus replied tightly, feeling defensive about a brother's reputation. "In fact, he was once like you, a man who carried a sword and slew the enemies of God, before he found his true calling."

Titus was still inclined to argue, but he realized that he was too tired; just this brief exchange had exhausted him.

Instead, he therefore asked, "Where is Ranulf now? Can I see him?"

"He is in Saint-Omer, where his wife is caring for him.

Brother Membresius gave his permission since there is nothing more that we can do for him. It is," he repeated, "in God's hands now."

Titus felt a stab of guilt, realizing that he had not asked about, nor had he thought about Yanna until this moment, and he asked the monk, "Brother, may I ask a favor?" Albertus nodded, although if Titus had been in better shape, he might have noticed the cautious expression on the other man's face, the monk guessing what the request would be. "Can you get a message to my..." suddenly, Titus stopped, understanding the awkward situation he was in, but he would not lie and call her his wife, saying instead, "...friend? She is in Saint-Omer as well. Her name is Yanna, and she..."

"Unless she is your wife," Albertus cut him off, "I am afraid that Father Rudolf would never agree to send me, or any member of our order, to this...woman."

Fighting an almost overwhelming urge to reach up and grab this monk by the throat, Titus did not because he recognized the futility of doing so; besides, he reasoned, I'd probably pass out before my hand touched his scrawny neck. Instead, he did not say anything, but turned his face away to stare at the wall, sending another kind of message to the monk.

Whether this was why, he would never know, but Albertus asked with a sigh, "Where can she be found?"

"She lives on the main road, a quarter mile from the northern wall. Her house is on the left hand side facing the town, and has a small garden in front of it."

"I cannot make any guarantees, my son," Albertus said honestly. "I cannot leave and you are not the only wounded man in my charge, but I will do what I can."

Titus thanked him, then said quietly, "I am very tired, Brother. I think I will sleep some."

Understanding, Albertus rose from the stool and exited the small chamber that was normally reserved for highborn patients, which the Count had ordered reserved for the Saxon, returning to the larger room where the rest of the wounded were being cared for, by Albertus, Brother Membresius, and two other monks. It was from one of these men that Albertus had heard about the Berserker's exploits, even as the fate of this warrior, Méliau his name, and whether he would keep his leg hung in the balance. Of the ten men who made their way into the town, only three lived, and of those, only the archer named Josse was unwounded, and of the other two, only the Berserker had a chance to survive *and* return to full strength to continue their service for the Count. While Albertus was not the most experienced among the monks, he had treated enough wounds to know that the kind of penetrating stab wound that the Berserker had suffered to his right side more often than not became corrupt, and that was a death he would not wish on any man, even a pagan, which was what he strongly suspected that the Berserker was; after all, he had not been wearing a cross under his tunic. Regardless of this evidence, what was clear was how highly regarded this strange Saxon was by their Count, so Brother Albertus' suspicions did not matter; what did was that he be seen to do everything in his power to help the Berserker recover.

Chapter Six

Uhtric's initial reaction when boarding *The Redeemer* was relief that he was a passenger, and not expected to sit at the bench of this, the largest ship in the Saxon fleet, although he took a great deal of pride that he had been there for the birth of the still-nascent idea concocted by their King, that the best way to combat the Northern invaders was to meet them on the terrain that was preferred by the pagans, the sea...and to defeat them. They had done so during the raid by Sigurd the Bold, and while there had not been any other opportunities since then, the King had not been idle, commissioning ships that were a compromise between the traditional Saxon design, with their wider beam and shorter length, but which made them ponderously slow when facing the sleek longships of the Northmen that could sail in knee deep water, and were far more maneuverable. These new ships were not the equal of the longships, but they were not hopelessly outclassed as they had been before, although Alfred had still been sure to augment Saxon numbers by capturing every longship he could find, and repairing those that were damaged. When Uhtric recognized the sleek lines of *Sea Viper*, which, to his disgust, he had learned had been renamed by the pious King as *Ærendgaest*, their word for Archangel, he felt a surge of affection mingled with pride, realizing that he still thought of it as *Sea Viper*, and that it was *his* ship.

He had been told by Lord Eadward that they would be leaving from Hrofescester immediately; instead, he ended up waiting for two days, although Eadward had no more idea why than he did, and the ship's master, named Ragnulf, was similarly in the dark. They got their answer on the third day, shortly after the departure of the Wiltun men back home, with the arrival of a member of the nobility, along with his entourage. Uhtric was in an alehouse inside Hrofescester that serviced the docks, engaged in what could only be described as a sulk at the thought of being left behind and unable to return home, although he consoled himself with the task he was being sent to perform, and how it was a virtual certainty that Leofflaed would forgive his extended absence since he would be returning with her brother; it never occurred to him, or to Lord Eadward for that matter, that Titus might demur on the offer to return home. A crewman of *Ærendgaest* entered The Happy Seafarer, which was run by neither a seaman nor anyone who could be described as happy under any circumstances, informing Uhtric that the party they had been waiting for had arrived, though he could not give their identity, other than to say they were clearly high ranking. With an exaggerated sigh, the one-eyed warrior drained his cup and indicated the crewman to lead the way, following him out of the alehouse and the short distance to where the ship was moored. Even from a distance, he could see the at least dozen servants, several of them unloading the wagon that had been pulled up to the quayside, and he could not stifle his groan.

"God's blood," he murmured to the crewman. "Who are we sharing this ship with? The King doesn't even bring this much baggage."

He got his answer when he was about twenty paces away and saw his first familiar face, and despite the circumstances, he felt his face split into a grin.

"Godric, you thieving bastard!" he called out, normally fighting words, but the warrior, a man of Alfred's bodyguard who had served with Uhtric on *Sea Viper*, responded with a grin of his own, striding towards Uhtric with his hand out. "What are you doing here?"

"Making sure you don't fall in and drown," Godric retorted.

"That only happened once!" Uhtric protested. "And that was when Einarr was making us oar dance!"

"Bah!" Godric gave him a shove. "So *you* say! I remember differently, you *burlofotr*."

The use of that term that they had been introduced to by Einarr and Dagfinn made them both laugh, but Uhtric quickly became serious.

"So, why *are* you here, and why are you coming with us?"

In response, Godric turned and pointed at the stooped figure with the shining bald head whose back was turned to them as he was helped up the plank onto *The Redeemer*.

"I'm escorting Lord Eardwulf," he explained.

"Where is he going?" Uhtric asked, thinking he knew; he was quickly proven wrong.

"He's going to Saint-Omer," Godric explained, which surprised Uhtric considerably, certain that the old nobleman, who was one of Alfred's longest and most trusted councilors, would be going to Paris to consult with the Frankish king, Charles the Fat.

What little knowledge Uhtric had of Frankish affairs meant that he considered this Count, an unfamiliar term to the Saxon, to be a minor nobleman, so he was hard pressed to understand why Lord Eardwulf wanted to meet with him. On the heels of this thought came another, though he dismissed it almost immediately; was King Alfred sending Lord Eardwulf with him because he was involved with the effort to bring Titus home? Any other thoughts in this direction were cut short when Lord Æthelweard saw them standing there.

"You two! Help get Lord Eardwulf and Father Æthelred's baggage aboard. Master Ragnulf says that the tide will be going out soon, and he intends to be on it! Quick now!"

As unusual as it was for Lord Eardwulf to be on *The Redeemer*, the fact that the King's personal chaplain would be accompanying them gave Uhtric a sense of even deeper unease, though he could not have articulated why. Nevertheless, he and Godric gave each other a resigned glance, and trotted over to the wagon to help the small army of servants and slaves shift the boxes and leather satchels that, from the feel of them contained scrolls of varying thicknesses, making Uhtric wonder if the Father could not go anywhere without a copy of the Scriptures. Whatever they were, they were loaded and stowed, and the men were already at the oars, *The Redeemer* shoving away from the dock shortly after midday, with Uhtric, Godric, and the half-dozen other men of Alfred's bodyguard, none of whom Uhtric knew by name but recognized, left to find a spot out of the way. There was no question that they would be allowed to share the tent where Lord Eardwulf was already installed, the flaps drawn to give him privacy, so Godric and Uhtric made their way to the bow, the only other place where there was ample room, ample being a relative term.

The oarsmen began stroking their way down the Medway, moving even more quickly aided by the outgoing tide, while the two warriors chatted quietly, talking about everything other than the thing that was most on their mind, the crossing of The Narrow Sea. On a large ship like *The Redeemer*, the risk was, while not nothing, minimized, but they had all heard the many stories of the ships that had been caught by sudden storms, and in their case, they had survived such a storm on *Sea Viper*. Thankfully, at least as far as they were concerned, they would be able to hug the coast, heading due east along the headland of Thanet that jutted out towards Frankia, then turn directly south, still hugging the coast, until they reached the most famous landmark in this part of the island, the white cliffs of Dover. Then, they would turn east again to head across the twenty miles of open water, and that would be when the praying began. Which, Uhtric thought idly as he watched the scenery slide by off the right side of the ship, means that it's a good thing that Father Æthelred is with us; surely the King's confessor had a special relationship with the Almighty! He could deny to himself that he was excited at the prospect of seeing his brother-in-law again, yet at the same time, he worried; how much had Titus changed? What had he been through the previous two years? Later, he would remember these thoughts and ruefully acknowledge that even in his wildest imaginings, he did not come close to the reality.

A week after the battle, Titus was strong enough to begin taking broth; the next day, he insisted that he was strong enough to get off his cot, which he did, but only after two attempts. His face glistened with sweat, but to Brother Albertus, the clearest sign of his distress was that when the monk reached out to steady him, the Saxon did not shake his hand off, giving him a grateful look instead, though he did not say anything. Ever so slowly, he made his way out of his private chamber into the larger room, where Méliau was fighting his own battle, having come dangerously close to losing his leg, but he was on the mend now, although it was still an open question whether he would be able to walk without some sort of aid.

"Berserker!" he called out when he saw the towering figure, although Titus was slightly hunched over, and the monk was huffing and puffing just as much as his charge from the effort of supporting him. "You," Méliau said cheerfully, "look like the turd I left in the bucket this morning!"

"And you think you look better?" Titus challenged, but with a smile, though it might have been a grimace.

With Albertus' help, he lowered himself down onto a stool that one of the other monks, seeing where the Saxon was heading, had hurried over to place next to Méliau's cot. The largest room in the hospital was now less than half full, but while all of the men present knew who Titus was, he did not recognize most of them, informing him that they were men of the *lantweri*, which made sense. None of them besides Méliau were *Eques*, so he confined himself to giving the men of the *Pedes* who he recognized a nod of recognition before turning his attention to Méliau, who was propped up with his back to the wall that his cot was placed against.

"It is good to see you, Berserker," Méliau said quietly. "I wanted to thank you in person, and I was worried that you would go and die on me before I could."

"Thank me for what?" Titus asked, though he suspected he knew.

Méliau gave him a searching look, then glanced up at Albertus, who was lingering nearby, glaring at the monk until Albertus got the hint and, with a hurt expression, drifted away.

Once he was a few cots away and involved with checking on another patient, Méliau asked quietly, "Do you not remember what you did?" When Titus shook his head but did not reply, the other warrior asked, "Was it the same thing that happened at Watten? And why you are called Berserker?"

Knowing there was no point in denying it, Titus nodded again, but he also was unwilling to delve into the matter, so instead he asked, "Have you heard anything about Ranulf?"

He did not expect that Méliau would have any useful information, so he was surprised when the warrior replied,

"Yes. Theutbald and Wala came to visit yesterday." Suddenly realizing how Titus might take it, he added quickly, "You were asleep, and they did not want to disturb you. But yes, they went to see Ranulf."

"And?"

Titus got a hint in the way Méliau suddenly became interested in his hands, which were laced together and in his lap, and he braced himself, but to his intense relief, Méliau replied readily enough, "He is still alive. But," his expression turned grim, "aside from that, there is not any change. Theutbald said it is like he looks at you, but he does not see you."

Titus had plied both Brother Albertus and Brother Membresius with questions, so he felt he was qualified to say, "Both Albertus and Membresius say that that is to be expected, that it takes head injuries much longer to heal. And," he admitted, "they say he may never get better. But Brother Membresius told me he knew of at least two men who suddenly got better, and one of them he witnessed himself! The man woke up one morning, and was able to talk and recognize people around him." Remembering the cautioning words he had received, he went on to acknowledge, "The Brother said that the man was not able to go back to his normal occupation. He was," Titus explained, "a smith who was kicked in the head by a horse. He could not be a smith anymore, but at least he got to see his children grow up."

"May God make it so with Ranulf," Méliau responded, with a quiet intensity that said more than the actual words. Thinking to get away from a potentially distressing subject, Méliau asked, "So, what do you know about everything that happened?"

Titus knew what the other man was doing, but he also was consumed with curiosity, since Brother Albertus had been singularly unhelpful, refusing to discuss it because, he claimed, it might harm his recovery.

"Only that we are back in Saint-Omer," Titus began, then corrected himself. "Or, back in the Cell of Saint-Bertin. Who is holding Boulogne for the Count? Did they keep the *lantweri* under arms?"

Méliau shook his head.

"Nobody is holding it, because there's nothing to hold," he explained grimly. "The Count ordered the entire docks and buildings along the river burned and razed."

Titus was surprised, but only mildly so, because there had been a great deal of discussion among the *Eques* about this very thing, and the consensus had been that, given all of the other commitments the Count had made, both in giving his word that the series of fortified towns that dotted Flandre would be under his protection, and the practical costs of making sure that his word meant something, holding Boulogne was a task that could only be accomplished by requiring the *lantweri* to remain under arms. Similarly to the *ceorls* of the Saxon *fyrd*, the Franks of the *servii* class made their livings as farmers or artisans and not warriors, and keeping them under arms was an expensive proposition, in more ways than one, especially with harvest season approaching. However, Boulogne was the largest port facility in this part of Frankia, but that also meant that it was likely, bordering on a certainty, that the Northmen would make a concerted attempt to take it back. No, Titus reflected in that moment, the Count was wise to do what he had done. Even if he denied the Northmen its use for a period of a few months, it was a blow.

"So the *lantweri* have been released?"

"Yes," Méliau nodded, then added offhandedly, "all but yours."

"Mine?" Titus frowned, confused. "What do you mean, 'mine'?"

Méliau shifted on his cot, suddenly realizing that perhaps he had made an error.

"You mean, you do not know?" he asked Titus.

"Know what?" the Saxon cried in frustration, and now Méliau was definitely regretting bringing anything up, but he also understood that he had to tread carefully.

"About Bent," he replied, then added carefully, "and what happened to him."

Titus' initial reaction was to stare as his mind tried to grasp what he thought the other man was saying.

"You mean," he asked dumbly, "he is dead?"

"So you do *not* know," Méliau breathed, wondering how

to frame it.

Deciding that the best approach was to plunge right in, he described what he, Josse, and the smith Gilo had witnessed from their spot hard against the wall next to the gateway, how, like every other man of the *Eques* who did not go off in pursuit of the fleeing Northmen, they sat there, enthralled by watching him, Titus the Berserker, slaughter any Northman who was foolish enough to try and stand up to his onslaught. Talking about it later, none of the three remembered seeing the young spearman of the *lantweri*, not until he played his part in the drama that was still the talk of the men of Baldwin's bodyguard, although he ultimately failed to stop Bent from flinging the spear at Titus' unprotected back.

"Wait." Titus held up a hand. "You are saying that Bent *tried to kill me*?"

Méliau nodded, saying honestly, "We thought he *did* kill you, because we saw him draw the spear back and prepare to throw it, but then that *lantweri* boy began moving, and," he shrugged, "our attention was on him. So when we looked back to where you had been and saw you lying there, we all thought that Bent had killed you."

"So," Titus said slowly, still trying to comprehend, "Bent is dead." Méliau nodded, and Titus asked, "What about Sigismund?"

"Sigismund tried to stop Bent, and he almost lost all the fingers of his left hand for his trouble," Méliau replied.

"By who?" Titus asked. "The *lantweri*?"

"No, by Bent. He pulled a dagger and chopped down on his hand when Sigismund grabbed his arm to try and stop him from throwing the spear."

Titus' head had already begun swimming from this period of time sitting up, but now it was so severe that he felt the need to grab the edge of the stool. It was at this moment that something else occurred to him.

"What did Count Baldwin do to the *lantweri*?" he asked, thinking that there was something he should do for this anonymous youngster, though he had no idea what it might be.

"Actually," Méliau spoke carefully, "there is a...disagreement between the Count and Lord Baudelius. The

Count wanted to release him to return with the other men from his village, but Lord Baudelius had him seized and put in irons. He is demanding a trial for him."

Titus' initial reaction was to become indignant; the idea that this youth would be punished for at least trying to save his life, especially when Titus and his men were the reason why Boulogne had fallen so cheaply in terms of lives, was deeply offensive to him. Nevertheless, almost as soon as this ran through his mind, he understood the deeper ramifications of what was taking place. It was no secret to anyone with eyes and a modicum of sense that, as the Count grew older and more confident, he deferred to Baudelius less, something that clearly irritated and offended the older nobleman. In fact, it had been Ranulf who had predicted that there would be some sort of confrontation between the two coming.

As usual, he had put it in his normal, earthy manner. "It's like the old bull and the young bull of the herd, deciding who gets to fuck the cows."

At the time, this had elicited some chuckles from the others gathered at Melisandre's, but it had been Titus who pointed out, "You know that depending on how you look at it, we could be considered the cows who are getting fucked."

"That," Ranulf replied after a deep belch, "is why I said it. We are *always* the cows!"

The chuckles had turned to roars of laughter, and the memory of that moment struck Titus with the same kind of force, and pain, as the stab to his vitals had...if he could have remembered it.

Unaware of Titus' musings, Méliau continued, "Lord Baudelius wanted to execute the lad straight away, but the Count refused to authorize it. Now?" He shrugged. "I have no idea where things stand. I have not heard anything for the last two days."

With this, Titus returned, this time without the help of Brother Albertus, back to his cot in his chamber, and even after he regained his breath, his head continued to spin, though not because of the exertion. Bent was dead, he kept repeating to himself, and as he did so, he started feeling a flicker of anger, not at the dead man, but at this unknown *lantweri* spearman, because Titus had long before resolved that, if anyone was going to kill that miserable bastard Bent, it would be him. And now, he had been deprived, and he was unhappy.

Going by the route that *The Redeemer*'s master had plotted, hugging the coast all the way to Dover before making the straight crossing of The Narrow Sea, Uhtric and the other passengers had been told to expect to be aboard ship for six days, weather permitting, although they would put in at night so that they could sleep on land, the normal method for Saxons. On the second day, they rowed past Sceapig (Sheppey), the island that, as every Saxon knew, had served as a base of operations for Danish raids thirty years earlier. Now part of Cent, the remnants of the Danish camp were visible as the ships rowed past, and Uhtric and Godric stood in the bow, watching silently.

The bodyguard broke the silence, saying quietly, "We've been hearing some things in Wintanceaster, Uhtric, and I wanted to talk to you about them."

"Things?" Uhtric echoed. "What things? And why haven't you said anything until now? We've been on this cow for the better part of two days!"

"Because it concerns Lord Einarr," Godric replied quietly. "I know you consider him a friend."

"And you don't?" Uhtric replied harshly. "I thought any question about his loyalty had been settled!"

"It has been," Godric protested. Then, realizing how this sounded, he amended, "Nobody questions his courage, and nobody questions his loyalty...to King Æthelstan. That's who the talk is really about, Uhtric."

This settled Uhtric down, though he still was cool towards Godric as he said, "Go ahead."

"The talk is that the so-called King of East Anglia and the Danelaw has been under a great deal of pressure by other Northmen to repudiate the treaty he made with Alfred." He paused, not particularly happy about how the conversation was going, but he felt it was important that he communicate to his former shipmate what was going on. "According to spies, Lord Einarr and Dagfinn disappeared from Lunden, and the rumor was that they were sailing to Frankia."

"Frankia?" Uhtric frowned, though not in a disbelieving manner; he had learned during their time together that the men who were part of the King's bodyguard were unsurprisingly much better informed about larger events than a warrior from Wiltun. "Any idea why?"

"No," Godric shook his head. "But there are some men who think it has to do with Sigfred the Úlfhédnar. Have you heard anything about what he might be up to?" Again, Uhtric shook his head. "Apparently, he took most of his ships from Boulogne and sailed up to Frisia, but nobody seems to know why. And," he added carefully, "some men think that Einarr was sent there to find out exactly what Sigfred is doing."

"What he's doing," Uhtric spat over the side, "is offering a hundred pounds silver for Titus' head, so I hope he's sucking Satan's cock in Hell right now!"

Godric laughed and slapped Uhtric on the shoulder.

"Hopefully, God is listening, because that's a happy thought!" Turning serious, he continued, "What the King is most concerned about is what Æthelstan is up to. As I said, he's under a great deal of pressure from his *Jarls* to repudiate the treaty and join forces with the Northmen in Frankia and elsewhere. Yes, he's held to the terms so far. But," Godric shrugged, "for how much longer?"

As troubling as this was to Uhtric, he also realized that there was precious little that he could do about it standing here on the deck of *The Redeemer*.

It was the next day, shortly before midday, when they were approaching the headland called Thanet by the Centishmen that a lookout shouted a warning about seeing several sails on the horizon to the northwest, back in the direction of the huge estuary of the Thames and Medway...back, Uhtric thought grimly, in the direction of Lunden. Knowing that there were no other Saxon ships that originated back in that direction, they could only have come from Lunden, or somewhere along the long coastline of the estuary. The initial reaction was for Lord Æthelweard, acting as the overall commander of this small fleet, to order the pace of the oarsmen to quicken, in an attempt to round the Thanet headland and turn south, thereby taking them away from Lunden and the Danelaw and deeper into Cent. There was, Ragnulf had assured the King's representative, several spots where they could put in, although that held its own risks.

"We can go a short distance up the Stour, which is south of Remmesgat (Ramsgate) in Pegwell Bay," Ragnulf had explained. "Depending on who these spawns of Satan are, they're likely to steer clear because of the sandbars and low tide bogs that are all over the place."

"Very well," Æthelweard said, though he was not happy at the idea of running and hiding, "let's do that."

Ragnulf held up a hand and cautioned, "There is a risk, Lord."

"Which is?" Æthelweard snapped, regretting yet another time his eagerness in volunteering for this duty.

"If we go up the Stour, and they figure out that's what we've done, they can bottle us up," Ragnulf explained. "And depending on whether there are other ships besides those four we can see, we may have to fight our way out."

Æthelweard silently mouthed an oath, then thought for a moment before asking, "When do we need to make a decision?"

Ragnulf rubbed his chin, staring at the landscape for a moment, before he said, "We're about a mile from the end of the headland where we turn south. Once we turn, it's about five more miles to the bay, which is about two miles across and almost as deep. And," he indicated the white line of the chalky bluff that was a much lower imitation of the famed white cliffs some twenty miles away, "the headland is like this all the way around, until we get to the bay, so there is no other place to put in." He thought for another heartbeat then said, "We'll decide as soon as we reach the northern side of the bay."

With this, there was nothing else to do except to relay the orders to the other four ships, which was accomplished in a rudimentary fashion by a series of colored pennants that were hung from the rear stay that ran up from the stern to the single mast, whereupon a crewman on each of the other four ships signaled their acknowledgement. From Uhtric's perspective, still in the bow with Godric, there was an air of tension that had him checking his *seaxe* Eagle's Claw, making sure that it slid easily from the scabbard. His longer sword was with his baggage, but as he had learned aboard *Sea Viper*, for the kind of fighting that was a feature of seaborne combat, the shorter, single-bladed *seaxe* was better suited for the closer quarters aboard ship. Otherwise, there was nothing they could do but wait and see what, if any, threat these strange ships posed. The crew of *The Redeemer* were not actually members of the King's personal bodyguard, but they were more skilled warriors than the normal complement of men who manned Saxon ships, and were paid accordingly. Uhtric was skeptical, but Godric had assured him that these men knew what they were about, while the men seated at the benches of the renamed *Sea Viper* and the other were of a similar quality, but it was what they were not that convinced Uhtric they could be trusted to put up a fight.

"And there's not one Centishman among them," Godric had assured him, reminding Uhtric once more that the King's guardsman had been with *Sea Viper* when they had been betrayed by Beorhtweald and the crew of *Dragon's Fang*.

That assurance alone put Uhtric more at ease; nevertheless, he still hoped that there would be no fighting at all. Despite the fact that he barely got his longsword, which he had named Dane Slayer, wet during the battle at Hrofescester, the circumstances of the death of Lord Eadwig haunted him, because he had been next to Eadward's father when they made their dash for the longships to cut off Hallsteinn's escape, and he had seen the expression on his lord's face just before he literally threw himself at the Northman leader, leaving him to wonder what he could have done differently to prevent his lord from doing that. The fact that Eadward was next to his father, protecting Eadwig's weak side did not matter to Uhtric, knowing from experience how difficult it is for a son who admires his father to see what others can see quite plainly, which in this case was that Eadwig was determined to make this his last battle. Uhtric became lost in his brooding, barely noticing the turn to the south, which also meant they turned more into the wind, rendering the single sail useless, and Ragnulf ordered it struck, relying on oar power now. After perhaps an hour, the lookout, who as was customary, was a youngster who was small and nimble enough to clamber up the mast to stand on the impossibly narrow platform, called something down to the master, who happened to be Ragnulf. Since the youth was facing the stern, Uhtric could not make out what he said, but he came to his feet nonetheless, peering back towards the stern himself, where he could see the masts of the four other Saxon ships, who were acting as a screen protecting *The Redeemer* from the strange vessels, but he could not see their sails beyond them, although he knew it was likely they had furled them as well.

"Let me go to the rear and see what's happening," Godric commented, waving an acknowledgement at Uhtric's request he share the information on his return.

Because *The Redeemer* was a Saxon-built vessel, and served as the King's personal flagship, there was a centerboard that was not present in Danish longboats, which Godric used to trot to the stern, though he was not there long, returning with a thoughtful frown on his face.

"The ships that appeared to be following us didn't round the headland. They kept sailing due east."

To Uhtric, this was good news, yet he could tell that Godric was troubled.

"That's a good thing, eh? That must mean they're heading to Frankia."

"They could be," Godric admitted. Then, he shook his head as he added, "But Ragnulf said that if they were heading for Boulogne, they would have turned south, and if they were heading for Frisia, they wouldn't have come in this direction at all. Besides, there's nothing much due east along the Frankish coast, except for the mouth of the Scheldt."

While this was slightly troubling, it did not concern Uhtric overly much; in fact, he was far more concerned about when they made their own turn eastward to cross The Narrow Sea. Although it was still somewhat early, Ragnulf gave the order to put ashore about a quarter mile from the mouth of the Stour, close enough that he could send their small boat upstream to replenish their fresh water supply, but not trapping them upriver in the event the strange ships came back. Grumbling good-naturedly about being expected to do so, he helped erect the shelters for Lord Eardwulf, who barely acknowledged the presence of anyone save Lord Æthelweard and Father Æthelred, the latter with whom he had the most congress, huddling with the priest as they argued over one of the scrolls, while a scribe who was part of the old nobleman's entourage took copious notes, as Uhtric recalled that this was at the behest of King Alfred, who had what most of his unlettered subjects considered an obsession with recording every event, great and small in his kingdom. Once camp was made, he became bored trying to listen in on their back and forth, hoping to hear something, anything, that might give him a clue about why these two men were on *The Redeemer* with him. He had learned from Godric that this Baldwin was not a minor member of Frankish nobility, like a Thegn; from what he could tell, a Frankish Count was essentially the same as an Ealdorman, who ruled over a territory that was granted to him by the King, in this case Charles the Fat, who, Uhtric would be the first to admit, the Saxon would dearly love to see in person to determine how accurate the nickname was. Still, he thought it odd that they would be going on this moderately perilous journey, especially Lord Eardwulf; any kind of journey could be dangerous for the elderly.

Finally, Uhtric got up from his spot by the fire and began walking along the beach, completely unaware of the fact that it was on this very beach, several centuries earlier, that the Roman general Caesar led two of his Legions ashore, or that in the ranks of one of those Legions was the ancestor of his brother-in-law and best friend who bore that ancestor's name, his size and strength...and the dark gift that earned them renown among their fellow warriors. For a moment, as the sun slid below the horizon, he unwittingly stood at the very spot where Titus Pomponius Pullus stood in the ranks of the First Century, Second Cohort of the famed 10th Legion, but when he felt a shiver go up his spine, he put it down to the drop in temperature and the stiffening breeze. After a moment, he turned and wandered back to the camp, where Godric and the other men of the bodyguard were gathered, about to eat the evening meal.

"At least I don't have to stand guard shift," Uhtric laughed to himself, wisely murmuring this before he got within earshot of the others.

Tomorrow, he thought, we cross The Narrow Sea; by the

time he fell asleep, he had completely forgotten the strange ships.

On that same day, and in the evening, Father Memberius removed the sutures from Titus' side, but despite cautioning the warrior that he should stay there overnight, this week of inactivity after he regained consciousness was the longest time he had spent prone, and he insisted that he was ready to be released. What he did not say was that this period of enforced idleness also reminded him of the time he was chained to the mast of Leif Longhair's ship in Lunden, a time he did not like thinking about. Walking the two miles to Saint-Omer was out of the question, but Brother Albertus made arrangements with one of the servants who lived in Saint-Omer and was responsible for hauling supplies from the town to the monastery to give Titus a ride, and the monk escorted his former patient to the cart, carrying Titus' helmet, armor and Wyvern's Fang for his charge. During their time together, Titus had become fond of the monk, and his solicitude and obvious worry for the Saxon he found endearing, and touching in equal measure.

None of this was something that Titus would betray, of course, but he did elbow the monk in the ribs as he said with a grin, "I don't remember my mother, Brother Albertus, but I cannot imagine that she would fuss over me as much as you have."

Albertus reddened, but he replied proudly, "You are the most seriously injured man I have ever had in my care, Titus my son, so I am just happy to see you on the mend!"

"So am I," Titus replied fervently.

Then, while he did not really need it, he allowed Albertus to help him up onto the bed of the open-ended cart, but he was forced to scoot back farther because his legs were too long and his feet would drag on the ground otherwise. On an impulse, Titus offered his hand to the monk, which Albertus took, a solemn expression on his face as they shook hands.

Leaning forward, Albertus whispered, "And do *not* let Otran here convince you to hand him any silver. He has been paid already, and quite handsomely!"

Privately, Titus was not so certain about this; he had seen

just how parsimonious monks could be, and he knew that what a monk like Albertus would consider "handsome" payment would be viewed by the recipient of that payment in quite a different light. The fact that he did not have his coin purse with him meant that it was not an issue anyway. The jolt of the cart starting to move caused Titus to gasp, but he pointed at Albertus in a manner that the monk understood was a command to stop moving towards him, the pointing turning to a wave.

"Be sure to send for me if you become feverish!" Albertus called out, the third or perhaps the fourth time he had issued this reminder. "And avoid...

"Yes," Titus cut him off. "I know! I need to avoid sudden movements for the next week!"

And with that, the cart reached the gateway, exiting through it as Titus nodded to the man of the *Pedes* who was part of the permanent garrison that protected this cell of the abbey, who watched him with curiosity and a bit of caution as the cart rattled down the road, heading south towards Saint-Omer. Titus passed the time looking at the scenery, such as it was, which consisted of a scattering of buildings consisting of a farmhouse and perhaps a shed or, in the case of a more prosperous farmer, a barn that was separate from the house. Just as with Wiltscir, and in fact all of Wessex and Angle Land, most Frank *servii* were too poor to afford an extravagance like a separate barn, the animals sharing space in the farmhouse with the family. This was how Titus had lived, but even by these mean standards, Titus and his sisters lived in abject poverty as the children of a one-hide *ceorl*, the lowest requirement to be considered a free Saxon. Now, as he looked around in the growing twilight, he felt a stab of envy at what he saw, thinking, I would have thought I had died and gone to Heaven if I was able to live in a house like that when I was growing up.

While he could not turn around comfortably to see where they were, he could tell by the landmarks they were approaching the cluster of houses that were just outside the northern walls, one of them belonging to Yanna, and he briefly considered telling the cart driver to take him into the town to where Ranulf lived, but quickly discarded it. Yanna and Emilde had become good friends, with Yanna helping Ranulf's wife with their babe, so she would have undoubtedly been to see Ranulf this day; besides, he did not want it getting back to Yanna that she was second on his list of people to see. The carter drew up in front of her house, where the door was closed but the shutters were open, so he saw her shadow through the linen curtain that he had bought for her, an extravagance that kept the bugs out but was semi-opaque, and he felt his heart start to thud heavily against his ribs just at the sight of her shape. He took his time climbing out of the cart, ignoring Otran who, while he did not hold out an outstretched palm, still looked at him expectantly, then muttered under his breath when Titus looked pointedly away from him, pretending instead to be involved with dragging his equipment off the cart. Slapping the reins, the single mule moved away at a trot, and Yanna must have heard the noise, because he was still a pace away from the door when it opened, and he saw her there, framed in the doorway. Unbidden, he felt the tears come rushing up to push against the back of his eyes, while her own eyes began to shine, her full lips turning up in a smile, and he was sure that he could never love her more than he did in this moment.

She proved him wrong when, rather than rushing to him, or crying out, she said simply, "I've made that stew that you like, with the pork, and I just baked two loaves. I suppose you're hungry."

"You," he said fervently, "have no idea."

And he could tell that she knew he was not just talking about food.

After they ate, and he learned that, while his spirit was oh so willing, his body was still not ready for making love, they instead lay together, her head on his right shoulder instead of his left since the cut along his left ribcage was still so tender, and he told her about their infiltration of Boulogne, then moving through the sewer; in general terms, of course. He did not mention the wolves, which naturally meant that this was the first thing Yanna brought up, though she did so carefully.

"Theutbald and Wala came to visit the day after the Count returned to Saint-Omer," she began, feeling him stiffen, not much, but enough she knew he was alert. She kept her voice neutral as she continued, "They brought me a gift."

"A gift?" Titus frowned, not sure he liked where this was going, though he had no idea why. "What kind of gift? And why?"

"Do they need a reason to bring the Berserker's woman a gift?" she asked teasingly.

"If they know what's good for them, they do," he growled, but she heard the humor in his tone.

Nevertheless, she hesitated a heartbeat, then said, "They brought me three pelts."

"Pelts?" Titus echoed, but with a guarded quality.

"Wolf pelts," she continued. Then, she sat up and propped herself on one elbow so she could look down at her man, trying to keep her eyes from fastening on the fresh scar that ran from the middle of his ear to the corner of his eye just above his beard, thinking that, if anything, it made him even more attractive, though she could not have said why this was the case, just that it was. "Is there any reason they would bring me three wolf pelts?"

She was disappointed that Titus did not fall for it, instead countering immediately, "Are you saying they didn't *tell* you why they brought them to you?"

Knowing that she was outmaneuvered, she sighed, "No, I'm not saying that. They did tell me. You killed these wolves?"

"Isn't that what they said?" he asked, smiling now.

"Yes," Yanna answered crossly, "but I want to hear it from you! How did you manage to kill three wolves?"

"I didn't," Titus replied, waited a heartbeat, then grinned. "I killed four."

She slapped him playfully on the arm, and he gave a mock groan, crying out, "Is this how a hero should be treated? Beaten by his own woman? And when he's already wounded at that?"

"If he tries to be clever when he's not," she shook a finger at him, "then he deserves it!" Turning serious, she said, "Now, tell me about these wolves. And why did you go find trouble with a pack of wolves?"

"I didn't!" he protested. "I didn't go looking for them; they just found me." His smile faded as he began thinking about it, and he decided to tell the truth, or at least part of it. "You know about Sigfred, the Northman?" Naturally, she nodded. "And you know that he put a price on my head." This time, she was unhappy, but she still nodded. He debated for an instant, then realized that if she did not already know, she would soon enough, so he continued, "He raised the bounty on my head. But," he hurried on in an attempt to avoid the details, "he's nowhere near here. The Count's spies were right. He and most of his men are up in Frisia, so he's far away. And," he assured her, "he's got bigger things on his mind than me."

His hope that Yanna would be more interested in learning what Titus knew about why Sigfred was in Frisia lasted only long enough for her to ask, "How much is he offering for your head?"

"It's...a fair amount," he admitted, but she was not thrown off by his evasion, demanding to know the exact amount. He took a breath, then said, "He's offering a hundred pounds in silver."

This brought her bolt upright, the cover falling away from her breasts, forgotten as she stared down at him with wide eyes, gasping, "*A hundred pounds?*"

"Well," he joked mildly, "when you say it like that, I suppose it *is* a lot."

"Titus," she shook her head with such vigor that her hair, which was a rich, lustrous brown with tints of red that he adored, flew around her face, and despite the subject, he felt a stirring in his groin. "That's more than 'a lot'! That's a *fortune*! For that much money, you will have to watch your back from other Franks as much as from any Northman or Dane!" She saw his expression alter, turning hard, but while she still believed that there were Franks who would succumb to the temptation created by such a vast sum, she did allow, "At least Bent is dead. He would be the one I consider most likely to try and stab you in the back for that much."

"Are you mad?" Titus scoffed, but he was grinning. "He would have done it for a *denier*." The grin did not vanish, but it changed, becoming something that Yanna had never seen on her lover's face, a cruelness that, as much as she loved him, sent an involuntary shiver up her spine. "But that whorespawn shit licker is dead now, and he's burning in Hell."

Proving that she had not been diverted, Yanna returned to the original subject. "About these wolf pelts. You mentioned Sigfred as if there is some sort of connection. Why?"

Titus stifled his groan of frustration, and he did not answer immediately, trying to choose his words carefully.

Finally, he began, "Do you know what they call Sigfred?" She shook her head, and he said, "Sigfred the Úlfhédnar. Do you know what that means?" Another shake of her head, and he explained, "It means 'Wolf Warrior,' I suppose is the best way to put it." Suddenly, he was inspired to point at himself. "They call me Berserker, yes?"

"Yes," Yanna agreed, "but you said you do not care for that name."

"I don't," Titus answered, then surprised himself by adding, "at least, I didn't. Now, I suppose I've learned to...accept that that's how men will view me, and," he shrugged, "it has its uses. But in the Danish tongue, the word for bear is the root of the word for Berserker, so what it means is basically 'Bear Warrior'." Realizing this was not enough, Titus spent the next few moments explaining the cult of warriorhood devoted to the spirit of the bear, although he did not dwell overmuch on what it took to be initiated into the cult, mainly because, once he had learned about it, he understood why Einarr, who had failed his year-long trial, had been so offended at Titus being awarded the nickname. He finished by explaining, "The Úlfhédnar are their other spirit animal cult, and it's similar to the Berserkers, but they're devoted to the wolf, and what men say is that Sigfred completed their initiation to earn that title."

Yanna did not reply immediately, regarding her lover thoughtfully, so that Titus, who recognized that look, was not altogether surprised when she said flatly, "You *want* Sigfred to know that you killed four wolves on your own...don't you?"

"Yes," Titus answered simply. "I do."

"Won't he consider that to be a challenge to him? That you are taunting him?"

"He might," Titus was forced to admit. "But I think it will also make him more cautious." He hesitated, then decided it was time for full honesty. "Especially once he hears about what happened at Boulogne. I mean," he added quickly, "what I did there."

"I knew what you meant," Yanna replied, but she was still thinking, and Titus braced himself for her to bring up something else he had not considered, something she did with annoying regularity. "But it is still a risk, that he will consider this an insult and a challenge." Titus opened his mouth to argue the point a bit more, but before anything came out of his mouth, she added briskly, "But I believe you are right. Between what you did killing those wolves, and then at Boulogne, he is going to be cautious about doing anything to you."

Titus had been prepared to talk more about the Úlfhédnar's presence in Frisia and the rumors about what he was doing up there, but decided against it now that Yanna was in agreement. Consequently, he finally brought up the other subject he had been dreading, for different reasons.

"What about Ranulf?" he asked quietly. "Is what I heard from the monks true? That he's lost his wits?"

"Is that what they say?" Yanna, who had finally settled back down next to Titus, sat back up, clearly angry. "Is that what those stupid, stupid men who think they know so much say?" Before Titus could respond, she shouted, "How would they know? Do you know how many times they have come to check on Ranulf since they threw him out of their precious hospital? *None!*" This got her up off the bed, and she began pacing in the small space available, arms folded against her breasts as she scowled down at the floor. Wisely, Titus said nothing, just watched her going back and forth until, finally, in a softer tone she said with a sigh, "But they are not wrong, not completely. He cannot feed himself, he cannot control himself, and Emilde must clean him up. All he does is watch her as she moves around the room, but at first, he could not move his head, and now he turns it to watch her, and he can move his right hand some."

Not knowing what else to say, Titus tried to sound optimistic, reminding Yanna, "It hasn't been that long since he was wounded, my love. So any progress is good progress, isn't it?"

"I suppose," she sighed, coming back to the bed. "I just worry about Emilde and baby Amis. Who will take care of them now?"

"You know that I will," Titus replied, without any hesitation, and for that he received a grateful smile and a kiss.

All that Titus could say later was that he was absolutely sincere when he said it, but neither of them knew that, even then, his future, and hers, was about to be upended yet again.

In the aftermath, the one thing that Uhtric and Godric agreed about was how, if this had occurred before their service aboard *Sea Viper* and their training by the group they referred to as "Alfred's Danes," the results of the sudden attack by four longships might have turned out quite differently. However, neither of them could deny, nor could anyone present, that no matter how quickly they responded, or how well things turned out, they had been caught by surprise, early the next day after they set sail from their camp at the mouth of the Stour. As they learned, the four longships had only sailed east long enough to get out of sight, then turned south to parallel the coast, but several miles offshore, and as the Saxons of Alfred's first attempt at a navy had learned, Danes and Northmen had no compunctions about spending the night at sea. This did not mean they spent the dark hours resting, however, instead moving southward several miles, so that when the Saxons resumed sailing and their lookouts watched to the north and east, not only were the longships able to get closer than they should have because they were approaching from the opposite direction than the Saxons expected, they had the stiff morning breeze filling their sails. What was not clear was whether these raiders recognized *The Redeemer* as the Saxon king's flagship, or they assumed that, being the largest ship it would provide the most plunder, but what was beyond argument was that all four enemy ships pointed directly for *The Redeemer*, surrounding it so quickly that *Ærendgaest* and the other four ships, which had been trailing the flagship in a semicircular protective screen from the expected direction of any attack, could not reach *The Redeemer* in time to interpose themselves between the attackers and their flagship. Surrounded as quickly as they were, in some ways, it made matters straightforward, and to his credit, Thegn Æthelweard did not hesitate to respond.

"King's Guard, all but Godric to me here at the stern! We must protect Lord Eardwulf and Father Æthelred! Godric, you command the left side oarsmen!" He was pointing with his *seaxe* as he spoke, and he shifted it slightly to point at the one-eyed warrior from Wiltun. "Uhtric, you command the steerboard side, but wait for my order!"

Despite his surprise, Uhtric did not hesitate, shouting down to the men on the benches lining the right side of the ship, "All right, boys, stay on your benches, but make ready!" Suddenly realizing that he had not paid attention to the arrangement of the men who comprised the crew, he asked, "How many of you have spears?"

To his intense relief, every other man, fifteen total, raised their hands; more importantly, they were distributed evenly on every other bench, which told him that this was not random. He did not bother glancing over his shoulder to Godric's side, both because he was certain that the arrangement would be the same, and because it was not his concern. Among the many things he had learned as a man of *Sea Viper*, which was how he would always think of that ship that, even now, was rowing at full speed from off their left stern, being part of a good crew meant trusting your fellow shipmates when it came to doing their jobs; the second was why he had asked about the spears, because their period of greatest utility was in the moments when an enemy crew was trying to board, the extra reach the spear provided crucial in fending off an attack. Once they managed to get aboard, that was the time for the *seaxe*, or in the case of Northmen, an ax, which they actually favored for shipboard combat; and, as Uhtric had seen during the fight that ended with Titus' actions saving the crew before being struck in the head and falling overboard, then saved by Einarr who dove overboard to save Uhtric's best friend, it was an effective weapon. The Berserker, for that was how Uhtric thought of him in those moments, as if he was not Titus but another man or being, had snatched up an ax and used it to devastating result during that fight, and since that time, Uhtric had begun training with an ax as well, though he did not carry one. However, if the chance arose, he would not hesitate in grabbing one, preferably from the hands of a dead Northmen.

"Ship oars!"

This order came from Ragnulf, who by prior agreement and custom, maneuvered the ship, taking control of the steering oar himself, the oarsmen on both sides obeying instantly by pulling the oars in, doing it earlier than some masters would because the loss of mobility was instantly felt by all of them, including Uhtric, feeling the large ship settling into the water under his feet. However, this was by design, because there were no circumstances under which *The Redeemer* could either outrun or outmaneuver the sleek ships that were knifing through the water in their direction, so the time could be better spent in other ways.

"Shields!" Lord Æthelweard bellowed, and the men lifted their shields from the strake, followed immediately by his order. "Brace!"

Everyone, including Uhtric, grabbed for something; in his case, it was the aft mast stay, but because his attention was naturally on the side of the ship for which he was responsible, he did not see that the longship on the opposite side, its steersman seeing that there would be no opportunity to maneuver so that his vessel was turned parallel but only a matter of two or three feet from the side of *The Redeemer* and with their higher speed able to shear off several oars, instead did not turn at the last instant, so that its dragon prow slammed into the side of the larger Saxon craft, striking *The Redeemer* about midway between mast and stern. The blow was massive, but the oaken timbers that, in future centuries would become famous the world over, withstood the force without buckling, although more than one man, despite bracing themselves, was thrown off of their feet. Uhtric was one of them, but he was to suffer a further indignity because, just as he scrambled back to his feet, the leading enemy ship on his side slammed into *The Redeemer*, but at a shallower angle so that it essentially caromed off and slid several feet towards the bow, gouging the timbers of the Saxon ship. For a second time in as many heartbeats, Uhtric found himself falling to the deck, though he managed to regain his footing just in time to see a bearded Northman with several arm rings, wearing a helmet that shielded his eyes like a mask and wielding a long-handled, double-bladed ax in his right hand, with a round shield painted in the colors of black and red, with the black as a background and the red in a spiral pattern, attempt to leap upward from the side of his ship right next to the snarling dragon's head to land on the side of *The Redeemer* that was at least two feet higher and perhaps four feet away.

One of the oarsmen armed with a spear, timing his thrust perfectly, met the Northman at the top of the arc of his leap, and while the warrior did an admirable job of bringing his shield up to block the thrust, the opposing force from the spear thrust that struck just next to the iron boss stopped his momentum, and he fell backward, knocking two other Northmen who were trying to scramble aboard backward and down into their vessel. The Northmen on the opposite side used their oars to swing the rear of their ship closer to *The Redeemer*, so that it finally was parallel to the larger vessel, whereupon the attempt to board began in earnest. This was when Uhtric saw the third Northman ship, which had seemingly been hanging back but in fact was waiting to slide up to the left of the first vessel, placing itself so that the stern was even with the mast of *The Redeemer*, move into position. Within the span of perhaps fifty heartbeats, the large Saxon ship was completely surrounded by the four enemy vessels, Uhtric being struck by the thought that this was very similar to how a pack of hounds attacked a bear. Hard on the heels of that was another; this would be a good time for another "bear" to be present, but even as this ran through his mind, he was moving towards the bow, *seaxe* in one hand, shield in the other, arriving barely in time to assist a spearman who had just been knocked backward, falling back onto his bench so heavily that his shield was out of position as a Northman, this one with flaming red hair and a shortened spear that some warriors used for shipboard combat, pulled his arm back in preparation to thrust it into the oarsman's chest.

Uhtric did not have time to think, essentially throwing himself at the Northman while leading with his *seaxe*, and Leofflaed would have insisted that God was truly with him because it was the sloppiest thrust he had executed since he was a pimply faced lad and using nothing but the strength of his arm, yet the point somehow went straight and true, burying itself in the armpit of the Northman, his head whipping around in astonishment at Uhtric and dying in that state, his last thought being, where did he come from? Twisting the blade, Uhtric used his shield, putting his shoulder hard up against it as he slammed into the dying Northman with enough force to send him staggering backward and blocking another of his comrades, this warrior armed with a sword, from dropping down from the high side of the Saxon ship down onto a bench. With nowhere to go, this warrior was teetering on the edge, faced with the choice of dropping back down into his ship or shoving his dying comrade aside. He did not hesitate, giving his comrade, blood now pouring out of his mouth, a brutal kick that sent him tumbling down into the bottom of the ship facedown in the filthy water that was a combination of spray from the sea and piss from the crew. Knowing he could not hesitate, Uhtric was already moving, and was consequently in position to meet the sword-wielding Northman, even as other enemies were making their own leaping attempts to board on either side of the pair. Deliberately shutting out the frenzied movement all around him, Uhtric was in a perfect position to block his opponent from dropping down into the ship, earning a snarled series of curses, some of which the Saxon understood, but he quickly learned that there was a disadvantage in his proactive move, because his foe effectively had the high ground up on the side of *The Redeemer*. The Northman rained down blow after blow with his sword, and in such rapid succession that Uhtric could not even contemplate an offensive move of his own, feeling his left arm growing tired from the unusual posture of having to hold his shield higher than normal. There was a great deal of power behind the blows, and Uhtric was further hampered by the fact that he could not see his foe's face, especially the eyes, which was crucial to the chances of seeing another day, so it was more out of desperation than any real plan that he lashed out with his *seaxe*, aiming for the narrow space under the Northman's shield, his foe holding it lower than normal because of Uhtric's position.

Somehow, even without aiming, the point of Uhtric's *seaxe* struck the Northman just above his left ankle, and while it was not a particularly damaging blow, the Northman howled in pain and instinctively shifted his weight to his right leg as he lifted his injured leg in a reflexive and understandable act. Uhtric did not hesitate, stepping forward despite the fact that it was on the back of the Northman he had just slain, feeling the body shifting under his weight and unconsciously compensating for it as he shot his fatigued left arm forward, striking the Northman's shield with his own. Without the stability of both feet on the four-inch-wide edge of *The Redeemer*'s side, Uhtric heard his foe give an alarmed shout, then he was gone, falling backward and down into the gap between the enemy ship and *The Redeemer* with a tremendous splash that was audible even over the shouting and other din of the fighting that was now taking place along the entire length of the Saxon ship, as the crews of the Northmen vessels made their attempt to take the Saxon flagship. Uhtric took this moment for a brief glance about, looking for any trouble spots, but within a heartbeat, he knew that the fight, while not over, was definitely won, as the *Ærendgaest* and the other ships had arrived, and were now on the opposite sides of the four enemy vessels, surrounding them in an outer ring of Saxon wood and iron. If he had thought to do so, he would have barely reached the count of a hundred before the Northmen broke off their attempt to take *The Redeemer*, intent on escaping while leaving their dead and wounded behind.

"Let them go!" Lord Æthelweard bellowed over and over, which both Godric and Uhtric began repeating, grabbing their men to break off their attack.

While Uhtric understood that this was the right decision, that forcing these Northmen to choose between fighting to the death or a life of slavery by keeping them engaged, it did not sit well with him, and he could see that Godric and the other men of Alfred's bodyguard felt the same. The raiders had barely set foot on the ship's stern, and Lord Eardwulf and Father Æthelred had not even emerged from the shelter they shared, while the highest concentration of dead and wounded Northmen was from around the mast forward. Naturally, no prisoners were taken, the wounded men having their throats summarily cut, although Uhtric surreptitiously allowed the three Northmen he dispatched to clutch their weapon in one hand, although his boot was on their wrist as a precaution. All told, out of about two hundred warriors spread among their four ships, the Northmen lost twenty-six of their own, while the cost to the Saxons was astonishingly light; four men from *The Redeemer* died, one of them a few hours after the fight, with another three Saxons wounded seriously enough that they would not be able to man the oars. Among the other four ships, five men died, though one of them drowned when he slipped leaping from the side of his ship into one of the Northmen's vessels, with as many wounded, though none of them were from the *Ærendgaest*. Afterwards, it was also agreed that this had been a foolish venture on the part of the Northmen, but what troubled Uhtric, which was shared by Lord Æthelweard, Godric, and the other men of Alfred's bodyguard was how the Northmen fled due north, back in the direction from which they had come.

"They're going back to Lunden," Alfred's Thegn had said, his tone grim at the implication. "That's the only place where they can recover and replace their crews."

Thinking of Einarr, Dagfinn and the rest of Alfred's Danes, Uhtric interjected, "That doesn't mean that Guthrum is involved, Lord. They may lie and say we attacked them without provocation when they get there and hope that Guthrum believes them."

"That's true," Æthelweard allowed grudgingly. He hesitated, then pointed out, "But it's also true that Guthrum *might* be behind this. It's no secret that he's been under a lot of pressure from his own *Jarls* to break the treaty."

This was also something that could not be denied, so Uhtric did not even try.

In a subtle move, Godric changed the subject by asking, "It's still early, Lord. Are we going to keep sailing?"

Rather than answer directly, Æthelweard turned to Ragnulf, and asked the shipmaster, "What say you, Ragnulf?"

The mariner did not reply immediately, examining the men, most of whom were sprawled on their benches catching their breath and excitedly recounting their exploits to their comrades, who were barely listening because they were doing the same, then turned his attention to the coastline barely a mile off to their right, while Father Æthelred moved among the slain, who were now arrayed on the centerboard, murmuring the prayers for the dead. To Uhtric's eye, there was absolutely nothing distinguishing about the area: a strip of golden beach, then the green of the Centish countryside, with no variation in the form of hills, or even forests.

Ragnulf broke the silence, saying slowly, "We're about a mile north of Addelam (Deal). There's a good anchorage there, and we can put the dead ashore and at least give them a proper burial instead of at sea." There was a ripple of disapproving muttering from the men around him, but Ragnulf was uncowed, asking bluntly, "Do you want to keep sailing as their bodies start to stink, then dump them overboard anyway? Where would you rather put them? In the ground? Or?" He jerked a thumb eastward to the open sea, but said nothing else.

This ended the argument, the small fleet rowing to the village of Addelam, a miserable collection of weather-beaten huts, with a dozen small fishing vessels pulled up above the high tide line and turned upside down. By midday, the ships were anchored, and parties of volunteers composed of the close friends of the dead crewmen from each ship went ashore to bury their fallen comrades, accompanied by Lord Æthelweard, Godric, Uhtric and a half-dozen bodyguards. Addelam, which was smaller than Wiltun, was large enough for a village priest, a scrawny, underfed and filthy man with a wandering eye that meant Uhtric was not sure where he was looking, while his church looked to Uhtric as if it had begun life as a stable, and it smelled as bad inside, but there was a wooden cross against the wall opposite the door, and a wooden lectern that was clearly two crates cobbled together. What mattered was the presence of the graveyard adjacent to the church, and while some of the surly villagers looked on with an air that communicated that their interest was based only in this as a break from the boredom and monotony, the crewmen dug one large grave. It took some persuasion on the part of Lord Æthelweard to coax Father Æthelred from *The Redeemer* to officiate the burials, the King's personal chaplain insisting that he needed to stay with Lord Eardwulf. Only after Lord Æthelweard informed the cleric that the village priest clearly had a woman did Æthelred deign to get into the small boat to be rowed ashore.

"How did you know that would work?" Uhtric asked the

Thegn as they stood a short distance away from where the cleric made his preparations for the burial rites.

"I overheard him telling Lord Eardwulf about how it's a sin for a priest to take a woman," Æthelweard confided, giving the other man a rare grin.

"*Cum lā*," Uhtric exclaimed. "Every priest I've ever met has a woman. Or," he grinned and gave the Thegn a nudge with his elbow, "a 'cook'."

Æthelweard chuckled at this but said, "There are men of the clergy who believe that to truly be a man of God, they can't have any congress with a woman." Using his head to nod at the cleric, he added dryly, "And the good Father there is one of them."

The bodies, hastily cleaned up and wrapped in their cloaks, were lowered into the ground into the large pit that allowed them to be laid side by side, as those closest to each of them stood at the foot, heads bowed as Father Æthelred intoned the words that none of them understood yet mouthed anyway. By the time they had finished, the rain had begun falling...and it would continued to fall for the next two days, further delaying their progress in reaching Flandre.

Two days after Titus returned to Yanna's cottage, he felt strong enough to make the relatively short walk into Saint-Omer to where Ranulf and Emilde lived, in a small dwelling just inside the northern wall that had once belonged to a grain merchant who had been slain in a raid on one of the coastal towns, where he had been buying a consignment of grain. His widow had chosen to return to Paris, where she was from originally, and Ranulf's pay as a member of the Count's bodyguard was sufficient to support his small family without Emilde having to take in work. This was something that Yanna refused to stop doing; she worked as a seamstress and a laundress, and despite Titus' ability to support her, she insisted on continuing to work, something that aggravated Titus, while at the same time was a source of secret pride for him, admiring her stubborn independence that reminded him of his oldest sister. They took their time on the walk, Titus having to stop twice to rest, but he could tell he was regaining his strength, though no matter how quickly it came back, Yanna would say tartly, it would never be fast enough for him. Which, he thought ruefully as he leaned against a tree that provided shade for the yard of one of the five smiths that worked in Saint-Omer, is certainly true. Their spot for stopping in turn made him think of Gilo, and he wondered how he was doing on his way to wherever he was going. It had taken some doing, the difficulty compounded by the fact that the only man who might have been able to prevail on Count Baldwin was Titus himself, and he was incapacitated, but in the end, it was Josse, the only other survivor of the men who had gotten into Boulogne who had gone first to his commander in the *Pedes,* Liébaut, to plead the smith's case. He had been persuasive enough to convince Liébaut to seek out Lord Baudelius, so that Gilo was one of the very fortunate few inhabitants who had been allowed to load one wagon with his family and personal belongings, and another with his tools and anvil.

The town's other occupants that were Franks were spared being put to the sword, but they were turned out after being given an hour to gather whatever they could carry with them before the port, and the primary source of income for the inhabitants was put to the torch as punishment for their choosing to stay in Boulogne, though the lighthouse was left intact, although Titus suspected that this was due more the enormous effort it would have taken to bring it down. In Titus' view, this was a harsh punishment, but he had learned during his time among the Franks that it was a customary one, the people on the eastern side of The Narrow Sea taking a much different view of such matters than the Saxons. The noncombatant Northmen, mostly women and children, were put in chains, while those who had been slaves, mostly Franks but with a fair number of Saxons and a smattering of Frisians, suddenly found themselves free...but that was all, being left to fend for themselves, and as Titus had also learned, a fair number of these people would be forced into banditry to survive. The new Norse slaves found themselves marched to Paris, home to the largest slave market in West Frankia, under guard by a combination of *Pedes* and men of the *lantweri* who volunteered for the extra pay offered by the Count for the duty. While it was possible that Gilo had come here to Saint-Omer, Titus suspected he would choose someplace else, perhaps Bruciam, or Ganda, both of which were growing rapidly, although it was because more *servii* were fleeing their homes in the surrounding countryside due to the near-constant raiding by the Northmen. With the destruction of Boulogne's port, Titus thought as they resumed their walk, *maybe Flandre will see some peace and quiet*. To his surprise, this thought did not displease him; in fact, he felt a surge of anticipation at the idea that he and Yanna could spend more time together, without the specter of going off to fight and kill the Northern invaders constantly hanging over them. Titus had been wounded before, but never to this degree, and he wondered if this sudden complacency was a natural part of a serious wound. He was still turning this over in his mind as they reached the northern gate, and to his surprise and delight, he saw the gap-toothed grin of Josse, one of the four men standing guard.

"*'Allo*, Berserker!" the *Pedes* called out when Titus and Yanna were still a few paces away. "You," he said with a wide grin, "look like shit, but you still look better than the last time I saw you!"

"At least I can improve," Titus countered, but also with a grin. "You are as ugly as the day you were born."

Josse did not answer Titus, turning instead to Yanna and giving her an awkward bow from the waist.

"I apologize, Lady," he said earnestly. "We are two *vulgari* who don't know how to behave in polite company."

"Oh, that is quite all right," Yanna assured him, with the kind of gleam in her eye that Titus had learned meant she was feeling mischievous. "I have become quite accustomed to such things now that I have been with this Saxon here. I realized that he cannot help himself, being what he is." She gave a mock shudder, and with eyes quite wide she whispered to her fellow Frank, "They are such *savages* on that island of theirs!"

"All right," Titus growled, though he was jesting...for the most part. "You two Franks have had your fun."

Turning serious, Josse asked, "Are you going to see Ranulf?"

"Yes," Titus nodded, then without thinking asked, "how

about you? Have you seen him yet?"

"N-no." Josse shook his head, his face flushing. "Not yet, at least. We were not that close before...well, before..."

His voice trailed off, but Titus felt badly, and he put a hand on the other man's shoulder, assuring him he understood.

"Besides," he added, "he probably wouldn't know you'd visited."

They parted then, entering through the gate, taking a left turn and walking a short distance down the street to Ranulf's home, where they could see that the door was open from a few paces away, which was somewhat unusual, yet neither of them were alarmed. This changed when, from inside the cottage came a sharp cry, almost a scream, but while it was not clearly of fright, or pain, it was alarming enough to get both Titus and Yanna running the last few paces, wrenching a gasp of agony from him that was severe enough that he staggered for several steps, which meant that Yanna reached the doorway first...then came to an abrupt stop, where Titus saw her standing, hand to her mouth. Titus arrived a couple heartbeats later, but despite Yanna blocking the doorway, he could see over her head, and he only dimly heard a gasp that he recognized as coming from his own mouth. His first immediate thought was that the man who was standing there just inside in the main room was weaving as much as Titus; his next thought was how ugly his best friend looked with a poorly shaved head, with tufts of hair sticking up and a misshapen skull from where one of the monks had tried to piece it back together.

Emilde, standing next to the single table where they took their meals and holding infant Amis, whispered, "What did you say, my love?"

For a long, long moment, Ranulf stood there, blinking in what appeared to be dull surprise, reminding Titus of someone who had just awakened from a deep sleep to find something unexpected.

Ranulf's mouth worked, but nothing came out at first, then finally, he pointed at Titus as he croaked, "I just asked Emilde where you were. I...I do not remember anything after we climbed out of that sewer in..."

He stopped, and Titus, despite the lump in his throat,

supplied, "Boulogne."

Ranulf's eyes lit up, and he nodded.

"Yes! That was it!" Suddenly seeming to notice, he indicated the scar on Titus' face, and asked, "How did you get that?" Then, as he took in how Titus was standing, favoring one side by clutching it with his right hand, and weaving a bit like Ranulf, he added, "You do not look very good."

Before he could stop himself, knowing that it would hurt, Titus began to bellow with laughter, to which tears were quickly added from the relief at what would immediately become termed a miracle, and not only by Father Rudolf and the monks of Saint-Bertin, when by what could have only been by the grace of Almighty God, Ranulf the *Eques* miraculously regained his wits.

The Redeemer and its escorts departed Addelam on the tide shortly before dawn, and while the storm of the previous two days had broken in the middle of the night, there was a tension among those for whom this was their first crossing of The Narrow Sea, which included Uhtric. First, they had to resume sailing south until they saw the white cliffs of Dover, the northern end of which also marked where the Centish coast curved from a north/south axis to more of an east/west orientation, at a bay that would be named for Saint Margaret of Antioch, five miles south of Addelam. While maintaining a generally southerly course, they would turn slightly east, sailing across the narrowest part of The Narrow Sea, reaching a point of land that jutted out just west of a place the Franks called Wissant, so-named because, while they were not cliffs, the land along the shoreline was sparkling white sand. If nothing occurred, namely another storm, or while it was not said aloud, what Uhtric was certain was the more likely event, interception by more Northmen's ships, Ragnulf estimated that they would begin the crossing just before midday, and reach sight of land long enough before sunset to send a scouting party ashore. Wissant was only ten miles overland from Boulogne, but by sea, because of that jutting headland west of Wissant, it was more than fifteen if the Northmen were alerted to the Saxons' presence. There were many questions that had to be answered before the decision was made about whether or not they would be spending the night at anchor offshore, or it was felt to be safe enough to make camp. For Uhtric, Godric, and most of the other warriors, it was an easy decision, but they also understood that it was not theirs to make, and what they had all learned during their time aboard, or in the case of Godric and the other men of Alfred's bodyguard, had learned long before, Lord Eardwulf was a man who liked his comforts, and his advancing age had only served to exacerbate this. First, however, they had to make the crossing, which was spent with Uhtric constantly straining his lone eye as he scanned the horizon for sails, then the sky for the sight of dark clouds. And, while he would never speak of it, he spent an equal amount of time looking astern and a bit to the right at the looming white cliffs, thinking of home and Leofflaed.

"I hope she appreciates what I'm doing," he muttered. "Saxons aren't meant for the sea!"

"Truer words," Godric said from behind him, making him jump, which earned him a laugh from the bodyguard.

They stood for a moment, then Godric cleared his throat, a nervous habit that Uhtric had learned meant that he was about to deliver news that was either unwelcome or possibly contentious.

"Lord Eardwulf is insisting on making landfall, regardless of what's waiting for us," he said finally.

While this was what Uhtric had expected, he still let out a string of oaths, but he quickly learned that his companion was not through.

"And Ragnulf admits that he doesn't know anything about inland beyond about a mile up the Aa River." When Uhtric frowned, Godric interpreted the meaning, and explained, "He knows that Saint-Omer is about twenty miles upriver, but he doesn't know if it's navigable for a ship this size."

"And how far is the mouth of the Aa from this Wissant place?" Uhtric asked in growing dismay at the thought that they would be stuck aboard this ship even longer than he had anticipated.

"Another twenty miles," Godric replied sympathetically, feeling the same way.

"So we're going to be stuck on this cow for at least two more days?" Uhtric blurted out, receiving a glare from Godric.

"Keep your voice down," he hissed. "Do you want to hear these bastards around us moaning about that too?"

Frankly, Uhtric did not care all that much, but he realized the position it put Godric in as the ranking member of the King's bodyguard, not to mention the tension between the commander of bodyguard, Lord Cyneweard, and Lord Æthelweard, who it was rumored lusted to command both land and sea forces in the name of King Alfred.

"I apologize," Uhtric said with as much sincerity as he could muster, but he was still preoccupied by the idea of even more time on *The Redeemer*.

They lapsed into silence, sitting on the side of the ship, rocking with the rhythm of the waves as the oars dipped, rose, and dipped again to the rhythm called out by Ragnulf's first mate, a swarthy man who was so taciturn, it was rumored that Ragnulf had cut his tongue out, which was something that seemed in keeping with the shipmaster's personality. It was about an hour later when Ragnulf's son shouted from his spot on the mast, and Uhtric looked up to see him pointing straight ahead, but despite getting to his feet then leaping up next to the prow that, instead of a dragon, had a cross nailed to it to go with the large cross painted on the sail, now furled since they were heading into the wind, he still could not see anything. Reasoning that he would likely spot a sail, or sails more easily than land, he stared in the general direction of where Boulogne was located until his eyes watered, but he still saw nothing.

"Anything?" he asked Godric, having learned that, while his acuity was not impacted by the loss of his eye, his range of vision was, and it had required an adjustment when it came to judging close distances.

"No," Godric replied, but even as he said it, Uhtric realized that what he thought were whitecaps were actually not moving.

"There!" He pointed after a moment to make sure his eye was not playing a trick on him, just to the left of the prow, then moved his finger in a line to their left. "See that white strip? I think that's the sand they were talking about!"

Over the next hour, the coastline slowly materialized, but

now most of the attention was to their right front quarter, the direction from which any ships from Boulogne would materialize. The headland that jutted out had a hill on it, a perfect place for a signal fire since it blocked the view between Wissant and Boulogne, yet there was no sign of one, or once they were close enough, to see any movement at all. *The Redeemer* hove to, dropping anchor a half-mile from the beach, where a row of small fishing boats that, to Uhtric's eye, looked identical to those at Addelam or any other fishing village on the other side of The Narrow Sea had been pulled up beyond the high tide line and left, bottoms up. What was different was the cluster of figures standing there, at the top of a low rise, beyond which was a similarly weather-beaten collection of huts, with one stone building that, while there was no cross on it, Uhtric and his fellow Saxons knew was the village church. It was, he thought with sour amusement, understandable, especially since Saxon churchmen did the same thing, but taking down the cross, or removing all signs that the savage pagan raiders learned meant a Christian church did not matter; a stone building in their world meant wealth, and wealth was what the Northern invaders were after, in any form.

"Lord Æthelweard wants you as part of the shore party," Godric informed him, which did not surprise Uhtric, and he quickly dragged out his mail vest, strapped on both *seaxe* and longsword and put on his helmet, while leaving his shield behind.

The landing party was not solely composed of men from *The Redeemer*. Along with *Ærendgaest*, the ship formerly known as *Widow Maker* that had been renamed as *Se Wrecend*, or *The Avenger* sent over boats, each with five men, but most importantly, two men who spoke the Frankish tongue, and the sun was a finger's width above the horizon when the three-boat party rowed ashore...whereupon the small party of a half-dozen men and at least two women who had been watching turned and fled.

"By the Rood," Godric groaned. "Now we're going to have to hunt these fools down and convince them we mean them no harm!" He glanced at the sun, adding anxiously, "We don't have much time."

They beached their vessels, and since there were two men who spoke Frankish, they split into two parties, with Lord Æthelweard in command of one, and Godric the other, Uhtric naturally joining Godric's, and without any order to that effect, they headed in two opposite directions, with Godric leading his group towards the western side of the village, while Lord Æthelweard led his men directly for the stone building, which, as was also the custom, was built on a low rise so that about half of its height stood above the thatched roofs of the other dwellings. The light took on the golden quality of sunset, adding to the urgency they felt, but while they moved quickly, they performed a thorough search of each dwelling lining the muddy street that ran perpendicular to the beach and ended where the sand began.

"No doubt they have all sorts of hiding spots," Godric said bitterly, while Cuthfrith, a crewman on *Se Wrecend,* called out in the Frankish tongue, a few words that Uhtric understood, like "*amicis*" for friends, and "*pax*" for peace, but it had no discernible effect.

Fortunately, Lord Æthelweard and his party had better fortune, which they learned when they heard shouting in the direction of the church. Moving at a trot, they reached the building, and to their collective chagrin, they found most of the villagers huddled inside, along with the village priest, a lad that Uhtric was certain could barely be out of his teens with buck teeth and a spotty complexion who, while he was clearly relieved that these were Saxons and not Northmen, still looked shaken.

"We're putting ashore tonight," Æthelweard began, and with a broad smile on his face, but before Godric could ask, he explained, "Father Bernier here just told me some good news, *very* good news indeed." He paused for effect, but Uhtric could not fault him once the Thegn explained, "Count Baldwin attacked Boulogne and destroyed the port. There will be no threat from there."

This elicited gasps and cries of delighted surprise, and Uhtric's voice was among them, but Godric's voice cut through the small celebration that was a repeat of the one that had just taken place when Æthelweard's party learned the truth.

"So Sigfred is dead? Or was he forced to run? Where to?"

"No," the Thegn replied. "Neither of those because he wasn't there. In fact, he only left a thousand warriors behind, and..."

"Half of them went to Hrofescester with Hallsteinn," Godric interjected, but if the Thegn was irritated, the news that this thorn in their sides, on both sides of The Narrow Sea, was removed was sufficient to overlook the interruption.

"Exactly," Æthelweard nodded. "And when Count Baldwin learned about Hallsteinn's betrayal of Sigfred, he didn't hesitate."

That night, Lord Eardwulf slept in the village church, and Uhtric was closer to reuniting with his friend.

While Ranulf's recovery was nothing short of miraculous, it did not take Titus long to feel that his friend's days as a warrior were over. Aside from the significant gaps in his memory that went beyond the fight in Boulogne, he could not recall other things, like how he and Titus had met. He suffered debilitating headaches that sent him to his bed, vomiting from the pain, to which all Father Rudolf, who insisted that this was due only to God's intervention, could offer was a shrug and a promise to offer up another prayer to ease his suffering. Nevertheless, it was a marked improvement from how he had been just a matter of a couple days before. Oddly enough, Titus' own recovery seemed to accelerate, so that by a week after his return to Yanna's cottage, he was working at one of the stakes outside the Count's residence, and it was on his first day that a moment he had been dreading occurred. He was at the stake with a wooden sword, but he was performing the movements that were second nature to him as if he was a new man called to his first *fyrd*, which was how he still thought of it and not the Frankish term. As always happened, he quickly lost himself in the exercises, although there was still a fair amount of pain, especially when he performed a twisting motion at the waist, so he barely noticed the figure who appeared to stand at the edge of his vision. Finally, he had to stop to catch his breath, silently cursing the lost fitness, but when he turned to see that it was Sigismund, it was as if he had suddenly sprinted a hundred paces, and without thinking, he felt his grip on the wooden sword alter in the slightly looser grip that he would use in combat. The other man stood there, his expression unreadable, yet Titus had the strong sense that he was every bit as discomfited about being there as Titus was seeing him standing there.

Without thinking, Titus spoke in his native tongue, saying cautiously, "*Wes hal*, Sigismund."

Sigismund's reaction was a narrowing of eyes, and he asked suspiciously, "What does that mean, this *was hel*?"

Despite himself, Titus chuckled at the mispronunciation, but he said quickly, "I apologize. That was in my tongue. I just was...surprised, that is all." Somehow understanding it was important, he added earnestly, "No offense was intended, Sigismund. It is just a greeting that one man gives another man...a friend."

"Ah," Sigismund mumbled, coloring slightly and shuffling his feet. "I...see. I understand." Suddenly, he looked up at Titus, who was almost a head taller, but his gaze did not waver as he asked directly, "Are we, Berserker? Friends, I mean?"

"That," Titus replied honestly, "is up to you." Thinking it important, he said, "Sigismund, I have *never* borne you any ill will, I swear it. I know that you and Bent were friends, good friends long before I arrived here. As far as Bent and I?" He shrugged, waving his free hand, Sigismund noticing that he had not dropped the wooden sword. "I cannot pretend that I am sorry that he died."

A part of him, a very tiny part of Titus, the cruel part, the part of the Berserker that was with him all the time, something he would never divulge to anyone, not even Uhtric, or Leofflaed, and especially not to Yanna, wanted to add, "I am just sorry that I was not the one who killed him!"

He did not, though when he thought about it later, he had the strong sense that, even if he had, this would have neither surprised nor offended Sigismund.

"I do not expect you to be sorry," Sigismund assured him. He heaved a sigh that, to Titus' ears, seemed to carry a deep emotion, but he was completely unprepared for his fellow warrior to say simply, "Bent was a bully, he was cruel...and he was a prick. But," he finished with a helpless shrug, "we grew up together. We were cousins, you know."

"No," Titus said in surprise. "I did not know that."

"Yes," Sigismund nodded. "His father and my father were brothers. They both served Count Baldwin's grandfather, and his father." He looked away then, and Titus saw the gleam in the man's eyes. "But I told him more times than I can count that he was a fool to torment and taunt you as much as he did." He looked back at Titus, as he added, "And that was before I saw you at Watten...then when I watched you at Boulogne, I actually thought for a moment that it would drive this...madness that was in Bent about you from his mind, that he would know he could never defeat you." Sigismund laughed, but it was a bitter one, laced with anguish. "Although maybe he did understand that, which was why he tried to kill you with a spear to the back. And," he added with even more bitterness as he held up his left hand, which was still wrapped in a bandage, "I got this for my troubles at trying to stop him."

"I did not even know he had done it," Titus told him honestly. Indicating the other man's hand, he asked, "What about your hand? What do the monks say about it?"

"The fingers should heal," Sigismund replied, then tried not to sound worried as he added, "as long as they don't become corrupt. It has just taken longer for them to heal than I expected."

He demonstrated that they were on the mend by wiggling the fingers that peeked out from under the wide bandage, earning an approving nod from Titus.

While he was reluctant to do so, Titus felt that it was necessary to ask, "And what about that boy? The *lantwerus*?"

"What about him?" Sigismund asked cautiously.

"Has he been executed yet?"

"No." Sigismund shook his head, which surprised Titus a great deal.

"Why not?" he asked, although even as he did, he felt conflicted about it.

Now that he had learned everything that had taken place, he knew that the boy with the spear had not really saved his life, because he had executed his thrust right after Bent hurled his own spear, but at the same time, he could not discount the idea that Bent might have drawn his sword and attacked him on horseback before anyone around him, like Sigismund, could have reacted.

"Because Lord Baudelius and Count Baldwin are at each other's throats right now," Sigismund replied, and while his tone was neutral, Titus sensed some resentment on Sigismund's part, and he wondered where his sympathies lay, recalling how Bent made no secret that he felt more loyalty to Baudelius than the Count. "Baudelius wants the boy's head, literally, but the Count has not rendered his decision yet. And," he sighed, "now that he has left for a tour of the *pagus*, who knows how long it will be before the boy is punished?"

Titus was curious about something, thinking he heard something in Sigismund's voice, but at the same time, there was something else, and he asked in surprise, "Wait. The Count is not here?" Sigismund shook his head, and he asked, "When did he leave?"

"At dawn this morning, actually," Sigismund replied. "Why?"

Titus was uncertain how to approach what was in his mind; while he understood why he had not been informed and was not riding as part of the *Eques* that would have been expected to go with the Count on a trip like this, which could take weeks, he was unsure how to broach the question, so he asked carefully, "How many of us did the Count take with him?"

"All of them," Sigismund replied, then he smiled, but it was one with a bitterness that was impossible to miss, "save for you...and me. I," he sighed, "was...excused, because of my grief at losing my cousin. At least," Sigismund gave an elaborate shrug that did not fool Titus in the slightest, "that is what Lord Baudelius told me."

On an impulse, Titus asked, "What do you think should happen to that *lantwerus*?" Realizing he had no idea, he added, "Do you know his name?"

"Yes, it is Eudes," Sigismund replied, but with an absent air that made it clear to Titus that the other man was considering his first question. Finally, he sighed. "Honestly, I do not know, Berserker. I know that I am supposed to want to avenge Bent's death, and that means that Eudes should die...but he is just a youth. Besides," he shook his head, "what Bent did was without honor. I just want him gone, one way or another, so that I am not reminded of him."

When he thought about it later, Titus would understand that this was the moment the seed for the idea was planted, even if he had no idea what his own future held for him.

"Do you think Lord Baudelius will go ahead and execute the boy while the Count is gone?"

Sigismund gave Titus a sardonically amused look.

"That," he answered dryly, "will be difficult, since Lord Baudelius is with him."

"What?" Titus gasped. "He took Baudelius with him? He's never done that before. At least," he added as he thought about it, "not since I have served him."

It was the standard practice, he had been told; since Saint-Omer was the Count's headquarters, whenever the Count was gone, Lord Baudelius stayed behind, while the opposite held true as well, that when Lord Baudelius was out in the *pagus,* the Count was in Saint-Omer, the only exception being when they marched to war as they had at Boulogne.

"I think that the rift between Count Baldwin and Lord Baudelius is much deeper than because of one *lantwerus*," Sigismund said soberly.

"I do not remember who told me," Titus lied, "but they said they thought that the Count has realized that he does not need to rely on Lord Baudclius as much as he has in the past, and Baudelius is not happy about it."

"That," Sigismund agreed, "is my assessment as well. But," he lowered his voice, taking a look around as he continued, "I think that Lord Baudelius is not likely to step aside gracefully, if you take my meaning. I also believe that the Count is aware of this, and that is another reason he is with the Count, so that Baudelius cannot make mischief."

This also made sense to Titus, and he said as much; then, they stood there awkwardly, eyeing each other until, without planning on it, Sigismund offered his hand, which Titus took without hesitation.

"I hope you recover from your wounds soon...Titus,"

Sigismund said, but before the Saxon could respond, the Frank turned and walked away, leaving Titus feeling as if a weight had lifted from his shoulders.

At least I won't have to look over my shoulder for Sigismund, he thought, then returned back to the stakes.

Chapter Seven

The Redeemer entered the mouth of the Aa River shortly before midday, and while they did not need the sail, Ragnulf had it unfurled so that the cross was plainly seen by the inhabitants of the small village at the mouth of the river. Thankfully for Uhtric's impatience, the question of the Aa's navigability upstream by the large Saxon ship had already been determined, by *Ærendgaest*, which Lord Æthelweard ordered sent ahead, along with Ragnulf's first mate to determine whether *The Redeemer* could navigate it. They were waiting at the mouth, and Uhtric, Godric, and the other warriors who did not have duties stood evenly distributed along both sides of the ship as the oarsmen began working against the current, which, as expected, was much stronger here at the mouth. This slowed their pace down to the point that, while the adult Frankish *servii* stopped whatever they were doing to watch the ships, with *Ærendgaest* leading the way followed by *The Redeemer*, in silence and with suspicious stares, their children were able to caper alongside, shouting crude insults while making faces that only a couple of men with the Saxon party understood or, in the case of some of the older boys, baring their backsides or waving their tiny penises and making vulgar gestures that they had learned from their fathers. Despite himself, Uhtric could not help grinning, as did most of the other men, until the children, panting from the exertion of running almost a mile upstream, finally dropped off and trotted home, their fun over, while the memory of this unusual event would be discussed for days. Despite the presence of these people, Uhtric also could not miss the signs of destruction that, while these were not his folk, still ignited a flare of anger in him, particularly when they would spot the gutted, blackened stone buildings that had once been a church, although the buildings around them had been either

251

repaired or rebuilt.

"They probably don't see the point in rebuilding a church when they know that these Northern whorespawns are going to be drawn to it like bees to honey," Godric commented.

The sun was close to going down when they were signaled by the master of the *Ærendgaest,* who pointed ahead to where a solid line on the lefthand bank of the Aa that Uhtric knew was a wooden wall.

"That is a village they call Watten," the master of the *Ærendgaest* called out. "Do you want to put in here for that night?"

"How much farther is Saint-Omer?" Æthelweard asked, cupping his hands around his mouth to be heard.

"About six miles," the master replied. "But about five miles from here is a monastery they call Saint-Bertin."

The news that there was a monastery made the Thegn stifle a groan, and he counted the heartbeats for the appearance of both Lord Eardwulf and Father Æthelred from the shelter, their ears alerting them to this news; he did not reach five before the chaplain materialized at his side.

"Did I hear correctly, Lord Æthelweard? That there is a monastery nearby?"

"There is a monastery, but it's not nearby, Father," the Thegn replied, but he was not surprised when the chaplain said irritably, "Surely it can't be *that* far."

"It's far enough that we would arrive in the dark, and unless we send word ahead, it's entirely possible that they'll think we're Northmen, Father," Æthelweard snapped.

He had endured the sniveling and carping of both Alfred's chaplain and councilor for as long as he could take it; the end of this journey could not come quickly enough, and while there was a part of him that thought to just acquiesce and order the ships to resume rowing upstream, he was sufficiently irritated to turn away from the cleric and ignore Lord Eardwulf, who had just tottered up, ready no doubt to add his own weight to the idea of a soft bed and the kind of food that monasteries were known for, to order Ragnulf to put in at the lone wooden dock that lined the river. By the time the plank was lowered and Æthelweard had descended, there was a party of four villagers, regarding the Saxons with a mixture of apprehension and curiosity, while one of the Frank speakers in their party served as translator. Arrangements were made, silver was paid, and the two men most concerned with their comfort were escorted to, once again, the stone church, and as Uhtric and Godric walked through the gate to the dock, they saw that the wall was relatively new. Calling to one of the translators, through him, Godric asked a villager who reeked of urine, betraying his profession as a tanner, what had prompted the construction of the wall.

For the first time, the Frank showed some animation, talking rapidly, making several gestures that Uhtric could not understand, but he heard the tanner mention a Northern word he did understand, though in the moment, he did not make the connection, the tanner referring to the Berserker several times until the translator lifted a hand, cutting him off. There was more back and forth, and Uhtric was beginning to regret bringing it up when a look of dawning understanding crossed the translator's face, and he said excitedly, "I know where the Berserker is!" The story came out as they walked to the church, the translator explaining, "This wall was built last year, after Watten was attacked by Northmen who sailed upstream. It was the deepest they had come for some time, and the Count that we're going to see lives north of here in Saint-Omer."

"We know that," Godric interrupted impatiently. "That's why we're here!"

Chastened, the man went on, "The Northmen were in the process of sacking the town when the Count showed up with his men. There was a battle, and the Count found himself surrounded and cut off from the rest of his men." Showing he had a flair for storytelling, the crewman turned translator, whose mother had been a Frank, paused just long enough for both Godric and Uhtric to start opening their mouths to demand he continue, when he finished with a broad smile, "But then the Berserker showed up on that horse of his, and singlehandedly cut his way through those Northmen savages to the Count." He indicated the villager who had related this to him, saying, "He saw it all happen with his own eyes!" When the Frank only stared blankly at the two Saxons looking to him for confirmation, the translator spoke rapidly, earning an emphatic nod from the man. "See?" the translator said triumphantly. "He saw it all happen. And now," he finished by pointing in a generally northern direction, "the Berserker serves the Count and lives in Saint-Omer." As an afterthought, he added one tidbit of information the villager had related, "He has a woman there, this man says."

Uhtric stifled a curse, certain that this had now become a more complicated mission of retrieving Titus back to Wiltun and wondering if this woman would be willing to come with his brother-in-law, it never occurring to him that Titus would not have developed strong feelings for her; he knew Titus well, and knew that if he had taken up with a woman, it would be serious. Still, it was also nice to have confirmation that Titus was definitely nearby, and it took him some time to fall asleep, rolled up in his cloak aboard *The Redeemer* since there was no more room in the church. His last thought before he finally dropped off was that tomorrow should be an interesting day.

Titus was at the stakes again when there was a shout by one of the *Pedes* at the gates of the Count's palace, which were open, and he turned in time to see another man of the *Pedes* come through them at a brisk run.

"Where is Liébaut?"

The *Pedes* at the gate pointed in the direction of another large building only slightly smaller than the Count's residence, one of two that served as the barracks for the *Pedes* who did not have families and lived in Saint-Omer.

"I saw him go in there."

Since the newly arrived man had to pass by him, Titus called out, "What is it? What is happening?"

Even if he was not the Berserker, the *Pedes*, who had been sent by the commander of the guard at the town gate, would not have been eager to refuse the huge, scarred warrior; besides, he thought, what harm could it do to tell him? In the moment, he did not make any kind of connection between Titus and the newly arrived party.

"Saxons!" he said excitedly, though he slowed but did not stop. "From their King, Alfred! Five ships full of them! They are here to see the Count!"

It struck the messenger as somewhat strange how, even before he was through, the Berserker had dropped his wooden sword and was moving at a fast walk towards the gate, but he quickly forgot about it.

Titus' heart was pounding, though not from the exertion; while he was not at full strength, he had seen marked improvement every day, and his left side only ached after his exercise sessions. His lower right side still pained him all the time, but Brother Albertus had told him this was to be expected because of the scar tissue, and the only way to get his mobility back was to break apart the hard lump at the site of his wound, which was an angry pink knot. None of this was in his mind now as he hurried down the street leading to the river, where there were three wooden piers reserved for merchant ships, though there were precious few of those because of the stranglehold that the Northmen had on the Flandre coast that had just been broken by the Count's bold action against Boulogne. It was far too soon for them to see the benefits of the destruction of that important base for the Northern raiders, although it did explain how these ships managed to sail from Wessex, across The Narrow Sea, and up the Aa, he thought, wondering what ships they might be? He knew of Alfred's ambition to build an all-Saxon navy, and it had been more than two years since he had left, but given the other challenges facing any leader during this age of Northern depredations, he felt certain that he would recognize at least one of the vessels that were tying up at the dock; maybe even the *Sea Viper*, he thought with a peculiar mixture of emotions. His view was blocked by the slight curve of the street that terminated at the river, so it was only when he negotiated the curve that he got his first sight of the prow of a large ship, of a clearly Saxon design, although it was the cross attached to the spot where the Danes and Northmen put a dragon or some other snarling beast's head that told him the identity.

"*The Redeemer*?" he murmured to himself, suddenly trying to recall exactly what the messenger had said; he had thought he said someone had been sent *by* King Alfred, but was it possible that the King himself was here?

This thought was so overwhelming that he had to stop for a moment and lean against the side of a dwelling; after a few heartbeats, he was able to resume, but at a slower pace, as if his feet were trying to keep him from finding out. It took him a long moment to recognize the figure who was standing facing in his direction as his former shipmate from *Sea Viper* Godric, although he was wearing the scarlet tunic that marked him as a man of Alfred's bodyguard, but he did not see Titus because he was talking intently to another man whose back was turned. There was something about the way this second man carried himself, along with his lean frame, that brought Titus to a halt for a second time, and now his heart felt as if it was in his throat, but it was not confirmed until Godric, looking over the man's shoulder, took in Titus standing there, and he was close enough to see Godric's eyes widen, then almost shove the other man, who turned around to look directly at Titus...but with only one eye, the other one obscured by a patch.

Without a flicker of surprise, Uhtric called out, "You look terrible."

Titus desperately wanted to say something clever in return, but not only could he not say anything, his throat suddenly closing up, Uhtric himself seemed to dissolve in a shimmering curtain, and he was so overcome that he did not even sense Uhtric running to him. His next memory was of being swept into an almost choking embrace, one that he returned with equal fervor, and it was their touching that seemed to unleash the dam that had blocked off the words, except they were both speaking at once, babbling, laughing, and crying in what, even in the moment, in the back of Titus' mind he chided himself for an unseemly display. Really, the part of him that worried about such things asked crossly: is this any way for the Berserker to behave? Crying like some *woman* just because he was seeing someone he had not seen for some time, especially in front of others? This did not stop him, and when they finally broke their embrace, something Uhtric had said during their babbling at each other seemed to penetrate, although it did not make any sense.

"Wait," he interrupted Uhtric, who was describing the trip, "what did you say?"

"I said," Uhtric smiled, "we've come to take you home, Titus. You're coming home with me back to Wiltun."

As Titus, and Uhtric, would learn, it was not nearly that simple.

"What do you mean, Count Baldwin is not here?" Father Æthelred demanded.

This *Saxon* is behaving as if it's my fault! thought Father Rudolf, suddenly regretting his decision to invent an illness to keep from accompanying the Count and sending his acolyte, Father Guibaud, instead.

Aloud, he adopted the tone of the professional courtier, saying with feigned cordiality, "It is as I said, Father Æthelred. As regrettable as it is, I am afraid that the Count was called away on urgent business elsewhere in the *pagus*. Which," he added helpfully, and with the kind of smug sense of superiority that comes from a man who lives in a kingdom so vast, "is quite large compared to what you might be accustomed to in Wessex."

They were speaking in Latin, the language of the Church and of the Frankish nobility at moments such as this, which meant that Lords Eardwulf and Æthelweard were forced to look to Father Æthelred to translate. For this first meeting, they were actually not in the Count's palace, but in the church of Saint-Bertin, which was about three hundred paces from the southern wall of the palace, both structures some two hundred paces west of the river.

Father Æthelred ignored the jibe, repeating, "We are here at the order of our King, Alfred of Wessex, who has directed Lord Eardwulf and myself to approach Count Baldwin on a most urgent matter, and it is absolutely imperative that we deliver our message directly to the Count."

"Yes," Rudolf replied dryly, "so you have said. But," he held both hands out, as if inviting the others to search for themselves, "as I have said, the Count is not here. He left two days ago, and I regret to say that he travels quite swiftly." He paused, then behaving like it was an afterthought, he added helpfully, "Perhaps if you tell me what this matter is about?"

"What is he saying?" Eardwulf interrupted loudly enough

to be heard by the two clerics a half-dozen paces away, obviously irritated, which unfortunately made his voice seem even more querulous rather than commanding.

"I will explain later, Lord," Father Æthelred murmured in Saxon. To Rudolf, he again ignored the other cleric's attempt to pry information from him, asking, "Who is the Count's second in command...of matters *secular*, I mean?" Proving Rudolf was not the only one who could behave as a courtier, he smiled. "I do not have to ask who the Count relies on for matters pertaining to Mother Church."

"Is there truly such a thing as a matter *secular*?" Rudolf countered, which oddly enough, put Æthelred more at ease, long accustomed to this kind of sparring among men of God, most of whom would argue that, ultimately, all matters of the flesh were matters of the Spirit since all roads and paths led to God. And, it was something that Æthelred wholeheartedly believed himself, but he was not there as a fellow cleric; he was there representing his King, which meant that on this occasion, he did not.

Consequently, he replied, "In this matter, I believe there is."

There was no mistaking the rebuff, but Rudolf said stiffly, "I am afraid that Lord Baudelius, who fills that role for the Count, is with him and not here."

"Is there anyone else of gentle birth here? Who is not clergy?" Æthelred added quickly.

"No," Rudolf snapped, finally losing his composure. "And I am afraid that if you are unwilling to divulge why you have come all this way to speak to my liege lord, who," he added acidly, "I serve just as I serve God, then I am afraid I must ask you to leave in the morning."

While they could not follow the words, the other Saxons present had no trouble deciphering the tone, and they all looked at Æthelred, who gave an audible gasp.

"What is it?" Eardwulf demanded. Raising his hand covered with the spots that plague old people and pointing a shaking finger at the Frankish priest, he asked Æthelred, "What did he say that has you looking like you swallowed a rat turd?"

A shaken Æthelred explained, eliciting a hissed curse from

Æthelweard, who muttered under his breath, "No wonder he brought us here to the church. He didn't want me striking him down for his insolence!"

Unusually, it was Eardwulf who recovered his composure first, and gave his companions a glimpse into why the King still valued his counsel.

"You must tell him, Father Æthelred," he said calmly. "He holds the power here because I am certain that he knows where Count Baldwin is. And," he reasoned, "I don't think it's unreasonable to assume that the Count will be telling him what the King is offering him very soon after we tell the Count. This," he finished with a shrug, "is just telling him sooner rather than later."

The trio of Saxons did have the satisfaction of seeing the Frankish priest gasp, then stagger over to sit down on a bench against the wall once he had been informed.

"I...I...the Count is heading for Cortryk, one of our fortified towns. From there, he is going to Ganda, then will finish his tour in Bruciam before returning back here."

Since none of them knew where any of these towns were located, or how far they were from Saint-Omer, Æthelred asked, "How long is he supposed to be gone?"

"He was going to attend to several administrative matters in each town," Rudolf answered, his lips turning down into a frown as he thought about it. "The estimate he gave me was that he would be returning to Saint-Omer anywhere between four and six weeks from now."

It was the turn of the Saxon priest to gasp, but he was quickly joined by the other two men when he translated for them, and Eardwulf said, "We can't possibly wait that long!"

"I...I...I will send a rider after the Count immediately!" Rudolf assured them. "And while I cannot speak for the Count, I am certain that he will make all haste to return to Saint-Omer."

While it was not exactly what they were looking for, the three Saxons wordlessly agreed that this was the best for which they could hope, and considering the prize being offered the young Count, they were as close to confident as it was possible to get that he would be returning shortly. It was only when they emerged from the church that they learned that the other mission that, as far as Lord Æthelweard and Father Æthelred knew, was something about which their King had no interest, the retrieval of the Saxon warrior with the unusual name and even more unusual, and to the cleric at least, sinful nickname that glorified the pagan savagery, had been at least partially accomplished, seeing Uhtric, Godric and Titus standing together. In fact, of these three, only Lord Eardwulf knew that, while it was not his primary goal, their King was keenly interested bringing the hulking warrior back to Wessex to serve the new Lord of Wiltun...and the Lord's King.

This was what prompted Eardwulf to murmur, "I believe I might have an idea."

"Are you sure you're fit to ride?" Uhtric asked for what Titus was certain was the fifth or sixth time.

They were in Yanna's cottage, it now being late afternoon, after what could only be described as a dizzying series of events that culminated with Titus packing his saddlebags. Uhtric felt badly for Yanna, who was sitting at their table with a dazed expression on her face, one that he could certainly understand; after all, he thought as he watched her surreptitiously, *I had more than a week to prepare for seeing Titus again, and I still was shocked when it happened.* Now, within the span of a couple of hours, this poor woman's entire life had been turned upside down, her lover was now about to leave to go find this Count Baldwin to bring him back to Saint-Omer...and then? While Titus had not given him any indication about whether he planned to return to Wiltun with him, Uhtric felt cautiously optimistic that he would, and if the impediment to that proved to be Yanna, he would do whatever he could to assure both of them that she would be welcomed in their household. *Although,* he thought ruefully, *I suspect that Leofflaed and I will be having a...discussion about my promising such things without her input.* Yes, he was the master of his household, but as he had heard from other men who preceded him in the state of matrimony, the key they all agreed was how having a happy wife made for a happy home. Besides, while her temper was nowhere nearly as terrifying to behold as her brother's, Leofflaed still was formidable when angry. Nevertheless,

Uhtric felt he was doing the right thing, and Yanna *was* a beautiful woman, with an air of self-possession that, while Uhtric would never say as much to his brother-in-law, reminded him of Isolde, although he was intensely curious about whether or not Titus saw the same thing in her. Otherwise, they were nothing alike in appearance, though Uhtric would not have said Yanna was more beautiful than Isolde had been, or the other way around; they were just different. Now, she sat there watching Titus, who was doing his best to pretend that bending over to roll up his cloak did not cause him any discomfort, her eyes wide and blinking rapidly in the sign she was fighting her tears.

"Do you have time to eat?" she asked in the Saxon tongue, but Titus shook his head.

"No, my love. Sigismund is waiting already, and I still have to saddle Thunor." Addressing Uhtric, he added, "The Count's stable has plenty of spare horses, so you won't have trouble finding one."

For that was the one concession that Titus demanded when Lord Eardwulf approached him about accompanying whoever Father Rudolf was sending to find the Count, that Uhtric go with him, although the elderly nobleman only put up a token resistance. Not surprisingly, it was Father Rudolf who objected most strenuously, giving Uhtric the impression, which was later confirmed by Titus, that the priest thought the Saxons planned something for Sigismund while on the road, but when Uhtric asked why, Titus said he would explain later.

"Why are you putting on your armor?" Yanna asked, glancing at Uhtric with an anxious expression.

Without pausing, Titus shrugged and replied absently, "Out of habit, I suppose."

"My wife, Leofflaed is her name," Uhtric put in, smiling as he spoke to put her at ease, "she complains that I do that all the time. 'Why are you putting on your armor to go into town?'" he mimicked, or attempted to mimic his wife, which earned him a chuckle from Titus. "'Are you hoping that Danes show up?'" Shaking his head in mock exasperation, he said, "It is a habit, Yanna, nothing more. We would feel naked without it." Thinking to lighten the mood, he complimented her. "You speak our tongue very well, Yanna. Did you know it before this big lump showed up?"

"No." She shook her head, though she smiled shyly. "Everything I learned, I learned from Titus."

"She picks up languages faster than anyone I've ever met," Titus said proudly. "She can even read some."

"Really?" Uhtric asked, in real surprise this time, this being rare for someone of their class, and exceedingly so for a woman. "Where did you learn that?"

"From my father," Yanna replied, her tone vague. "He was a priest."

"Really?" Titus echoed, clearly startled to the point where he stopped tightening the straps of his saddlebag. "You never told me he was a priest."

"You never asked," she replied evenly, but Uhtric sensed there was something more than just her words, that there was a hidden warning in her tone.

Which, he was relieved to see, Titus understood and heeded, not saying anything more. He was ready then, and Uhtric said quietly, "I'll be outside."

He was not there long before Titus emerged, and while his eyes were shining a bit, there were no tears, but the same could not be said for what was taking place inside, as Uhtric heard weeping.

"She knows we're coming back, doesn't she?"

"She does," Titus replied shortly.

Uhtric followed his lead, not having any idea where the stables were, taking note of how the townspeople responded to the sight of the large Saxon, although Uhtric got a fair amount of attention, which he put down to being a stranger, knowing that it would be the same if a Frankish warrior was wandering down the street in Wiltun.

They had gone a few paces when Titus added quietly, "She's worried that I'm going to leave and not take her with me."

"Is she right to be worried?" Uhtric asked, matching his friend's tone.

He was relieved to see the startlement on Titus' face, and he turned his head to look at Uhtric in astonishment.

"By the Rood, no, Uhtric! I'm not going to leave her behind! Not now! She already has a...reputation as it is because she's with me."

Although Uhtric had suspected as much, he replied, "Ah, I see. You aren't married."

"No," Titus sighed.

"Why not?"

"Because she didn't want to be married!" Titus said indignantly.

"Wait, are you saying that it's not because of you?" Uhtric asked in real surprise.

"Yes, that's what I'm saying," Titus snapped. They reached the stables then, and Titus said in a tone Uhtric knew meant he was serious, "It's complicated, and I don't want to talk about it anymore. I need to think about things first."

Then, they stepped inside, and Uhtric heard Thunor before he saw the horse, but while his friend walked over to his horse, Uhtric, who had a good eye for horses thanks to his time with Otha, spotted a black gelding, which he would not normally have chosen for his warhorse, but there was not much chance of a fight, or so he hoped. And, he thought with grim humor, even if there is, he was back with Titus, and even a not fully recovered Titus would be more than a match for all but a large band of Northmen.

"What about the black?" Uhtric pointed to the animal, immediately noticing how Titus stiffened.

"That belonged to...someone," Titus said carefully, "who died at Boulogne."

"Then he won't mind me riding his horse, will he?" Uhtric replied, somewhat jokingly, though he was serious.

Before they could discuss it any further, a figure appeared in the doorway, and Titus responded by calling out a greeting in Frankish, then in Saxon told Uhtric, "This is Sigismund. He's going to be with us."

Uhtric nodded a greeting, which the Frank, who was a couple years older than the Saxon, returned, but then Titus said something more in the Frankish tongue that, if Uhtric was any judge, disturbed Sigismund, followed by a lengthy exchange, and it was when Sigismund's eyes went to the black gelding that Uhtric thought he understood, at least partially. Finally, Sigismund gave a nod, and Titus turned back to Uhtric.

"Sigismund was close friends with the...previous owner of the black," he explained. "And he says that he would be happy to let you ride Noir. That," Titus explained, "is the horse's name."

"Thank you," Uhtric addressed Sigismund, nodding his head in a bow of thanks, which Sigismund returned by inclining his own head.

Whereupon they busied themselves saddling up, then led their animals out, having decided that they did not need a packhorse or spare mounts. When they mounted, a low groan escaped from Titus' lips, causing both of his companions to look at him in concern.

"Don't tell me that you haven't ridden since you were wounded," Uhtric said severely, earning a wan smile from Titus.

"All right, I won't tell you."

Titus turned Thunor's head and, without warning, kicked his sides, sending the horse into a trot, the other pair united, at least temporarily, in their exasperation with their large companion, sharing a rolling of eyes as they urged their own horses to follow. They left Saint-Omer in the mid-afternoon, the idea being they could make at least ten of the forty-five miles to Cortryk before nightfall, making it possible to reach the Count the next day, albeit late, and for perhaps the hundredth time, Uhtric wondered just what King Alfred was offering that would elicit this kind of reaction.

Before they had gone three miles, Titus was regretting agreeing to Lord Eardwulf's request that he accompany Sigismund, which Father Rudolf had surprisingly, at least to Titus, agreed was a good idea, although the Saxon did not much care for how the Frankish priest had put it.

"I cannot understand why, but the Count and the Berserker here have a friendly relationship, so I suppose it makes sense that he goes along."

They moved at a fast walk, followed by a short period at a trot, then a walk, eating up the distance riding east until shortly before sundown, when they stopped at a small village. As tempting as it was, Titus refused Uhtric's offer to unsaddle Thunor, sharing a barn that belonged to the headman of the village, who behaved as if he was conferring a favor on the occupants, despite the fact that Sigismund handed him a silver *denier* for the forage the horses would require, and another one for the privilege of sleeping in a smelly barn.

"It's the Count," Titus explained tiredly. "He insists that we pay the *servii* for lodging and the like. Even," he added with a sour glance at the headman, who was understandably curious and nervous in equal measure about the large warrior, "if it's no skin off their ass to give it."

The headman bustled out of the barn, the two coins in his hand that he was already planning on spending at the lone wineshop, and on the lone whore who was near the end of her time as a serviceable fuck, but as eager as he was for the romp, he was even more eager to spread the news *that the Berserker was in his barn!*

This was the explanation for the moment when the three warriors roused themselves just after dawn the next morning, and in a small act of revenge, pissed in a corner of the barn, then saddled their mounts before leading them outside, where there was a small crowd outside, all of them pretending to be involved with some morning chore, though it did not fool Sigismund, who for the first time Uhtric had seen in his short association, actually laughed and pointed at Titus as he said something in Frankish.

"What did he say?" Uhtric asked, but Titus did not want to answer, which earned him a chiding from the Frank, and he finally relented, grumbling, "He says this happens all the time when the *servii* figure out who I am."

"So it's no different than Wessex." Uhtric laughed as he mounted.

They broke their fast as they rode, while Titus resigned himself to a long day of misery. He had slept poorly, his side keeping him from finding a comfortable position, despite lying in a fairly deep pile of straw.

Sensing Titus' mood, Uhtric decided to keep his friend from dwelling on his discomfort, saying, "You've mentioned a word a couple of times now that I don't understand." He thought for a moment, then remembered, "*Servii*?" Taking Titus' grunt for acknowledgement, he asked, "What does that mean?"

"They're basically the same thing as our *ceorls*," Titus explained. "But they don't have the same requirements, like how a *ceorl* has to own at least one hide to be considered a free Saxon." Shrugging, he added, "Honestly, I've never taken the time to understand it because it doesn't really have anything to do with me. As long as I have," he tapped the scabbard, "Wyvern's Fang, I'll always have enough food to eat."

Not surprisingly, Titus' sword had been one of the first things he had shown Uhtric, who could not help admiring it, nor did he try to hide his envy; Frankish craftsmanship with edged weapons was known throughout their world, but it did not stop there. His friend's mail shirt, which he had tried on, earning a laugh from Titus, and a giggle from Yanna at the sight of a man wearing a shirt that hung down well below his knees, while the sleeves, which came down to just above Titus' elbows, extended a couple inches below Uhtric's, was almost as beautiful, and as finely worked as Wyvern's Fang.

"Why didn't you get it made with scale armor?" Uhtric had asked.

"I don't like scale," Titus had replied without hesitation. "I had to wear one the first year before I had enough money to have this made, and I never could get used to it. It didn't let me move the way I can with mail."

Titus' explanation of the social system used by the Franks left Uhtric with more questions than answers, though it was more due to Uhtric's curious nature than anything else, but with that topic exhausted, they fell silent again, which was another difference with Titus. He supposed his condition had much to do with it; Uhtric could see that he was in some pain, and he had heard his friend tossing and turning, but he did wonder if this was another change that he would have to learn to live with in their time together, because it still had not occurred to him that Titus might not want to leave.

Baldwin, Margrave of Flandre, had a horrible headache, his ass was sore, and he was about as bored as he thought it was possible to be. He was seated in the large chair in the hall that ostensibly belonged to the headman of Cortryk but had been taken over by Lord Dalmatius, who held Ypres as its *Dominatius* some sixteen miles west of Cortryk, and who was now the commander of the garrison of this fortified town. There was nothing much to recommend Cortryk aside from its strategic location between Ganda and Saint-Omer, providing a series of inland fortified positions that roughly paralleled the coast, though far enough away that they were not under threat from Northmen raiding upriver. It was, Baldwin knew very well, a reactionary strategy, spreading armed men in protected positions, placing them in spots from which they could respond. It was also the best strategy with which he could come up, because if he had learned anything, it was that to try and meet the savages on the water was an invitation to disaster, something his father had learned the hard way. Now, here he was, sitting there trying to be interested when a *fidelis* of Lord Dalmatius was arguing why he should have the rights to a portion of the harvest from a set of fields just outside Cortryk, based on some promise that Baldwin's father had supposedly made after the *fidelis* had performed some heroic deed against the Northmen. It was, he thought, tediously boring, but he could not say that his father had not warned him that most of his duties as the Count of Flandre would consist of such moments.

As he pretended to listen, he idly watched Baudelius, who was standing at the back of the room with Dalmatius, whispering something while the *Dominatius* listened intently, reminding Baldwin that the two men had been close friends during their younger days serving his father. That, he thought with some concern, is something that bears watching. When the commotion erupted at the back of the room but outside the closed double doors to the hall, Baldwin's first thought was, Maybe there's another raid, and the tedium was such that he welcomed the thought. One of the doors opened, and because it was broad daylight outside, while the figure was framed in the doorway, the glare was such that Baldwin could not immediately identify who it was; in fact, it was the giant standing just behind the first man that Baldwin instantly recognized, and he felt his face split into a smile, even as he wondered why the Berserker was here. Hard on the heels of that thought was a rush of concern; when he had left Saint-Omer, the Berserker was still recovering and hardly seemed up for what had to be a hard ride, given that he himself had just arrived the day before. This brought him to his feet, and in that time, he recognized Sigismund, whereupon he was struck by yet another thought, that it had to be something indeed momentous if these two were here, together.

It was Baudelius, who, recognizing the pair, rather than letting them enter, suddenly moved to block their path, his back to Baldwin, making it clear that he intended to stop them, and Baldwin barked, "Lord Baudelius! For what possible reason would you bar Sigismund from entering?"

Even in the dim light, Baldwin saw the older man stiffen, then turn with a deliberate, and insulting, slowness to face the Count.

"I simply wanted to make sure that whatever Sigismund is here for is worth interrupting your duties, Lord Count."

"I believe that I am the best judge of that...wouldn't you agree?" Baldwin asked, in a deceptively mild voice that he was pleased to see Baudelius interpreted correctly, both of them behaving as if neither of them heard the rustling of whispers from the men who were present at this court.

With a stiff bow, he replied tonelessly, "I would, Lord Count. Forgive me."

He stepped aside without a word, but while he barely glanced at Sigismund, Baldwin saw the poisonous glare he gave to the Berserker, at his back, Baldwin noted with amusement, eloquently communicating his feelings for the large Saxon...and his fear. Consequently, Baldwin did not immediately notice the rangy, one-eyed warrior, like the Berserker wearing a mail shirt and not the scale armor that Sigismund was wearing, though none of them were wearing their helmets, but now his curiosity was at a peak.

Stopping two paces from Baldwin, who had resumed his seat, Sigismund went to one knee, but when the Berserker made to do the same, Baldwin stopped him with a gesture, while the one-eyed warrior, who was undoubtedly a Saxon as well, also went to a knee a pace behind the other two men.

"Lord Count, Father Rudolf sent me and the Berserker," Sigismund began, then fumbled to add, "and this Saxon warrior from Wessex, with a message of utmost importance."

"Oh?" Baudelius put in caustically. "Did the good Father see a shadow lurking outside the walls and think that Saint-Omer is under attack? And why would we need *Saxon* help?"

Because of their respective positions, Baldwin was in a perfect spot to see Sigismund's face darken, his lips twisting into a scowl, but his voice was even as he replied, "No, Lord Count. There is no attack on Saint-Omer. But," he reached down to his sword belt, and for the first time, Baldwin noticed there was a scroll tucked into it, which Sigismund retrieved and extended to Baldwin, "he wrote this message for your eyes...and your eyes alone, Lord Count. He was very insistent on that."

Even with the distance, Baldwin heard Baudelius' muttered curse, but he ignored it, standing up and taking the message. Snapping his fingers to beckon one of the servants hovering in the shadows to bring a lamp closer so he did not have to strain his eyes, Baldwin unrolled the scroll, noticing that Father Rudolf had taken the time to seal it, not with the seal of Saint-Bertin, but with the seal of Flandre created by Baldwin's father that, frankly, was either a poorly rendered lion or an equally poorly rendered dragon. Most importantly, it told Baldwin that the priest considered this a matter of state, and it was with a slight tremor that he broke the seal, unrolled the scroll and began to read. He heard someone gasp, unaware that it came from his own lips, but it was the manner in which he collapsed back onto his chair that caused a minor uproar among the onlookers, all of them members of the lower nobility, or *servii* who had some sort of business before the Count at this *contio*, the term the Franks used for what the Saxons called a Hundred Court.

"Lord Count," Baudelius called out, with what Baldwin dimly heard was real alarm. "What is it?"

Baudelius was now walking up the aisle towards Baldwin, but the Count had no intention of letting Baudelius know what was contained in this message, not until he had time to think...and to talk to someone who had been mentioned by the priest in his message. It was, Baldwin knew, a name that would incite Baudelius to object as strenuously as he could, and perhaps do something rash. This thought almost convinced Baldwin to let Baudelius know what was contained in the message, because it was entirely possible he would behave in a way that gave Baldwin the pretext he had been searching for to remove Baudelius and replace him as his *Primores* among the *Nobiles*, but the problem was, with whom? He had been considering Dalmatius, but watching how he and Baudelius had been behaving moments before, now he was not so sure. Deciding that this was not the time, instead Baldwin held up a hand in a silent command to Baudelius.

"*Nobiles*, I am afraid that I must put an end to this *contio* at this time to deal with a very urgent matter that has just come to my attention." As he expected, this was met with unanimous dismay and general unhappiness, which Baldwin ignored for the most part, but he did turn to the *fidelis* of Lord Dalmatius, raising his voice to be heard, "While I must end this, I have heard enough of this matter to render a decision, Lord...?"

His voice trailed off, and he did not have to feign his look of embarrassment for forgetting the man's name, who supplied it, saying stiffly, "Marquin of Ypres, Lord Count."

"Yes, Lord Marquin." Baldwin nodded. "After listening to your claim, and the counterclaim of Lord Sebastien," Baldwin inclined his head in the direction of the older man, with an iron gray mustache that hung down well below his chin and whose name he did not have to struggle to remember because Sebastien had been a fixture of his early life, one of his father's longest and most trusted *fideli*, which also made this easier, "I rule in favor of Lord Sebastien. Your claim to those fields is based on nothing more than your assertion that my father was so impressed with your deeds in the battle at Carcehuttes (Ambleteuse) that he ceded the fields west of Cortryk north of the Lys totaling three hundred *arpent carré*, yet you have provided no documentation of this event. On the other hand, those fields have been in the possession of Lord Sebastien's family for several generations, going back to the time of the blessed Carolus Magnus, so I find it difficult; no," he held up a hand as he corrected himself, "I find it *impossible* to believe that my father granted you possession. Therefore, your case is denied. Now," he raised his voice, ignoring the spluttered gasps of Marquin, while noticing that Baudelius seemed equally displeased, although he understood that it could be for unrelated reasons, "please depart and consider this *contio* concluded, since I am returning to Saint-Omer immediately." Turning to where Titus was standing, while both Sigismund and the Saxon whose name he still did not know had continued to kneel, he commanded, "Berserker, you will stay behind and attend to me. There are matters I must discuss with you...in private. Everyone else will leave."

"Lord Count!" Baudelius, perilously close to shouting, called out over the hubbub of other voices. "I must protest! As your *Primores*, it is my duty to be at your side when matters of import are being discussed. Not," he pointed directly at Titus, who studiously ignored the nobleman, "some lowborn *foreigner*! What could he possibly have to contribute to whatever this is?"

Just in time, Baldwin realized that Baudelius was baiting him in an attempt to divulge why he wanted to speak to the Berserker, and he replied calmly, "That is for me to decide, Lord Baudelius. Now," he pointed to the door where the last of the occupants were filing out, with Sigismund and the one-eyed Saxon bringing up the rear, although Baldwin noticed the Saxon had exchanged some words with the Berserker, "I will call you should you be needed...but you will not be."

For a long moment, Baudelius gave every indication he intended to refuse his Count's command, and Baldwin glanced at the Berserker, instantly seeing how the huge warrior had turned his body slightly, while his hand moved to hook a thumb in his sword belt, placing his hand mere inches from the hilt. It was something all warriors did without thinking, sending a signal to others that they were always ready for a fight, but Baldwin knew this was not what the Berserker was doing, that this was a deliberate move on the Saxon's part. Otherwise, his face revealed nothing, not even anticipation at the prospect that Baldwin might unleash him on Baudelius, which was tempting for the Count, but he was not ready to take such a drastic step, not yet. And, Baldwin acknowledged to himself when, without a word, Baudelius turned on his heel and stalked out, this would not have been the place even if he was ready. After the noise and mild uproar that marked the abrupt end of this *contio*, the silence was profound as the Count and his most feared warrior eyed each other. Finally, it was Baldwin who broke it.

"We have a few things to discuss, Berserker."

It would be an understatement that Titus would long remember.

"Your Saxon King Alfred has made me an offer," Baldwin began, but not after bidding Titus to pull up a chair and place it directly across from him.

The fact that he was still seated on the raised platform while Titus' chair was on the floor was not lost on Titus, nor did it change that, even with this advantage, he was still looking Baldwin almost directly in the eye.

When Baldwin did not expand, Titus could only think to reply, "Oh? That is...interesting, Lord. But I am not certain what it has to do with me."

"How well do you know Alfred?" Baldwin asked suddenly. "What is he like? I mean, as a man?"

"I...I barely know him at all, Lord!" Titus replied in a deep surprise bordering on shock. "I have been in his presence a few times, but I am sure he does not even know my name!"

Even as he said this, Titus realized that this was, at best, something of a falsehood, remembering how, when the Wiltun men had arrived to become part of Alfred's first attempt at building a navy, not only had the King remembered his name from four years earlier, but had remembered a conversation with a fourteen year-old son of a one-hide *ceorl* from that time at Ethantun.

Baldwin, however, would not have accepted this anyway, and Titus learned why when Baldwin held up the scroll and said, "He knows you well enough to mention you by your name...Titus." He paused, then asked curiously, "I realize I have never asked you before; do you know where that name comes from? I confess I do not know much about Saxon names, but that does not sound like one. In fact," he smiled, "it sounds more like a Frankish name."

This, Titus knew, was true, because he had heard this

sentiment expressed more times than he could count since his arrival in Frankia.

Aloud, he answered honestly, "I do not know, Lord, other than it was a name from my mother's side of the family, and she made my father swear he would name me Titus before she died."

Sensing this was a sensitive topic, Baldwin continued, "Yes, well, as I said, you are mentioned by name, and you are mentioned as part of a...proposition that King Alfred is making." Seemingly out of nowhere, Baldwin asked, "What do you know of Alfred's children?"

"His children?" Titus echoed, startled and even more confused, but he thought for a moment before answering, "He has five children, alive, I mean." He counted them off. "There's Æthelflæd, she's the oldest daughter and oldest child. Then there's Eadward, and I suppose he's the Ætheling..."

"Ætheling?" Baldwin interrupted, unfamiliar with the term.

"The heir," Titus explained, "the crown prince. Saxons call that the Ætheling." When Baldwin nodded his understanding, he continued, "Then there's Æthelgifu, another daughter, Ælfthryth..."

"Yes!" Baldwin interrupted again, but this time with an animation that Titus did not understand. "That is her!"

"Oh?" It was all Titus could think to say.

"That," Baldwin explained, "is who King Alfred is offering to me as my bride."

In that moment, Titus was glad he was seated, yet he could not stop himself from gasping, "But she is a child! She could not be more than seven or..."

"She is eight," Baldwin cut him off, his face coloring. "But she would not become my wife until she is of a proper age! Berserker, this is not at all uncommon with...people of my class," he finished weakly.

Titus knew this was the case, though it did not make it seem any less unseemly in his mind, even as he recognized that it was not just people of the nobility who, for lack of a better term, sold their daughters into wedlock, often well before they were of a marriageable age. It was the way of their world, one that men did not think about overmuch, yet it had always bothered Titus, though he never divulged this to anyone of his own sex, which he ascribed to the fact that he had two sisters, and neither of them had been shy about expressing their own feelings to their younger brother on the matter.

"I still do not understand what I have to do with this, Lord Count," Titus said as a tacit way to change the subject.

"Because one of the conditions the King is putting on this agreement is that I release you from your oath to me so that you can return to Wessex." He consulted the scroll again, then shook his head as he explained, "Since this is not the proposal from Alfred and only Father Rudolf's note, it does not say what he has in mind for you, and until I see the proposal with my own eyes, I cannot tell you what it may be. Now," he set the scroll aside, leaned forward and put both elbows on his knees to stare intently at Titus, "tell me everything you know about King Alfred."

They did not leave the hall for another two hours, emerging into the darkness to find that the only people remaining in the area were the *Eques* who had been assigned as Baldwin's close guard that day, the one-eyed Saxon, Sigismund...and Lord Baudelius.

"We are returning to Saint-Omer in the morning," Baldwin announced. "I have an important decision to make."

Titus knew that the ride back would be difficult, though not because of his physical condition, but from the constant badgering by the men he had come to consider his comrades and friends, although a fair amount of time was devoted to talking about the miracle with Ranulf. Once that was dissected, however, Theutbald, Wala, and not coincidentally, the other men who had been with him the night he had been attacked by the wolves as *Exploratores* relentlessly pressed him for information on the cause for their early return. The fact that he had sworn to Count Baldwin to not divulge anything about the offer from King Alfred meant nothing to them, as they attempted anything and everything—cajolery, flattery, bluster, guilt, and outright bribery, nothing was off limits—yet Titus maintained his silence until, finally, with varying degrees of grace or ill humor, they left him alone. Throughout it all, Uhtric had ridden beside his brother-in-law, aided by the fact that he did not understand a word of what was being said.

Once they were left to their own devices, the others communicating their displeasure by drifting away to talk about other matters, the two Saxons rode in silence for about a mile when, finally, Uhtric asked, "Well?"

"Well what?" Titus sighed.

"I know why you didn't tell them, but are you going to tell me what's going on?"

"You mean you don't know?" Titus looked at him in surprise. "You were on *The Redeemer* with Lord Eardwulf and Father Æthelred, and they didn't tell you why they were with you?"

"They weren't with me." Uhtric laughed. "I was with them. Surely you don't think that King Alfred would send five ships, including his favorite ship just to bring you back for Lord Eadward, do you?"

When put that way, Titus realized how ridiculous it was, but he still did not answer immediately.

When he did, it was to ask, "Do you know how old Alfred's daughter Ælfthryth is?"

This startled Uhtric, but he thought a moment and answered, "She has to be around eight. Why?"

Titus did not say anything, instead regarded Uhtric steadily for a long moment until, finally, his friend gasped in shock.

"Wait," he did think to pitch his voice just above a whisper, "are you telling me what I think you're telling me? That Alfred is offering his daughter to Count Baldwin as a *bride*?" Titus nodded, and Uhtric let out a low whistle, but then he thought about it for a bit, the pair riding in silence until, finally, he allowed, "Well, I won't say that it's the worst idea. This Count Baldwin is young, but he holds an important...what do they call it? Not a shire."

"No, they call it a *pagus*," Titus provided. "But it's basically the same thing...just bigger. Flandre is bigger than all of Wessex."

"I wonder what kind of dowry he's offering your Count," Uhtric mused.

"He's not *my* Count," Titus replied absently, which Uhtric thought might be meaningful...or it might not. After another silence, Titus said, "There is a...condition that Alfred is requiring, which is why Count Baldwin wanted to speak to me privately."

"He's demanding that the Count release you from your oath to him," Uhtric said evenly.

Titus' head swiveled to stare at Uhtric, gasping, "How did you know that?"

"I didn't." Uhtric laughed. "Not until you told me what Alfred is offering, and that there was a condition. That's the only one that makes sense. Lord Eadward never hid the fact that the only reason he hadn't sent for you was because of his father, and you know that our King knows everything that goes on in Wessex...and beyond."

"Lord Eadwig," Titus said disgustedly. "If he was still alive, and even if he *begged* me to come back, I wouldn't! Maybe I'll go back so that I can piss on his grave!"

Uhtric shifted uncomfortably in his saddle, because while he understood and sympathized with his brother-in-law, he took a longer, more mature view, but decided against trying to argue that view right then. There will be time for that later, he told himself.

Instead, he probed, "So? I can't see Count Baldwin being so stiff-necked that he would risk offending King Alfred, not when his daughter is the prize, so I'm certain he'll release you." He hesitated, hoping that Titus would speak, but when he didn't, he asked quietly, "What do you want to do, Titus?"

"I don't know," Titus replied honestly. "A lot of it depends on what Yanna wants. Because," he turned and gave Uhtric a challenging look, "*if* I go back to Wiltun, she's coming with me."

"I don't think anyone will argue that she can't come," Uhtric assured him, although at the same time, he imagined what Father Æthelred would have to say when he learned that Yanna and Titus were not married.

That, however, was a problem for later.

"Why would a *Saxon* king offer you his daughter? What

gain does he see for himself?"

Despite who was asking the question, Baldwin recognized that Baudelius' query was not only a good one to ask, as his senior councilor, he was the appropriate man to be asking it. They were back in Saint-Omer, having arrived barely an hour earlier after a hard ride, departing Cortryk at dawn with Baldwin setting a blistering pace. The Count had only taken the time to wash the dust from his face and hands, gulp down some wine, and was still wearing his traveling clothes as he sat in the room he used for councils and for his meals. Seated at the table was Baudelius, Father Rudolf, and Father Guibaud, who was acting as a scribe, though he was at the far end of the table in the sign that he was part of the furniture and not to be heard from, but it was the fifth man who was the surprise, one that Baudelius immediately understood was a signal by the young Count. While Baldwin was tired, Lord Sebastien, almost thirty years older than the Count, was sitting there gray-faced from exhaustion, yet his eyes were alert, and his color was gradually returning. It had been a spontaneous decision for Baldwin to ask the old nobleman to accompany them back to Saint-Omer, yet Sebastien had not hesitated to accept. For Baudelius, Sebastien's presence was close to a mortal insult, an almost literal slap in the face, their rivalry going back to even before the young Count was born, when Baudelius was a teenager and Sebastien in his twenties, both of them knowing that they would be succeeding their fathers as the lords of their domains and were maneuvering to win the favor of the old Count. Sebastien had won that battle, while Baudelius exacted his revenge by positioning himself as a mentor to the current Count, relying on his youth to insinuate himself into the young Baldwin's confidence, something that Baldwin had only begun to see for what it was recently. His inclusion of Sebastien performed a dual purpose; he did value the old nobleman's counsel, finding his incisive insight and sardonic humor a balm to the glowering bluster of Baudelius, but he also knew that Baudelius would be nettled by the other man's presence. This was being borne out as the two men sat on opposite sides of the table, exchanging baleful glances as Father Rudolf read the contents of King Alfred's message, which was what had prompted Baudelius' question as soon as he finished.

"That," Baldwin was forced to admit, "is a good question. And," he added as he looked directly at Sebastien in another signal, "is what I want to discuss first."

The older nobleman stroked his long mustache for a moment before he spoke, his words having a sibilant quality now because he had recently lost one of his front upper teeth.

"There are rumblings about why that demon Sigfred is currently up in Frisia, gathering men and ships," he began. "And what I have heard is that he has been in secret negotiations with the Dane Guthrum, urging him to break his treaty with the Saxon king and join him in an attack on Wessex."

Baldwin nodded in agreement.

"Yes, I have heard the same thing," he replied.

"So has every washerwoman and butcher," Baudelius put in dismissively. "But," he added with mock courtesy, "thank you so much for that observation, Sebastien."

"I was not finished," Sebastien replied quietly, and Baldwin ducked his head to hide his smile as the older man continued, "The reason I brought it up is that I believe this offer is to give the Saxon king a safe refuge where he can at least send his family if those rumors turn out to be true."

This had occurred to Baldwin as well, but he pointed out what he had thought of when he considered it. "But Alfred has been working very hard at fortifying his key towns, and he has built up his army. Wessex today is not the Wessex of before the Battle of Ethantun."

What Baldwin did not say was that his own actions had been partially inspired by the news of what the Saxon king had done, creating what the Saxons called *burhs* and the Franks called *urbs*, like what he had done here at Saint-Omer, Cortryk, Ganda, and Bruciam, where, against his better judgement, he had installed his sixteen-year-old brother Ralph as the commander at Bruciam, although his second in command, Ymbert, was an experienced veteran who had been one of his most trusted subcommanders of his *Pedes* and had been given strict instructions to keep Ralph, who was impetuous even for a teenager, from making a serious error. And, he would admit, if a bit reluctantly, Alfred's strategy had served as a model for his actions.

"That is true, Lord." Sebastien nodded. "But from everything we have seen and heard, Alfred is also a prudent man who plans for as many outcomes as he can. And this," he pointed to the scroll, "can be seen as an example of his prudence. After all," he finished with a slight shrug, "you and he obviously are of a similar mind, what with your fortifications here and elsewhere."

How, Baldwin thought with some alarm, does he know that Alfred's example is what made me think of doing the same? Following hard on the heels of this was another: or, is it just that obvious? Setting it aside as unimportant in the moment, he acknowledged, "That makes sense. What are the risks of accepting?"

"How old is the girl?" Baudelius asked, a question that Baldwin had dreaded, even as he understood that it was a valid, and important one to ask. When he told Baudelius, the nobleman made an exclamation that gave Baldwin forewarning. "God's blood! She won't become beddable for five years, or perhaps four if she matures early!" He shook his head and said emphatically, "That's far too long to wait, Lord! There is so much that can happen! Including," Baudelius indicated Sebastien, "as Lord Sebastien has already mentioned, the fact that Wessex may not survive that long! If the Úlfhédnar is indeed gathering an army to attack Wessex in conjunction with that dog Guthrum, it does not matter how many towns Alfred has fortified, or how many ships he builds! He was almost conquered once, and if the Danes *and* the Northmen join forces?" He shook his head as he concluded, "You may very well end up with nothing from this other than that piece of vellum, Lord."

It was, again, a valid issue, Baldwin knew, but the fact was that his mind was made up, yet he also knew that he must at least appear to consider the matter. However, he had to convince Baudelius, and to a lesser extent Father Rudolf, who it was rumored was being considered for the Bishopric of Saint-Bertin, that office currently being filled by some fat cleric in Paris who Baldwin had only seen once on his investiture, that he was still seriously weighing his decision.

Aloud, he allowed, "That is also a valid concern, Lord Baudelius. And," he sighed, "if my mother was still alive, or if Guinidilda were not in Barcelona with her husband, I believe I would be within my rights to have the girl brought here to live, with a Saxon chaperone, of course." And, he thought, it would be a good way to have the Berserker nearby, because I would suggest to the King that a bodyguard as formidable as the Saxon, and one that the King obviously knew and held in high regard, would be a perfect solution, but since this was out of the question, he put this aside. "However, if Alfred survives any attempt to defeat him and remains in power, what do I stand to lose in my refusal to this offer? And," he pointed to the scroll, "his dowry offer is adequate; perhaps it could even be called generous. Father, will you inform Lords Baudelius and Sebastien?"

"Five hundred pounds of silver," Father Rudolf read from the vellum. "And the incomes from estates in Ashton, in Wiltscir, which would include the income from Saint Michael's, which is in the Ramsbury diocese, along with an estate in Wellow, on the Isle of Wihtwara (Wight), and the income from the All Saints Church in Freshwater." The priest cleared his throat, and finished, "All told, these should yield the equivalent of a thousand *livres* a year, depending of course, on a variety of circumstances."

"Like Wessex being crushed by the heathens," Baudelius muttered, but Baldwin ignored it.

"There is the other matter, Lord Count," Father Rudolf said quietly, but when Baldwin only gave him a quizzical glance, the priest could not stop from glancing over at Baudelius, who was paying close attention before reminding Baldwin, "The King's condition that you release the Berserker from your service so that he can return to Wessex."

The truth was that Baldwin had not even considered this being worthy of mention, so certain was he that Baudelius would be only too happy to be rid of the Saxon, who, while Baudelius did not say as much, Baldwin knew he blamed for Bent's death. Immediately after this thought, the memory of the young *lantwerus* who was languishing in the cellar of this very building, in the single cell, came back, and he resolved that he would make his decision on this matter immediately afterward.

He was completely unprepared, and was deeply shocked when Baudelius snapped, "That is out of the question, of course!"

For a long moment, Baldwin could only stare, open-mouthed, yet even in the moment, he saw both Father Rudolf and Sebastien had similar reactions; even the young priest Father Guibaud at the opposite end of the table looked startled.

Baldwin finally found his voice, though he could only ask dumbly, "But...why?"

"Yes, Baudelius," Sebastien echoed, though he looked more amused, "please tell us, why would you say that it is out of the question to let a man return to his home? A man," his voice hardened slightly, "you have made no secret that you loathe and have wanted to see dead almost since he arrived."

"This has nothing to do with my personal feelings," Baudelius declared loftily. "My concern is only what value he provides as a member of the Lord Count's bodyguard. And," Baldwin saw the older man's jaw suddenly bulge slightly, the sign that he was clenching his teeth, "my personal feelings for the brute aside, he *is* valuable as a warrior."

"Yes," Sebastien seemingly agreed, but now it was his turn to be under Baldwin's scrutiny, and the young Count saw the slight narrowing of his eyes that he knew meant the old nobleman was feeling a bit mischievous, "quite formidable indeed. So formidable that your man Bent tried to murder him from behind because he could not defeat him face to face...even in a brawl."

As personally satisfying as it was to see Baudelius go pale, Baldwin did not want, nor did he need the kind of confrontation that was likely heartbeats away, so he spoke more harshly than he needed to. "Lord Sebastien, that is quite enough!" Turning to Baudelius, he lied, "I truly appreciate your concern, Lord, and I agree that the Berserker is our most valiant and formidable warrior, but I have many valiant and formidable men in my bodyguard." He took a breath, then said with a tone that the others understood, "If the Berserker chooses to return to Wessex and his fellow Saxons, I will not stop him. However," he finished, "if he chooses to stay, I will be happy to keep him in my service. The decision is his."

For the first time in days, Titus felt like he could relax; the only thing missing was Ranulf, although his recovery seemed to be progressing, but he tired very easily and Emilde informed them that he had fallen asleep shortly after dark. Titus wanted to introduce his longest friend and brother-in-law to the man who had befriended him during a time when he needed a friend most, but he was not about to rouse Ranulf. Instead, they sat down to a meal prepared by Yanna, who was more relaxed this time, which Uhtric put down to her having more time to absorb the sudden arrival of these Saxons, and the change to her life it represented. And, Uhtric thought, to himself, *she's a better cook than Leofflaed*, as he asked for another helping of the suckling pig she had roasted, done so that the skin was crackling but flavored with seasonings that he had never tasted before. The only thing missing was a good cup of ale, but aside from that, he had no complaints, in both the food and the company. It was September, now, getting close to October, which meant there was a snap in the air; it also meant that they would have to leave soon, sailing back down the Aa, then back across The Narrow Sea.

It was with this in mind that he asked Titus with a feigned casualness that did not fool his friend, "Does your Count take a long time to reach a decision? Although," he chuckled, "I don't see how this is something that he can say no to, not unless he's a fool."

"He's no fool," Titus countered, perhaps a bit more sharply than he intended. To make up for it, he grinned as he gave Uhtric a shove, "And he's not *my* Count. I've told you that already." He paused to take a sip of wine, then answered, "And no, he doesn't. When he was certain that Hallsteinn had left Boulogne, he didn't hesitate to call the *lantweri*." Before Uhtric could ask, he explained, "It's the Frankish version of the *fyrd*. So," he shrugged, "no, I don't think it will take him long to give an answer."

"Are you all packed?" Uhtric asked Yanna, who only gave him a blank look. "Ah, I mean, have you gotten your belongings together that you'll be bringing to Wessex with you?"

It was a fleeting look, one that later Uhtric was able to convince himself that he imagined, although Yanna answered readily enough, "No, but it will not take me long." She waved a hand at the room. "As you can see, there is not much to...pack." She smiled when she used the unfamiliar word, and Uhtric quickly forgot it, moving on to something else.

"Yanna, has Titus ever told you about the time that I thrashed him so badly when we were sparring that he couldn't walk right for a day?"

"Oh, lick my ass!" Titus groaned, immediately falling back into the pattern that the two had followed for years. "I was fifteen!" he protested, then turned to Yanna and pointed an accusing finger at Uhtric. "He beat me when I was barely a man! What do you say about a man who would beat a child?"

"You were only about three inches shorter than you are now, and about as heavy," Uhtric snorted. "And," he winked at Yanna, who immediately understood what was taking place, "you had a big mouth back then! Someone needed to shut it. And," he shrugged, "I just happened to be available."

"That was the last time you were able to thrash me," Titus pointed out with a grin.

"Bah!" Uhtric snorted. "That's not it at all. I saw how badly you took it, and I just wanted to spare your feelings, that's all."

By this time, Yanna's giggling had become outright laughter, and the rest of the evening was spent in the same fashion, with Uhtric telling stories about her lover, while Titus protested that his brother-in-law was either exaggerating or was understating the circumstances, and Yanna noticed that it depended on whether or not it painted Titus in a good or bad light. She also could tell this was not the first or the second time the pair had plowed this ground, and she realized in that moment that there was no way she could do what she had planned, to beg Titus to stay here, in Saint-Omer, with her. No, she realized, if they were to be together, she would have to be the one to uproot herself. Somehow, she managed to enjoy the night immensely, and once Uhtric fell asleep in the large room, for the first time since his wounding, she and Titus made love. It was, in most ways, a perfect night.

The summons for Titus to come to the Count's residence came from Theutbald, who had guard duty that morning, delivered in mid-morning, but for once, Titus was not at the stakes, which meant that the *Eques* had to saddle his own mount to ride outside the walls to Yanna's cottage. Yanna opened the door, and while there was no missing how pale she was, Theutbald made no mention of her pallor, although he would have been hard-pressed to think of a time where he had exchanged more than a half-dozen words with her at any time, despite knowing her dead husband Maló and considering him a friend. What was even more striking was how Titus was dressed in his best tunic and freshly cleaned trousers, with his hair braided, his beard trimmed, and wearing his arm rings, one of the things he did despite them being objects of suspicion by the Franks around him. He was expecting someone, Theutbald thought, but again did not make any mention of it. Titus disappeared around the back of the cottage, returning with his horse, which had to have already been saddled given how little time it took, another sign that the Saxon was prepared for this summons. He also noticed that Yanna disappeared inside, closing the door before Titus returned with his horse, but he gave the house barely a glance as he swung up into the saddle.

For Titus' part, he was secretly thankful that it was the taciturn Theutbald who was his escort back, but Theutbald was the one who broke the silence by asking bluntly, "You are leaving, aren't you?"

Startled, Titus stammered, "I...I...yes," he finally said, with an exhalation of breath that was a sign of the tension that had been building inside him. "I am, Theutbald. I am going back to Wessex." He thought to add, "That is, if the Count releases me."

"What if he does not?" Theutbald asked, which Titus took as a sign that, somehow, the contents of Alfred's message had remained a secret.

"He will," Titus replied confidently, then more to forestall what he was certain was coming, with Theutbald demanding to know how he could be so certain, he added, "But in the event I am wrong, then," he shrugged, and grinned at the warrior, "I stay."

"What do you want to do, Titus?" Theutbald asked quietly,

but it was the use of Titus' given name that was so unusual, and a sign that Theutbald had his own thoughts on the matter that Titus would remember.

Titus did not reply for several paces, but it was the gate to the palace approaching that prompted him to reply honestly, "I wouldn't mind going home, Theutbald, but only if Yanna comes with me."

Theutbald considered speaking up then, telling Titus what he had seen in Yanna, how she looked as if she was dreading something in her future, but he quickly convinced himself that he was just putting his own feelings onto her, because despite his initial resistance to Titus' appearance, the truth was that he could not imagine not having the huge Saxon around. While Theutbald was not a deep thinker, nor was he adept at expressing what thoughts he did have, he understood that there was something about this huge warrior riding next to him that went far above and beyond what was obvious to the eye. Yes, he was physically formidable, with larger arms, chest and thighs than anyone Theutbald knew, and there was that...thing in him that had not only earned him the appellation, but had been responsible for a feat inside Boulogne that he knew from experience would be the talk in Melisandre's for not just this coming winter, but for winters to come. Yet, it was more than that, and while he did not have the words to express it, what Theutbald, a Frankish warrior who served Baldwin, second of his name and second Margrave of Flandre, understood was that Titus the Berserker was greater than the sum of his parts and skills.

Bent had thought himself to be the unofficial leader of Baldwin's bodyguard, based in his belief in his prowess on the battlefield, which *was* considerable, but also through his domineering, brutal bullying of his fellow warriors, backed up by his willingness to resort to violence to resolve any and every dispute. Then, the strange Saxon had appeared, and it was now to Theutbald's shame that he had been one of the men with Bent that night at Melisandre's who set upon the Saxon, and while Bent had been the instigator, Theutbald and the other four men, including his brother and Ranulf, had been eager and willing to participate. It still ranked as the worst beating Theutbald had ever endured, but it was a shade compared to what happened to Bent, who along with the savage beating, had endured the destruction of his myth of invincibility, and even now Theutbald could understand why Bent had bore Titus an undying enmity; after all, any warrior worth his salt would bear a grudge towards the man who had robbed him of his belief in himself. Then had come Watten, and the first time that the Franks in Baldwin's service witnessed why the large Saxon was called the Berserker, something that they had actually learned from a merchant who plied his trade between Lunden and Frankia early during his time in Baldwin's service. That had spelled the end of Bent's grip on the men of Baldwin's bodyguard, and only now was it clear that it had begun Bent's obsession with destroying the Berserker, culminating in what, by any definition, was a cowardly attempt to murder the Saxon with a spear in the back. Now, Bent was dead, and the Berserker was leaving; who, he thought miserably, was going to lead them now? Who could they look to? Ranulf would have been the most likely candidate, but in this, Theutbald and Titus' outlooks were the same; despite never speaking of it, they were equally certain that Ranulf would never fully recover.

By this time, they had reached the Count's residence, and they both dismounted, where on impulse, Theutbald thrust his hand out, saying awkwardly, "No matter what happens, it has been an honor to fight alongside you, Berserker."

Moved, Titus accepted the hand, replying hoarsely, "No more than it has been mine, Theutbald."

They parted, Theutbald leading his horse back to the Count's stable while Titus was waved through the door by the *Pedes* at the door, exchanging a quiet greeting, but he came to a stop just inside to let his eyes adjust, and it took a moment for him to spot Lord Baudelius, standing in the doorway that led to the room where the Count held his private meetings. Approaching cautiously, Titus' first thought was that he should have at least worn a dagger based just on the way Baudelius was glaring at him, and he braced himself for some sort of onslaught, hoping for the most part that it would be verbal. However, when he reached the entrance, Baudelius continued to glare at him...but stepped aside to allow Titus to enter the room.

It was as he passed the nobleman that Baudelius whispered, "Do you think that you can run off to Wessex without that bounty Sigfred the Úlfhédnar put on you following you, *Saxon*? You will spend what's left of your miserable life looking over your shoulder...and I will laugh when some savage earns that hundred pounds!"

Too shocked to reply, Titus passed him, entering the room to see that Baldwin was not alone; both Lord Eardwulf and Father Æthelred, as well as Father Rudolf were all present.

"Please shut the door," Baldwin was seated at a small table that served as his desk, but when Titus started to beckon Baudelius, assuming that he would be in the room, the Count said sharply, "Lord Baudelius will not be joining us."

As startled as he was at this, his mind began racing with what it could mean even as Titus was pulling the door shut and, since Baldwin's view of him was blocked, while Baudelius was staring at him with undisguised hatred, Titus told himself that it was no longer his concern, or his problem.

Unsure what to do, once he closed the door he stood there, bowing from the waist instead of his more normal inclining of his head that sufficed for the Count as far as obeisance, saying as he did, "You called for me, Lord Count?"

"I did," Baldwin nodded, his tone brisk and somewhat detached. "And I know I do not have to tell you why you are here."

"No, Lord Count."

"I have decided to accept the gracious and generous offer made by King Alfred of Wessex for his daughter, the Princess Ælfthryth, although the ceremony will take place by proxy, and the marriage will not be consummated until she is of proper age," Baldwin said, but if there was a hesitation there, it was barely noticeable before he continued, "And as part of that agreement, I hereby release you from your oath to serve me. You are now free to return to Wessex...if you so choose. However," he turned to look at the two Saxons, "if you choose to remain here, of your own free will, know that you will always have a place in my service...Titus of Cissanbyrig."

This was clearly unexpected on the part Lord Eardwulf and

Father Æthelred, but before it could become a point of contention, Titus answered quickly, "I appreciate the honor, Lord, but I want to go to Wessex. I want," he had to swallow the sudden lump, surprised at the welling of an emotion he did not realize he had been holding in, "to go home."

Baldwin looked disappointed but not surprised, only nodding, then the next few moments consisted of Father Rudolf and his Saxon counterpart speaking in Latin as the terms of the agreement were formally accepted, while unusually, the Frankish cleric served as his own scribe. It was as they were finishing that Titus made his decision, making it difficult to wait through the last-moment courtesies before the parties were ready to part company.

"Lord Æthelweard intends to depart tomorrow," Father Æthelred told Titus. "So you need to speak to him as soon as possible to make arrangements for your baggage."

"I will," Titus promised, "but I would like to speak to the Count first...alone. If," he looked to Baldwin, "that is acceptable, Lord."

"It is," Baldwin agreed, intrigued by what it might be.

Father Rudolf was the last to leave, reluctantly, and Titus had the pleasure of turning to the door to shut it in Baudelius' face when he began to move towards the doorway. Bracing himself, both for Baudelius to pound on the door, which he did not, and for what he was about to do, Titus took a breath before he turned to face the Count.

"Lord Count, first I want to tell you that this was not a decision I made lightly, and it has been the greatest honor of my life serving you. I," he had to pause to collect himself, "have made good friends here, and that is what I want to speak to you about now."

"You want to speak about Ranulf," Baldwin said evenly, and it took an effort on Titus' part not to sag in relief.

"Yes, Lord Count. I...I want to do something for him, but he is a proud man, and I know that if I approached him, he would refuse my help."

"Ranulf will have nothing to worry about, Berserker," Baldwin said with a stiffness that told Titus that he had offended the Count. "I always take care of those who suffer in my service."

"Lord," he gasped, "I know that, and I apologize if it sounded like I was implying otherwise!"

"Well, it did," Baldwin snapped.

Knowing that he was in dangerous waters, Titus spoke hurriedly, "I know that his basic needs will be cared for by you, Lord, and for his wife and child as well. But, you see," he offered a brief prayer for forgiveness for the lie he was about to tell, though it was not a total fabrication, "Ranulf had...plans, for when he could no longer wield a sword."

"Oh?" Baldwin asked, one eyebrow lifted. "What kind of plans?"

"He wanted to become a smith, specializing in weapons," Titus replied. "But, as you know, he's too old to be taken on as an apprentice, and, well," he shrugged, then said simply, "I do not believe that he will ever again be able to serve you as a warrior, Lord."

"I had heard he was making a miraculous recovery," Baldwin said. Frowning, he added, "In fact, that is exactly how both Father Rudolf and Brother Membresius described it, as a miraculous recovery!"

"And, it is, Lord," Titus agreed, then added quietly, "but to what degree? Yes, he can speak now, and he knows Emilde, and his son Amis. And he knows me, but he has large gaps in his memory, and he suffers from terrible headaches. *Can* he completely recover? Anything is possible with God," Titus said with a piety that he hoped did not sound as false to Baldwin's ears as it did to his own. "But I wanted to do something to help him in the event that God has other plans for him."

Baldwin was silent for a long moment, then he finally asked, "So, what is it you are saying, Berserker?"

"I want to give you the sum of twenty *livres*, and request that you keep it for the day that Ranulf decides to become a weaponsmith, which he can use to purchase the tools he will need, and to bribe a master to take him on as an apprentice."

Baldwin sat back in his chair, putting the tips of his finger together as he looked up at Titus for a span of several long heartbeats, his expression unreadable.

Finally, he said, "Very well. Bring it to me, and I will honor your request, you have my word on it."

"Thank you, Lord Count," Titus said hoarsely, then did something that he normally hated to do, dropping to one knee and bowing his head. "Words cannot express my gratitude, and if there is ever anything that I can do that is in my power to do, and it does not violate my oath to Lord Eadward or to King Alfred, I will do should you ask it."

Baldwin gestured for him to rise, and it was as he was doing so that it came to Baldwin, an idea so simple yet so audacious in a way that he had to fight a smile at the thought of the look on Baudelius' face.

"Actually, Berserker, there is one thing you can do for me now."

When Titus left the Count's presence, he had to make a concerted effort to not glance over at Baudelius lest his expression give the nobleman a hint about what was in his future. Mounting Thunor, it was not until he exited the gate of the Count's palace that he began to laugh.

Chapter Eight

"What did you say?"

"I said," Yanna replied calmly, making it a point not to look into Titus' eyes, knowing that his expression of utter bafflement and budding sense of hurt might dissuade her, "I am not going to Wessex with you, my love."

She braced herself for the explosion of the temper that she had heard so much about yet had never seen for herself, but what came was so much worse.

"B-but...why?" he asked in such a way that she could easily imagine him as a child, looking up at his mother when she said something that broke his heart. "I...I don't understand."

How could she explain? she wondered. How could she tell him that she was doing this *for* him, and not *to* him, no matter how it might seem at this moment?

Hardening her heart, she said with as much coldness as she could, "Because I do not want to go to Wessex, Titus. I will not know anyone there. I will be away from my family."

"Your family?" he echoed, and Yanna saw the first glint of something besides hurt. "You told me yourself that you don't get along with your sister, and that your brother hasn't been sober in years! He only lives a few miles from here in Isbergues, and you haven't seen him once since we have been together!"

"They are still my family!" she insisted stubbornly.

They stood there, in her cottage, glaring at each other, then Titus asked gently, "Tell me the real reason, my love. You owe me that much."

Oh, why did he have to say that?

Steeling herself, she began, "I cannot give you children, Titus."

"I know that," he replied. "But that doesn't matter to me!"

"It matters to me, my love," she said quietly but with an

underlying intensity that was impossible for him to miss. "It is all I think about, how much I want to give you a child." The tears came then, hot and in a rush, along with a welling of such strong emotion that she thought it would choke the life from her. "I thought I could live with the shame of not being a full woman, but then Emilde had Amis, and I lie awake at night, hoping that I will die!"

By the time she was finished with this, she had begun wailing, and the grief was so real, and so raw, that it shook Titus to his very core, filling him with such a sense of helplessness at seeing her anguish that he was paralyzed, rooted to that spot and unable to move, to reach for her, to hold her. The thought flashed through his mind: what good would it do anyway? This is the one thing that I can't fix. I can't make her not want a child as much as I don't want a child, he thought miserably. They stood there then, less than two feet apart but separated by a gulf that neither of them knew how to cross. Finally, Titus broke the awkward silence, though he had to swallow twice before anything came out.

"I need to go speak to Lord Æthelweard. He commands the ships and I need to make arrangements for Thunor and find out when we are leaving." Because she was standing between him and the door, Yanna took a single step to the side, and as he walked past her, he impulsively reached out to grab her hand, not caring that he was begging, "Please come with me to Wessex. I know we can be happy!"

"I am going to my sister's," she said dully, refusing to look at him. "My mother is already living with her and my sister's husband."

"To Paris?" he gasped. "You're moving to Paris?"

"I cannot stay here," she answered miserably. "Not when you are not here. And," she did look up at him then, "I will be spending the night with Ranulf and Emilde."

There was nothing more to say then, and Titus the Berserker went to make the arrangements to leave Saint-Omer.

Eudes had long since lost track of all time in his filthy cell in the basement of the Count's palace, the only light coming from the single lamp carried by his jailer, a brute of indeterminate age who was hampered in his ability to communicate by virtue of the fact that his tongue had been cut out. Once a day, or night—Eudes was unable to tell—the man, whose name he did not know, not that it mattered, showed up carrying a bucket of water and a bowl of barely edible slops. Then, even when it was unnecessary, the jailer would use his short club to strike Eudes, and if Eudes was fortunate, it would strike him on the back or legs; if he was not, he would be knocked senseless for varying lengths of time. He was still recovering from the savage beating by Lord Baudelius, who had shown up the night during which Boulogne was burning after it fell, where he sent the two *Pedes* guarding him back at the camp away. He was bound, but even if he had not been, the youth was no match for the nobleman who rendered Eudes unconscious for...who knew how long? All Eudes could say was that when he had awakened, he was not in a tent in camp, tied to a center pole, but in this dark, dank, and filthy place that he had resigned himself to becoming his home for the rest of his days. That those days were numbered he also knew, because he had been told of his fate, again by Lord Baudelius, except this time, he had not been beaten, and he was not alone. With him was Sigismund, who did not say a word, only stared at Eudes as Lord Baudelius informed him with undisguised relish that he would personally be parting Eudes' head from his shoulders.

Eudes would never know where he got the courage from, but he did manage to say, "I do not deny I killed Bent, my Lord, but he was about to kill the Berserker!"

"That is what you say!" Baudelius snapped, then slapped Eudes across the head with his gloved hand. "Nobody else saw him doing anything like that!"

Since his hands were bound, Eudes indicated Sigismund by using his head, protesting as he did so, "That is not true, Lord! Sigismund here tried to stop him, and Bent almost chopped his fingers off!" Looking directly at the warrior, he did not try to hide his desperation, "Please! Tell him!"

Sigismund said nothing, looking away in an unmistakably pointed manner, and while he did not know the warrior other than by sight and from their brief conversation that night, he was certain that Sigismund looked ashamed.

Seeing there would be no help from Sigismund, Eudes also realized that he was doomed, yet he still said stubbornly, "I know what happened, and," summoning all of his courage, he looked directly into Baudelius' eyes, "God knows what happened. And He will punish anyone for killing unjustly, no matter what their station."

He was pleased to see Baudelius flinch, although his satisfaction only lasted the amount of time it took for Baudelius to strike him again, knocking him down, and when he regained his senses, the pair was gone. He had been largely ignored since then, and he spent his time in something of a stupor, while his times of full consciousness were spent trying to think of the few happy events in his short life, like the time that one of the daughters on the farm next to his father's, Joaïa was her name, had let him reach under her shift to touch her breasts, *and* let him stick his tongue in her mouth when they kissed. Aside from that, he would occasionally think with understandable sadness, there was precious little, which meant his memory of Joaïa was replayed over and over in his mind. Despite the fact that he did not know whether it was day or night, the lack of activity above him informed him that it was night, which meant that he was asleep when he was jerked awake by a sudden noise, one that was not part of the night sounds of tiny feet scrabbling across the packed dirt floor, or the creak of a floorboard above his head as one of the guards walked his post. No, he realized with thudding heart, this was footsteps descending the wooden stairs, yet despite his first instinct being to open his mouth to call out, he stopped himself, instead straining his ears to listen.

"Eudes!" a voice whispered, but he still did not answer, the whisper becoming more insistent, "*Eudes!*"

Was that...?

"Sigismund?" he whispered back, certain he was mistaken.

"Yes," the voice whispered back, then he heard halting footsteps before Sigismund whispered, "Say something so I can find you!"

"Say something?" Eudes did keep his voice down. "Like what?"

The footsteps increased in speed, then he sensed a dark bulk just on the other side of the bars.

"That works," Sigismund whispered, then Eudes heard the rattling sound of metal on metal, followed by a rasping sound, and ending with the creak that Eudes knew meant that the door was opened. "Follow me," Sigismund commanded, though he offered no explanation.

Which meant that Eudes did not move, asking suspiciously, "Why? Where are you taking me?"

He heard the hiss of frustration, followed by a brief silence before Sigismund, still whispering, demanded, "Do you want to get out of this place, Eudes?"

There was an obvious answer, but the Eudes that was in this cell was not the same callow, inexperienced Eudes of a couple months earlier, which was what prompted him to say, "Yes, but not if you're taking me to get my head chopped off!"

It is difficult to express one's chagrin in a whisper, but not impossible, which was what Sigismund did then as he admitted, "That's a fair point, Eudes. But no, I'm not taking you to be executed. I'm taking you away from here so you *won't* be executed. Now, come on!"

Oh, how Eudes wanted to simply obey, but there was a mulish streak in the youth that tended to come out at times that were not to his advantage, but too much had happened, and Eudes recalled how Sigismund had looked away from him that time when just perhaps his speaking up would have kept Eudes out of this cell, which was what prompted him to demand, "Why should I believe you now? You could have helped me earlier when Lord Baudelius came to tell me I was being executed, but you didn't!"

There was a brief silence, then Sigismund sighed, not loudly but Eudes heard it.

"Bent was my cousin, Eudes, and we had been together since we were children. But," Sigismund's voice rose above a whisper, "that's no excuse. My...my nerve failed me."

It was such an astonishing thing, Eudes thought; the idea that a warrior as experienced as Sigismund, a man of the *Eques* of the Count's bodyguard should admit such a thing was so astonishing that this more than anything else got Eudes to move towards the opening, reaching out like a blind man. Sigismund let out a barely audible gasp of surprise when the youth's hand brushed his chest, but he recovered quickly.

"Grab my belt," he commanded as he turned around. "Hold on to it until we're outside."

Eudes did as he was told, finding the warrior's sword belt after some fumbling, then obediently followed Sigismund as they crossed the basement, reached the wooden stairs, then slowly ascended them. It was not until Sigismund opened the door that led out into the courtyard that Eudes fully realized that it was dark, but to his eyes, it was almost as bright as daylight.

"Stick to the shadows," Sigismund commanded. "We have to leave through the gateway, then get to the river."

This brought Eudes to a stop, staring at Sigismund in the light of a quarter moon, which was almost as much light as the lamp used by his jailer, and as much light as the youth had seen in more than a week.

"Why do we need to get to the river?" Eudes asked, but Sigismund shook his head, whispering sharply, "There's no time for that right now. Once we get there, then I'll explain to you."

It was far from satisfactory, but Eudes sensed that he had no choice, so he nodded, and Sigismund resumed moving along the wall of the palace until reaching the end of it near the outer wall that protected the palace, barracks, stables and other outbuildings.

"Wait here," he commanded, then strode off to the gateway.

Eudes heard him, speaking in his normal voice, "I need you two to go check the kitchens. I heard something rooting around in there. I think that pack of dogs is back."

"Both of us, Sigismund?" Eudes heard one of them ask.

"I'll stay here," Sigismund replied, then said with a feigned casualness, "Unless one of you wants to go by yourself and it turns out that the pack has grown since the last time they made a raid."

As Sigismund knew it would be, this was enough, and the pair went trotting past, not even glancing in Eudes' direction as he crouched at the base of the outer wall of the Count's palace. Only after the sound receded in the distance did Sigismund whistle, and Eudes hurried over, almost immediately becoming winded. The thought came suddenly; I hope I can make it to the river! Sigismund turned and began moving at a brisk trot, and Eudes decided that he would have to find a way, following behind the warrior. Eudes did not know Saint-Omer very well; he had spent time here during his period of training after the calling of the *lantweri*, and when he thought about it, that brief time seemed as if it was ten years earlier. The town was utterly quiet, Eudes estimating that it was at least an hour before dawn, so their footfalls were the only noise, along with Eudes' panting, but just before he was about to gasp that he had to stop to catch his breath, Sigismund rounded a corner, and when Eudes followed him, he saw they were at the dock. And, he saw with a surprise close to shock, there were ships tied up at three piers, one on each side of two of them, and one big one at the third pier.

Sigismund pointed to the large one and said, "Go over there. You'll see two Saxons there, and one of them has an eyepatch. The other one speaks our tongue, and he'll explain what to do."

Eudes felt dizzy, and before he moved, he asked, "What's happening, Sigismund? I don't understand."

Sigismund replied immediately, his tone matter-of-fact, "You're going to Wessex, Eudes. You're going to serve the Berserker. Do whatever he tells you to do, and do it to the best of your ability, and you'll do well."

If anything, the youth was even more confused.

"The Berserker? Serve him? I don't understand!"

"Go speak to that Saxon," Sigismund repeated, for the first time showing some impatience, "and he'll explain it to you. At least," he thought to add, "part of it. The Berserker will be here soon, and he'll tell you the rest as soon as it's safe to do so." Before Eudes could say anything, Sigismund spun about and began walking away, but he only went a half-dozen paces before he stopped and faced the youth. "I failed you the first time, Eudes. I should have spoken up, but I didn't. This is my way of making up for that mistake. And Eudes?" He hesitated, then said, "May God protect you. You did the right thing when you tried to stop my cousin from a foul deed that would have stained his honor forever. I thank you for that."

Then, he turned his back and walked away, leaving Eudes in some ways more confused than ever. Nevertheless, he walked to where the two Saxons were standing next to the gangplank where one of them, a bit taller than average and lean in build, was wearing the eyepatch.

In an oddly accented but understandable Frankish, the Saxon without the eyepatch asked, "Your name is Eudes?" The youth nodded, and the Saxon continued, "Follow us onto *The Redeemer*. We will wait for Titus to join us, and I will translate everything."

It took Eudes a heartbeat to recall who Titus was, never thinking about him as anything other than the Berserker, the most formidable and courageous warrior in Count Baldwin's service. And, even in his confusion, Eudes understood that if the Berserker was joining them, it meant he no longer served Count Baldwin. That it also meant he was leaving his home, the only place he had ever known, was something that was too enormous to consider in that moment, so he merely nodded and meekly followed the two Saxons onto the ship. Eudes had never been on a ship before, and the first thing he noticed was how it rocked, even in the river, making him wonder how bad it would be on the open sea. The next thing he noticed was that the ship was already crowded with men, although they were almost universally reclining on one of the narrow benches that lined both sides, and while the Frankish youth had never been on a ship, he had seen them before, so he knew that these men would be doing the rowing. The Saxon with the eyepatch pointed to himself, and said, "Uhtric," which prompted Eudes to supply his own name, though he felt foolish for doing so since they had already addressed him.

Uhtric had an exchange with the other Saxon, whereupon the second man explained, "Uhtric is married to Titus' sister." He made a gesture, apologizing, "I do not know the word for that in your tongue. But he wanted me to tell you that if you have any questions, you are to come to him and not bother Titus. Uhtric says that he has much on his mind and needs to be left alone for a time."

Although this suited Eudes, given that as much as he admired the Berserker, a larger part of him was terrified of the

298

Saxon, but he felt compelled to ask, "What if I just want to thank him for taking me with you to..." He had to think for a moment before he recalled, "...Wessex?" Before the Saxon could answer, he asked, "Where *is* Wessex?"

This clearly surprised the translator, because he turned and said something to Uhtric, whose one eye visibly widened, but Uhtric spoke for a few heartbeats, then shrugged.

"It is across The Narrow Sea, of course!" the translator finally said. "You did not know that?"

"I...I had never even seen The Narrow Sea until..." he had to think, "about ten days ago, when we marched to Boulogne." As his mind caught up to the conversation, he felt a lump forming in his throat, which he had to swallow down before he asked nervously, "How narrow *is* The Narrow Sea?"

The Saxon laughed, then translated to Uhtric, who chuckled as well, though it was not an unkind one to Eudes' ear, while the translator said, "I do not know for certain, but I heard one of the shipmasters say that where we crossed is twenty miles of open water." He shrugged and added, "I do not know if we will take the same route back. If we do and it is daylight, you can see Dover, but I have heard that is a dangerous thing to do because of those Northern *bâstarts*. Although," he smiled at Eudes, "we heard that your Count took care of that vipers' nest near here once and for all."

"He did." Eudes nodded, then added with what he felt was justifiable pride, "I was there."

"You were?" the translator asked in what sounded to Eudes as real surprise, offending him slightly, and the Saxon relayed this to Uhtric, which prompted Uhtric to respond.

The translator listened, then turned back to Eudes.

"Uhtric asked if you got your blade wet?"

"My blade?" Eudes echoed, confused for a heartbeat before understanding. "Ah, you mean my spear. I am a *lantwerus*," he explained, quickly realizing this would mean nothing to two foreigners, amending it to, "I am a spearman. And," he hesitated then said, "yes, I did...that."

It was, he thought, the truth; that it was the blood of one of his own did not change the fact that what Eudes had done was done to protect their fellow Saxon, but he decided in that moment to keep this to himself.

Besides, the pair seemed suitably impressed, both of them nodding their approval, and this did embolden Eudes to address Uhtric as Titus' friend, "Sigismund said I will be serving the Berserker?"

Uhtric either knew a bit of the Frankish tongue, or more likely to Eudes, he made an assumption based on Eudes' tone, because he nodded before the translator related his question.

They had a brief exchange then, and the translator confirmed, "That is what Uhtric was told. He said that once Titus is with us, he will explain everything. Now," the translator pointed almost directly down at the deck, "we are going to hide you. If you need to piss, do it now, because we will not be letting you out until it is safe, and I do not know how long that will be."

"Hide me? Hide me where?" Eudes asked, more surprised than alarmed, though that would quickly change.

"Underneath the deck," the translator indicated again. "Now, hurry up and piss. Or shit if you have to shit. The shipmaster said that we will be leaving just after dawn."

To Eudes' intense relief, both mentally and physically, he did not have to ask how he was supposed to do that, because even as the translator was speaking, he watched no less than three of the ship's crew get up, pull down their trousers then perch on the edge of the ship on the river side, and Eudes followed suit. He was just finishing when, out of the darkness, he saw two shapes, one large led by another even larger, materialize from down the street that terminated at the dock. It took a few heartbeats for his eyes to confirm what his mind already had assumed, that it was the Berserker, riding his horse while leading a pack animal with him. Hurriedly finishing his business, he hopped down as he pulled up his trousers, intending to go to the plank to speak to the Berserker, but he was stopped by the translator, who pointed to where one of the crewmen had lifted up a timber on the centerboard while Eudes had been busy.

"You need to hide now," the translator said, but Eudes resisted.

"I just want to speak to the Berserker! To thank him!"

"You can do that once we are downriver and the master says it is safe," the Saxon said firmly.

Eudes glanced at Uhtric, but he had already turned away and was walking towards the plank to greet his friend. With a sigh, Eudes allowed himself to be led to the spot, finding that it was cramped, and while it was dry enough, that would be changing shortly, but it was when the board was lowered back into place and the dim light of predawn became total darkness that he felt a rush of panic. It was as if he was back in his cell, but with even less room to move, and it took every bit of his willpower, aided by a whispered prayer to God that He give Eudes strength for him to lie down and allow the plank to be replaced over him. As it would turn out, it consigned Eudes to being only an auditory witness of what was coming; if he had noticed that for some reason the Berserker was wearing his armor and had his sword strapped to his waist, it might have made him worry even more.

Titus had not gotten any sleep, though it had not taken him very long to pack his belongings. The rest of the time had been spent at Ranulf's, where by unspoken consent, neither he nor Yanna talked about her decision. Instead, they sat together as they had so many evenings before, with Yanna helping Emilde prepare the meal, while the baby slumbered in the crate that served as his crib, and Titus and Ranulf sat at the table talking. It heartened Titus to see how Ranulf's memory seemed to be coming back, but at the same time he noticed how his friend seemed to have difficulty judging near distances, having to reach for his cup twice, for example, yet while he wondered about it, he did not mention it. They talked about everything other than what lay in their immediate future and what it meant for all of them, or their immediate past that had led them to this point, instead choosing to share their last moments together reminiscing about the previous two years. The meal consumed, and with several cups of wine behind them, Titus cleared his throat, which caused the two women to exchange a glance, both of them knowing that when he did this, it had some meaning.

"I talked to Count Baldwin earlier today," he began. "He gave me his assurances that you and your family will always be under his protection, and won't want for anything."

"Yes, the Count sent Lord Sebastien to tell us," Emilde said for the both of them. "Ranulf is going to speak to the Count tomorrow to express his thanks."

"Yes, well," Titus fumbled, feeling awkward, "there's more. I gave him twenty *livres* as well, which he will set aside for you when, I mean *if* you decide that it's time to hang up your sword."

"*Twenty* livres?" They both gasped in almost perfect unison, looking across the table at each other, but it was Ranulf who asked, "But why? You said yourself that the Count will pay me a *pensio*! No, we won't live like a lord, but it will be enough!"

"Don't you remember?" Titus asked, beginning to feel a little foolish. "You talked about becoming a weaponsmith, specializing in swords."

For a long moment, Ranulf's face was blank, his jaw hanging open and reminding Titus of how he had been all the time just a matter of about ten days earlier.

Fortunately, it did not last that long, his expression clearing, and he said, "I remember talking about it a time or two, but as I recall, whenever I did, I was drunk!"

"Well," Titus replied stubbornly, "the fact that you mentioned it more than once means that you must be interested in doing it. And," he pointed out, "you're not only long in the tooth, but you're too stubborn and set in your ways for a master to apprentice you outright, so," he shrugged again as if it was no great thing he was doing, "you'll have enough to buy your tools, and to bribe a master who's stupid enough to take you on. But," he pointed, "I'm reserving a blade, and I expect it to be something that the Count would be proud to carry."

Ranulf's eyes filled with tears, while Emilde had already begun quietly sobbing, leaning against Yanna, and Titus reached over and gripped his friend's forearm, squeezing it.

"And," he said quietly, "you know that I'm not one for prayers, but know that I will say a prayer every day for your full recovery, my friend. Every. Day."

Ranulf frowned, wiping his tears away as he asked in puzzlement, "Recovery? Recovery from what?"

Before Titus responded, he glanced over at Emilde, but she only shrugged and shook her head.

"Recovery from what that whorespawn Northman did to you, of course!"

"Northman?" Ranulf echoed, now cocking his head, and it was his turn to look at Emilde and ask, "What is Titus talking about, wife? What Northman?"

"The one who did that!" Titus pointed to Ranulf's skull where, while the swelling had gone down, the sutures that had sewed the flap of scalp back into place were gone and the hair was growing back, there was still the misshapen skull that would never look the same.

Ranulf reached up, still obviously mystified, and tentatively touched his skull with his fingertips, his expression transforming as he felt the scars and the ridges where Brother Memberius had done his best to rearrange the pieces back together, his eyes going wide in disbelief.

"W-what happened to me?" he gasped. "When did this happen? How? Why are you just telling me about this?"

The other three adults seated at the table were frozen in shock, Titus' mouth hanging open in an unintentional imitation of Ranulf a moment before, and once more he looked over at Emilde, who was as distressed as he was and only able to offer a helpless shrug. Titus was about to say something, though he had no idea what that would be when the silence was broken by a roar of laughter, from Ranulf, causing Titus' head to snap around to see his friend, his face red as he pointed back at him, guffawing and slapping the table with his other hand.

"You should see your face!" He hooted. "You look like you swallowed a turd whole!"

"You...*bâstart*!" Titus gasped. "You were playing the fool all along?"

"Of course!" Ranulf replied. "Just because I took an ax to the head, it doesn't mean my brains leaked out!"

Torn between being angry and relieved, before he could think about it, Titus found himself joining in with his friend, while the two women glared at the men.

"That was *not* funny," Emilde protested, but then Yanna began giggling, and before long, the four were laughing so uproariously that it woke baby Amis, who proved to be the one member of their party who could not be persuaded to see the humor.

Finally, Emilde solved the problem by pulling out a breast and offering it to her son, who immediately stopped squalling. A silence descended on the table, each of them becoming absorbed in their own thoughts, and not long after that, Titus said his farewells.

Yanna rose, but told Titus firmly, "I am coming back here, but I will walk with you back home first."

They did not talk on the way back, and Yanna refused Titus' plea to spend one last time together as man and woman.

"It would be too hard," she said honestly.

Interpreting her tone, Titus signaled his surrender by changing the subject. "Do you have the money I gave you in a safe place?"

"Yes," she assured him. "It is safe. And...thank you."

"Here." He rummaged in his pouch and retrieved an arm ring, the last one made of gold besides the one Einarr had given him. "I want you to take this as well. But," he continued, "I want you to use this for one thing and one thing only."

"What is that?" Yanna asked cautiously.

"If you decide to come to Wessex, this will more than pay for your passage, and I'm hoping that you will use it," he said earnestly.

Oh, how she wanted to; so, so badly did she want that, but she also felt in her heart that she was doing the right thing. Still, she thought, it wouldn't do any harm to accept it, and she would always have it to remember him by since she was certain she would never use it, for anything, so she took it from his hand. They did kiss, but it was more melancholy than passionate, and Titus held Yanna in his arms for a long time before reluctantly letting her go. He did not stop to watch her vanish into the night, turning to finish packing, then lying down for a short rest, though sleep never came.

There was a brief argument between Titus and the shipmaster of *The Redeemer*, based mainly in Ragnulf's ire in not being told he would be transporting a horse, which meant that cargo had to be shifted to make room. Thunor had just been led up the plank, only after Titus had unsaddled him then covered his horse's eyes with a cloth, a common method of loading horses, and Titus was in the process of hobbling both front and back legs, which would be followed by snubbing his horse to the vertical pole that was used for such purposes when transporting animals, this capability being one of the few where Saxon vessels were superior, when there was a shout from the direction of the buildings nearest to the dock.

"This is for your own good, boy," Titus whispered, patting Thunor on his neck as he stepped away to peer into the darkness.

He saw movement much sooner than Eudes had because it was lighter, and was able to identify that it was a group of men more quickly as well, the light of the predawn growing by the moment, but it was the manner in which one man was leading what he counted to be a half-dozen other men that told him who it was; more importantly, he knew why they were approaching, and he moved quickly to the plank to intercept them.

"It's Baudelius," Titus said quietly to Uhtric, who was not wearing his armor, but had strapped on his sword. "He must have checked the cell and seen the boy was missing."

Lords Eardwulf and Æthelweard had not arrived yet; they had been the guests of Count Baldwin in his residence, nor was Father Æthelred present either, the cleric staying with Father Rudolf in the cleric's house next to the church, and Titus' hope was that they would not arrive until after this matter had been resolved. When the party was within about thirty paces, Titus recognized Sigismund, Theutbald, Wala, Hekfrid, who was still limping slightly from the wound he had taken during their fight with the Northmen's scouting party, and another *Eques* who had been close with Bent, Artald. None of whom, even Artald, Titus noticed, looked happy to be there, which gave him some satisfaction.

"You there! Berserker! We have come to search this and every other Saxon ship!" Baudelius called out as he was still striding towards the plank.

Forcing himself, Titus inquired politely, "May I ask why, Lord?"

"You know why!" Baudelius snarled, but Titus refused to respond, turning instead to look at Uhtric as Ragnulf came hurrying from the stern, and Uhtric shook his head in a clear signal.

"Lord?" Ragnulf, who as a shipmaster that sailed between Angle Land and Frankia, and other points as well, spoke Frankish, though he professed to dislike doing so, arrived to stand at the head of the plank, feet apart and hands on hips in a clear signal. "You seem to think the Berserker knows why, but I assure you that I do not. For what reason are you demanding to search these ships? And," he added, "is Count Baldwin aware of this?"

It was, Titus thought with some chagrin, the first thing he should have said himself, bringing Baldwin into it, even though the Count had been explicit that he had no intention of being involved any more than he already was.

"It will be up to you to get the *lantwerus* out of here," he had told Titus. "If Baudelius manages to find where you have him hidden away, I will *not* intervene, is that understood?"

"No," Baudelius snapped, "I have not informed the Count...*yet*. I am giving you the opportunity to turn the prisoner over before I find him myself! And then," he finished threateningly, "it will be worse for all of you!"

By this time, Baudelius had reached the base of the plank, but instead of waiting, Titus gently moved Ragnulf aside and descended slowly, grimly pleased to see how suddenly Baudelius removed his foot and took a step backward.

"Are you accusing us of something, Lord?" Titus asked softly. "Or are you accusing *me*?"

"I have no doubt you are involved, Saxon!" Baudelius shot back, but Titus noticed that he was still moving backward; more importantly, he saw how the *Eques* that Baudelius had brought with him were shifting from one foot to another, looking at each other, and in general showing how little they wanted to be involved, something that Titus prayed would hold, having no desire to cross swords with any of these men he considered friends, even Artald. "And I intend to prove it!"

"You are not setting foot on this or any other ship unless Lord Eardwulf gives me orders to allow it, Lord," Ragnulf spoke up from behind Titus. "And," he asked challengingly, "what proof do you have that the Berserker is involved?"

"That is none of your concern," Baudelius answered, but Titus heard the first glimmering of doubt in Baudelius' voice.

"Lord Baudelius," Titus sighed. "Go back to your home. Let us leave in peace."

"And let you take that murdering lickspittle *vindjû* with you?" Baudelius shouted, using a gutter slang term that was most unseemly for a nobleman. He pointed directly in Titus' face, and the Saxon felt the stirring in his gut, while behind him he heard a gasp, knowing that it had to be Uhtric, who knew exactly how much his brother-in-law despised this. "You are *happy* that he murdered Bent!"

"There are not many people who are unhappy that he is gone," Titus retorted, then regretted it, glancing over at Sigismund, but he was expressionless and looking at Baudelius. Nevertheless, he felt he was on firmer ground when he reminded Baudelius, "And he tried to murder me with a spear in the back, so some might say he got what he deserved for that cowardly act."

"He was a great warrior!" Baudelius shouted. "He was a loyal Frank, and he was..."

"A bully who liked to pick on people weaker than he was."

It was not said loudly, but the effect was the same as if Sigismund had shouted the words, causing Baudelius to wheel on Sigismund to snarl, "Bent was always right about you, Sigismund! He said that you were weak, and I see that he was right!" Wheeling back about to face Titus again, he shouted, "Now, step aside, Saxon. I will search your ships, starting with this one!"

What sealed the fate of Lord Baudelius was that he made the decision to draw his sword; whether or not he actually intended to use it, or if it was to emphasize his intentions, none of those watching would ever know. Before it was halfway out of his scabbard, Titus had drawn Wyvern's Fang, rammed it into Baudelius' chest, driving the point through his heart, all of it happening so quickly that even if the watching *Eques* had been inclined to intervene, they could not have stopped him. Baudelius, bearing the look of shock that Titus had seen so many times before, tried to speak, to curse this Saxon interloper with his last breath, but he dropped to his knees, then collapsed facedown before he could do anything other than utter a soft moan.

"Oh, Titus," Uhtric said softly, "what have you done?"

As usual, it was Lord Eardwulf who was the cause for the delay, complaining incessantly about being rushed, yet somehow, both Lord Æthelweard and Father Æthelred managed to rouse the old man, and with the help of his small army of servants and slaves, they departed the Count's palace shortly after the sun rose. Count Baldwin was present to bid them a safe voyage back to Wessex, yet for some reason, he did not seem all that interested in accompanying them the short distance to the docks, but the two Saxons were sufficiently distracted dealing with Eardwulf that they did not put much thought into it. They arrived at the docks within a matter of heartbeats after Lord Baudelius was slain, and they were greeted by the sight of one of the Frankish warriors of Baldwin's bodyguard, whose name they learned was Sigismund, standing over the prone body, bloody sword in hand.

"What is this?" Lord Eardwulf demanded. "Who has struck down Lord Baudelius?"

Since he was speaking in the Saxon tongue, his words had to be translated by the nearest man who spoke both tongues, the Berserker as it turned out.

"Lord," Titus' voice was choked with some emotion that Eardwulf, nor the others who did not know him, could have identified, "Lord Baudelius tried to kill me because of a long-standing grudge he has held for me. This man," he pointed to Sigismund, who was standing with his sword in his hand, looking slightly stunned, "stopped Lord Baudelius from murdering me when my back was turned."

"Grudge?" Eardwulf frowned. "What kind of grudge could a man like Lord Baudelius possibly hold against a...against you?"

"It's...complicated, Lord," Titus replied.

"Lord Eardwulf!"

The old nobleman looked towards the ship, where Ragnulf was standing at the plank. "If it's your pleasure, Lord, we're ready to depart as quickly as possible."

"But there's a dead man lying there!" Eardwulf protested, pointing down at Baudelius. "Surely the Count should be informed. Shouldn't he?" he asked more hesitantly.

It was never spoken of, by any of the men standing there witnessing this, but somehow Æthelweard understood the essence of what was taking place, because he was the one who answered Eardwulf, "My Lord, I do not believe this is a matter that concerns us. And," he added what was the most important part, "we have the Count's agreement, do we not? The sooner we return to Wessex, the sooner we can give our King the good news."

"I suppose you're right," Eardwulf murmured, then after a brief moment, he turned and beckoned to the men carrying his baggage who had been standing there, open-mouthed and, understandably, extremely nervous, and they resumed moving towards *The Redeemer*.

Titus, who was standing next to the plank, bowed his head as the aged nobleman passed him, but Eardwulf stopped, clearing his throat in the signal that Titus should raise his head. When he did so, Titus was astonished; gone was the doddering old man and in his place was a man, old certainly, but without the rheumy gaze of the elderly, who was instead fixing him with a shrewd gaze that did not seem to miss anything.

"I don't know what happened here," Eardwulf said softly, "but I would suggest that you take it to the grave with you. Do you understand me, Titus of Cissanbyrig?" Titus, not knowing what to say, only nodded dumbly, though this seemed to satisfy Lord Eardwulf, who resumed ascending the plank. "King Alfred," he murmured, "has plans for you."

Lord Æthelweard followed Eardwulf, and though he did not say anything, he gave Titus a knowing look, followed by a curt nod, but the priest, who took up the rear of the party of three, did not deign to look at the large Saxon. The servants followed next, and as they secured the boxes and bags that accompanied men of noble rank, Titus was left standing on the dock with Sigismund, and the other Eques who had gathered around the corpse of Baudelius.

"Are you certain about this?" Titus asked Sigismund, but the Frankish warrior nodded, and replied firmly, "I am. This is for the best, for everyone."

"Not for him," Titus remarked, looking down at Baudelius' body, but before Sigismund could respond, he added, "I know that this solves a problem for the Count, but are you certain that the Count will not punish you?"

"Baudelius' fate was sealed before this," Sigismund replied elliptically, but while this was intriguing, Uhtric called out that they were ready to depart.

Before he ascended the plank to board *The Redeemer*, Titus took the time to clasp hands with the other men, saving Sigismund for last.

"If you are ever in Wessex," Titus said, half-jokingly, "you can find me in Wiltun."

"I think it is more likely you come back to Frankia," Sigismund said with a smile, which Titus knew was true.

Then, it was time, and he walked up the plank then helped the crewmen drag it aboard the ship. As a pair of crewmen used poles to shove *The Redeemer* away, the sun rose on Saint-Omer, but Titus refused to look at the town, preferring instead to walk to the bow and look downstream. It was not how he had planned it, but Titus was going home.

Now that they were aware of the fate of Boulogne, the mood was certainly more relaxed, but for Eudes, who had not been freed from his hiding place until they were well downstream beyond Watten, it was almost overwhelming. Part of it was his certainty that the ship he was on would suddenly come to a stop somewhere along the riverbank, and he would be put off the ship to fend for himself. When that did not happen, it was not until the second day that he worked up the nerve to approach the Berserker, who had settled himself in the bow, with Uhtric and another warrior whose name Eudes learned was Godric. The large Saxon watched him approaching, his face giving nothing away of his thoughts, which was even worse for the youth, but without remembering walking half the length of the ship, Eudes suddenly found himself standing a pace away from where the Berserker was leaning against the side next to the prow. He still had to grab the side to steady himself, and for a terrible moment, he was certain he had forgotten how to speak, but he finally managed, "I want to thank you for what you did...Master."

Titus held up a hand, and he said firmly, "You are not a slave, Eudes, so I am not your master."

While this was good to hear, Eudes was also puzzled.

"But I was told by Sigismund that I am to serve you. So, if that is true, but I am not a slave, then I am your servant."

To Titus' embarrassment, he realized this was the first time he had given the matter any thought; when Baldwin had broached the subject and said that Eudes would be told by Sigismund that he was in Titus' service, he had not spent a moment thinking about what that would mean.

"You are not my slave, and you are not my servant," Titus said slowly. "You are my...apprentice, I suppose."

If God struck him down in that moment, Eudes was certain that he would have died happily; after all, this was his dream! From the first moment he had seen the Saxon about whom he had heard so much, young Eudes longed to be considered worthy of being trained by the Berserker, and here was the moment!

Aloud, he managed, "T-thank you. I will not let you down, I swear it! But," he added, "I still do not know what to call you."

"Titus is fine," the Saxon replied, and for the first time, he smiled, but it was not one that Eudes found all that comforting. "Although I promise that you are going to be calling me all sorts of names...behind my back."

Eudes tried to laugh, but all that came out was a weak chuckle.

"Is there anything I can do now?" he asked. "Does your armor need scrubbing? Or is there something I should be learning?"

While he did not show it, Titus was impressed; when he related the conversation to Uhtric and Godric after Eudes left, they were as well.

He thought for a moment, then pointed to the stern.

"Do you see that man sitting right outside Lord Eardwulf's

shelter? The one with the bald head and gray fringe?" Eudes nodded. "That is Deorwine. He serves Lord Eardwulf, but he speaks Frankish." Titus paused to dig into his purse, peering down into it until he found what he was looking for, then handed Eudes a silver coin that was slightly larger than the Frankish *denier* and held it up for Eudes to take. "Give him this shilling, and tell him that you serve me, and I want him to start teaching you some words in our tongue. That," he had shrugged, "should keep you busy until we make landfall in Wessex."

"Yes...Titus," Eudes remembered to use his name, but then he bowed, which was bad enough; he also had the misfortune that this was the same moment that the prow of *The Redeemer* smashed into a wave.

Already off-balance from the bow, the shuddering of the ship sent him staggering, and he stumbled directly into the Saxon, who managed to catch him before his momentum sent him overboard over Titus' shoulder.

"Steady, boy." Titus laughed. "You need to get your sea legs. Although," he added as he helped steady the mortified youth, "once we're back in Wessex, I doubt that we'll see a ship again."

Mumbling an apology, Eudes retreated back towards the stern, clutching the line that Saxons rigged to run parallel to the centerboard at waist level; later, both he and Titus would have cause to remember this conversation, and their thoughts would run along similar lines.

While it was noticeably colder, the weather held, and there were no sails, either foe or friendly, spotted by Ragnulf's son, which Father Æthelred made sure to ascribe to God's grace, not mentioning his own part in this minor miracle through his almost constant prayer. With Eudes occupied, there was little for Titus to do other than catch up with the situation facing him, with Uhtric supplying the information about Lord Eadward, while on larger events, it was Lord Æthelweard who gave Titus the insight that their King was of a like mind as Count Baldwin, that Guthrum was wavering in his commitment to the treaty that, astonishingly enough, was now in its eighth year. What could not be denied was that more Danes than ever had grown restless, and were conducting *vikings* on their own, while Guthrum was either powerless or was too disinterested to intervene and bring them to heel. As fractious as Saxons could be, and from Titus' experience, the Franks were only marginally more disciplined and unified, the invaders from the North were next to impossible to control by a single leader, and the fact that Guthrum had managed to the degree he had was considered a minor miracle, but what was now accepted as fact as that these days of relative peace were coming to an end.

"And you say that Hallsteinn never returned to Boulogne?" Æthelweard had asked.

"Not that I'm aware of," Titus had answered him. "Although I was unconscious for two or three days after we took the gate, and when I woke up, I was at the cell hospital at Saint-Bertin. But," he added, "I'm sure if he had been there, I would have known. His second in command was Bjorn Sigurdson, and I faced him in single combat. If Hallsteinn had gotten back in time for the battle, I would have faced him."

"And," Uhtric had spoken up, a grim smile on his face, "we would know he was dead."

"How did he manage to get away?"

The answer to his question, Titus would learn, was the part of the story that Uhtric had yet to tell him. What Titus knew at that point was that, their plan to take Hrofescester foiled by Alfred's tactic of surrounding the besiegers, Hallsteinn and his surviving warriors managed to break out, and that it was in this battle that Lord Eadwig had fallen. What he did not know, until that moment, was that it had been Lord Eadwig and the Wiltun men who had been assigned the part of the battlefield where the Northmen's ships were beached, or that the King had given his instructions, not to Eadwig, but to his son, that they not sacrifice themselves needlessly to keep Hallsteinn from escaping. As Uhtric described it, Titus understood that this was quintessential Alfred of Wessex; win, but win while limiting the cost in blood because, as Titus had learned during his time in Frankia, there seemed to be a never-ending supply of Danes and Northmen streaming down from their frigid, barren home, lured by the lush, green lands of Frankia and Angle Land. It was something that worried the Count of Flandre as much as the King of Wessex, yet Titus could not deny that this caution did not sit well with him, and as he watched Uhtric's face as he talked about it, he knew that he was not alone. Destroying your enemy, crushing them and slaughtering every man who chose to stand before you with a weapon in their hand; for Titus, and most of the warriors of that age, there was nothing else. Mercy, or at least their version of it, was for the weak, and these pagan invaders were neither weak nor deserving of anything but a shallow grave as their piece of land. Now that he was a father of two, Uhtric did not carry the same fire he once did, yet he also knew that even before Leofflaed and children, he never had what his brother-in-law had inside him, and he had worried about telling him the full story of Hrofescester.

"The King put us on the right wing, because that was closest to Hallsteinn's ships, and when Hallsteinn made his run for them, we were in position to stop them, but then Lord Eadwig shoved Eadward out of the way so that he could face Hallsteinn first...and face him alone."

"But why?" Titus frowned, not understanding. "He was too old for that kind of thing. He was too old at Ethantun, so he was certainly too old at Hrofescester."

"You weren't there," Uhtric replied, not accusingly but as a statement of fact. "You didn't see how Lord Eadwig had just been...withering away the last year. So," he shrugged then looked away, over the side of the ship at the coast of Frankia sliding by, "he chose how he died."

"Wait." Titus sat up suddenly. "You mean he...?" He did not finish, instead glancing over his shoulder, but Father Æthelred was at the opposite end of *The Redeemer*, yet he still did not even want to utter the word, since as every Christian knew, suicide was a mortal sin that consigned that person to eternal damnation.

Uhtric, understanding, still spoke harshly, telling Titus, "He died with his sword in his hand, facing his enemy, just like any warrior would want to die."

This was something that Titus could not argue, so he did not try.

"I suppose it's better than dying of piles," he agreed,

causing Uhtric and Godric to laugh.

Uhtric quickly became sober again as he continued, "Once Lord Eadwig fell, Lord Eadward didn't even try and rally us to stop Hallsteinn, so they managed to get away."

Titus considered this, yet he could not find any fault with the new Lord of Wiltun, especially knowing that Alfred did not want him and the Wiltun men to put up a bloody fight.

"Well," he asked, "if he didn't get back to Boulogne, then where did he go? To Frisia?"

"And tell Sigfred the Úlfhédnar that he abandoned the town and took half the garrison with him?" Uhtric replied pointedly, and Titus nodded his agreement at the unlikelihood.

It was Godric who spoke next.

"Naturally, none of us here know since we've been in Frankia, but I do know that the King was concerned that they went to Lunden, and," he added ominously, "that Guthrum gave him refuge."

"If that happened," Titus wondered aloud, "what will that mean? Would Alfred consider it a breach of the treaty?"

It was, the other two agreed, a good question, but it was one that would not be answered until they returned to Wessex at the earliest, and this was the last they talked about it on this voyage.

As the white cliffs of Dover loomed larger ahead of them and off their left bow, Titus' nervousness and anticipation grew. It was the third day, in mid-afternoon, when the small fleet, instead of turning to the right and following their course back to Hrofescester, turned left, heading ultimately for Hamtun, or so that was what Lord Æthelweard had told them.

"The King is no doubt back in Wintanceaster by now," he had said. "So we will tie up in Hamtun, and the King has instructed that you and Uhtric be allowed to make your way to Wiltun while we return with the news that his offer has been accepted."

With no duties and limited opportunities for diversion other than playing dice or some other game, most of their time had been spent talking about the possible reasons for Alfred's marriage offer of Ælfthryth to Baldwin, and Titus found himself in the unexpected position of being the young Count's principal defender.

"Yes, he's young," he had argued. "But he's got a good head on his shoulders, and now that that piece of weasel shit Baudelius is dead, he's in a good position because Baudelius was dripping poison in his ear for his own ends. After all, the *pagus* of Flandre is bigger than all of Wessex, and a *pagus* is basically our shire, so imagine Wiltscir being the size of Wessex! Besides, he's descended from royalty himself."

"Oh?" Godric sat up, suddenly interested. "How so?"

"His mother was the sister of the old king, Charles the Bald," he began, which prompted a gasp from Godric, who demanded, "What's her name?"

"She's dead now, but her name was...Judith," Titus answered after thinking about it, puzzled, but this got an exclamation not from Godric, but Uhtric.

Seeing their reaction, yet completely confused by it, Titus demanded, "Why are you two acting like that?"

"Titus, you don't know who Judith was?" Uhtric asked, but Titus could only shake his head and reply, "Baldwin's mother."

"What was your Count's father's name?" Godric asked.

"He's not my Count!" Titus snapped, then saw the other two exchange a grin and realize they were having fun. "But his father's name was Baldwin as well."

"Before Judith was married to Count Baldwin, first of his name," Uhtric explained, "she was a widow of Æthelwulf."

"Æthelwulf?" Titus echoed, not remembering immediately, but then he gasped, "*You mean she was married to Alfred's father?*"

"Yes!" Godric exclaimed, but then he glanced at Uhtric, giving him a slight nod.

"But when he died, then she was married to..."

Suddenly, Titus remembered, groaning the name, "Æthelbald...She was married to Alfred's brother after she was married to his father!"

"And then," Godric resumed the story, "she was kidnapped by your Count's father."

This much Titus knew, and he shook his head, saying emphatically, "That's not how it happened. She wasn't kidnapped. They ran away together. And, they were very happy together, the Count told me that much, that his parents had a good marriage. Besides," he pointed out, "if the version about her being kidnapped was true, how willing do you think Alfred would be to give the son of Judith's kidnapper one of his daughters?"

It was as much the manner in which Titus said this that informed both Uhtric and Godric that this was not a point to argue with their large friend, but neither could they refute his logic about Alfred's unwillingness to reward the son of a kidnapper.

In a tacit admission that the matter was closed, Uhtric stood and pointed at the white cliffs, gleaming in the afternoon sunshine, asking Titus, "Did you ever think you'd see home again?"

For a long moment, Titus did not reply, prompting Uhtric to look away from the sight to him, and he saw the glint of tears in his friend's eyes.

"No," Titus said softly, "I really didn't."

Their first sighting of the eastern coast of Wihtwara evoked a host of memories among the three men who had been part of Alfred's first attempt at creating a Saxon navy as members of the crew of *Sea Viper*, which was how they referred to it, refusing to call it *Ærendgaest*.

"If you had told me that I would become friends with Lord Einarr," Titus mused ruefully as the fleet entered The Solent, "I would have probably done the same to your balls that he did to mine that day."

As he hoped, this evoked a roar of laughter, though not just from Godric and Uhtric, but from the men manning the benches who heard his comment, though it was left to Uhtric to explain to the crewmen the story of the contraption that the Danes loaned to Alfred by Guthrum that was designed to teach the *burlofotr* Saxons how to leap from one ship to another when both were rocking from the action of the waves and the movement of men within the ship, and how the Dane deliberately mistimed the motion so that when the young Titus, who had already been given the Berserker name, which was the initial source of Einarr's hostility, made his leap, making his balls the first casualty of what would turn out to be a bruising, grueling period of training. However, from that beginning of mutual distrust, with the Danes' contempt for their ostensible Saxon allies' abilities in nautical matters, which none of them, including Titus, would have argued were skimpy, and the Saxons' resentment at being in a position of taking orders from these pagan interlopers who, by a quirk of fate and an unexpected victory at Ethantun, were temporarily stopped from trying to take their homes, as they toiled, sweated, and bled, to become a cohesive crew, a mutual respect, and regard, grew. For Titus, this was magnified by the events of the fight by *Sea Viper* against the *viking* originally led by Sigurd the Bold, who Titus had slain at Stanmer, when Einarr had unhesitatingly gone overboard after Titus suffered a blow to his head, saving him, first from drowning, then from having his throat cut by Leif Longhair by lying to Leif and telling him that Titus was actually a Saxon Thegn, worthy of being ransomed.

As Uhtric told the story, Titus found himself reaching into his pouch and fingering the arm ring Einarr had given him, thinking about all that had transpired, and how the Danes talked at such length about fate, and the Spinners who sat at the Tree of Life, weaving the threads that represented the lives of every man, woman, and child in existence into a vast tapestry, snipping one thread short here, then interweaving one thread with another, like a Dane's and Saxon's, then with another, like Leif Longhair's, although Titus still felt a surge of satisfaction that he had been the man the Spinners had chosen to snip his thread short. Hard on the heels of that thought came another, less pleasant one, that Leif's thread had originated through the loins of his father, Sigfred the Úlfhédnar, the man who was offering a fantastic sum to snip Titus' thread short, despite the fact that by all accounts, the father loathed his son. If anyone needed an example of how complicated a man's life could be, he thought, even as he laughed at Uhtric describing the oar dancing the Danes required the Saxons to do, this mess with Einarr is a perfect example, because Titus had reached a conclusion. He no longer believed Einarr's story about why he was in Boulogne, that Guthrum was concerned about Sigfred's plans and did not want to be involved and had sent Einarr to send the message that Guthrum was not interested in an alliance. Although, he allowed, the last part might have been true; no, what he was afraid of was that, at last, Einarr had grown tired of serving his King. Yes, he had been unwaveringly loyal to Guthrum, but every man, especially a man like Einarr, who as Titus had learned during his time in Lunden, had his own formidable reputation, had his limits, and while he could not have articulated it, Titus felt certain that Einarr had reached his limit. He offered up a prayer then, to both his own God and to the Spinners, that he never be in the position where he and Einarr faced each other across a battlefield, whether it be on land, or on water.

It was as they rowed into Hamtun that Titus got his first hint that his homecoming would be different than what he had envisioned by the small crowd on the docks, but it was the composition of them that caught his attention.

Uhtric, who was standing next to him, murmured, "How would Lord Eadward know that we'd be arriving today? Or," he added, "this week for that matter?"

"He's grown," Titus commented, feeling his mouth turn up into a smile. "And I see he's a proper Saxon lord now with that mustache."

"You have no idea how long it took him to grow that." Uhtric laughed. "But yes, he's a man grown now. And, Titus," he warned, "he's...changed since you last saw him."

Titus considered this, then nodded, though he also replied, "So have I."

Eadward was not alone, though they did not see either Otha or Ceadda, but the other men gathered there made more sense, since one of them was Cyneweard, who they both assumed was there to escort Lord Eardwulf and Father Æthelred the twelve-mile ride to Wintanceaster to inform the King of the presumably happy news of Baldwin's acceptance.

"Wait," Uhtric said excitedly, grabbing Titus' arm. "Is that who I think it is? There near the rear of that bunch? Is that...Dagfinn?"

"It is!" Titus exclaimed, but after a scan of the other faces that were becoming easier to recognize, he said, "But I don't see Einarr. Do you?"

"No," Uhtric replied. "Maybe he's in that alehouse he and the other Danes liked because they served mead."

While this was possible, Titus did not think this was the case, thought he could not have said why. Staying out of the way to allow the crew to throw out the mooring lines, once *The Redeemer* was secured, they had to wait for Lord Eardwulf to be helped off the ship, tottering over to Cyneweard, who offered his bow, while Father Æthelred was met by a gaggle of priests, monks, and scribes that high-ranking men of the Church deemed to be indispensable, although, Titus was certain, it was an affectation of their own importance and not a necessity. They had to wait for the more important figures to drift away from the bottom of the plank, but Titus was too distracted to notice how they were huddled together, speaking in hushed yet excited tones, unsure as he was about how to approach the new Lord of Wiltun.

Who, he was happy to see was smiling as broadly as he was, and without thinking, he dropped to one knee in front of Eadward, bowing his head as he said in a choked voice, "Lord Eadward, I want to thank you for this gift, allowing me to return home."

Eadward, who, like Titus, had not been certain what to expect, blinked in surprise, his own voice becoming husky as he said, "Is that any way to greet someone who was your friend before he was your Lord?"

Titus stood, then they wrapped each other in an embrace, laughing and talking over each other.

"Uhtric told me that this thing took two years!" Titus pointed to the mustache, but Eadward was unfazed. "And you still look like a pagan, and," it was his turn to point to the pink scar on his cheek, "I see you've been trying to improve your looks too."

"While you've been lolling about in Wiltun, *I've* been fighting Northmen," Titus sniffed. "And they make Danes look like a pack of nuns."

Eadward's smile faded, and he looked about them before he lowered his voice. "That's good to hear then, Titus. Because I'm afraid that I'm not here to greet you. In fact," he confirmed

Titus' suspicion, "I had no idea that you would be showing up today." Gesturing to Uhtric, Eadward waited until he was close enough so that Eadward could whisper, "Titus, Uhtric, I'm sorry to tell you that you won't be returning to Wiltun immediately. We are going to sea again."

They retired to the Hart and Hound, the inn that Lord Eadwig had favored and had become the unofficial spot for the Wiltun men during their time in Hamtun. They were on the first floor in the room where meals were taken, and most importantly for Titus, where ale was served, although he was quietly admonished by Uhtric after his third cup that he needed to slow down.

Eadward seemed content to let Titus drink for a bit, then he took a careful look around before he began by asking Titus, "Did Uhtric tell you about Hrofescester?"

"Yes, Lord," Titus nodded, then said solemnly. "And I grieve for you. Your father was a great man, Lord, and I admired and respected him."

This earned him a peculiar look from Eadward, who said coolly, "I'm surprised to hear you say that since he was the reason that you couldn't return to Wiltun."

"Oh, I was angry at first, Lord," Titus allowed. "But then, as I thought about it, I realized that he only did what he thought was right, and what was best for all of his people, not just for me." Shaking his head, he finished, "I can't blame anyone for doing what they thought was right."

This both surprised and impressed Eadward, especially given what he had planned for the large warrior.

"I...appreciate that, Titus," he said sincerely. "I truly do." They were silent for a moment, absorbed in their own thoughts before Eadward gave a slight shake of his head, then continued, "Yes, well, as I was saying, since Uhtric told you, you know that Hallsteinn got away from Hrofescester."

"Yes, Lord," Titus nodded, and he thought it important to add, "and Uhtric told me why, that it was because the King didn't want to lose more men than necessary to stop him."

"That's right," Eadward affirmed. "But the mystery has been, where did Hallsteinn go?"

Realizing that he might actually have information that would be useful, Titus said, "He didn't go back to Boulogne, Lord. I know that."

"That was what we had assumed," Eadward replied. "But then we learned something. And," he hesitated, "we learned it from someone we both know, but from someone who you spent more time with than either Uhtric or I did."

This was the moment that Titus understood, thinking back to no more than an hour before when he spotted someone in the crowd.

"Dagfinn," he breathed. "You heard from Dagfinn."

"Yes," Eadward confirmed. Suddenly, he looked into his own cup, trying to decide how much to share, then decided that Titus was going to learn sooner or later. "I didn't know this until yesterday when I was summoned to Wintanceaster, where I met with the King." Looking embarrassed, he thought to add, "I mean, it wasn't just me. There were other Ealdormen there as well. But that was when the King told us that Dagfinn has been in his service, and it's Dagfinn who came to tell us that Hallsteinn fled to Lunden...and that Guthrum has given him shelter."

Despite the fact that he had suspected as much, Titus still reacted with surprise, realizing that suspecting and knowing were two very different things.

"What does the King have planned, do you know?" Uhtric asked, but it was Titus, who, thinking that he had an idea, gasped, "Are we assaulting Lunden?"

"No," Eadward answered immediately, and firmly, then hesitated a heartbeat. "At least, not right now. No, we're going back to sea, because there's a *viking* force of sixteen ships, and the King has ordered that we sail as soon as possible to hunt them down." Before either of them could ask, he said, "Otha and Ceadda are bringing our men from Wiltun. They should be here tonight at the earliest."

"What ship are we going to crew?" Uhtric asked. "The *Sea Viper* already has one."

"They do, but they just returned from bringing Lord Eardwulf from Frankia, and Cyneweard told me that the King has instructed him to leave immediately. And," Eadward grinned, "I *may* have suggested that it makes sense that we replace them since we know her so well and we're fresh. Cyneweard," he finished with a satisfied smile, "agreed."

"How immediately?" Titus asked.

"If Otha and the others arrive tonight, we'll leave on the first tide," Eadward replied. "The supplies are being gathered now, and *The Redeemer* and the ships that were with you are being recalked and checked for seaworthiness." Turning to address Titus, Eadward said, "And once we're all back together, I'll be taking your oath of fealty."

"Of course, Lord!" Titus assured him. "I'd be happy to give it here and now."

"No," Eadward replied quickly, and Titus missed Uhtric's look of alarm. "That's not necessary right now. Let's wait until everyone is here, eh?"

Titus also did not notice how Eadward immediately moved the topic of conversation to something else, telling both of his companions, "Leofflaed told me to tell you that Wiglaf is still angry with you for not taking him with you to get his uncle."

"That boy," he sighed. "He's worse than his mother about holding a grudge." He turned to Titus and said, only partially in jest, "I don't envy you, Titus. He stayed angry about you leaving for months. But," he added hurriedly, realizing he had unintentionally wounded his friend, "he'll be so happy to see you that I'm sure he'll forget."

"He must have grown a lot," Titus said softly, his eyes taking on a faraway expression. He held his hand out, "So, I imagine he's what? About this tall now?"

"If you're talking about him six months ago." Uhtric laughed, then nudged Titus' hand up a couple of inches.

"God's blood!" Titus gasped. "Leofflaed isn't much taller than that! And he just turned eight!"

"She thinks he's going to be about your height," Uhtric said proudly. "But he's slender, and she said you were never slender, even as a boy."

"No," Titus agreed absently, staring down into his cup. "I was never slender."

What Uhtric had learned from Leofflaed was that Titus' build and musculature was due as much to his father Leofric's use of him as another beast of burden, which, even for the time in which they lived, when children were expected to pull their own weight and then some, had been excessively harsh and cruel.

From outside of the inn, there was a commotion, but the three of them were still turning towards the door when it was flung open, and standing in the doorway was the only man who, even now, Titus of Cissanbyrig, the Berserker, was scared of, yet he was the first to get to his feet and cry out, "Lord Otha!"

With an impassive expression, the Thegn entered the room, and while Titus could see the other Thegn of Wiltun, Ceadda, along with Hrothgar, Ealdwolf, and the other familiar faces crowded around behind him, his attention was on Otha as he stood. Otha looked essentially unchanged, though Titus thought he saw a few more strands of silver in his hair and mustache, while Otha examined Titus for a long moment without so much as the hint of a smile.

He finally broke the silence by commenting, "Well, you don't have as many scars as I thought you'd have. Just that one," he indicated Titus' cheek, "that I can see anyway. And you still look like a fucking Dane." He leaned forward to make a show of sniffing Titus. "But at least you don't smell like a Frank. I heard their men like to wear perfume."

Now aware of what Otha was doing, Titus stifled his grin, replying seriously, "Some do, but only their nobility, like their *Domini*. That's what they call their Thegns, so if you were in Frankia, you'd be wearing perfume like them, Lord."

"Then thank God I was born a Saxon," Otha growled, then without warning, he reached out and pulled Titus into an embrace. "It's good to see you, boy," he whispered to the man who, even now, he still sometimes thought of as the huge youth who had walked from Cissanbyrig to Wiltun, full of anger and a hatred towards his father that Otha would come to understand as he learned more about Leofric, but it was the ambition in the lad that burned so strongly in him it was impossible to miss and which Otha recognized because it was in himself. "And I'm glad that you're back, and you and I will be..." he stopped himself then, aware that he had almost given the secret away, but he managed to recover quickly enough to change it to,

"...standing together and killing Danes."

"And Northmen again," Titus replied. "We're going to be fighting Northmen again if Hallsteinn is part of this *viking*, just like with Sigurd."

"They bleed and die just the same," Otha said dismissively, breaking the embrace then turning to bow to Eadward. "Lord, we're here. Where are we staying? And for how long?"

"I need to go speak to Cyneweard and find out," Eadward said, rising from his chair. "So I should do that now." Raising his voice, he addressed the men who by this time had entered the inn, taking up every available inch of space, "Lads, I know you want a cup to cut the dust, but we need to go back outside. There are some things that need to be taken care of first. Once that's done, then we can spend the evening welcoming our very own Berserker back among us!"

The roar of approval shook the rafters, while Titus had to look at his feet to hide his embarrassment at this display of affection. Consequently, he missed the quiet exchange between Eadward, Otha, and Ceadda that clearly involved him, as their eyes were exclusively on him as they spoke. It took a moment for the Wiltun men to file out, whereupon Eadward led them back to the docks. He had not been telling the truth about needing to speak to Cyneweard; he already knew what would be happening, and more importantly, where the men would be spending their one night in Hamtun, but he was confident that what he had planned, about which only Otha, Ceadda, and Uhtric knew about, would be so noteworthy that he doubted any of them would remember that he did not go speak with the commander of the King's bodyguard.

Leading them to the spot where Alfred had pitched his tent almost three years earlier, which was still left as open space, Eadward ordered the men to gather in a circle around him, then called out, "Titus of Cissanbyrig, come attend to your Lord, and make your oath of fealty!"

Titus naturally complied, while the comrades immediately around him clapped him on the shoulder, and once again, he knelt on one knee in front of Eadward, who drew his sword, then held it with the hilt up, point touching the dirt, both hands around the hilt. Clasping his own hands around Eadward's hands, as Titus had seen and done before, first with Eadward's father, then with Otha, and with Count Baldwin, this being the custom in Frankia as well, though the words were slightly different and, of course, in Frankish, Titus prepared to say the ritual words.

"By the Lord before whom this sanctuary is holy, I will to Eadward, Lord of Wiltun, be true and faithful, and love all which he loves and shun all which he shuns, according to the laws of God and the order of the world." Titus spoke from memory, his voice strong and clear. "Nor will I ever, with will or action, through word or deed, do anything which is unpleasing to him, on condition that he will hold to me as I shall deserve it, and that he will perform everything as it was in our agreement when I submitted myself to him and chose his will. Before God and all of His Saints, and in the name of Our Savior Jesus Christ, I swear this."

This, as they all knew, was only half of the ceremony, it now being Eadward's turn, his voice equally carrying and conveying this most solemn of moments in their world.

"It is right that those who offer to us unbroken fidelity should be protected by our aid. And since Titus is a faithful one of ours, by the favor of God, coming here before me with his arms, has seen fit to swear trust and fidelity to me in our hands, therefore we decree and command by the present precept that for the future, Titus of Cissanbyrig be counted among the number of warriors sworn to me, Eadward of Wiltun. And if anyone perchance should presume to unlawfully kill him, let him know that he will be judged guilty of his *wergild* of six hundred shillings." Eadward paused, scanning the faces around him, while Titus remained, kneeling and with his head bowed, the young Lord's gaze stopping at Otha, who gave a barely perceptible nod. Looking down at Titus' head, which even when he was kneeling came up to the middle of Eadward's chest, Eadward said more softly, "Rise...Thegn Titus of Wiltun."

For a long moment, Titus did not move, nor did he respond in any way, his head still bowed as he stared down at Eadward's feet, but while his body was motionless, his mind was racing, his first reaction a stab of anger, thinking that Eadward was making some sort of joke at his expense. Fortunately, for Titus, for Eadward, and for the onlookers, of whom only three men had known what was coming, a part of his mind chided him for that thought. What could he hope to gain by that? For what purpose? Eadward's never lied to me, and he's never been cruel or held his position over me.

Finally, he lifted his head, and while he had deduced it was no jest, he still heard what sounded like his voice ask, "L-Lord? Did I hear you correctly?"

"You did," Eadward assured him. Then, not unkindly but firmly, he said, "Titus, you're making us both look a bit foolish. Would you stand up, please?"

He did so, which was the signal for the assembled men to burst out into a roar of cheers, then the pair was surrounded as Titus, still dazed, thought, I'm a Thegn.